The Hills Of Refuge
A Novel

by

Will N. Harben

Double 9
BOOKS

The Hills Of Refuge
A Novel
by Will N. Harben

Copyright © 2024

All Rights reserved.

ISBN: 978-93-62206-87-9

Published by

DOUBLE 9 BOOKS

2/13-B, Ansari Road
Daryaganj, New Delhi – 110002
info@double9books.com
www.double9books.com
Tel. 011-40042856

This book is under public domain

ABOUT THE AUTHOR

William Nathaniel Harben was an American writer who lived in the early twentieth century. He specialized in stories about the people who lived in the mountains of Northern Georgia. He was sometimes attributed as Will N. Harben or just Will Harben. Harben was born in 1858 in Dalton, Georgia, to a wealthy family. He grew up to become a trader in the same town. At the age of 30, Harben began composing stories. His father, Nathaniel Parks Harben, was a notable southern abolitionist who worked as a spy for the Union and then a scout for General Sherman. When William was a tiny child, his family was forced to flee to the north, but they finally returned to Dalton during restoration. Harben's first book, White Marie, a narrative about a white girl raised in slavery in the American South, was written in 1889. After the work was published, he relocated his family to New York City. Harben's subsequent novel, Almost Persuaded (1890), was a religious novel. The novel attracted enough notice that Queen Victoria requested a copy. Harben later wrote Mute Confessor (1892), a romantic romance, and Land of the Changing Sun (1894), a science fiction novel. Throughout the decade, he also wrote three detective novels. Harben's greatest literary triumph was Northern Georgia Sketches (1900), a collection of short stories about Georgia "hillbillies". He became a protégé and friend of William Dean Howells.

CONTENTS

PART I

CHAPTER I

The house, a three-story red-brick residence, was on Walnut Street, near Beacon. Its narrow front faced the state Capitol with its gold-sheeted dome; from its stoop one could look down on the Common and, from the corner of the street, see the Public Gardens. It was a Sunday morning and the Browne family were at breakfast in the dining-room in the rear of the first floor, just back of the drawing-room. The two rooms were separated by folding-doors painted white, as was the wainscoting of the dining-room. There was a wide bay window at the end, the sashes of which were up, and the spring air and sunshine came in, feeding the plants which stood in pots on the sill.

William Browne, the head of the family, a banker of middle age, slender, sallow of complexion, partially bald, and of a nervous temperament, his mustache and hair touched with gray, sat reading the *Transcript* of the evening before.

Opposite to him sat his wife, Celeste, a delicate woman somewhat under thirty years of age. She had once been beautiful, and might still be considered so, for her face was a rare one. Her eyes were deeply blue, and now ringed with dark circles which added to the beauty of her olive skin. The hand filling her husband's coffee-cup was thin, tapering, and almost as small as a child's. Her lips had a drawn, sensitive expression when she spoke as he lowered his paper to take the coffee she was holding out to him.

"You have not told me how your business is," she said.

"Why do you want to know?" His irritation was obvious, though he was trying to hide it, as he dropped his paper at his side and all but glared at her over his cup.

"I think I ought to know such things," she answered. "Besides I worry considerably when—when I think you are upset over financial matters."

"Upset?" He stared, it seemed almost fearfully, at her, and then began to eat the brown bread and fish-cakes on his plate. "Why do you think that I am upset?"

"I can always tell," she faltered. "When you are disturbed over business you don't notice Ruth when you come in. You almost pushed her from your lap last night when she went to you in the library. It hurt the little thing's feelings. She did not know what to make of it."

"A position like mine is full of responsibility," he said, doggedly. "Hundreds of things go wrong. Mistakes are made sometimes. We are handling other people's money. The directors are harsh, puritanical men, and they are very hard to please. They want me to do it all, and they think I am infallible, or ought to be."

"You didn't sleep well last night," Celeste continued, still timidly. "I heard you walking to and fro. I smelled your cigars. I couldn't sleep, for it seemed to me that you were unusually disturbed. You may not remember it, but you ate scarcely anything at supper, and, although I asked you several questions, you did not hear me."

He bolted the mouthful of bread he had broken off. His eyes flashed desperately. "Oh, I can't go into all the details of our ups and downs!" he blurted out, shrugging his shoulders with impatience. "When I leave the bank I try to shut them in behind me. If I go over them with you it is like living through them again."

"Then—then it is not your brother this time," Celeste ventured. "I thought perhaps the directors had spoken of his conduct again."

"Oh no. On my account they allow him to go and come as he likes. When he is not drinking he does splendid work—as much, often, as two men. The directors know he is worth his pay even as it is. Sometimes he gets behind with his work, but soon catches up again. In fact, they all seem to like him. They think he can't help it. It is hereditary, you know. Both of his grandfathers were like that."

"You knew that he was drinking yesterday, did you?" Celeste inquired, with concern in her voice and glance.

"Oh yes. He wasn't at his desk at all. I heard him come in and go to his room about three this morning. I knew by his clatter on the stairs that it was all he could do to get along. I think he came home in a cab; I heard wheels."

"Yes, he came in a cab," Celeste said. "Some friend brought him. I was awake. I heard them saying good night to each other. So it was not *that* that worried you?"

William shrugged his shoulders. "I have given him up," he said. "I almost envy him, though—he has so little to worry about."

"How can you say such things?" his wife demanded. "I shall never give him up. He has such a great heart. He is absolutely unselfish. He has given away a great deal of money to people who needed it. You know that he helped Michael send funds to his mother in New York last month. Michael worships him—actually worships him."

Browne took up his paper again. It was plain that he had dismissed his younger brother from his mind. At this moment the servant just mentioned, Michael Gilbreth, came to remove the plates. He was a stout, red-faced Irishman of middle age and wore the conventional, though threadbare, jacket of a family butler.

"Have you inquired if Mr. Charles wants any breakfast?" Mrs. Browne asked him, softly, as he bent beside her for the coffee-urn.

"Yes, m'm," he said. "I was up just this minute. He wants coffee and eggs and toast. He said to say that he would not be down to breakfast."

"Is he sober? Is he at himself?" the banker asked, in a surly tone, from behind his paper.

For a bare instant the servant hesitated. His entire bent body seemed to resent the question. "Yes, sir, he is all right; a little sleepy, I think, but that is all. He'll be around later. He is a fine young man, sir; he has a big heart in 'im, sir. He is a friend to the poor as well as the rich."

"A very poor one to himself, and us," Browne retorted, irritably. "But it can't be helped. He is done for. He will keep on till he is in the gutter or a madhouse."

"Take the coffee and warm it again, Michael," Celeste said, a subtle stare of resentment in her eyes. "He was to go to church with Ruth and me, but say to him, please, that we are not going this morning."

"Very well, madam, I'll tell him, though he will be ready to go, I'm sure. He always keeps his engagements. He intended to go, I know, for he had me get out his morning suit and brush it."

"Tell him I have other things to do and won't have time to get ready this morning," Celeste said, firmly. "Remember to say that, Michael."

The butler had just left when a child's voice, a sweet, musical voice, came from the first landing of the stairs in the hall.

"Mother, please let me come as I am. I have my bathrobe on, and my slippers. I have bathed my face and hands and brushed my hair."

"Well, come on, darling—this time!"

"When will you stop that, I wonder?" The banker frowned as he spoke. "What will she grow up like? What sort of manners will she have? You are her worst enemy. A habit like that ought not to fix itself on her, but it will, and it will foster others just as bad."

"Leave her training to me," Celeste said, crisply. "You don't see her once a week. She is getting to be afraid of you. You are upset now by some business or other, and it is making you as surly as a bear."

"Do you think so—do you really think that?" He laid the paper down and gave her a steady, almost anxious look. "I don't want to get that way. I know that hard, mental work and worries do have a tendency to spoil men's moods."

"Oh, it is all right," Celeste said, her eyes on the doorway through which her daughter, a golden-haired, brown-eyed child of five years, was approaching. She was very graceful, in the long pink robe—very dainty and pretty. She had her mother's slender hands and feet, the same sensitive lips and thoughtful brow. She ran into her mother's arms, was fondly, almost passionately embraced, and then she went to her father, timidly, half shrinkingly kissed his lowered cheek, and then pushed a chair close to her mother's side.

"Shall I have coffee this morning?" she whispered.

"Yes, but not strong, dear." Celeste's lips formed the words as they played over the brow of the child. "I must put a lot of milk in it."

Browne bent forward tentatively. It was as if the sight of his child had inspired him with a softer mood, as if her sunlight had vanquished some of the clouds about him. He smiled for the first time that morning.

"Don't you think you could have dressed before you came down?" he gently chided the child, reaching out and putting his hand on her head caressingly. "Naughty, careless little girls act as you are doing."

"I didn't have time," the child said, leaning against her mother's shoulder and causing his hand to fall from her head. "If I had dressed, both of you would have been gone from the table before I got ready, and I don't like to eat alone; besides, Uncle Charles was talking to me."

"Talking to you? Where?" Celeste asked, surprised.

"In my room. What is the matter with him, mother?"

"Matter? Why do you ask that?" Celeste inquired, her face grave, her voice sinking low.

"Because, mother, he acts so strangely. He came in while I was asleep. I don't know how long he was there. When I waked up he was seated on the foot of my bed. He didn't see me looking at him, for he had his hands over his face, pushing his fingers into his eyes, this way." The little girl put her hands to her face, the wide sleeves of her robe falling down to her shoulders and baring her beautiful dimpled arms. "He was talking to himself in the strangest way, almost ready to cry. 'I'd like to be a child!' I heard him say that, mother—I'm sure I heard him say that. I closed my eyes, for I didn't know what to do. Then I think—I think he must have been praying or something. He bent down a minute, and then sat up. I could feel him moving and I heard him groaning. Presently he was still and I peeped at him. He was looking at me with tears in his eyes, mother—great big tears. They came on his cheeks and fell down on his hands. He saw that I was awake, and put his hand on my head and brushed back my hair. Oh, I was so sorry for him, and I don't know why! He kissed me. He took me in his lap and hugged me, holding my face to his. Then he put me back, and I heard him say: 'I have no right to touch her. She is pure, and I am'—he said some word that I do not know. He got my robe and slippers and helped me put them on, awfully sweet and nice, mother. Then I told him I was going down to breakfast. I offered to kiss him, and at first he wouldn't let me. He stood shaking his head and looking so sad and strange. 'You ought not to kiss me, if you *are* my little niece,' he said. 'I am not a good uncle, Ruth. You will be ashamed to own me when you are a young lady and go to balls and parties. People will not mention me to you. But I will go away and never come back. Mother, is he going off? I hugged him and begged him not to leave, and he began to cry again. He was trying not to, and he shook all over. Presently he said he might not go away if I wanted him to stay. Oh, mother, what is the matter with him? What is the matter with *you*? Why, you are crying, too! Don't, mother, don't!"

Celeste, her handkerchief to her eyes, had turned her face aside.

"Oh, why do you do this?" Browne asked, impatiently. "Don't you see how emotional the child is? All this can't be good for her. Charles ought to be kicked, the rascal! Why doesn't he keep his remorse to himself? He is like this after every spree, and he will do it all over again."

Celeste, as if regretting her show of emotion, wiped her eyes, straightened up, and forced a smile. "You must eat an egg this morning, darling," she said to her daughter. "Don't worry about your uncle. He is not very well, but he will be all right soon."

"And he won't go away?" Ruth asked, anxiously.

"No, he won't go away, dear," Celeste said. "We'll keep him. You must love him and be kind to him."

CHAPTER II

With a tray holding the breakfast of the other member of the family, Michael ascended the stairs, the heavy carpet muffling his steps. In a room at the end of the house, on the second floor, he found the younger brother of his master nervously walking to and fro across the room. He was tall, strongly built, and had a well-shaped head. He was clean-shaven, blue-eyed, and had a fine shock of brown hair through which he was constantly pushing his splaying fingers.

"Come in, come in! Thank you, Mike!" he said, drawing his long gray robe about him and retying the silken cord at the waist. "I can't eat a bite, but I want the coffee. Wait; I'll clear the table."

He made an effort to move some books from the small table, but he fumbled them and they slid from his trembling hands to the floor, where he let them lie in a heap. The servant heard him sigh dejectedly and then he said:

"I'm all in, Mike; I'm done for."

"Oh no, sir!" Michael said, with emotion, as he put the tray on the table and proceeded to gather up the books. "You feel bad, I know, sir, but it will wear off by to-morrow."

A low groan escaped the young man's lips. "No, it is too late now, Mike. Give me a cup of coffee, please—strong and hot. Oh, Mike, you can't imagine how I feel. Mike, I am at the end of my rope. I am the greatest failure in Boston. My old college friends shun me. Ladies I used to know drop their eyes when I pass, as if they are afraid of me. The other day I insulted one by staring in her face, not conscious of what I was doing. Her brother resented it yesterday in a café before several people. He struck me—I struck him. We went to the police court. I was fined, and scolded like a dirty street loafer."

"Here is your coffee, sir," Michael said, sympathetically. "Drink it right down, sir. You are nervous again."

Charles obeyed, as a child might. "Thank you. You are too good to me, Mike," he said, returning the empty cup and beginning to stride back and forth again. The butler was about to leave, but he stopped him. "Don't go yet," he pleaded. "Oh, I must talk to somebody—I must get it out. It is killing me. I've been awake here since three o'clock. I can't sleep. Yesterday they turned me out of my club. I'm no longer a member. I am the only man who has ever been expelled. I've been a gambler, Mike. I've been everything except dishonest. I'm rotten. I don't blame the club. I deserved it long ago. I ought to have had the common decency to send in my resignation."

"You need money, I'm sure," Michael broke in, "and I owe you five hundred dollars. I've been hoping—"

"Don't mention that," Charles broke in. "I'm glad I lent it to you. If I'd had it it would have been thrown away, and, as it was, it helped your mother, you say. No, no, never bring it up again. Let it go."

"I'll never let it go," the servant gulped. "I'll pay that debt if I work my fingers to the bone to do it. Everybody else refused to let me have it; even your brother didn't have it to spare. My oldest and best friends turned me down."

"Cut it out! cut it out!" Charles frowned. "Give me another cup of coffee. Yes, I thought it all out here this morning, Mike. I am imposing on William. They keep me at the bank only on his account. He used to protest against the way I am acting, but he has given me up—actually given me up."

"I've heard him say you did a lot of work," objected the servant. "Don't underrate yourself. It isn't right."

"Oh yes! I work when I am at it," Charles admitted. "Remorse is a great force at times, but it is the other thing, Mike. The damnable habit gets hold of me. For hours, days, and weeks I fight against it. I've even prayed for release, but to no purpose. Last night I was consorting with the lowest of the low. I had the money and they had the rags, the dirt, and the thirst. A friend found me and brought me home, or God only knows where I would have been by this time. They say it is in my blood; two grandfathers fell under it—one killed himself. Yes, I've decided—at last I've decided."

"Decided what, sir?" anxiously questioned Michael, as he took the empty cup and placed it on the tray.

"I've decided to be man enough to leave Boston forever. I shall not inflict myself longer on William and his wife and that angel child. Listen to me, Mike. There is such a thing as a conscience, and at times it burns in a man like the fires of hell itself. Do you know—you must know it, though—I practically killed my mother? She used to spend night after night awake on my account. Worry over me actually broke her down. She was always awake when I was out like I was last night. Mike, I was drunk the day she was buried—too drunk to go to the service. Yes, I am going to leave Boston before I am discharged from the bank, and I shall go away never to return. I want to—to blot my name from the memories of all living men. I am a drunkard and I may as well live like one. I am a disgrace to every one of my family. Uncle James, when he was here last, told me that he had cut me out of his will and was praying for my death. Great God! I was drinking at the time and I told him I didn't want his money, and I don't, Mike, for I am unworthy of it. He is a harsh old Puritan, but he is nearer right than I am or ever can be. Yes, don't be surprised if you miss me some day. This cannot go on."

"Surely—surely you can't be in earnest, sir—"

"Oh yes, I am. Mike, do you believe in dreams—in visions, or anything of that sort?"

"I think I do, sir—to some extent, at least. Have I never told you? Well, when I was trying to get the money for my mother, and was so miserable about it, I went to bed one night and prayed to the Lord to help me, and do you know, sir, I dreamed that a young girl all dressed in pure white, and shining all over with light, came and handed me the money. And it seemed to come true, for you gave me the money at breakfast the very next morning. Do you have dreams, sir?"

"Always, always, Mike. I am always dreaming that I am alone among strangers, away from kindred and friends, but always happy and care-free. I can't describe the feeling; it is wonderful! I know what I want to say, but I can't express it. Say, Mike, William is a good old chap. You may not believe it, but I love him. He has other troubles besides me. I don't know what they are—financial, I think. He never speaks to me of his ventures. In fact, I think he tries to keep me from knowing about them. I find him at the bank late in the night, sometimes. Yes, he is all right, Mike. I would have been kicked out of my job long ago but for him. Yes, Mike, I'll turn up missing one of these days. I've had enough."

"You'll feel differently by to-morrow, sir," the servant said, gently. "You are nervous and upset now, as you always are after—"

"After making a hog of myself," Charles said. "No, I'll not feel better, Mike. It is my very soul that is disgusted. I know that I'll never change, and I shall not inflict myself on my family any longer. Don't speak of this, Mike—it is just between you and me. Oh, they will be glad that I've left! Ruth will miss me for a little while, maybe, for the child seems to love me, but children soon forget, and I don't want her to grow up and know me as I really am. If I stay she will hear about me and blush with shame. Think of what a crime that would be, Mike—killing the ideals of a sweet, innocent child. Yes, I'm going, old man. It will be best all around. I'll be dead to everybody that has ever known me. I've lacked manhood up till now, Mike, but I'll use all I have left in trying to make restitution. Obliteration—annihilation! that is the idea, and somehow a soothing one."

The kind-hearted servant was deeply moved and he turned his face toward the open window, through which the cries of the newsboys came from the streets below.

"Anything I can do for you before I go down?" he asked.

"Nothing, thank you," was the answer. "I shall stay here all day, Mike. I don't want to show myself in town. The news of my expulsion from the club will be known everywhere. I don't want to look in the faces of my old friends. Some of them have tried to save me. This will be the last straw. They will give me up now—yes, they will be bound to."

"You will be all right by to-morrow, sir," Michael said, huskily. "Lie down and sleep. You need it. You are shaking all over."

When the servant had left the room, closing the door behind him, Charles began to walk to and fro again. Presently he paused before the old mahogany bureau and stood hesitating for a moment. "I must—I must," he said. And opening a drawer, he took out a flask of whisky and, filling a glass, he drank. Then holding the flask between him and the light, he muttered, "Oh, you yellow demon of hell, see what you have done for one spineless creature!"

Restoring the flask to the drawer, he sat down in an easy-chair, put his hands over his face and remained still for a long time.

CHAPTER III

He threw himself on his bed. He was lying with his dull stare on the white ceiling when he heard the voices of his sister-in-law and her child in the hall below. The front door opened. They were going out—out into the open air with free consciences, he told himself, with a pang of fresh pain. He stifled a groan with the end of a pillow into which he had turned his face. Then he sat up to listen. It was a step on the stair—a step he had known from childhood. It was that of his brother William.

"He is coming! He is coming up here," Charles muttered, aghast. "Well, it is his right. He waited till the others went out so that he can rave and storm to his heart's content. Yes, he is coming. He has heard about the club, and all the rest. This time he will kick me out. He has stood me long enough, in God's name."

Charles sat erect and adjusted his dressing-gown with nervous hands. The step was now near. The top of the flight of stairs was almost reached. Charles stood up as a gentle rap was sounded on the door.

"Come in," he called out, his husky voice cracking in his parched throat. The door was slowly opened and William Browne, pale, haggard, and trembling nervously, entered.

"Sit down, old man," Charles said, indicating a chair. "Sit down. I thought you'd come."

"Thank you." The movement toward the chair conveyed an idea of almost helpless groping.

"I am sorry I wasn't fit to come down," Charles faltered. "I don't show your house much respect, Billy, but at least I can hide myself when I have sense enough left."

The banker groaned as he sank into the chair and sat staring at the floor. His brother took another chair close to the table. He lowered his tangled head to the table and waited. But no further sound came from his companion.

"Oh, I've hit him hard—I've hit him hard this time!" Charles thought to himself. "He has lost all hope of me now. It is hard for him to say what he has to say, but he is going to say it. He looks like Uncle James now, with those grim lines about his mouth. Poor Billy! he deserves a better deal from me, for God knows he has been a good brother. No one else would have borne with me as he has all these years. But he has reached his limit. His endurance is ended. In the first place, I must leave the bank. Yes, that is first—then, then, yes, I must leave this house. He will say I have turned it into a hog-pen. He is calm. God! how calm he is! He is choosing his words. He has determined to speak gently. I can see that."

"Lessie and Ruth have gone out," William presently said, without raising his eyes. "Michael said you were here, and I took this opportunity to—to—"

"I know; I expected you," Charles heard his own voice as from a great distance, so faint was his utterance. He cleared his throat. "Yes, I knew you'd come. There was nothing else for you to do."

William's head rocked to and fro despondently.

"I don't think you know why I've come," he said, grimly, and he raised his all but bloodshot eyes and fixed them on his brother's lowered head.

"Oh yes, you have heard of this last debauch of mine, and the damnable acts that went with it—my expulsion from the club, the trial at the police court, along with other common loafers, and—"

"I hardly know whether I heard of them or not," William said, his stare now on his brother's face. "You speak of yourself. What about me? My God! Charlie, what about me?"

"Oh, I know that you've gone the limit."

"Gone the limit? Then you know," William broke in, his lower lip hanging helplessly from his gleaming teeth. "You know about *me*—but how could you know? It is my own private matter, and—"

"I know that your patience is exhausted, Billy. I know that you are sensible enough to see that I am no fit occupant of your house. Your wife is a sensitive, delicate woman. Your child is—"

"Oh, *that* is what you think I mean!" William broke in. "Great God! you think that I am worried about *that*! Listen to me, Charlie. You sit there accusing yourself, perhaps feeling that you have committed unpardonable sins, but look straight at me. As God is my judge, I'd be the happiest man alive if I could exchange places with you this morning. You have done this, and you have done that, but you have been honest—honest—honest—honest! I've seen you tried. I've seen you need money badly, but you have never touched a penny that was not your own. Charlie, I am a thief!"

Charles straightened up in his chair. He laid his slender hand with the long fingers and curving nails on the table and stared, as if bewildered by what he had heard.

"I don't know what you mean, Billy," he said, slowly shaking his head. "You can't be in earnest."

"But I am," the banker groaned. "I have wanted to tell you for a week past, and I would have done so if you hadn't begun to drink again. Do you remember when I came to your desk Friday afternoon? I wanted then to ask you into my office, but I saw you had been drinking, and I knew that you'd not understand. I've taken money from the vaults, Charlie. I'm short sixty thousand dollars, and there is no chance now to avoid detection."

It was as if the declaration had completely sobered the younger man. He rose to his feet, towering above the shrunken form in the chair.

"You can't mean that seriously," he faltered, his drink-flushed face paling. "Oh, you can't, Billy!"

"But I do. My transactions have been secret; through a broker in New York I bought copper on a margin. It kept going against me till all my funds and available collateral were used up. I was sure it would win. All hell told me it would win. I couldn't stand the disgrace of failure. It meant losing my position, too. I struggled with it all one night in the bank, and the next morning, when the time-lock opened the vaults, I took the money and, with it in my pocket, I went to New York and put it up."

"You did? You did? My God! Billy, and lost it!"

"Within twenty-four hours. Charlie, you have been a drunkard, but your soul has remained clean. But I'm lost—I'm lost. I'll be sent to jail. My wife will shrink in shame from the public gaze. My child will grow up to see that I have set her, by my own act, into a despised class. Great God! that little trusting thing will have to bear my just punishment! So—so you thought I'd come here to reproach you, eh? You say you have been turned *out* of a club. I am being turned *into* a prison. Charlie, I was a coward when I took that money. I am a coward now, and I cannot face this thing. You must not object to what I have to do. It is dishonorable, but it is more honorable than the other."

"You don't mean—you *can't* mean—"

"There is nothing else to do, Charlie. Don't you see that in this way it will be all over at once? Think of the arrest, the long trial, the certain conviction, the parting, the stripes, the clipped hair! No, no, you must not oppose me. Ruth will forget me then, but, alive and in jail, I'd be a canker on her young soul. Lessie could marry again. God knows I'd want her to do so. Yes, it is the only way out, Charlie."

The drunkard seemed a drunkard no longer. He might have been an impassioned young priest full of a holy desire to comfort as he stood before the wilted man and clasped his hands. He knelt at his brother's knees, he caught the tense fingers in his.

"You shall not kill yourself!" he cried. "God will show you a way to avoid it. I feel it within me. There must be a way—there must!"

"There is no other way!" William groaned. "I've thought of everything under heaven till I'm crazed with it all." He stood up. He put his limp arm about the shoulders of his brother.

"Will it be known at once? Do the directors suspect?" Charles asked.

"Not yet, but you know the bank examiner will be here Thursday. It can't be kept from him. If I were unmolested for three months I could replace the money. I'm sure more than that amount will come out of the Western mining lands I hold. The sale is made, and only a legal technicality holds back the final settlement."

"Ah, then if you confessed the truth to the directors, and promised to replace the money, would they—"

"They would send me to jail, just the same," William answered. "They are that sort, every man of them. In their eyes a man who will steal once will steal again, and they may be right—they may be right."

"Nevertheless, you must not think of—the—the other thing, Billy. For God's sake, don't!" Charles pleaded.

"What else can I do?" William swayed in his brother's embrace and turned toward the door. Charles released him, and stood speechless in sheer helplessness as his brother stalked to the door, opened it, and went slowly down the stairs.

Left alone, the younger man turned to a window and stood staring blankly out into the sunshine. Presently he went to the bureau, opened a drawer, and took out the flask of whisky. Taking a glass, he poured some of the fluid out and then stood staring at it in surprise. A strange thing had happened. It was like a miracle, and yet psychologists have said that it belongs to the regular order of nature. Charles was conscious of no desire for the drink before him; in fact, he was averse to it. He was under the sway of a high spiritual emotion, which the thing in his hand seemed vaguely to oppose. He marveled over the change in himself as he held the glass up to the light.

"I'm asking poor Billy to be a man," he said, "while I am less than one myself. Strange! strange!" he muttered, wonderingly, "but I feel as if I shall never drink again—never, never!" With a hand that was quite steady he took the glass to the window and emptied its contents on the grass in the little plot below. Then he began to shave himself, and after that was done he dressed himself carefully.

The church-bells were ringing.

"Oh, I must save him—I must save them all!" he kept saying. "Something must be done. But what?"

CHAPTER IV

It was Wednesday night. William Browne had not come home to dinner. Charles looked into the dining-room. Celeste and Ruth were in their places at the table.

"William telephoned that he could not come up," Celeste said, as he sat down. "He says he has work to do at the bank to-night."

"Yes. I'm going back myself at once," Charles answered. "In fact, I am not a bit hungry. I had something late this afternoon—sandwiches and tea. If you will excuse me, I won't stay."

As he rose, Celeste lifted an odd stare to his face, but simply nodded as he was leaving the room.

"Don't go, Uncle Charlie," the child protested. "Stay for your dinner."

"No, I must go." He came back, bent over her chair, and kissed her on the cheek, and then hurried away.

It was eight o'clock when he reached the bank. The outer doors were closed, but a dim light could be seen through a plate-glass window in front. Softly inserting his key, he turned the bolt and entered.

"My God! he may not be here, after all!" Charles thought, as he shut the door noiselessly. Then he saw a light in the direction of his brother's private office and went toward it, now more hopefully. He was near the office door when he heard a sound like the hurried closing of a desk drawer.

"Who is that?" a startled voice called out.

"It is I, Billy. May I come in?"

There was no reply, and Charles pushed the door open. The banker sat at his desk in the glare of a green-shaded electric lamp. His face was ghastly pale, and rendered more so by the greenish light that fell upon it.

"What did you come for?" he asked, almost doggedly, and yet without a trace of impatience or anger.

"Because you didn't come to dinner, and because—"

"Because you are still watching me. Say it and be done with it," broke in William, in a tone which was scarcely audible as it rose from his husky throat.

"Yes, Billy. That's it. You have scarcely been out of my sight since Sunday morning. The examiner will be here to-morrow. I know how you feel about that, you see. You told me what you wanted to do. I have seen the thought in your eyes often since then. But it shall not be so, Billy. I love you. You are the only one in the world whom I do love very much. You shall not kill yourself, Billy."

William lowered his head. His chin rested on his chest. "There is nothing else to do," he groaned. "I cannot face this thing. They say men are always insane who do such things, but it is not so. I am mentally sound. I see all that lies ahead of me—everything, even the thoughts that will spring to life in the minds of my wife and child. Go away and leave me, Charlie. I want to be alone."

"What did you put into that drawer just as I entered?" Charles asked, leaning forward.

"Never mind," William said. "Go away."

"I want to know what it was," Charlie protested. He reached down and caught the handle of the drawer.

William made a slight movement as if to stop him, but desisted, uttering a low groan as he did so. Charles opened the drawer. A long revolver lay on the papers within. He took it out, and shuddered as he held it behind him.

"You are not going to shoot yourself, Billy," he said, firmly. "I am not going to permit it."

William made no reply, and with the revolver in his hand, Charles went into the adjoining counting-room and turned on the light at his own desk. For twenty minutes he sat resting his head on his hand, his elbow on the desk, the weapon before him. Presently his eyes began to glow, his face was flushed, his pulse was throbbing. "I have it," he said. "I have it."

Laying the revolver on the desk, he turned back to his brother's office. William sat as he had left him, his limp hands on the arms of his chair, his disheveled head lowered.

"Listen, Billy, listen!" Charles began. "I want to tell you something about myself first, and then about you. You must listen. It is important. It is your chance, and a splendid one."

"My chance?" echoed the banker. "What chance?"

"Billy, I am down and out. I've lost all my friends and social standing. I don't want to remain here longer. I want to go away off somewhere among strangers and begin life over again."

"Well, well, why tell me about it when you see that I—"

"Because it concerns you, Billy. Listen, it is both your chance and mine. I want to live a decent, sober life, and you say if you could stave this thing off for a few months you could replace the missing money."

"I could, but—"

"Then it will be done, and I'll tell you how. It is very simple. I am just now the talk of the town on account of the life I have been leading. People will not be surprised at anything reported of me, the directors least of all. You know they would have discharged me long ago but for your relation to me."

"I don't understand. I can't see what you are driving at," William stared with his bloodshot eyes. "You say you see a way. For God's sake, for God's sake—"

"Yes, but you are not listening. I am coming to it. I am going away to-night, Billy. I'm going away never to return. I am going out of your life as completely as if I'd never been in it. I'll never write back. You will never know whether I'm dead or alive."

"*You* are going away? Why are *you* going? I thought of it myself, but I couldn't stand it. No, there is no other way than to end it all."

"Don't you see what I mean, Billy? It is known that I have access to the vaults during business hours, and when I turn up missing to-morrow the examiner will logically couple me and my bad record with the money that is gone. Now you understand."

With his hands on the arms of his revolving-chair the banker drew himself to his feet. A wild look of hope was in his eyes and on his ghastly face. He groped his way to his brother, his hands outstretched as if to prevent himself from falling.

"You—you can't mean it, Charlie!" he said in his throat. "And if you *do* mean it I can't let you—I can't, I can't!"

"You must, because I wish it. I want to be of some use to you and to Lessie and the baby. Oh, I owe you a lot—a lot! Think how you have borne with me—how I have disgraced you."

"I can't let you—I can't," William cried, and yet he was panting with a vast new joy. His eyes bored into those of his brother. "What, let you do *that*? No, no. I could not permit it."

"Billy, you see, I want to do it as much for myself as you. I want to be absolutely free from old associations. You can replace the money. You can claim that you are doing it, you see, because you were responsible for my staying on when I ought to have been discharged. It will all seem so—so plausible—so very natural."

Turning, his eyes on the floor, William stalked back to his desk. He drew his chair around. "My God! My God!" his brother heard him muttering as he lowered himself into it. Dropping his head to the desk, he was still for a moment. Charles went to him.

"You have nothing to do with it." He touched his brother's bowed head. "I am going, whether you consent or not. I am going to-night. When I am missed in the morning that will tell the tale. You won't even have to explain. They will sympathize so much with you that they will not ask you many questions. Oh, it is all right now! You will have a chance to pay a just debt and I'll have a chance to make a new life for myself. They can't catch me, Billy. I know how to dodge the slickest detectives on my trail. The world is big and full of adventures. Do you know, Billy, I have always been haunted with the idea of freedom like this? Don't you worry. I'll be all right, whatever happens. And listen, Billy. I swear to you by the memory of our mother that I'll never tell a living soul of this agreement of ours. Never!"

William raised his head. He clasped his brother's hands and pressed them convulsively. "Oh," he gulped, "if I want to escape my just punishment, forgive me—forgive me, Charlie, for I am afraid of death. I have faced it for more than a week. It is an awful thing to think of all that it means, its effect on Lessie and the baby. Oh, Charlie, Charlie!" His lower lip was twisted by suppressed emotion. His eyes were filling with tears.

"I am going. That is settled," Charles said, with feeling. "And there is no time to lose. I'll hurry home and pack a few things. There is a train for New York at midnight. I can hide there safely enough for a while. I know the ropes. Good-by, old chap."

William stood up. He clung to his brother's hands for a moment, then put his arms around him. "Good-by," he gulped. "I hate to let you do it, but I am a coward—not only a thief, but a weakling and a coward. You must have money. Wait. I'll—"

"No, no, Billy." The other shook his head. "I sha'n't take a cent from the bank, under any consideration. You must begin anew as I am going to begin anew. You will owe to these men every cent you can get till that debt is paid. Besides, I have a little money and I shall not need much, for I am going to work for my living. I'll find something to do. It won't be an indoor job like this, for I am tired of it. I want to use my body instead of my brain. I want to tramp from place to place in the open sunlight and free air. I want to be a hobo. I want to put myself down on the level of the most unfortunate of men. I want to wring the poison of my past out of me. This chance seems a godsend to me. It will save Lessie and little Ruth from great sorrow and humiliation, and you from a desperate act. Life is a short thing, anyway, isn't it, Billy? Don't ever expect to hear from me again. In addition to the risk, it will be best for your state of mind. Think of me as dead."

William made a feeble effort to detain him, but he was gone. The banker heard him softly closing the big front door, and he sank back into his chair, tingling under a growing sense of vast relief. To be sure, he was losing his only brother, but he was retaining countless other things. He told himself that the plan was a marvelous one. Every flagrant act of his dissipated brother gave color to the implied charge against him, while his own high standing and the agreement of restitution he was to make would lift him above all possible suspicion.

CHAPTER V

Outside, the sky was clear. The stars were coming out. Their light was pale by contrast to the street-lamps. A cool breeze fanned Charles's hot face as he made his way with a step that was almost buoyant toward the Common. Some students on one of the walks were singing a college song he used to love in those gay days which now seemed so far away.

He was passing a little wine-room where he had been fond of going with certain friends, and almost by habit he paused and faced its lighted windows. Then he was conscious again of that strange experience which had immediately followed the tragic revelation his brother had made to him. He had no desire to drink. He laughed as he turned and strode onward across the street to the Common. Was there really such a thing as a new birth in which, under stress of some rare spiritual experience, a man was completely changed? It might really be so, he told himself, for nothing like this had ever come to him before. He was happy. Indeed, something like ecstasy had come upon him; it was in his very veins, hovering over him like indescribable light. He thought of William's dumb look of relief, and a joyous sob rose and hung in his throat. It was pain and yet it was not pain. How wonderfully beautiful the whole world seemed! There was really nothing out of order. Till a few minutes ago all was meaningless chaos and tragic despair, and yet now—now—he could not put it into words. He thought of the action of the club which had turned him out, and smiled. Why, the officials were merely puppets of convention, and he had been a naughty child. The police court! How funny the grave, fat judge looked as he delivered that fatherly lecture and imposed that fine! Oh, it was all in life, and life was a mosaic of rare beauty!

When he reached Beacon Street a night policeman was on the corner. Charles saluted him and gave him a cigar. "Fine night, fine night!" he said.

"It is indeed," the man answered.

Charles found the house dark, save for the gas which was turned low in the hall. He let himself in softly, and ascended the thickly carpeted stairs to his room. Turning on the electric light, he looked about him. He must hurry.

"Yes, I'll write a note and leave it here for William," he reflected. "It will help him explain to-morrow. He need only direct the examiner's attention to it, and they will understand, or think they understand."

He sat down at a little table, drew some paper toward him, and began to write.

> My Dear Brother [ran the note],—When you get this I shall be gone. I need not explain. When the examiners get to the vaults they will see why I had to leave. I have been going from bad to worse, as every one knows. I have abused your confidence, love, and hospitality. You will never see me again. Sixty thousand dollars is a large amount, I know, but on my honor I am not taking all of it with me. Most of it is gone already. Good-by.
>
> C.

He put the note into an envelope, sealed it, and directed it to his brother. He had just done so when he heard a soft step on the stairs leading down from the servants' rooms above. There was a rap on the door. He opened it. It was Michael.

"I thought I heard you come in," Michael said, lamely. "I was about to go to bed, sir. But is there anything I can do for you to-night—a cup of something to drink—coffee or tea?"

"Not to-night, Mike," Charles answered. "The truth is that I am off for Springfield—on a little business of my own. I must get away at once. I may have to stay there a short while—several days, in fact, and I want to pack a few things. Pull out my dress-suit case from the closet, will you, and dust it off. Then put in half a dozen shirts and underwear."

"Your evening suit, sir?"

"No, oh no, not that," Charles smiled. "I'm not going into society on *this* trip. I'll get out what I need."

Taking the articles from a drawer of the bureau, Charles tossed them on the bed near the suitcase which the servant had brushed and opened. "Put them in, please, Mike. It will save time."

The suitcase was packed and locked. Charles suddenly observed that Mike was eying the addressed envelope curiously.

"Oh, that note?" the young man said, averting his eyes oddly. "That is for my brother. Will you hand it to him—not to-night, I mean—at the breakfast-table in the morning? Don't fail, Mike. It is rather important."

The servant took it up. He held it tentatively. He hesitated. "He does not know that you are going, sir?" he asked.

Charles stared straight at the floor. "This will tell him all that he need know, Mike."

Putting the note into his pocket, Michael stolidly faced his companion. "Of course it does not concern me," he faltered, "but somehow you talk and act like—?" He went no further.

"Oh, you are afraid I'm off on another spree, eh?" Charles laughed. "But I'm not, Mike. It is business, this time, and serious business at that."

The servant was not satisfied, as was evident from his unsettled glances here and there, now on the young man's face, again on the suitcase or the floor.

"You may have forgotten it, sir, but only the other day you spoke of wanting to go away for a long stay, and the little unpleasantness at your club and the police court—"

"I see, I see, you don't forget things. You put two and two together," Charles interrupted. "What is that?"

It was a child's startled scream from Mrs. Browne's room, followed by the assuring tones of the mother.

"It is Ruth," Michael explained. "She screams out like that now and then when she is dreaming."

"I wish I could see the little thing," Charles seemed to be speaking to himself now. "They are a beautiful pair—that mother and child. Ah, and they have been sweet and good to me!"

"Now, I *am* afraid, sir. Indeed, I am," Michael said, with feeling.

"Afraid of what, Mike?"

"I am afraid it is not Springfield you are going to, sir."

"Ah, you are suspicious!" Charles said, in ill-assumed lightness.

"I haven't known you from boyhood up for nothing, sir," Mike said, with emotion. "Ever since your talk Sunday I have been afraid you'd leave."

"Well, then, what if I am going, Mike? The world is big and full of opportunities, and I am tired of this—I really am."

"But why leave like this, sir?" Mike demanded, gently. "Surely you won't go without telling your folks of it and saying good-by! Why, this note to your brother looks as if—as if—"

"Well, I do want to slip away, Mike, and I'm going like a thief in the night. You will understand to-morrow. Everybody in Boston will. As for that, Mike, a drinking-man will do many things that he ought not to do, and—and I handle money at the bank. Don't push me further now. Let's drop it. I have to go, and that settles it."

Michael failed to understand, for he was thinking of something else. "You will need the money I owe you, sir, and I've been trying to get it up. I see a chance now, sir. My sister out West feels that she owes at least half of that debt to you, and her husband has been doing well. She wrote me—"

"Drop that, Mike," Charles cried. "I don't need that money. You shall never pay it—never. I've given that to your mother, do you understand, not to you, but to her?"

"It shall not be that way, sir," the other pleaded. "I will send it to you. But as for your doing anything wrong at the bank"—Charles's statement was dawning on him slowly—"nobody on earth could make me think so."

"Well, never mind about that, Mike. The fact is that I must go—now and at once. Let me out at the front door."

"Do you want a cab, sir?"

"A cab?" Charles smiled. "Not to-night. In fact, I am going through the darkest streets I can get into. I know every alley in this old town. Good-by, Mike. Deliver the note to my brother in the morning."

CHAPTER VI

It was near midnight when he reached the station. He had met no one on the way whom he knew. He was tired and his arm ached from the weight of the bag, for he had taken a long, roundabout way to avoid being seen. Few persons were at the station, for it was not a popular train that he was to take. He bought his ticket at the little window, glad that the clerk was too busy to look up as he pushed the exact fare in to him. This done, he took up his bag and hastened for the train. He sought the smoking-car, feeling that he would be less conspicuous there than in the coaches set aside for the accommodation of women and children. He had the car almost to himself and was glad of the fact. Seated in one corner, he lighted a cigar. Somehow he was impatient for the train to move. He was not guilty of the crime he had shouldered, but he had a guilty man's fear of detection at that moment. He almost felt as if he and William were identical, for, after all, would not William's arrest and exposure have been quite as painful to him? The train did not start. He was becoming seriously alarmed now. He went to a window and looked out. An attendant with a lantern stood close by.

"What is the delay?" Charles asked.

"Accident ahead," the man answered. "Train off the track ten miles away. The wrecking-train has gone on. They will have the road clear before long. May as well wait here as farther on."

Charles went back to his corner. Why was he nervous? he argued. What was there to fear, since the exposure would not be made till the following morning after the bank opened? Why, nothing—nothing at all. He puffed at his cigar. The only thing was to avoid being seen by any passing acquaintance; but his face was known to many of all classes and he must be careful. He pulled the brim of his cap down over his eyes; he raised the collar of his light overcoat above his ears, and crouched down as low as possible. The train still lingered. His watch told him that it was two o'clock. He stretched his legs out on the seat in front of him and tried to sleep. He was quite fatigued, and yet his brain was too active to permit it. He thought of little Ruth. Again he heard her startled cry and pictured the child as lying in his arms and being soothed back to sleep. A sob filled his throat. Was it possible that she was going out of his life forever? Was it possible that he was actually renouncing home and home ties and going out into a new world in which he would be absolutely unknown, a veritable babe of mature age born among strangers? A mood of deep dejection was on him and it seemed to thicken and become more depressing as the hours stretched along. Then terror filled him, for he had a facile imagination which reached out for the disagreeable as well as the pleasant. What if the train were not to go for hours? What if the dawn of day found him still in Boston? He sat up. He rose and went to the platform of the car. The brakeman with the lantern was chatting with a man at a trunk-truck several car-lengths away. He descended and sauntered up to them.

"Any news?" he asked the man with the light.

"Yes. We will move soon," was the answer. "I see you are sticking to it. Most of the passengers went home, to take a morning train. You could take it yourself, if you are bound for New York, and get there almost as soon as by this train."

"Oh, I'm here now and will go this way," Charles answered. He turned away, for he realized that he had made his first serious mistake in talking to the man about his destination. The fellow might remember it later. He might even give the information to the police when they got on his trail. If the train were delayed between Boston and New York a telegram might be sent on and he would be arrested upon his arrival. He shuddered—not for himself, but for his brother. How the news would stagger William! He would confess, then. He would tell it all rather than permit the punishment to fall where it was not merited. Poor haggard, nerve-torn William! He would kill himself, and the black tragedy would settle upon the old home. Charles went back to his seat in the corner. His brain was whirling and pounding like that of a madman capable of half reasoning. Another hour passed. It was three o'clock. A desperate idea flashed into his mind. What if he should leave the train and take to the country roads? Might he not escape arrest in that way? He was about to resort to it when he heard a shout outside:

"All aboard!" A bell on the locomotive rang. Steam was heard escaping. The cars began to jerk one against the other, then to move steadily and to pick up speed. He looked through the open window. Through a shower of fine cinders and wisps of steam and smoke he saw the street-lamps dancing past, whirling, waltzing to the roar and clatter of the cars. Soon they were left behind. Fields and country roads lay dimly visible in the darkness. He was now conscious of a feeling of boundless elation. It amounted almost to ecstasy. He chuckled. After all, his brother and the others would escape the thing William had dreaded. They would live in happiness, and why should not he manage to exist in the new life before him? There must be a God, and a God of love and pity and mercy; surely some one, something, was holding the black curtain of fate aside for both William and himself, that he might enter upon a further probation and have one more chance to make good.

The conductor was coming, his ticket-punch in hand.

"What time shall you arrive in New York?" Charles asked, as casually as was in his power.

"About eight o'clock," the conductor answered, punching the ticket and handing it back. "That is the best we can do now."

CHAPTER VII

Reclining on the two benches, Charles managed to fall asleep, and in spite of his worries he slept soundly. The gray morning light crept in at the open window and swept his dust-coated face, but still he did not wake. The light grew yellow and warm as the sun rose, but still he slept. He waked and sat up as the train was entering the suburbs of New York.

"Safe—still safe!" was his first thought, as he looked about him. The car was now half-full of passengers, many of them commuters going in to work. How fresh, clean, and contented they looked with their cigars and damp papers, and what a dismal tramp was he, at least in his own eyes! There was a little lavatory at the end of the car, and his first impulse was to go to it, wash the dust from his face and hands, and brush off his clothing; then it occurred to him that, as he was, he was less recognizable than otherwise, and he gave up the idea.

Slowly the long train clattered over the switches and crossings and pulled into the station at Forty-second Street. The vast roof cut off the direct rays of the sun and the forms and faces of the passengers became indistinct in the shadow. He followed the others down the packed aisle and joined the stream of passengers on the platform, all forging their way to the street. Covertly, as he hurried along, holding his bag in his right hand, he watched the crowd of bystanders to see if any one wore a police uniform. He was gratified to notice that the way seemed clear in that respect. And then he smiled at his imagined fears, for how could the police be on his track before the opening of the bank? No, no, he was safe so far, and he would soon be hidden from sight in the slums of the great city, for it was the slums that were to shelter him. There no one would look for a man of his type.

He was soon out in the crowded thoroughfare. Somehow it appealed to him to-day more than ever before. He walked along the street until he reached Fifth Avenue, and then he realized that he was not going in the direction he desired and turned back. He walked on till the buildings began to look more antiquated and shabby, and then he turned south. He pursued this direction till he had reached Twenty-eighth Street, and then turned east again. The surroundings were now decidedly squalid. The street was unclean and thronged. The houses were old three-story-and-basement residences, the ground floors of many having been turned into shops, the upper floors being rented as sleeping quarters at a very low rate as was shown by the soiled cards placed against the window-panes to catch the eye of passers-by.

Suddenly he became aware that he was hungry, and he looked about him for a place to break his fast, for he had eaten scarcely anything since noon the day before. Presently he descried a restaurant. It was located on the first floor immediately above a delicatessen shop. The street in front of it was unclean, ash-cans and garbage-pails flanking the crumbling brownstone steps to the entrance; and yet his aversion to these unsavory surroundings was conquered by his hunger and the security that such a place afforded him.

He went in and was surprised at the inviting appearance of the room. It was clean. The walls were snow white. White-clothed tables stood close together, some small, some long and narrow. He put down his bag and hung his hat and overcoat on an upright rack. The tables were nearly all filled with a motley assortment of human beings. The table near his bag had a single occupant, a young man of about his own age. Charles sat down opposite him. The fellow's face appealed to him vaguely, as reminding him of some countenance he had once seen and forgotten. It was a rather round face, blue-eyed, clean shaved, and crowned by light-brown curly hair.

A waitress in spotless apron and cap came to Charles. "You forgot to get your check," she said.

"Check? What is that?" he asked.

"Oh, I'll get it for you," the girl said, hurriedly, and she went to the glass-inclosed desk by the door at which another girl sat.

The stranger across the table held up his own check and smiled. "It's like this," he explained. "You see the prices, from five cents up to one dollar, are printed on it. The girl who waits on you punches the amount you order, and that is what you pay as you turn the check over at the desk when you go out."

"Oh, I see! Thank you!" Charles liked the face more than ever. Its underlying humor and good nature at once soothed and attracted him. The waitress came back with the check, and with it brought a printed bill of fare which she gave to Charles. While he was looking it over she bent near the man across the table.

"You can't keep this up," she said, gently. "It will kill you. I've been watching you for a week."

"Oh, leave that to me," he answered, with a smile that Charles now saw was drawn and twisted by manly embarrassment. "I've been this way before and pulled through."

The waitress sighed. "I wish I could manage it," she said in an undertone, "but I can't. That woman at the desk is a cat. She has it in for me."

"You don't think I'd let you do anything like that for me, I hope," he said, sensitively. "I appreciate it very much, but no working-girl shall lose through me."

Without replying she came around and bent over Charles. "Ready to order?" she asked.

"Eggs and bacon and coffee with cream," he said. As he spoke he noticed that his table companion had apparently ordered nothing but the few slices of bread and butter which he was slowly eating. A goblet of water was all the man had to drink. Charles now understood the situation and he wanted to assist, but Boston men of his class are not as free with strangers as Western and Southern people, and he found himself unable tactfully to accomplish what he desired.

"You are not quite on to the ropes," the stranger remarked, his eyes on the dress-suitcase which Charles had put down. "It was all new to me when I came here, but it doesn't take long to get the run of things. God knows it is simple enough if you have the money to do it with."

"I suppose so," Charles responded. "I've just come in."

The waitress was bringing his breakfast. She placed it before him, handing him a paper napkin and leaving spoons and knife and fork. "Anything else?" she asked.

"Nothing now, thank you," Charles answered.

Instead of going on to the next table at which a man and a woman with drink-flushed faces were seating themselves amid the soiled dishes left by others, she leaned again over the shoulder of the young man opposite Charles.

"You must let me help," she whispered. "I know you are all right, and you will never get work if you are underfed. You see, I know because I've been there myself."

"Please, please, don't mention it," the young man said, his face drawn and flushed with chagrin. "I assure you I am all right. That's a good girl—let it drop."

She said nothing, but moved on to the new arrivals and began to place the soiled things onto a tray preparatory to taking their order.

"Do you intend to stop in the city awhile?" the young man asked Charles.

"I may," the Bostonian returned. "I am looking for a room in this neighborhood."

"Oh, there are plenty of them," the other smiled, "but you don't always run across clean ones. I've tried several places and left. The house where I am now is clean and cheap, and I think there are plenty of vacancies. I have the landlady's card, if you care to look her up."

"Thank you, I'd like to do so." Charles had the feeling that he would like to see more of the stranger, and living in the same house might afford him the opportunity. The young man took a card from his pocket, and as he got up he laid it before Charles. "I hope you will find a room you like," he said, wearily, as he reached up for his hat, which Charles noticed was dented and frayed on the edges of the brim. As he went out Charles watched him, and saw him push a five-cent piece across the desk to the cashier. He looked very thin and his step seemed uncertain, like that of a convalescent.

The waitress came back to Charles. "He is in bad shape," she sighed. "He has been coming here for two weeks and eating like that. He is silly. He won't take help from any one. He has been well brought up, I'll bet."

"I wanted to help him, but I didn't see an opening for it," Charles said. "It was kind of you to offer it."

"Oh, I'd break if I owned this joint," she laughed. "I see things like that every day. Our cook used to make pancakes in the window. It was pitiful to see the people stand watching him with their poor mouths open."

Her voice shook and she suddenly turned away. As he was leaving the restaurant a wonderful sense of peace and quiet was on him. Already his new life was full of attractive novelty. How could he account for it logically? He was a fugitive from law, without any income to provide for his needs;

he had renounced every tie of blood and former associate; he was a man without a home, without a prop to lean upon, and yet an inexpressible content was his. Was it due to his disgust over his past life and the sense of having put it behind him, or was it on account of the sacrifice he had made for his brother? He could not have said.

Glancing at the card, he saw that the rooming-house was quite near, and he turned toward it.

CHAPTER VIII

The house was a red-brick building like all the others in the block. The steps were of the conventional brownstone with rusty iron railings. The front door over the basement entrance was open, and he rang a jangling bell, the handle of which was so loose in its socket that it was drawn almost out of place. While he waited he looked into the hall. It was clean, though the carpets on the floor and visible stairs were worn and the massive hat-rack of walnut leaned forward from the wall as if about to fall. The basement door was opened and a portly woman with a red face and tousled yellow hair climbed the stair to the sidewalk and approached him.

"I understand you have rooms to rent," Charles said.

The woman eyed him curiously, evidently surprised at the elegance of his clothing and the politeness of his attitude, for he had taken off his hat in greeting her.

"Top floor back, three a week; hallroom back, next to it, two," she answered, wiping her fat hands on a white apron. "Want to see 'em?"

"If you please," Charles said.

"No trouble. That's what I'm here for," she smiled pleasantly. She came up the steps and led him into the hall. "Three flights up," she explained. "Will you leave your bag? If you do I'll have to lock the door. Roomers can't leave overcoats or hats on the rack now. Thieves are as plentiful as mosquitoes in Jersey—some in the house, as for that. My folks keep their rooms locked."

"I'll take the bag up with me," he said, feeling that, no matter what the rooms were like, he would take one.

The stairs were dark. A wire hanging down the shaft was attached to a bell at the top in order that it might be rung from the basement by the landlady as a signal to her few servants who might be working above when needed below. Immediately over the stairs in the roof was an oblong skylight of variegated glass through which the tinted rays of sunlight came. The woman pushed open the door of the larger room.

"The girl hasn't had a chance to get at it yet," she apologized. "The bed hasn't been made up, and the man that is in it has left his things lying around. He is going away this afternoon. If you like the room I'll put his things out. He is unable to pay and I can't run my house on nothing."

Charles saw an open unpacked trunk of very cheap quality in the center of the room. The sight of the chamber in its disorder was decidedly unpleasant, and Charles did not enter it. "What is the other like?" he asked.

"I'll show you," said the woman, and she opened the door of the adjoining room. It was very small, and it had only a single chair and one window with a torn shade and cheap cotton-lace curtains. The only place to hang clothing was the back of the door, into which hooks had been screwed. There was a tiny wash-stand with a bowl in which a pitcher stood, and a rack holding two thin cotton towels.

"This will do very well," he said. "It is large enough for me. I want to cut down expenses. I am out of work at present."

"Oh, I see!" the landlady said, sympathetically. "A good many young men are out of work. That is what is the matter with the fellow next door!"

Charles paid for a week in advance, and when she was about to leave she said:

"Is your trunk coming? If it is, I'll send it up."

"No, I don't happen to have one," he said, trying to summon a casual smile.

"Oh," she exclaimed, avoiding his eyes, "I make a rule to insist on that. I've had trouble with some roomers, and it was always them that just had hand-baggage."

"I can pay you more in advance, if you wish," he proposed, anxiously. "I don't want you to break any rules on my account."

"Oh, never mind!" she said. "I know you are all right. I'm a pretty good judge. The Lord knows I see all sorts of folks in my business, and most of them will do me whenever they can. I've had thugs and counterfeiters in my house. One man that said he was studying to be a minister had six wives scattered over the country. They arrested him one afternoon while I was giving him a cup of tea down-stairs—the smoothest talker that ever lived, by all odds. I missed some trinkets, but, being a widow, I never mentioned it to the officers. You see, it was all in the papers and any little thing like that might have put my name on the list of his victims; as it was, the number of my house was all that got into print."

When she had left him Charles closed the door and softly locked it. He sat down in the chair and leaned back. The little walled space gave him an odd sense of security. It was his own, for the time being, at least. The window was open and a cooling breeze came in, fanning back the white curtains. He took out his cigarettes and began to smoke, and as he smoked his mind became very active in dealing with recent events. Two marvelous things had taken place. He was free from future contact with his Boston friends and acquaintances, who knew of his recent escapades and their humiliating consequences, and he had released his brother from conditions that were even worse. The memory of William's open-mouthed stare of hope as he clutched at life anew drenched his soul with joy inexpressible. What did it matter that he was never again to see William, or his wife or child, or that he was never again to walk the historic streets of his native city? What was to become of him he knew not. Somehow it did not seem to matter. For the first time in his existence life had taken on a meaning that was worth consideration. It meant that by his persistent self-obliteration another man might reach readjustment, and a woman and a child would escape pain and disgrace.

"Good! good!" Charles exclaimed, and slapped his knee. "I haven't lived in vain, after all—that is," was his afterthought, "if I am not caught; but I shall escape. The infinite powers could not will it otherwise. William shall be a new man, and—why, I am already one! It is strange, but I am. This room"—he swept the walls with exultant eyes—"seems as natural to me as one in a fashionable club or hotel. It is all owing to one's point of view. I now live on this plane, and it is good. How amusing that woman was just now! How remarkable that I should feel inclined to laugh at her drollery! Another week and she would have been the seventh wife. The tea in the basement proves it. She is funny. I like her."

Then his facile mood changed. What was happening at the bank at that very moment? He looked at his watch. It was ten o'clock. The bank examiners were at work. The discovery was made. Poor, crushed William at his desk had only to say that the brother he had trusted had fled, and, understanding all, they would leave him alone.

CHAPTER IX

At nine o'clock that morning William Browne came down to breakfast. Celeste was already in her place, and smiled as he bent down and kissed her. As he drew out his chair he noticed on his plate the envelope in his brother's handwriting. He was not expecting any communication from Charles, and the sight of the letter startled him. What could it mean, his morbid fears suggested, unless it was that Charles had changed his mind, after all, and had not left the city? Perhaps he was now in his room, sleeping late, as usual. The thought was unbearable, for it brought back all the terrors which had beset him during the weeks just past. He sat down, and for a moment let the envelope lie on the plate untouched. Celeste was busy pouring his coffee.

Michael came in bringing toast. He indicated the note with a wave of his pudgy hand. "Mr. Charles asked me to hand it to you," he said, in a grave tone which caught the attention of Celeste and caused her eyes to linger on his face inquiringly.

"Is he coming down?" she asked.

For the first time in his experience as a family servant Michael deliberately decided not to answer. He pretended not to have heard and turned from the room.

William took grim notice of the failure on the man's part. He tore off the end of the envelope, drew out the note, and read it. A thrill of joyous relief went over him. With tingling fingers he folded it and put it back into the envelope, and then placed it in his pocket. The rays of the sun falling in at the window on the plants and flowers held a beauty he had never seen before. Life—life! After all, he was to live! Charles was gone and all would yet be well. His wife was looking straight at him now.

"Good news of some sort," she smiled, as she spoke.

"Why, why do you think that?" he inquired, his beaming eyes steadying into an uneasy stare.

"Because I saw it in your face just then," she answered. "But why is he writing you when he could have come down and seen you? Is—is he all right?"

William wondered what he could now say. Why had it not occurred to him that he must be as adroit in his explanations to his wife as to the bank examiners, the directors, the public in general?

His brain seemed too heavy to deal adequately with a situation so delicate and fraught with pitfalls, for Celeste had a subtle intuition.

"Yes, he is all right," William said. "That is, he is not—was not drinking yesterday or last evening when I saw him at the bank. In this note he tells me that he has left town. I don't think he slept here last night. Did he, Michael?" The butler was entering with the eggs and bacon. "Did my brother sleep in his room last night?"

"I think not, sir," Michael answered, stiffly, avoiding the straight gaze of his mistress as he put the platter down by his master. "At least he was not there half an hour ago."

"But he gave you the note," Celeste put in, insistently.

"That was last night," Michael said. "He gave it to me when he came in. I was to hand it to you, sir, at breakfast."

"It is all right," William said, evasively. He took up a spoon to help himself to the eggs, but awkwardly dropped it. Michael served him with steady hands and unruffled mien. "Yes, he is all right. He says he wants to leave Boston for a while. You know he has had some troubles of late."

"Gone without saying anything to me or Ruth?" Celeste said, her thin lips twitching. "Why, I can't understand it! Is there anything in the note about the length of time he will be away?"

"I can't explain now," William returned, frowning over his coffee-cup. "Perhaps later to-day I may tell you more. I—I don't want to talk about it now. I have hard work before me to-day at the bank—a meeting of the directors, and other things of importance."

Celeste stared stolidly. She sat a moment erect in her chair, then said, crisply, "If you will excuse me, I'll go attend to Ruth."

William half rose as she got up, and then with a limp attitude of relief he sank back into his chair. He had not touched his eggs and toast. He drank his coffee rapidly and signaled the butler to fill his cup again. "Strong," he said; "no cream or sugar."

"Very well, sir." Michael obeyed with sympathetic deliberation. He evidently wanted to talk to his master about his brother, but he could find no plausible excuse for so doing. William bolted a few mouthfuls of the food on his plate, finished his third cup of coffee, and rose.

"I shall not be here to lunch," he said. "We'll have something served in the bank."

"Very well, sir." Michael drew his chair back and bowed as his master left the room.

William was getting his hat from the rack in the hall when Celeste came to the top of the stairs. "Do you want to see Ruth before you go?" she called down. "She is awake, but not quite dressed."

"Not now, dear. I am in an awful hurry," he said, impatiently. "I have no time to lose."

"Very well," Celeste coldly replied, and disappeared.

Outside the sun was shining brightly; the air was invigorating with its bare hint of dewiness on the trees and sward of the Common which he was crossing. A wondrous haze draped the Public Gardens some distance away on his right. On his left, the golden dome of the State House blazed under its reflected fire. The city's dull hum fell upon his ears, punctuated by the far-off peal of a bell.

Was Charles safely away? he asked himself. If only he had one more day between him and discovery how much better it would be! But that was out of the question. The thing that was to be done must be done at once. After all, what was there so terrible about it? Charles would make his way in some fashion, and the family disgrace would be avoided. Suicide? Nothing could be worse than suicide. Ah, but Charles might be followed and detained! In that case he would be put on trial for the crime, and of course he could no longer play the part he had undertaken. Then it would be suicide for himself; yes, suicide was even yet a possible contingent. He shuddered; the sunlight lost its charm, the air its bracing quality. He plunged on now, glancing neither to the right nor to the left, and his step was heavy as he entered the bank. It was open for business, and very active in the counting-rooms. Typewriting and adding machines were clicking. In the office of the president, a raised voice could be heard dictating a letter in studied paragraphs. William hung up his hat in the little anteroom and sat down at his desk. Automatically he felt in his pocket for the note Charles had written. He understood the afterthought which had inspired its writing, but he shrank from availing himself of it. He must appear to be busy, he told himself, and yet what could be done by a man in his state of suspense? Could one dictate a letter or add a column of figures while momentarily expecting the verdict of a jury as to whether he should live or die? The bank examiners would soon come. The ordeal of meeting their experienced scrutiny would be impossible in his present state of mind. How could he escape it? The note! Ah yes, the note! With the revelation once made to the president, his privacy would be respected. It was a terrible thing for a brother to do, but as a matter of sheer self-preservation, it had to be done. The dictating in the president's office had ceased. The girl stenographer, with her notes in hand, was hurrying past his open door. Now was the time, but he must first set the scene for the drama. He got up, went to the vault, drew open the massive door, busied his distraught brain over a combination, opened an inner safe. He remained there for a moment and then came out. A clerk glanced up from a big book of commercial reports, bowed respectfully, and then stared almost in alarm at his superior.

"My God!" he heard the banker say. "My God!"

With Charles's note in his hand William moved on to the office of the president. The door was partially open. He pushed it aside and entered. A heavy-set gentleman past sixty years of age, with a reddish face and iron-gray hair, raised a pair of frank blue eyes. "Well, Browne, we've got to show a clean record to-day," he began, jestingly. "This fellow McCurdy thinks he is a regular Sherlock Holmes. You know he was the slick chap that exposed—" He suddenly checked himself. The jovial smile left his facile mouth, for William was now in the full light of the electric lamp on the desk.

"I have bad news, Bradford," William gulped, putting his bloodless hand on the roll-top of the mahogany desk, the hand clutching his brother's note.

"Bad news?" Bradford repeated, in slow amazement. "Why, what's happened? You look—look—"

"The safe has been robbed!" William's words tripped over one another, as they tumbled from his pallid lips. "I found this note, and went to see if— if what it says could be true. See! Look!"

William spread out the crumpled note, and laid it before Bradford's widening eyes, and then stepped back and stood still and silent behind him. There was only a moment's pause. Bradford whirled around in his revolving-chair.

"My God!" he cried. "Your brother! I was afraid something might go wrong. Several of us were; but on your account—"

"I understand," William leaned forward. There was almost unexpected support in the president's tone and phrasing, laden as it was with sympathy. "I have made a great, great mistake, Bradford, and I will do all in my power to make up for it. In a short while—a month, six weeks—I can replace that money out of my own funds, and I want to do it—I *must* do it. I want the directors and you to understand that. Will you tell them? Will you do that for me? The money is almost in sight. I'm sure it is coming. I only need a little time."

"That will be considered later." Bradford stood up. His hand was extended to the limp man before him. "I sympathize with you, Browne. I have been sorry for you all along on account of your brother's conduct, and of course I am more so now. You need not fear that the matter will impair your own standing with us. The fact that you propose to return the money is sufficient proof of your personal integrity. Now—now, leave everything to me. You are in no shape for business. Why, you have gone all to pieces! Leave it all to me. If I were you I'd go home. This will create a sensation—it can't be avoided—and why should you be in the midst of it?"

William heard himself muttering subdued words of thanks. He felt his hand warmly pressed; the arm of a friend and old associate was around his shoulders as he turned away.

Reaching his office, William entered, closed the door, and sat down at his desk, his fixed stare on the large, spotless green blotting-pad. What ailed him? Why was he so filled with excruciating agony? A better way of escape than he had hoped for had opened out before him. The bank examiners, the directors, the depositors would respect his feelings and think nothing prejudicial to him for absenting himself from the scene. They would regard him as a well-meaning man impoverished by the irresponsible acts of a drunkard relative. If anything, their respect would be heightened by his generous offer of reimbursement. He told all this to his benumbed consciousness, but it failed to revivify the soul within him.

"Sixty thousand dollars!" It was a voice from a telephone-booth near by, a voice unwittingly raised too high, through excitement. It was Bradford speaking to one of the directors at his suburban home.

"Yes, Davis, you must hurry in. We'll wait for you." Here some words became indistinct in the tread of hurried feet in the counting-room and corridors, then: "Oh yes, poor fellow! he is all broken up over it. Surprised him like all the rest. I must say I didn't think it of Charlie. I loved the boy, in a way, but I presume he got entangled in some—Well, you know what I mean. It will get the best of 'em down sooner or later. Yes. All right. Good-by. Oh, say, hurry in. We must decide what we are going to do about the police. We must be quick about that. Unpleasant as it will be for Browne, the boy must be caught. At least that is my opinion, and I think we ought to offer a reward. Think it over and hurry in. We need you. Good-by."

William, his stare still on the green pad before him, heard Bradford closing the door of the booth. He recognized the voice of one of the directors who had just come in and had met the president in the corridor.

"It has taken me off my feet," the man said, angrily. "What a bunch of fools we were! The young villain! What other bank would have allowed him to be around, after—"

"'Sh!" Through the very walls and closed door William saw the president's considerate thumb jerked in his direction. "'Sh! He'll hear. There'll be no permanent loss to us, you know. The newspapers must put that in. It will prevent a run on us. McCurdy is in my office. We'll get together soon."

Their voices died down. The telephone-bells were jingling from all directions.

"Is that police headquarters? Well, this is—"

William would have stood up, his ear to the door, had he not known so well all that was flying over the wires. The clerk at the 'phone in the nearest booth was now in communication with the editorial office of a leading daily.

"Yes, you can send him around," the clerk said. "I'll tell him all I know about it."

William clasped his hands between his gaunt knees. He had once deliberately planned suicide to avoid facing his accusers. Yet now, with safety in his grasp, how could he face the defamers of his innocent brother? Strange, but this was agony—even greater agony than the other situation. He told himself that he must get away from it, for the moment, anyway. Bradford had suggested a loophole. No man of refinement would want to be present during the investigation of his own brother's ill conduct. No, he would go out, home, for a walk—somewhere, anywhere. He had left Charles's note with Bradford. That was sufficient in all reason to absolve William from any suspicion whatever. Yes, he would go. There were situations under which a man's leaving such a scene would suggest complicity, but this would imply naught else than broken-hearted innocence burdened beyond physical endurance. Taking his hat, he went out into the street. As he passed the main counting-room many eyes were lifted from ponderous tomes and machines. Curiosity and sympathy combined were in the awed and stealthy glances. Outside, at the door, a group had gathered. It was as if a telepathic sense of the tragedy within had permeated the walls.

"There he goes! That's his brother!" reached William's ears as he elbowed his way to the pavement. "Hey! there comes the chief of police!" the same voice said. "Quick action, if he *is* fat, eh?"

William did not care to see the official in question even at a distance. He kept his eyes on the ground and hurried away. Home? he asked himself. No, not now—not now. Celeste would wonder. She would have to be told, and how could he tell her the thing that his reason assured him she would never believe? A woman's intuition! Ah, it was to be dreaded! It did not lend itself readily to practical subterfuge. Business men, bank examiners, skilled detectives would be led by mere physical evidence—a man's written confession, his open flight, his reckless past and inebriety, but a woman's faith was too deep and well-informed for that. What was to be done—what? He crossed the Common; he plunged into the Public Gardens; he strode through into Commonwealth Avenue, and on and on. He knew not where he was going or with what object in view, but he must keep in motion. He wanted to put a certain thing behind him, but that thing was in his brain and it was producing a thousand pictures—pictures of his boyhood with Charles as a toddling infant beside him; of his later young manhood with Charles, a careless school-boy shirking his studies for open-air sport; Charles as he entered the bank under his protection; Charles in the beginning of his reckless career; Charles as he had last seen him, drawing the accumulated burthen of another man's folly upon his sturdy, repentant shoulders. Great God! How could he go through with it? And yet it must be done. The terrible game must be played to a finish. After all, was the whole thing not right? Through this sacrifice were not a good woman and a helpless child escaping shame and misery? True, he had made a misstep, but so had Charles. It would be comforting to know that, in a sense, he and Charles were on a sort of level. Ah, but they were not—they were not! Pragmatically tested, they were different. Charles was now living in the joyful consciousness that a great good was to come out of his self-renunciation; but it was vastly different with the man for whom the renunciation had been made. William had never loved his brother so much as now. He had never before been capable of such a love. From the depths of the pit into which he had fallen Charles appeared as a far-off superman. William might have wept, but men do not weep while in terror, and William was afraid. After all, he asked himself, with a start, how could he be sure that his secret transactions in stocks might not be ferreted out by this same McCurdy, or some one else? These facts brought to light and the authorities would readily see through the thin ruse that was being perpetrated.

For more than two hours he walked, here and there. He crossed the bridge to Cambridge. His dull stare swept the various college buildings and stately clubs, but they only reminded him of Charles and what Charles was doing for him. Why, the day Charles was graduated his friends had honored him with—But why think of trivialities? Perhaps at the bank some further discovery was being made. Had he covered his tracks completely? How could he tell? He turned abruptly homeward. He would plead a headache; he would shut himself in his room; he would explain nothing to Celeste. She would wonder, but the newspapers would tell her all.

CHAPTER X

Alone in his little room, Charles became conscious of a vast sense of fatigue, induced, no doubt, by the fact that his fears concerning his brother's fate were now allayed. Removing his coat and shoes, he threw himself on the hard, narrow bed and was soon soundly asleep. He did not awaken till three o'clock in the afternoon, and might have slept longer but for the harsh sound of a truck delivering coal through a sheet-iron chute into the basement of a house next door. He lay for several minutes trying to recall some vaguely delectable and flitting dreams he had just been enjoying. Somehow, by sheer contrast to their evanescent quality, the sordid little room and its meager furnishings produced a depression that had not come to him since the beginning of his flight. His thoughts were on his home, and he was all but faint under the sharp realization that it was his home no longer.

Presently he heard a step on the stairs. It was a slow, discouraged one, and the man who made it opened the room adjoining his and went in, leaving the door open. Feeling the need of fresh air, Charles got up and opened his own door. And as he did so he saw the inmate of the other room standing over the open trunk. To his surprise he recognized him as the man whose acquaintance he had made at the restaurant. Their eyes met.

"I see you got fixed," the stranger said, with a smile that seemed forced. "Well, you will like it, all right, I think. As for me, I'm bounced. I've had my walking-papers. Mrs. Reilly is a good soul, but she has to live, and I don't blame her. Do you know, she was awfully good about it—tried to let me down easy, says I can take my trunk and all that, and forget what I owe her. Take my trunk! Huh! as if I'd carry it out on my shoulder, which I'd have to do or cheat the expressman out of his dues."

"I'm sorry you are going," Charles said. "I wish we could be neighbors."

"Well, so am I," the other responded, listlessly, "but we can't have everything our way. After all, the sleeping is good in the parks such weather as this. I've done it, and I can do it again, but I sha'n't need a trunk. I'll leave it. And I'll pay Mrs. Reilly some day. I've always paid my way."

Some one was coming. It was the landlady herself. Her face was very grave and full of feeling. She seemed slightly surprised at finding the two men together. Charles explained how they had met at breakfast.

"And he sent you to me?" she said. "He recommended me?"

"Yes, that is how I got the address," Charles returned.

She turned on the young man suddenly. She was trying to smile, though her face was full of contradictory emotions. "Mr. Mason," she faltered, as she touched him on his arm, "I must tell you the truth, and I'll do it right here, facing this gentleman. I hardly slept a wink last night, tired as I was from house-cleaning and beating carpets, because I said what I did yesterday about you leaving. And now I hear in this roundabout way that you have been trying to help me. Humph!" she laughed, making a sound in her throat like a suppressed sob, "do you think I'm going to let you go? Not on your life. I've never had a young man under my roof that I liked better. I'd rather keep you here for nothing than to get money for the room from some of the scamps that are floating about."

"You are very good, Mrs. Reilly," Mason said, with emotion on his part, "but I don't think, owing you for three weeks already, that—"

"Three weeks nothing! Cut that out!" she exclaimed. She strode to a window and examined the tattered shade. "There is no demand for rooms now, anyway. Do you hear me, you are going to stay? I've got to have new shades here, that's all there is about it. Yes, I want you to stay, Mr. Mason, and that settles it. You will find work, I'm sure of it. It is a dull season, that's all. Business will pick up later. It always does."

Mason was blandly protesting, his color high in his cheeks, when she suddenly whirled from the room.

"You are to stay!" she called back from the head of the stairs. "You talk to him, sir," she added to Charles. "He is a nice young man and needs a home of some sort."

The situation being embarrassing, Charles went into his own room. Mason, now without his coat and his shirt-collar open, stalked in after him.

"Sorry you had to hear all that," he said with wincing, tight-drawn lips. "Great God! do you know, sir, that the hardest thing on earth for an able-bodied man to do is to receive help from a working-woman? God! it stings like fire—it kills me!"

"I see, I see," Charles answered. "Your feeling is natural to your particular temperament. In your case you'd better owe it to a man. I want to be frank with you, Mr. Mason. You can do me a favor. I have the money to spare, and I want you to let me advance it for you."

"You? You? Great God! man, you are not in earnest! You don't mean it!"

"But I do," Charles said, firmly. "It is selfish on my part, too, for I don't want you to go away. I'm a stranger here and I'm lonely. I'm out of work myself; I want your companionship; strangers though we are to each other, I feel as if we were old friends. I can't tell why this is, but I do."

"I know, I guess," said the astounded man as he sank into the chair near the window. "I suppose we are both troubled to some extent. I thought you looked bothered a little at breakfast this morning. I'd like to be with you, too, but I couldn't start out in any stranger's debt like that, you know. It is—is almost as bad, you see, as owing a woman."

"You mustn't feel as you do in regard to me, at least," Charles said. "I am without a home. I don't want to be alone. I would love to share the little I have with you. Something draws me to you like ties of blood."

It was significant that Mason made no reply. He leaned forward, clasping his big freckled hands between his knees. He dropped his head, his reddish-brown curls lopped over his wide brow. He was silent. Charles saw his shoulders rise and fall convulsively, as if he were trying to suppress a tumult of feeling. Presently he raised his head. His hunger-pinched lips were twisted awry.

"My God!" he gulped, "I didn't know I'd ever run across a fellow like you. I thank you! I thank you! I thank you!" He got up; his knees, in his frayed, bulging trousers, shook visibly. He moved to the door, passed through it, and went into his own room. From his position near the door Charles saw him reel past the trunk, totter, and clutch a post of the old-fashioned bed. Holding it, he stood swaying back and forth, his head hanging low on a limp neck. Charles ran to him, caught his arm, and made him lie down on the bed. Mason was ghastly pale.

"It is nothing," he said, trying to smile carelessly. "It will pass over. I had it once yesterday in the street."

"I know what it is." Charles bent over him tenderly. "You are weak from hunger."

"Do you think that is it?" Mason asked, resignedly, doggedly.

"Yes, and it has to end right here and now. We are friends, aren't we? I'm going down and bring you something this minute. It is not a woman that is offering it, Mason. It is a friend who knows what suffering is. Wait! Lie still. I'll hurry back."

From the restaurant where he had breakfasted that morning Charles secured some hot chicken broth with bread and coffee. As he was hurrying back, he met a newsboy selling afternoon papers. The thought darted through his brain that the papers might contain an account of his flight which had been telegraphed from Boston, and he bought a paper and thrust it into his pocket. He met Mrs. Reilly as he was entering the front door. Hurriedly he explained the reason for his bringing the food.

"Good gracious!" she cried. "I thought he looked bad. One of my roomers said it was dope, but I didn't believe him. And I was turning him out in that condition! Think of it—just think of it!"

"I am to pay the back rent he owes, Mrs. Reilly," Charles said, putting the things down on a step of the chair and taking out his purse.

"You? Not on your life!" she threw back, warmly. "Do you think I'll let a stranger come and do more for that poor boy than I've done, when he was going about drumming up trade for me after what I said to him? Not on your life! I'll feed him, too, from this on. I'll bring him his breakfast if he ain't able to come down in the morning."

Seeing that she would not receive the money, Charles took up the things and ascended the stairs. He found Mason seated at the window in the cooling breeze from the open space in the rear.

His eyes held the eager gleam of a starving man shipwrecked on a raft. He tried to make light of his hunger as Charles hurriedly placed a small table near him and filled a soup-plate with the rich broth, which contained tender fragments of chicken.

"Here, tackle this, you chump!" said Charles, and he laughed as he used to laugh in his school-days. "The idea of your letting yourself starve in this great, enlightened, Christian city!"

Mason obeyed. A warm look of reviving health was in his face as he drank the soup. The plate was soon empty. Charles filled it again, and poured out the hot coffee. As he did so he felt the folded newspaper in his pocket, and a sudden cool shock of dismay went through him. What might not the paper say? Some one might have seen him take the train in Boston. Some one might have watched him on his arrival in New York. The very house he was in might already be shadowed by instructed officials. Men nowadays were captured easily enough in the vast network of the detective system.

As he crumbled his bread into the broth Mason's satisfied glance swept the face of his companion. "What are you worried about?" he asked. "I saw you change all at once like you was thinking of something unpleasant. I hope it ain't me. My God! I don't want to be a burden on a man as kind as you are!"

"You? No, no! But I have my little troubles, Mason," Charles admitted, frankly. "I try to keep my mind off of them, but they will sneak back at times. Don't think it is money; it is not that, and instead of being a burden you are just the reverse. You are a great help to me."

"I'm sorry you have worries," Mason responded, with a sigh. "But it seems to me that every one I meet has some trouble or other. The thing has its funny side, too. I could dance and sing with this feed in me, thanks to you. This morning, after I left you, I went looking for a job, as usual. I had failed to see the firms I had in view in Wall Street, and was standing in front of an old church down there when a shabbily dressed man with a red nose came up to me.

"'Say, boss,' he began, 'can you give a feller a dime to pay his carfare home? I'm stranded here and got to get back.'

"It struck me as funny—his wanting money to get booze with, and me without bread, and I laughed in his face. 'Say,' I said, 'I was about to ask you the same question, but I've never begged in my life, and I don't know how to go about it.'

"'Oh, is that it? New hand, eh?' he said, very cordially. 'Well, young feller, I don't mind giving you a tip or two to start you out. I was green at it once myself. Now look here. You are too timid. Brace up. Nothing ventured, nothing gained. Pick 'em out as they come along. Take the best-dressed first. Learn to know the labels on cigars and make a break for the costly smokers. If you see a feller smiling, he's your game. If you see two prosperous-looking guys chatting in a friendly way, strike 'em both. One will try to outdo the other. I won a dollar in a game like that once out of two fellers getting in a fine auto. Women are all right, too, but when you see one coming you'd better just hang your head and look sadlike, especially if you are at the lead-pencil game.'

"I thanked him," Mason finished, "but I never profited by his advice. I simply can't beg. Say, is that an afternoon paper in your pocket? I wonder if it carries want ads?"

"I don't really know," Charles replied, drawing the paper out slowly and awkwardly, for in some way it seemed to cling to his pocket and his fingers were not apt as usual. He spread it out, and as he held it toward his companion some large head-lines on the first page caught his attention and a cold wave of despair swept over him.

"Robbery of a Boston Bank! Absconding Clerk Makes Away with Sixty Thousand Dollars. Ten Thousand Dollars Reward Offered!"

Mason was taking the paper into his extended hand. It seemed to Charles as if the dismal room were enveloped in a mist. He heard Mason saying something as if from a great height or depth as he opened the rustling sheet.

"Excuse me," Charles managed to say. "I'll come back in a moment."

Mason made some reply which he did not hear, and Charles went into his own room, where he stood at the window, looking out over the back yards below. Why, he asked himself, was he so terribly alarmed all at once? Was not all this to be expected? To do him full credit, he was not even then thinking of himself. It was William. It was Celeste. It was little Ruth. They were first in his thoughts. Ah, after all, was his vicarious effort at rescue to fail totally? He stood at the window a long time, lost in a flood of reflections. It was now sundown. Lights in the rear rooms of the buildings across the court were flashing up. He heard a match being struck in Mason's room and the rustling of the tell-tale paper. He crept to the door, glanced in, and saw his new friend standing under a flaring gas-jet, with the first page of the paper before his eyes. Was he reading the Boston news? Would he couple his new friend's arrival on that particular train with the events described? Well, what did it matter? Something told him that even were he a murderer his secret would be safe with Mason; and yet, if possible to avoid it, Mason must not know, for Charles had promised his brother that no circumstances should wring the truth from him. Mason remained at the jet, reading as if wholly absorbed. There could be no doubt now that it was the Boston report that had caught his attention.

Suddenly, while he watched him, Mason lowered the paper, and Charles had barely time to step back to the window before Mason was on the threshold, the paper in his hand.

"Pardon me," he said, staring through the dusk at Charles, "I did not mean to take your paper from you. I was expecting you back every minute and got to reading about—about"—there was a slight pause here as it seemed to Charles's overwrought fancy—"about a poor chap in Boston who got away with a pile of boodle. It is interesting, the whole tale. Booze, booze! The old, old story—secret speculations, and women. Family broken-hearted. Went back on his best friend, his only brother, who stands at the top socially. Gosh! I've been reckless myself, but not like that, thank God! I've been my own worst enemy, but I never hurt my people like that. I'm sorry for the poor devil! I really am sorry! This paper speaks of the chap as having had lots of friends before he got to the bottom. They are usually like that, free and easy and kind-hearted. Oh, I guess he was tempted, poor devil! And he will be caught, they think. Left for New York last night and is hiding here."

Mason was offering him the open paper and Charles took it. Before a man so genuine as his new friend had shown himself to be, he could not bring himself to play a part. Silently he dropped the paper on his bed. He sat down by it, leaving Mason standing with a sort of dumb inquiry in his eyes. It was significant that Mason was now silent. It was significant that he seemed to be studying Charles's features in the dim light from the gas, studying them with an awkward, reluctant stare.

"I'll read it later—later," Charles said, faintly, taking up the paper and laying it on the pillow of his bed. "I hope you feel better since you've eaten," he went on, lamely. "I—I thought the soup would do you good, weak as you are."

The natural thing for Mason to have done would have been to reiterate his appreciation, but he only stood staring helplessly at Charles. Afterward Charles understood. The paper contained an accurate description of him— appearance, age, manner, and the very suit he was then wearing. Mumbling some excuse, Mason went back to his room. Charles heard him moving about, and now and then he saw his shadow flit across the floor of the hall.

Some one was coming up the stairs. Could it be an officer of the law? Why not? He stood up to meet whatever fate was in store. He dared not look toward the stairs. He pretended to be unconcerned. Then he saw that it was only Mrs. Reilly.

"You must have fresh towels," she smiled, genially. "I almost forgot them. I hope you like your room, Mr.—Mr.—I didn't get your name. I like to know who my roomers are, for parcels and mail are always coming."

"Browne," he answered, impulsively, and then bit his lip to keep the word back. But it was too late, and the situation was complicated by the sudden appearance of Mason in the doorway of his room behind Mrs. Reilly. The startled look in his face and the fact that he disappeared at once showed that he had caught the name and grasped its significance.

"Brown? That's common enough," Mrs. Reilly laughed. "I've had Browns and Whites and Blacks all at the same time. How is Mr. Mason? I'm going in to see him."

Turning, she went into Mason's room, and Charles heard her laughing and talking in her voluble way. He wanted her to leave so that he might read the printed condemnation of himself from his old home. She seemed to linger unnecessarily. Presently, however, she went down the stairs, and, lighting the gas, he read the article. Mason had given him a compact summary of the whole thing, but the details lashed him like whips of fire. It is one thing to make a sacrifice for a loved brother, but it is quite another to bear calmly such consequences as he was facing. It was plain now that even if he escaped he was forever lost to his past.

He heard Mason coming back. What could the fellow want?

"I see," Mason began, almost huskily, "that I am more deeply in your debt than I thought. Mrs. Reilly told me that you wanted to pay my back dues. I don't know what to say to show my appreciation. I have never, in all my knocking about, met a man with such a kind heart."

"Oh, don't mention that!" Charles replied. "It was nothing."

"But it is—it is to me, you may be sure. I'll never forget it as long as I live. I want to serve you. I want to be your friend as you have been mine. I've come here now to tell you that"—Charles knew what he meant in full—"that I will stick to you through thick and thin. I think I understand the—the trouble you spoke of just now. You will need a friend now, and I will be that friend."

Their eyes met. They both understood.

"Yes, I need a friend," Charles said, thickly, "and it is good to find such a one in you. Some time I may be able to speak more freely about myself than I can now, but I will say that, as I see it, I am not—not quite as bad as one would think."

"I know that. I'd bet my very life on it," Mason declared, warmly. "But let all that drop. Don't tell me anything. I know men, and I know you are pure gold. I want to help you and I will do it if it is possible."

Turning back, he entered his own room. A wonderful sense of security, blended with a sense of new-found comradeship, descended on the lonely, pursued man. He now had an adviser, a friend whom he could trust, and it was one who was capable of suffering, who even now was suffering.

That night he slept soundly, strangely free from the fear of arrest.

CHAPTER XI

When William Browne reached home, after his aimless walk which he had taken on leaving the bank that tumultuous morning, he endeavored to reach his room unnoticed by any member of the family, but on the landing of the second floor he met Celeste. She regarded him with a slow look of tentative surprise.

"I've been worried", she said.

"Worried, why?" he questioned, with a start.

"Because Mr. Bradford telephoned me two hours ago that you had started home and that you were not feeling very well. He seemed worried, from the excited way he spoke. Of course I looked for you at once. How could I tell but that you were seriously ill somewhere?"

"I thought a walk would do me good, and I took it," William bethought himself to say. "If I'd known he was telephoning I would have come directly home."

He started to pass her, but, touching his arm, she detained him. Her cheeks were pale, her thin lips were quivering.

"What *is* the matter?" she demanded.

"I told you I was not feeling very well," he answered, lamely, trying to meet her penetrating stare with an air of complete self-possession. "I've had a lot of head-work to do at night. I'm afraid I am near a breakdown. Bradford noticed it and advised me to come home."

He passed her now, and went into his room. She followed close behind him, and when he turned he saw her.

"Oh!" he exclaimed, in surprise, for he thought he had left her outside. "What is it now, Lessie? You know you are acting strangely."

The window-shades were drawn down, but she resolutely raised one, letting the sunlight stream in on him.

"If I am acting strangely, so are you—so are you," she said, desperately. "Something has happened, William, and you can't keep it from me. I have a right to know and I will know." She sat down in an arm-chair and folded her white hands in her lap.

He tried to smile, but his smile was such a ghastly failure that he gave it up. He turned to the bureau. He began to unbutton his collar and untie his cravat. His brain had never been more active than now. She would soon know the whole story through the afternoon papers, why keep it from her now? The only explanation was that William Browne could not find within himself the power and poise openly to accuse his brother. His conscience was against it and something else was against it—the fear of Celeste's shrewd condemnatory intuition. She did not leave him long to his turbulent reflections. "You may as well tell me," he heard her say. "I shall sit right here till you do. Is it about Charles?"

He was glad that she was behind him, since he had to speak.

"Yes, it concerns him," William answered. "He has gone away, no one knows where. You know how he has been acting of late? Well, well, he is gone this time for good, it seems."

"But that isn't all—it isn't all, and you know it isn't!" Celeste leaned forward and fixed him with a demanding stare. "That wouldn't make you act as you are now acting, or look as you look."

William jerked his cravat from his neck and stood folding it with unsteady fingers. "You may as well know the—the rest," he stammered. "It will be in the papers. He has been reckless. Half the time he did not know what he was doing. He must have been out of his head, for a large amount of money is missing from the vault. He had free access to it. The examiners were due here to-day, and—and the thing could not have been kept from them, so—so he left last night."

"I know. You told me this morning at breakfast," Celeste's tone was firm, impersonal, impatient. "He wrote you a note. Was it about that—about the missing money?"

William's eyes sought the carpet as he answered: "Yes, he didn't have much else to say. He seemed to think that would be sufficient to—to thoroughly explain why—why he was leaving."

Celeste stood up. She sighed. Her husband had never seen in her face the expression that was in it now.

"William, I am not a child. I am not a fool!" she said, fiercely. "I want you to be frank with me. He is your brother and we love him. Why are you not perfectly—perfectly, absolutely open about this?"

"Open? Am I not open?" he evaded, as stupidly as a guilty child facing indisputable proof. "What—what is wrong now? Haven't I told you all that I know about it? You ought not to—to expect me to be in a natural, normal state of mind after a thing like this has happened. Surely you see that it was all due to me—I mean that but for me the directors would not have allowed Charlie to be about the bank after he became so dissipated. As it is—as it is, I have agreed to repay the missing money. It will almost bankrupt me, but I shall do it some way or other."

"You did not know it before you got his note at breakfast?" Celeste asked.

"No, not till then. It was like a bolt from a clear sky," said William, slightly more at ease.

"I don't believe it—I don't believe a word of that," Celeste said, firmly.

"You don't? You think I am lying, then?" William gasped. "My God! that you should say that to me!"

"I don't believe it," Celeste repeated. "I don't, because this morning when you came down you were very dejected. I have never seen you look so much so. It lasted till you read Charles's note. Then your face fairly blazed with relief. If Charles told you for the first time in that note that he was a thief, you could not have looked like that. You say you are all upset now over it. Why were you not then?"

"I was—I was, but I tried to hide it from you," was the slow answer.

"I know you did, in a way, but you did not assume that first look of joy and relief. I see that you are bent on keeping me in the dark. I see a reason for it, but I won't mention it now. When you feel like putting complete confidence in your wife, let me know. This is our first misunderstanding, but it is a serious one."

She left him stupefied, unable to formulate any defense. He was aware, too, that his helplessness was in its way a confession that she was right in her contention against him, but what was he to do? Retaining her respect and love meant much to him, but the other horror quite forced it into the background. Celeste must wait. The first thing to be considered was the retention of his high standing at the bank and the respect of the public. The seed of suspicion and disrespect was sown in his own home, but that could not be avoided. Celeste had defended her brother-in-law before; she was doing the same now. She was pitying the absent man too much for the absolute safety of William's plans. The feeling Celeste was entertaining might leak out into public channels, flow here and there, and create dangerous pools of suspicion. William threw himself on his bed. He really needed sleep, but his brain was too active for repose. He was listening for the ring of the 'phone in the hall below—or, worse than that, the ring of the door-bell. What was to keep those shrewd men at the bank from seeing through a pretense already half punctured by a woman? William thought of the revolver, but that was at the bank. He thought of quick poisons, but he had none, then of gas, but the room was too large and airy. Suddenly he sat up on the bed, his stockinged feet on the floor, his ears strained to catch a sound which came from the street.

"Extra! Extra! Extra! Big Bank Robbery! Sixty Thousand! Thief in High Social Standing!"

The front door below was opened, but not closed. He crept to a window over the stoop and peered through the ivy hanging from the wall. It was Celeste buying a paper from a newsboy. She was reading it. Only the top of her head was visible, outlined against the paper. How unlike Celeste to stand like that on the stoop, in the view of people passing by! An automatic pang of pity went through the storm-tossed man. Could that really be the young girl whom he had loved so passionately—the frail, tender feminine creature he had taken from the care and protection of devoted parents, and brought to this? A dead ivy-leaf was swinging by a spider's web and spinning before his eyes. How odd that he should note it, that he should notice how the rays of the sun fell on the dome of the Capitol, that he should find his brain estimating how many copies of the paper the shouting boy could dispose of in that street! Celeste was coming into the house. She was out of his view now. He knew that she was in the hall below, still reading, still wondering, still bent on knowing more than the paper could reveal.

When she had finished reading the account, Celeste, white in the face and yet steady in her step, went back to the dining-room. Michael was there at work, a cleaning-cloth and metal-polish in hand, rows of knives, forks, and spoons ranged in perfect order on the table in front of him. His mistress faced him.

"Did you know, Michael," she began, spreading out the paper on the table, "that this paper says that Charles has stolen a large amount of money and run away?"

Instead of answering, he bent over the paper. His kindly eyes took in the head-lines at a glance and he looked up, slowly shaking his head.

"Yes, yes, I see it is here," he answered. "I was afraid something would be said. I was afraid last night that something was wrong, but I don't believe he took any money. I don't! I never will believe it."

Celeste stepped to him. He was merely a servant, but she put an eager hand on his arm and looked into his face steadily.

"I don't believe it, either, Michael," she said, huskily. "I'll never believe it. He's gone—he's gone, but something else was at the bottom of it. It may have been like this—don't you see? Don't you see my idea? I know that he was thoroughly disgusted over his dissipation—over what they say happened at the police station and his club; he made up his mind that perhaps he was a burden on us and determined that he would go away. And it just happens, you see, that the money was missing and they all connect him with the loss because he is gone?"

"It does look like that, madam," Michael said almost eagerly.

"But, Michael, Michael, what do you think of *this*?" and she pointed to a paragraph in the paper. "Here is what they say was in the note you handed Mr. Browne at breakfast. See! See! Look! Read it!"

Michael obeyed stolidly, then he looked up. "I know," he said, "and I think he wrote it. I think so from something he said to me about bank money last night, but still I don't think he is guilty. He didn't look it, madam."

"You say he didn't?" Celeste's fine features held an incipient fire which glowed through her thin skin and was focused in her eyes.

"No, madam, he was too—I might say, too happy-looking. Oh, I know the difference between the looks of a guilty man and an innocent one! I've run against both brands."

"And you say he was happy—happy over leaving us, perhaps never to return? Don't you think that is strange, Michael?"

"Yes, madam, that was odd. I must say that I could not make it out. He was jolly, and he was not drinking, either. If I never see him again, I'll never forget how he looked."

"I've been to his room," Celeste went on. "He took very few things, but do you remember the last photograph of Ruth that he had, in a silver frame on his bureau? He took that; at least it is missing."

"Yes, I saw him put it into his bag," said the servant. "Oh, he thinks a lot of the child!"

"And she almost worships him"—Celeste's voice shook at its lowest depths—"and she will never understand his absence. How am I to tell her? What am I to say? She may hear this"—indicating the paper with a gesture of contempt—"from other children. Oh, Michael, to think that her ideal is to be destroyed, and unjustly destroyed, for, as you say, and as I say, our Charlie is not a thief!"

Michael had taken up his cleaning-cloth and a silver platter. "I shall never believe that he is, madam," he faltered. "I shall not read that paper, either. It would upset me—make me mad."

"I had to," Celeste replied, dejectedly. "I see now that I'll have to read other things about him. He may be brought back to Boston, Michael. You see the mention of the big reward? They will search everywhere, and Charlie is too unsuspecting, too innocent, to get away—that is, if he really *wants* to get away. Did it strike you last night that he wanted to get away unhindered, Michael?"

"Yes, madam, he was anxious about that, and that is strange, too."

"Yes, it is strange," Celeste said, "for he is not guilty. He must have had a reason, but what could it have been, Michael?"

"I can't say, madam," answered the servant, applying his polish and rubbing the platter vigorously.

Celeste folded the paper. "This talk is just between us," she said, half questioningly.

"I understand, madam, I understand," Michael said, bowing as she was leaving the room.

In the hall she met her husband coming down the stairs, his trembling hand sliding on the walnut balustrade as for support. Their eyes met. "I am going back to the bank," he explained. "It is after closing-time, but the directors may be holding a consultation. It would be better, I think, for me to offer any assistance in my power. Bradford suggested that I stay away for a while, but I have thought it over and I think I ought to be there."

"Yes, it might be better," Celeste agreed, or seemed to agree. "If you hear anything bearing on—on Charlie's innocence—if they discover that the money was taken by some one else—I wish you would telephone me at once."

"Some one else?" he said, staring blankly. "But you see they have his note. Bradford wanted that to—to show to the rest."

"Yes, I know about the note"—Celeste was turning into the parlor, her eyes averted—"but something else may come up to throw light on even the note."

"Yes, perhaps," he admitted, stupidly, "and in that case I'll 'phone you."

She vanished through the door, and he stalked down the steps into the street. He walked slowly and with a self-imposed limp. He kept his head down.

"Something is wrong with her," he mused, turbulently. "She does not believe it all. She may never be satisfied, and in that case what am I to do? I can't keep this up. It is as unbearable as the other thing from which Charlie saved me. But I must not give in—I must not! He has given me his word of honor never to reveal our compact and never to return. If he is not caught I shall escape. I may lose my wife, but I'll escape."

CHAPTER XII

Two weeks passed by. For the most of the time Charles stayed close in the larger room, which he and Mason now occupied together, with a view to the utmost economy. They had become warm friends. When Charles's funds were almost exhausted Mason received a check for fifty dollars in payment of a debt owed him by a brother-in-law in the West, and Charles had to share it.

Mason never again alluded to the discovery he had made in regard to the trouble Charles was in, excepting once, when they were walking together in a crowded street on the East Side, and he had noticed that Charles seemed to be slightly nervous.

"Leave it to me," said Mason, suddenly. "I'll keep a sharp watch out, and I'll let you know if I see the slightest thing that looks fishy. Keep your mind off of it. I don't want to know any more about it, either. From what you say I gather that you are bound by some promise or other to keep your mouth eternally closed, even to a friend like me. That's all right. I admire you all the more for it. You may be a thief to those Boston folks, but you are not to me. The fact that you don't even deny the charge means nothing to me."

Upon another occasion, one rainy evening Mason took up the framed photograph of Ruth which Charles always had on the bureau, table, or mantelpiece, and stood admiring it.

"Say, pal," he said, suddenly, as he wiped the glass over the little face with his handkerchief, "if I ever leave you I'll want to steal this thing. It has grown on me. She must be a beauty, and so sweet and gentle."

Charles rose, took the picture into his hands, and stood looking at it steadily. "I wouldn't take the world for it," he said.

"I think I know something about her—I can guess. You say you used to drink hard at one time, though you don't now."

"Yes, that's true, but what else?" Charles went on, still feasting his homesick eyes on the picture.

"I don't want to bring up things that will pain you for no good in the world," Mason said, "so let's drop it."

"No, go ahead," Charles urged, half smiling. "I want you to finish, for I think, from some little things you have dropped now and then, that you are mistaken about me—in one particular, at least."

"Well," Mason went on, "I have an idea that you were once happily married and that—well, the old habit got the upper hand so far that your wife took the little girl and went away."

"Wrong, old man," Charles said, with a weary smile. "I've never been married."

"Ah, then she is a little sister?"

"No, only a niece," Charles interrupted, "but I love her and I think she loved me at one time, and may still, perhaps. They say that children soon forget those they love, and, as I shall never see Ruth again, she is sure to forget me; but I shall never forget her. Do you know, old man, that that very little angel has seen me drunk. She has crept into my arms and hugged me tight when I was too drunk to know she was near. I came to myself one day when she was crying in alarm because she could not wake me up. Oh, if I could blot that out! Perhaps when Ruth is grown she will recall that, scene more vividly than any other associated with me. It is odd, but I don't feel as if I shall ever drink a drop again—the desire has left me completely. I don't know why, but it has."

"Our talk is on the wrong line to-night," Mason said, sympathetically. "You said once that it was absolutely impossible for you ever to go back to your old friends, and if that is so this talk is doing you no good at all."

"No, it is doing no good," Charles admitted. "When I think of those old days my very soul seems torn apart. Lost opportunities—the 'what might have been' but wasn't! Yes, let's talk of the present. What chance for work now?"

Mason lighted his pipe, which he had been carefully filling. "There is a chance, but not here in New York. To tell you the truth, I rather like the idea, for it is the only thing I have seen in which we could stay together."

"A chance? What is it?" Charles demanded, putting the picture back into its place.

"You may laugh, but this monotony is killing me, and I am thinking seriously of taking the plunge," Mason said, as he puffed away. "I want you to come, but not if you don't like it. This morning I met a man in Union

Square who told me he was taking a week off from a job with a traveling circus and menagerie. It is now in Philadelphia. It will be in Newark, New Jersey, the day after to-morrow. He says men who are willing to do hard manual labor can always get employment, good food, fair sleeping-quarters on the train, and two dollars a day promptly paid. I've always liked outdoor work. The thing fairly charms me, for I want to see more of the country, but I don't want to throw you over. I've got used to you. I'd be lost without you. I've never had a real pal before."

Charles lighted his own pipe. He frowned as if in deep reflection. "I'm going to be frank," he said, presently. "I am like you. I like the idea of that sort of life immensely, and I am dying of dry rot. But I am wondering, would a man—well, a man like me, for instance—be as safe there as here."

"Safer, in my opinion," Mason declared, eagerly. "In a roundabout way I dug it out of the chap that many of the hangers-on were fellows who, for different reasons, were dodging officers of the law. He said he did not like that feature of the life, but that you don't have to associate with them unless you like. Gosh! you know, I like the idea, and I wish you did!"

"Newark, day after to-morrow," Charles said, thoughtfully. "That's close. Well, I'll think it over. It looks inviting, doesn't it? Yes, I'll think it over. What will we have to do?"

Mason laughed. "Feed the animals; drive stakes and pull them up; help about the big tent-kitchen; dress up like Turks or some other outlandish creature and march in the street processions, and Heaven only knows what else."

"It is getting interesting," Charles smiled. "I'll let you know soon. Keep it in view. It is the only thing in sight, and we will starve at this rate."

The two friends happened to be in Madison Square the following afternoon, and were attracted by the sight of several groups of people gathered around some "soap-box" orators in the space set aside by the city for such meetings. Speeches were made daily by the men and women on religion, science, philosophy and every form of politics from crass anarchy to ideal socialism. For the most part, the speakers were of foreign birth or the descendants of foreigners. Presently they were drawn into a group that was gathering about a blond-bearded philosopher who had the ascetic face of a mystic and who was telling how he had forsaken a life of practical activity and had found infinite peace. Men in the group who openly avowed themselves to be atheists began to laugh and jeer and ask pertinent questions. The speaker replied to them. A fierce argument arose. The noise of the discussion attracted persons in the other groups and Mason and Charles found themselves hemmed in by the close-pressing human mass.

Charles, who was deeply interested in the man's theory of renunciation, suddenly felt his friend nudging him with his elbow. Looking into his face he detected a queer expression in it.

"Let's get out," Mason said, in a low voice. There was no mistaking the insistent note of warning which it held, and, sure now that something was wrong, Charles quickly assented and began worming his way through the crowd. It was difficult to do so, for the spectators were all deeply interested in the argument and did not care to stand aside. As they laboriously moved forward, inch by inch, Charles noticed that Mason now and then cast a furtive backward glance into the throng, as if anxious to avoid some one.

"Come on, come on!" he kept urging. Finally they were free and on the open sidewalk. "Come on!" Mason repeated, his eyes on the ground.

"What is the matter?" Charles asked, bewildered.

Looking back toward the crowd, Mason suddenly lowered his head again and said, warningly: "Don't look back. I see him watching us. He followed us out of the crowd." Mason swore under his breath. "I don't like the looks of this a bit—not a bit!"

Further along he explained. "I was looking over that bunch of men just now when all at once I saw a short man a little behind us watching you like a hawk. He evidently didn't think we were together. He never let your face leave him for a minute. I saw his eyes gleaming, as if he had just discovered you and was studying your features."

"And you think—" Charles did not finish.

"He looked to me like a detective in plain clothes. I have seen some of them, and he was of that type. He couldn't hide his interest. You know your picture has been published. It looked to me like this fellow was comparing you to it in his mind. I don't know, but I am sure we must dodge him if we can."

"I ought not to have come out like this," Charles sighed, gloomily. "I've been a fool."

"Never mind, come on," Mason said, looking back. "I don't see him now. We'll give him the shake."

They went up to Central Park; they sat there on one of the benches till sundown, and then went back to their room. Both were very grave and neither had much to say.

CHAPTER XIII

At seven o'clock Mason proposed that he should go out and get something for them to eat, while Charles stayed in the house to avoid the possibility of being seen by any one who might be searching for him. Charles consented, but when his friend was gone his sheer loneliness became all but unbearable. The tawdry room with its cheap gas-fixtures of rusted cast iron, the machine-made oil-paintings, the tattered, dust-filled carpet, the cracked furniture, seemed a sort of prison cell in which he was confined. Not since his disappearance from Boston had the outlook seemed so hopeless. He told himself that it would only be a question of a day or so now before he would be caught and taken back to his old home. He shuddered at the thought of the scandal in the mind of the public. William, who no doubt had felt somewhat secure for the past two weeks, would find himself on that black brink again. Celeste—poor, gentle, sensitive Celeste—would suffer now in reality, and little Ruth! Why, the child might even ask to see him there in jail, and what reason could he give her for his incarceration? He paced the floor back and forth. How long Mason was in returning! Had anything detained him? Presently Mason came back. He brought nothing with him. He looked too much concerned to have thought of his errand.

"Say, it's serious," he began. "I didn't have time to go to the restaurant. As I went out, old man, I saw that same fellow standing in front of our door, across the street. He was in the shadow, but I saw him and recognized him by his build. I couldn't doubt it, for when he saw me come out he bolted. He turned and went straight to the corner and down the avenue. I've been watching outside ever since to see if he was coming back."

"Then he followed us," Charles said.

"Every step of the way to the Park. He had us under his eye while we were there, and he dogged our steps back here. Say, you've got to listen to me."

"I'm ready," Charles said, gloomily. "You can decide better than I can."

"Here is my idea," Mason said. "He evidently intends to get a warrant for you, but it may not be possible till to-morrow. We must get away from here to-night—at once. There is no time to lose. We are going to Newark."

"The circus?" Charles said, inquiringly.

"Yes, but we must not be followed by that fellow, or any one else. Now I'll pack a few things, and you do the same. Make a small parcel. Don't bother with your bag. Thank God, our rent is paid. We are not going by train. That would be risky. We are going to walk most of the way through the country. It will be safer than in the trains that may be watched by the police. Hurry now!"

Mason was soon ready. "Listen," he said, impressively. "I'm going outside now. You bring both parcels with you. I'll stroll along the street and make sure that the coast is clear. When you come out, if you see me with a newspaper in my hand it will mean that you are to follow me, and you do it. If I have no paper you are to go back and wait here till I come."

Ten minutes later Charles descended the stairs. He deemed it lucky that he met no one. A clock below was striking ten. Outside he looked up and down the street. Presently he saw Mason on the first corner. He was in front of a laundry, a newspaper in hand. He saw that Mason had seen him, for he turned suddenly and began to walk westward. Charles followed for several blocks. Presently Mason stopped in a spot where there was little light, and waited for him to come up.

"Coast is clear, I think," Mason softly chuckled. "That skunk thinks his game is safe till to-morrow, for he doesn't dream we are on to him."

"Where are we going now?" Charles asked, vastly relieved by his friend's confident tone, and the sudden sense of the freer life into which they were going like two children of Fate.

"We must cross the Hudson somewhere," Mason answered. "We could take the ferry at One Hundred and Thirtieth Street. It is less apt to be watched than the others, but still I want to avoid even that chance of detection. There are some small boat-houses near One Hundred and Eighty-first Street. I've hung about them a good deal. If we can get there unnoticed we can be taken across in a row-boat or small launch—easy enough to pretend to be camping out over there. Hundreds are doing it this summer. We could take a car up, Subway or surface, but I think we ought to make for the river-front and do it afoot. It is a long walk, but it is safe."

"It suits me," Charles agreed, and side by side they continued in their westward course.

Reaching Broadway, they walked northward till they came to Fiftieth Street; then they turned to the river-front. It was a fine night. The Albany excursion-boats, brilliantly lighted, were passing. Hundreds of smaller craft, yachts, sailboats, launches, and canoes, dotted the surface of the broad stream, and from some of them came strains of band music, the strident notes of a clarinet, merry voices singing to the accompaniment of stringed instruments.

"Fine! Fine!" Mason kept muttering. "We ought to have done this before. You can't beat it at this time of the year."

They were passing a small restaurant and Mason paused. "We've got to eat," he laughed. "I like the looks of this snug joint. What do you say?"

Charles consented. The haunting sense of danger was gone. He was hungry. They went in. The hour was too late, the single attendant said, for anything to be served except sandwiches and coffee. They ordered a supply, drank two cups of coffee each, and ate their sandwiches as they walked on.

They were soon in the neighborhood of Columbia University and Grant's Tomb. The moonlight on the river, the abrupt cliffs of the Palisades beyond, on the top of which gleamed the lights of an amusement park, drew Charles into a reminiscent mood which suddenly became painful in the extreme. He told himself that it was no wonder that Mason could be cheerful. He had a home and relatives to whom he could return when he wished, but with Charles the wide world was his only home. He was so bound by his promise to his brother that he could not reveal his entire past even to Mason, who had proved himself worthy of all confidence. Remorse over his ill-spent, dissipated youth was all but gone, for something told him that he was fully atoning for all the mistakes of the past. It was William he was saving, yes, and William's good wife and sweet child growing into promising girlhood. After all, what did it matter what became of him? Nothing, he thought, and with the reflection came a vast sense of peace and freedom from care. He was a man without home or kin now, but what did it matter? All sorts of interesting things could happen to a world-wanderer like himself. He could tell no one who he was or where he was from, but surely he need not be unhappy. Indeed, whenever he thought of William's escape from disgrace and death by his own hand, and realized that his vicarious sacrifice had made possible that escape, he felt wondrously happy.

It was midnight when they reached the boat-house where Mason intended to secure passage across the river. It was a long, narrow, two-story building, with a float at one end and a dance-hall on the upper floor. The hall was lighted up and a dance was in progress. Through the windows they could see the young couples waltzing.

"Glad it is going on," Mason said, reflectively.

"Our chance is all the better to get across. Some of these fellows live in tents on the Jersey shore and may be going back to-night. Stay down here on the float and I'll nose about. I know the owner of the house fairly well."

Charles sat on a bench on the float. The vast sheet of water was smooth. The larger boats were no longer in sight. Now and then a canoe holding a pair of lovers drifted by, or a sailboat almost be-calmed. The sound of a piano and a violin came through the raised windows of the dance-hall, and the low swishing of sliding and tripping feet, merry laughter and jesting, loud orders for drinks or cigars in the bar. Presently Mason came back. Charles saw at a glance that he was pleased over something.

"Boat-house man says he will take us across in a few minutes for a dollar. Cheap enough. He thinks we are out for a hike on the other side. He has a launch. He has to wait till the dance is over. It is breaking up now."

This was true, for the couples came down the stairs and began to get into canoes and launches. The sight of the lovers drew Charles's thoughts back to himself again. Why had he not thought of it before? Love and marriage were the things he could never expect to enjoy, and yet they now seemed to be essential to life. How lovely was the girl with the golden hair and brown eyes who laughed so joyously as her escort tripped over a coil of rope and all but fell into the water! And what a giant of a creature was the man himself as he lifted the slender girl in his arms and playfully shook her to silence her amused twitting.

"Here you are, young feller!" It was the boat-house keeper drawing his little launch alongside the float. "I'll spin you over in five minutes on water like this. You guys are taking an early start for a hike."

"Obliged to do it," Mason fibbed, with a straight face. "We have to catch some chaps at Alpine before they start in the morning. All right. We are ready."

The tiny engine began to rattle. The boat glided away from the float and was soon under way. Looking back at the almost deserted boat-house Charles had a sense of safety from pursuit that was very soothing. He saw, too, that the same thought was evidently in Mason's mind, for he was very easy in his manner and had much to say to the boatman in regard to fishing and boating. They landed at a little pier almost directly opposite the boat-house. Mason paid the fare and the boatman left them.

"Smooth, smooth! Slick, slick!" Mason chuckled. "We are safe now. What do you say; shall we lie down here and take a nap till morning, or go right on? It is six of one and a half-dozen of the other?"

"It is all the same to me," Charles replied. "I am not really tired."

"I am not, either," Mason said. "I'll tell you, though, that my choice would be to hike it by night. I've been over the road once before, and if we go now we will not be noticed by a single soul, while in the daytime we might accidentally be seen by some one on the lookout for you. It is a stiff climb to the top, but let's make it and go on to Newark. We'll get jobs. I'm absolutely sure of it, from what that fellow told me in Union Square. They happen to be very short on help. Well, it will mean three square meals a day, plenty of outdoor exercise, and a bunk to sleep in over rattling car-trucks, I'm going to take to it like a fish to water."

"I shall like it, too," Charles declared, and they set out for the road leading up the Palisades to the level country above. The joyous mood of his companion communicated itself to Charles, and he felt very light-hearted. The warm sense of a new existence tingled over him. He felt all but imponderable as he strode along by his friend in the clear moonlight and the bracing air from the river.

PART II

CHAPTER I

It was the beginning of the month of May, one year later. The two friends were still boon companions. They had joined the force of canvasmen of the circus and menagerie at Newark, gone with the organization to California, and were now in the mountains of Georgia, where the company was billed to exhibit and perform at the town of Carlin.

Their long train reached the place at three o'clock in the morning, drew up on a side-track near the circus-grounds, and the canvasmen were gruffly ordered out of their bunks to go to work. Charles and Mason slept opposite each other, and now stood dressing in their rough clothes in the dim light of a dusky oil-lantern at the end of the car.

"Dog's life, eh?" Mason said, recalling a remark Charles had made the night before.

"That and nothing else," Charles muttered; "I've had enough, for my part."

"Well, I have, too," Mason admitted, "and I'm ready to call it off. But I think I ought to stick till we get back to New York."

"I'm not sure that I ought to go back there," Charles said, in a more guarded tone, as they went down the narrow aisle to the door.

"Oh, I see what you mean," Mason said, "and after all, you may be dead right about it. But what would you do if you called it off right here to-day, as I know you are thinking of doing?"

But, somewhat to his surprise, Charles made no response. It was as if he had not heard the question, so deeply was he absorbed in thought. There was no time for further conversation. The foreman drove them like sheep to the work of unloading the canvas, ropes, and stakes, and the hasty erection of the tents. Seat-building, ring-digging, stake-driving with heavy sledge-hammers, kept them busy till after sunup. Then it was all over. They were permitted to go to the dining-tent set aside for the "razor-backs," as the canvasmen were called, to get their breakfast; and then they were free to sleep or amuse themselves till ten o'clock, when they were expected to get ready for the street procession. An event was due to-day which occurred only once a month, and that was the payment of wages, so, after breakfast, they joined the string of men waiting their turn at the windowed wagon of the paymaster to get their money. Mason got his first, and Charles found him waiting for him after he had been paid.

"What's up now—sleep?" Mason inquired.

"I thought I'd look around the town," Charles replied. "I'm tired, of course, but I don't feel sleepy."

"I'll go with you," Mason smiled. "I'm trying to get on to your curves. You mystify me to-day. I've never seen you look like you do now. What has happened?"

They were now entering the main street of the town, at the foot of which the circus-grounds were situated. Green hills encircled the place and beyond rose the mountain ranges and towering peaks. The spring air was quite invigorating; the scene in the early sunlight appeared very beautiful and seductive.

"I was going to mention it to you," Charles said. "I ought to have done so sooner. You see, in a way, it concerns my old trouble, and I've been trying to forget that."

"Oh, well, don't mention it, then," Mason said, sympathetically. "I know how you feel about it."

"But I must tell you this and be done with it," Charles went on. "Last night as we were loading I heard two of our gang talking on the quiet. It seems that some expert bank robbers are with us, using us as a shield. In fact, they are on the force itself. Telegrams have been sent out, and we may all have to stand an examination such as we went through in New Orleans. That was enough for me. It seemed to me that I got through that last ordeal by the very skin of my teeth. I can't answer all those questions again—I simply can't. It is different with you. You have a straight tale to tell, but I haven't!"

"Where did they think the examination would be made?" Mason wanted to know.

"Next stop—Chattanooga."

"Ah, I see," Mason mused, "and, as you have been paid off—"

"If I am going to quit, now's the time," Charles answered, gravely. "I don't want to part from you, but really we are not situated alike. You have been homesick for the last three months. You cannot hide it. You are always talking of your people."

Mason blushed visibly. "Well, so are you homesick. I wish I could see that fellow Mike you are always talking about. I know every story by heart that the Mick ever told, and the little girl and your brother and his wife—why, you think about them as often as I do about my folks."

Charles made no denial. They were passing one of the churches of the town. It was an old brick building with ivy growing on the walls, a beautiful sward about it. The front doors were open. They paused and looked in. A negro sexton was sweeping the floor near the pulpit. Mason was for moving on, but his friend seemed to linger.

As they left, Charles said, frankly: "I'm not a member of any church and I have no religious creed, but if I lived in this town I'd want to come here every Sunday morning and sit back somewhere in the rear and listen, and get into contact with the people, real people—not the sort we've been traveling with for nearly a year. O God! I'm weary of it—weary, weary! I want a home of some sort. You have one that you can go to. I haven't, but I want to make one. Strange idea, isn't it? But I want it."

Mason laid his hand on his friend's arm gently, tenderly. "Poor old chap!" he said. "I understand you better now. And you think you could make a permanent home for yourself in a place like this?"

"Something tells me to stop here—right here, old man. Something seems to say that it is to be my home for all the rest of my life. Ever since we turned northward I've felt uneasy. I've not slept so well. I've dreamed of disaster up there. I've not heard from home once since we left New York. I've seen no paper. I don't know what they think of me. Some of my people may be dead. I don't know. I don't dare to think of it. I want to blot it all out, for it no longer pertains to me."

"I see," Mason said, gloomily. "Well, you must be your own judge and I must be mine. Somehow I can't dig the homesick feeling out of myself. I thought I could stick to the gang till we got back to New York, but, as I have my pay, and some more besides, if you quit I'll follow suit and travel first-class, like a gentleman, back to New York, where I'll stop a while before going home. Have you made up your mind?"

"Yes, fully," Charles answered. "I'll find something to do. I'd like to work on a farm. Out in the country my life could be even more private and secluded than here in a town like this. See those hills? They seem made for me, old man. They seem to have fallen from the eternal blue overhead. They will shelter me. I'll work and sleep and forget. The inhabitants will never know who I am, but I'll like them. I'll serve them, and perhaps they will like me a little after a while. The manager can easily fill my place."

"Well, then, it is settled," said Mason, with a deep breath. "It seems strange to think of parting with a pal like you, and I guess it means for good and all. You don't intend ever to see your folks again?"

"My relatives, no," Charles said. "I've thought often of writing back to dear old Mike, but don't think it would be quite safe. If I had any way of communicating with him other than the mails I would let him know where I am. I could trust him with my life."

"How about letting me go to Boston? I could see him on the quiet and tell him about you."

"No, that would be out of your way," Charles protested. "Never mind. It is better as it is. I'd like to hear from Mike, but he belongs to the past with all the rest. Let's go to the car and pack."

CHAPTER II

The two friends parted at the train that night. Charles felt a pang of loneliness as his companion was borne away. He had his bag with him and he wondered what he had better do. There was a small hotel near by and he went into the office and asked for a room. The clerk handed a pen to him across the counter and turned the register around for him to inscribe his name. Charles hesitated for barely an instant, then decided to make use of his own name. It looked strange to him, for he had not written it since he left home.

"C. Brown," he smiled. "Too common to attract notice. I've given up everything else; I will stick to my name. I can't always be lying about it."

A negro porter showed him his room. It was on the second floor and looked out toward the circus-grounds. The windows were up and he could hear the band and the clapping of hands by the audience. The air of the room was hot, and so he threw off his coat and tried to be comfortable, but he was restless and had no inclination to sleep. He knew, from the changing airs of the band, every act that was on in the ring. He could hear the familiar voice of the clown, the crack of the ringmaster's whip, and the clown's comical cry of pain, followed by the moss-grown jests Charles had heard hundreds of times.

Finding that he could not sleep, he put on his coat and went out. The street below was quite deserted. The stores were all closed. Everybody had gone to the circus. He walked to the end of the street, then turned eastward and climbed a hill in the edge of the town. He had the square and the diverging streets before him, and an odd sense of part ownership in it all crept over him.

"It is mine, it is mine!" he whispered. "I'll live here or close by. I'll make a home of it."

The performance was over under the vast canvas. He knew it from the ceasing of the music and the far-away hum of voices as the crowd filtered back to the town. One by one the tent lights went out. He heard the rumble of the wheeled animal cages, the gilded band-wagon and gaudy chariots, as they were rolled on to the flat cars; the loud shouts of teamsters; the roar of a disturbed lion. He heard the clatter of the seat-boards and supports as they were taken down and hauled to the train, the crash of falling tent-poles, the familiar oaths of the foreman of the gang he had just left. Soon the lights were all out save those moving about the train. The bell of the locomotive was ringing a hurry signal. Charles had a mental picture of his former companions tumbling, half undressed, into their berths in the dimly lighted cars. There was a sound of escaping steam from the locomotive, a clanging of its bell. The train was moving. Charles waved his hat in the still air as the train was passing the foot of the hill.

"Good-by, boys!" he said, with feeling. "I'll never see you again."

The train moved on and disappeared in the distance. Charles sat down on a boulder. For a year past he had longed for just that sort of freedom, but, now that it was within his reach, it somehow lacked the charm he had expected. Suddenly he felt averse to the thought of sleeping in the room he had taken at the hotel. He wanted to lie on the grass there in the starlight, and greet the rising of the sun upon his new life. But he told himself that he had better go to the hotel. Not to occupy a room after engaging it might arouse suspicion, so he went back to the deserted square.

The clerk was behind the counter and gave him his key, "You was with the circus, wasn't you?" he asked.

"Yes, but how could you tell?" Charles answered.

"Oh, by your clothes," the young man replied. "All of you fellers look different from common folks, somehow; your hats, shirts, shoes ain't the sort we-all wear. Then you are as sunburnt as gipsies. You've quit 'em, I reckon!"

"Yes," Charles told him. "I'm going to try something else. I want to work on a farm if I can get a job."

"Easy enough, the Lord knows," said the clerk, smiling broadly. "Farm-hands are awfully scarce; niggers all moving off. Now I come to think of it, I heard to-day of a job that is open. Miss Mary Rowland is stopping here in the house now. In fact, I think she came in town to catch some of the floating labor brought in by the show. I know she didn't go to either performance. She is a friend of Mrs. Quinby, the wife of the feller that runs this hotel, and when she comes in town she always puts up with us. She is a fine girl and a hard worker. The Rowlands are one of our oldest and best families, but run down at the heel, between you and me. Her daddy lost a hand in the Civil War, and can't work himself. He's got two boys, and take it from me they are the limit. The wildest young bucks in seven states. The old man don't know how to handle 'em, and Miss Mary has give up trying. If she can keep 'em out o' jail she will be satisfied."

Not being in the mood to enjoy the clerk's gossip, Charles sought his room and went to bed. It was somewhat cooler now and he soon fell asleep. He was waked at nine o'clock by the sound of some enormous trunks being trundled into the sample-room set aside for the use of commercial travelers across the hall from his own chamber, and, rising hurriedly, he went downstairs. He was quite hungry and afraid that he might be too late to be served with breakfast. The same clerk was on duty; he smiled and nodded.

"I kept your breakfast for you," he said. "The dining-room is closed, but we make exceptions once in a while. Walk right in—just give the door a shove. I'll go in the kitchen and have you waited on. You take coffee, I reckon?"

Charles said he did, and went into the big, many-tabled room adjoining the office. The clerk followed and passed into the kitchen through a screened door.

He appeared again in a moment. "It will be right in," he said. "You can set right here by the window. This seat ain't taken. We've got a lot of town boarders. It helps out, I'm here to state. They get a low cut rate by the month, but it brings in money in the long run. Say, you remember you said you were looking for a job on some farm? That young lady I was telling you about, Miss Mary Rowland, was at breakfast just now, and I told her about you. She was powerfully interested, for, between you and me, she is in a hole for want of labor out her way. She missed fire in every attempt she made yesterday. She trotted about town all day, and had to give it up. She begged me to see you. She went out about half an hour ago to do some trading at the dry-goods stores. She said tell you she'd be at Sandow & Lincoln's 'most all morning, and hoped you'd come in there. I'll tell you one thing—you will be treated right out there if you do go, and they will feed you aplenty and give you a clean bed to sleep in. You just tell her Sam Lee sent you—everybody about here knows Sam Lee—and if you just said 'Sam' it would do as well. I get up all the dances for the young folks here in this room. We shove the tables back ag'in' the wall, hire a nigger fiddler and guitar-picker, and have high old times at least once a month. You see Mrs. Quinby favors that because it makes a pile of drummers lie over here, and they pay the top rate. What do they care? Expense-account stretches to any size."

Charles promised to look Miss Rowland up, and, being needed in the office, Sam Lee hastened away. Charles enjoyed his breakfast. The food was an agreeable change from the fare of which he had grown tired in the dining-tent of the circus. The clean white plates and dishes appealed to him by contrast to the scratched and dented tin ones the canvasmen had been obliged to use. The eggs, butter, and ham seemed to be fresh from the mountain farms; the coffee was fine, clear, and strong; the cream was thick and fresh; the bread was hot biscuits just from the range.

CHAPTER III

After breakfast Charles went out into the street. It was a clear day, and the mountains in the distance, the near-by green hills, the blue sky, appealed to him. His morbid mood of the night before was gone. Life seemed to promise something to him that had not been within his reach since the hopeful days of his boyhood. He wondered if he was already becoming identified with a locality which he could regard as a permanent home. He smiled as he asked himself who would look for him here among these buried-alive people. How simple and quaint the farmers looked as they slowly moved about their produce-wagons in front of the stores of general merchandise! How amusing their drawling dialect as they priced their cotton, potatoes, chickens, and garden truck! The sign of Sandow & Lincoln's store hung across the sidewalk in front of him. He turned in there. A number of country women with their children stood along the counters on both sides of the narrow room, all being waited on by coatless clerks. A clerk approached Charles.

"Something to-day, sir?" he asked.

Charles told him what he wanted, and the clerk nodded. "Oh yes!" he said, "Miss Mary was talking about you just now. She said you might come in, but she wasn't at all sure. She is in the grocery department, next door. She said tell you to wait back in the rear, if you came. You will find a seat there. I'll tell her when she comes in. No, Mrs. Spriggs, we've quit handling nails." This to a gaunt young woman at his elbow, with a baby on her arm. "When the new hardware started up we agreed to go out of that line and sold 'em our stock. It is right across the street. You can't miss it."

Charles went back to the rear of the long room and took one of the chairs. A country girl came with several pairs of shoes in her arms, and sat down near him to try them on. It amused him to note the way she pulled them on over her coarse stockings, and stood up on a piece of brown paper to prevent any scratching of the soles. Finally she made a selection, and went back with all the shoes in her arms. There was a long table holding suits of clothing against the wall, and a young farmer came back and began to pull out some of the coats and examine them.

Catching Charles's glance, he smiled. "Most of 'em moth-eaten," he said, dryly. "They've had 'em in stock ever since the war—mildewed till they smell as musty as rotting hay in a damp stack. Show feller, eh?"

"I was," Charles admitted.

"I heard the clerk talking about you just now," the man went on. "That was a good show, if I'm any judge. The best clown I think I ever saw. How any mortal man can think up funny things and fire 'em back as quick, first shot out of the box, as that feller did in answering questions beats me."

Charles explained that both the questions and replies had been in use a long time, and the farmer stared in wonder.

"You don't mean it," he said. "That sorter spoils it, don't it? Well, every man to his own line, I reckon."

He might have asked more questions, but Miss Rowland was approaching from the front. As he rose to his feet Charles was quite unprepared for what he saw. He had pictured her as an elderly spinster, somewhat soured by work, misfortune, and family cares, but here was a graceful young girl hardly past eighteen, with a smiling, good-humored face that was quite pretty. She was slight and tall; she had small hands and feet, hazel eyes, and a splendid head of golden-brown hair.

"I think you are Mr. Brown," she began, smiling sweetly. "Mr. Sam Lee said he would speak to you about what I want."

"He sent me here," Charles answered. For the first time since his exile he was conscious of the return of his old social manner in the presence of a lady, and yet he knew there was much that was incongruous in it, dressed as he was in soiled and shabby clothing.

"I certainly am glad you came," she said, in that round, deep and musical voice which somehow held such charm for his ears. "I tell you I am sick and tired of trying to get help, and our cotton and corn are being choked to death by weeds. If you don't come I don't know what I'll do."

"I am perfectly willing," he half stammered, under the delectable thrall of her eyes and appealing mien of utter helplessness, "but I must be frank. I am ignorant of field work. My idea was to offer my help to some farmer who would be patient with me till I got the hang of it. Of course, I could not expect wages till—till—"

"Oh," she broke in, with a rippling laugh, "you wouldn't have any trouble in that respect! A child can cut out weeds with a hoe. I did it when I was a tiny thing. All you have to learn is the difference between corn and cotton and weeds. I can show you that in a minute. Oh, if that is all, we can fix that!"

"That is the only thing I can think of," Charles answered. "I am tired of the roving life I've been leading with the circus and I want to locate somewhere permanently."

"Then we may as well talk about the—the wages," the girl said. "The price usually paid is two dollars a day for six days in the week, and board thrown in. How would that suit you?"

"I am only afraid I won't earn it—at first, anyway," Charles said. "I think I'd better let you pay me according to what I am worth. Money is really not my chief object. I only want a place to live. It happens that I am all alone in the world—no kin or close friends."

"Oh," Mary cried, softly, "that is sad—very, very sad. I sometimes think that all my troubles come from having so many dear ones to bother about, but it must be worse not to have any at all. What a strange life you must have been leading! And you—you"—she hesitated, and then went on, frankly—"you seem to be of a sensitive nature. And yet, from what I've always heard of showmen—"

Seeing that she had paused, he prompted her. "You were saying—"

"More than I have any right to say on such a short acquaintance," she replied, coloring prettily, "but I'll finish. Of course, we don't know about such things, but we have the impression that showmen are rough and uneducated; but you are quite the opposite."

"There are all classes among the workers about a circus," he said— "good, bad, and indifferent."

"Well," she smiled, "let's get back to business. When can you come? We live five miles out, at the foot of the mountains, and any one can direct you to our plantation—I say 'plantation,' because it used to be styled that when we owned a lot of slaves and land. Nowadays the slaves are all free and our land has been sold off, for one reason or another, till we have only a farm now."

"I can come any day," Charles answered. "I have nothing to do and would rather be at work."

"Well, then, suppose you come out in the morning," Mary said. "I'm going right home, and I want to fix a place for you to sleep. We've got a rather roomy house, but it is not fully furnished. Oh, you will find us odd enough! We used to have a lot of old furniture, but we got hard up a few years ago and sold it by the wagon-load to a dealer in antiques. We have some of the old things left, but very few. The man shipped the furniture to Atlanta and sold it at a very high price. A funny thing happened about it. I was down there visiting a cousin of mine, and we went to a tea given by a wealthy woman—one of the sort, you know, that says 'I seen,' and 'had went.' Well, you may imagine my surprise when I recognized our old mahogany side-board in her dining-room. She saw me looking at it, and set in and told me a long story about how it had come down to her through several generations on her mother's side. I was crazy to know how much she paid for it, to see how badly we were stuck by that dealer, but of course I kept my mouth shut."

Charles laughed heartily, and it struck him with surprise, as he suddenly realized that it was almost the first genuine laugh he had enjoyed since he had left his home. Then he became conscious of his incongruous appearance. He noticed the enormously heavy, unpolished boots he wore, with their thick leather and metal heel-taps. His nails were neglected, his hands as rough and calloused as a blacksmith's; he had not shaved for several days and his beard felt bristly and unclean. The shirt he wore was thick, coarse, and collarless; the trousers resembled the stained overalls of a plumber. He wondered that Miss Rowland should be treating him in such a cordial and even friendly manner, and he decided that it might be the way of the higher class in the South.

"Well," she suddenly said, turning toward the entrance of the store, "I'm going to expect you."

"I promise you that I won't fail," he said, earnestly, fumbling his coarse cap in his hands.

"And I believe you mean it." She smiled that entrancing smile again and, to his surprise, she held out her hand. As he took it an indescribable sensation passed over him. It felt soft and warm and like some sentient, pulsing thing too delicate and helpless for the touch of the rough palm which now held it.

"Many have fooled me, both white and black," she went on. "They swore they would come—even some of our old slaves—but didn't. However, I know I can count on you."

"You may be sure of it," he answered. "The obligation is on the other side. I want work badly and I am grateful to you for giving it to me."

"Oh, I hope you will like it out there!" she said, thoughtfully, as she lingered, and with her words she dropped her eyes for the first time. "We have our troubles and you will be sure to notice them. I have two brothers, Kenneth and Martin, both older than I am, and I may as well tell you that they are somewhat wild and reckless. I never know where they are half the time. Yes, they are bad—they are my dear brothers and I love them with all my heart, but they are bad. They drink; they play poker; they are always in fights. It was to get Kenneth out of trouble, to pay his lawyer and the fines, that we sold some of our best land. He wasn't altogether to blame, I'll say that; but he is quick-tempered and never could control himself. Martin is getting to be like him. He imitates Kenneth in everything. It all rests on me, too. My father is as easy-going as an old shoe and doesn't care much what happens. You will find him odd, I reckon. He has only one hand; he can't work, and so he is always at his books. He is writing a history of the Rowlands. He spends all our spare change for stamps to write to people of that name whenever he happens to hear of one. It is a fearful waste of time and energy, but it amuses him and I can't object. Well, I am going now. I'll count on you, sure."

"You may be sure I'll come," Charles repeated. He had the feeling that he ought to accompany her to the door, but at once realized that the instinct to do so came from the past in which he had the social right to consider himself on an equality with any lady. He sat down in his chair and watched her as she moved through the motley throng of country people in the store. How different she seemed from them all! Then an indescribable sense of dissatisfaction came over him. Why, he was to be her servant, nothing more nor less, and the freedom she had shown meant nothing. Yet surely it wasn't so bad as that, after all. She had said that he seemed to have a sensitive nature and that he struck her as being an educated man. Yes, she had said those things, and he was sure that the memory of them would never leave him. He was glad that he had parted company with Mason, as much as he liked him, for he wanted to hug this new adventure close to his own individual breast. She had her troubles, and was bravely bearing them. He would never complain again over his lot. He went through the store and out onto the street. There was something in the very atmosphere that seemed to shower down content and joy upon him. He spent the remainder of the day wandering about the old town, almost as one in a delightful dream. He was almost superstitious enough to think that some guiding angel in an invisible world had led him to this spot. Ruth, Celeste, William—they might remain out of his life forever. He had passed through a terrible travail to attain this new birth, but the whole ordeal was worth it. He told himself that no vastly good thing ever came till the price was paid, and he had paid long and well for this. Work? He laughed. He could work till he fell in exhaustion in such a cause. Then he laughed again.

"Why, she is only a girl!" he said. "Am I a fool? After all these years of common sense am I losing my mind? Now what is there about her that does not belong to the average woman?"

He did not attempt to fathom the mystery. He only knew that he was already itching with the desire to see her again. He wanted to serve her. She was a merry child and a thoughtful woman deliciously compounded. The lights of joy and the shadows of trouble seemed alternately to flit over her wondrous being. She had troubles, and so had he. He was almost glad that it was so, for he would kill his own in fighting hers. Her round, mellow accent sounded in his ears like dream music. The touch of her delicate hand remained, and thrilled him through and through.

CHAPTER IV

At dusk he was back at the old hotel. His strange happiness amounted to ecstasy. Sam Lee, at the cigar case and counter, the pigeon-holed key-rack behind him, filled him with a desire to laugh. How vain and empty the fellow's curling mustache and damp, matted hair made him look! Charles went into the dining-room for his supper. He was quite hungry and enjoyed the meal. When it was over he sauntered out on the veranda. Some one in the parlor overhead was playing the piano. It was an old instrument and the notes had a jingling, metallic sound. Through an open window came the merry, jesting voice of Sam Lee chatting familiarly with a drummer in flashy attire. Up the walk from the station came a negro pushing a two-wheeled truck laden with a mammoth trunk. The negro was humming a tune; his torn shirt was falling from a bare, black shoulder. Catching sight of a colored waiter idling at a window of the dining-room, he uttered a loud guffaw and continued to laugh as he trudged up the walk. Charles started out again to see the town. This time he strolled along the principal residential street. Many of the houses stood back on wide lawns. All had porches or verandas. Through the front windows he caught sight of families at supper. On one lawn a group of children was playing. Homes, homes! what a beautiful thing a home was! Why had he not realized this and made one for himself when he had a chance?

Turning back, he went to the hotel and up to his room. It was nine o'clock, but he was not sleepy. The room was close and warm, and he undressed and lay down. For hours he lay awake, thinking, thinking of the past and opening windows of hope for the future. Should he write to William? No, it would do no good and might lead to complications. William and Celeste might as well think of him as dead, and teach the child to forget him. A letter from him might upset his brother. He had promised to disappear, and he would keep his word. Besides, the budding joy of the new life depended upon a thorough detachment from the old. It was midnight when he fell asleep. It was early dawn when he waked. He knew that further sleep was impossible and he got up. Why should he wait longer? Why not be on his way to the Rowland farm? The idea appealed to him. He would walk the five miles through the country instead of hiring a conveyance, as he at first intended. He could have his bag sent out later.

Dressing and descending to the office, he found Sam Lee asleep in a big chair behind the counter. Hearing his step, the clerk waked and stood up.

"Early bird," Sam said, drowsily. "I guess you're anxious to get out to Rowland's. Miss Mary said she had hired you. She was tickled powerfully. There is a drummer that I got to call now. He is off for a mountain trip. His breakfast will be ready in twenty minutes and I'll have yours fixed at the same time. Have you hired a rig?"

Charles explained that he intended to walk, and made arrangements to have his bag forwarded. The sun was just rising into view as he fared forth, following the clerk's directions as to the way along the main-traveled road toward the east.

The five miles were soon traversed. It was barely eight o'clock when he came into sight of the Rowland home. It was a large, old-fashioned frame building, having two floors. It had once been painted white as to the weatherboarding and green as to the shutters, but time and rain had reduced the walls to gray and the shutters to a dark, nondescript color. There was a wide veranda which had lost part of its original balustrade, and had broken, sagging steps and tall, fluted columns, one of which was out of plumb, owing to the decay of the timbers at its base. Behind the house Charles noticed a rather extensive stable and barns, as well as several cabins which had been occupied by former slaves in the day when the place had seen the height of its prosperity. There was a lawn in front, or the remains of one, and the brick walk was moss-grown and weed-covered save for a worn path in the center; what was once a carriage drive from a wide gate on one side had quite disappeared under a wild growth of bushes.

As he entered the gate a gray-haired man of about seventy years of age, with a book and a manuscript under a handless arm, came out of the house and stood on the veranda, staring blandly at him. He wore a narrow black necktie, and a long broad-cloth frock coat, with trousers of the same material. The coat was threadbare, the trousers baggy and frayed at the bottoms of the legs. He stepped forward and smiled agreeably as he extended his hand to Charles, who was now ascending the creaking steps.

"Mr. Brown, I believe," he said. "My daughter told me about you and we were expecting you. I am Mr. Rowland. She has gone over to a neighbor's for a minute or two. Will you sit down here or go inside? It is about as comfortable here in the morning as anywhere about the house."

"I'll sit here, if you please," Charles answered, now noticing for the first time a deep scar under the old gentleman's right eye, which had been caused by a Northern minie ball.

"Yes, we were quite pleased to secure your help," Rowland went on, taking a chair and resting his book and manuscript on his gaunt knees. "We were really about to despair. You see," holding up his handless wrist, "that I am quite incapacitated for rough work, so I spend my time over my books and writing. I am preparing a rather extensive genealogy of the Rowland family. You may not be aware of it, sir, but it is certainly a fascinating pursuit. You never know, till you begin such research, how many of a name are in existence. I have written letters to more than two thousand persons, and had answers from a good many of more or less importance. What seems strange to me is that most persons are so indifferent on the subject. It seems to me the more worldly goods or standing they have the less they care about who they were at the beginning."

"It must be interesting," Charles agreed, vaguely pleased to find that the old gentleman was so kindly disposed toward him.

"It certainly is," Rowland went on. "I always ask strangers the question, and I'll put it to you. Do you happen to have met in your rounds (I understand that you have been a showman) any one by my name?"

"I can't recall any one just now," Charles said.

"Well, I'm not at all surprised," Rowland went on, "for the name is not a common one except in certain spots. Now they are thick in some of the Southern states. There was a governor and a general, but my daughter says all that sounds like bragging of our blood. She was looking over my work one day and said that I had not been so careful to record Rowland blacksmiths and carpenters as Rowland lawyers, doctors, and the like; but I reckon there is a good reason for that discrepancy, and that is that the lower classes don't really know much about their forebears. It is when a man starts to rise in the world, or is about to go down, that he sees the value of family history. My daughter will tease me. The last thing she said when she started away at breakfast was that I must not bore you with this work of mine if you came while she was out. I see her now, coming across the field over there. She is worried about her two brothers. They have been away for several days, and she went over to Dodd's to see if she could hear anything of them. Keep your seat, sir. I should have offered you some fresh water before this. I'll have Aunt Zilla, our cook, bring some out to you."

Glad of a chance to change the subject, Charles made no objection, and Rowland stalked, in his slipshod way, into the sitting-room. There he met the servant and gave the order for the water.

Charles heard a veritable African snort. "Who, me? You mean me, Marse Andy? Is you los' yo' senses? You 'spec' me ter draw water en' fetch it in fer dat new fiel'-hand wid clothes like er house-painter? What's he, anyhow? He gwine ter do his work, en' I'll do mine. Huh, I say!"

"Well, then, I'll have to do it with one hand," Charles was mortified to overhear. "This is his first day, Zilla. He has not set in yet. Until he does he is a guest under our roof."

"Well, let 'im set in now, den," Zilla cried. "He ain't de preacher; he ain't de school-teacher; he ain't nuffen but er rousterbout circus man."

Charles heard the sound of receding footsteps toward the rear of the house, and the soft slur of the old man's tread as he returned.

"Aunt Zilla appears to be busy back there," he said, blandly. "We'll walk around to the well and draw it ourselves, if you don't mind."

Deeply chagrined, Charles accepted the offer. The well was at the kitchen door and Charles lowered the bucket into it. As he was drawing it up Aunt Zilla, who was a portly yellow woman of forty, came out with a tin dipper. It looked as if she partially regretted her show of temper, for she had a softened look as she extended the dipper to her master.

Rowland filled it and offered it to Charles, but he declined to drink first, and as a matter of mere form Rowland drank and then refilled the dipper.

"Young miss is ercomin'," Zilla said, turning toward the front. "I wonder is she done hear sumpin' erbout de boys? Lawd! Lawd! what dey bofe comin' to?"

As she disappeared around the corner Rowland stroked his white goatee and smiled wearily. "We have to handle her with care," he said. "She is the only help we have now, and she threatens to leave us every day. She is getting tyrannical. They are all like that."

They were returning to the veranda when Mary came in at the gate.

"Put the table things on the line to dry, Aunt Zilla; there is no time to lose, if they are to be ironed to-day," Charles heard her ordering, in a hurried and yet kind tone.

He noted that she wore a somewhat simpler dress than the day before, a plain checked gingham, but it was most becoming, and her hat, a great wide-brimmed one, woven from the inner husks of corn without adornment of any sort, added to her rare, flushed beauty. Being in the shade of the house, she took the hat off and held it in one hand while she offered the other to Charles.

"So you didn't fail us," she said, but she seemed now to force the exquisite smile which the day before had been so spontaneous. "I was almost sure you'd come when I was talking to you at the store, but when I got home and saw how desolate our place looked I began to fear it would bore one who had traveled about a great deal, as you must have done. Well, if you don't like it, I'll excuse you. It looks like things simply will not go right, somehow." Her face had fallen into pensive solemnity, her pretty lip was drawn tight across her fine teeth.

"But I do like it very, very much," Charles heard himself stammering. "I am only afraid that I shall not be able to give thorough satisfaction with my work."

"Oh, that will be all right!" Mary smiled a stiff smile again, while a far-away look lay in her eyes.

"What is the matter, daughter?" Rowland asked, suddenly. "Have Lester & Hooker been bothering you about that account again?"

"No, father, I met Mr. Hooker, but he did not say anything about it. You know he agreed to give us another month."

"Then something else has happened," Rowland persisted, still staring inquiringly.

"No, nothing, father, nothing. I'm a little tired, that's all. Come, Mr. Brown, I know father has not shown you your room yet."

They left the old gentleman on the veranda, eagerly scanning a page of his manuscript, and Mary led Charles up the old-fashioned stairs with its walnut balustrade and battered steps. She smiled as she explained that the "Yankee soldiers" had occupied the house during the war, and that no repairs had been made since. There were six bedrooms on the floor they were now on, and the one at the end over the kitchen was to be Charles's. She led him into it. It was very attractive. An old-fashioned mahogany wardrobe stood against the wall near the single window, which was draped with cheap cotton-lace curtains. There was a walnut wash-stand with a white marble top holding a white bowl and pitcher, and a plain mahogany bureau. There was an open fireplace which was filled with boughs of cedar. Its hearth had just been whitewashed. There was a table of old oak in the center of the room, holding some books and an old-fashioned brass candlestick. On the white walls in various sorts of frames hung some of the brilliant print pictures which were popular in the South just after the war. In a corner stood a tall-posted bed, which, with its snowy pillows and white counterpane, had a most cool and inviting look.

"Do you really intend this for me?" Charles asked. "But you mustn't put me here, you know. You have no idea the sort of bed I've been sleeping in. If you have never seen a bunk in a circus freight-car—"

"All the more reason you should be comfortable here with us," Mary interrupted. "As it is, I'm afraid you will want to quit us. It is awfully, awfully dull and lonely out here—no amusements of any sort. Your life must have been a very eventful and exciting one, and this, by contrast, may be anything but pleasant."

"It is just what I want," he fairly pleaded now, as their probing eyes met like those of two earnest children. "I am sick of the life I was leading, while this—this somehow seems like—" He found himself unable to formulate what he was trying to say, and she laughed merrily.

"I hope it is not due to your fibbing that you are all tangled up," she said. "Well, let's go down-stairs. I've got to help Zilla get dinner ready, and then I'll show you our corn and cotton. You won't want to begin work till to-morrow morning, of course."

"But why?" he blandly inquired, as they were going down the stairs.

"Well," she returned, "people usually begin in the morning when they hire out, and it will take you one afternoon at least to get the lay of the land and see what is to be done."

"I feel that I ought to be at something right away," he said. "Besides, you remember that you told me your crops were suffering for lack of attention."

She laughed again. "I wonder if I have run across a real masculine curiosity," she said. She paused on the step and faced him, and he had again that magnetic sensation of nearness to her which he had experienced at the store the day before. "You see," she continued, "out here we have to drive men to work, negroes and whites, and you speak of it as if it were a game to be played. I wonder if you really know what you are about to tackle. The sun is hot enough some days to bake a potato, and there is no sort of shade in our fields."

"I don't think I shall mind the sun a bit," he said. "It is much cooler here than down in Florida where we were showing, and even there I enjoyed the days we had to work in the open more than those spent on the cars."

"Oh, well, we shall see," she said, smiling again. They were at the veranda now, and she added: "Wait here and I'll see Aunt Zilla, and then we'll walk down to the cotton-field that is suffering the most and I'll give you a lesson in hoeing and weed-pulling. Then if you really are daft about working, you may start after dinner."

CHAPTER V

Charles sat down on the veranda and Mary turned away. Rowland was bent over his writing and did not look up, so deeply was he absorbed in what he was recording. He had a small bottle of ink on the floor at his side, into which he dipped an old pen which was so sharp at the point that it kept sticking into the cheap paper he was using. Mary reappeared very soon, now wearing her becoming hat and a great pair of cotton gloves.

"Father," she said, teasingly, as she stood beside him, a hand on his threadbare coat at the shoulder, "I saw a list of men in the paper the other day that were being sent to the chain-gang for all sorts of crimes. There was a Jasper Rowland in the lot, and his son Thomas. Had you not better write to them? Perhaps they may furnish an important link in our history."

Rowland looked up and smiled indulgently at her and then at Charles. "She is always poking fun at me like that," he said. "Of course there are off-shoots from the main tree like those she mentions, but I assure you, sir, that they are rare. Besides, such cases often come from families who have once been high up in the world. I am afraid that the idleness and affluence of the old slave period have left their stamp on many of our best families. I know that my own boys—"

"Stop, father!" and Mary actually put her gloved hand over the old man's lips. "You must not bring Kenneth and Martin into such a classification. I know what you started to say, and you shall not to Mr. Brown. My brothers are idle, fun-loving, and wild, but they are not dishonorable."

"Oh, well, have it your way," Rowland gave in. "I think they are all right in many ways, but they are worrying the life out of you by the way they are carrying on. It seems to me that if they had a high sense of honor, they—"

"Now, Mr. Brown," Mary said, quickly, "I won't listen to what he is saying. You'll get the idea presently that my poor brothers are worse than thieves."

"Oh no," Charles tried to say, lightly, as they went down the steps and turned toward the side of the house. "I'm sure I understand about your brothers."

To his surprise, Mary's face had clouded over. It seemed as if she were about to shed tears, for her wondrous eyes were misty. He heard her sigh, and she was silent for several minutes as they went down the path toward the cotton-field. Presently she looked straight into his face. She tried to smile, and then gave up the attempt with a little shake of her head.

"I really am in great, great trouble over my brothers," she faltered. "I didn't want to tell my father, for it will do no good and it seems to me that he is already losing his natural love for them; but this morning I heard from Mrs. Dodd that they were over at Carlin last night, cutting up frightfully — drinking, gambling, and what not. Oh, I don't know how I can bear much more of it. Do you know, Mr. Brown, that since my mother's death these boys, although they are older than I am, have seemed almost like sons of mine? I worry, worry, worry. I lie awake night after night when they are away like this, and even when they are here I watch their every look and tone to see if—if they are about to break out again. I'll have gray hairs—I know I shall—and that very soon."

A keen pang of remorse passed through the listening wanderer. He was recalling certain incidents in his own life, the anxiety and tears of his own mother just prior to her death. For a moment he was almost oblivious of the sweet face into which he was blankly staring. But his expression must have been sympathetic, for Mary suddenly remarked:

"I don't know why I am talking so freely with you about them, Mr. Brown. I really never mention my brothers to my best friends—their faults, I mean—but here I am telling you the worst about them. You seem wonderfully gentle and sympathetic and—and—" She choked up, wiped her fluttering lips with her gloved hand and dropped her eyes.

"I want to aid you," he said, deeply moved, "and I will do everything in my power. Look at me, Miss Rowland. I don't want to pass for better than I am. I want to start right with you. The habits your brothers have were once my own. I owe my wandering life to them. For a year I have been free from the old habits. I hope I shall remain so. I sometimes feel that I shall never, never fall back. I feel so now more strongly than I ever did, because your trouble shows me so plainly how terribly wrong I was."

"Oh, it doesn't make any difference what you once were," Mary said, earnestly. "It is what you are now that counts. I understand you better than I did at first. I see why you are living as you are, away from kindred and friends, and I am glad you told me. It is a great thing to trample an old weakness underfoot and rise up on it. Oh, do you know, what you say makes me hope that my brothers, too, may change! Oh, they must, they must! They cannot go on as they are."

Nothing more was said till they reached the cotton-field, which was a level fertile tract of land containing about ten acres. Beyond it lay another tract about the same size, which was planted in corn, while another smaller field adjoining was given over to wheat. Under a tree at the side of the path lay some hoes, and Mary took one and gave him another.

"See, this is all you have to do," she began, lightly, going to the first cotton-plant in the nearest row and cutting the weeds about it with the hoe. "You can 'kill two birds with one stone'—loosen up the earth's surface and destroy the weeds at the same time. I'm sure you don't have to be shown which is the cotton."

"Oh no! I see that plainly," and with the other hoe Charles set in on the next row, and side by side they worked forward.

"Splendid! splendid!" Mary cried, pausing and smiling at him from her sweet, flushed face. "Surely you have used a hoe before this."

"Only once, in a little garden at a summer resort," he said. "Then it was cabbages and beans."

"But you really are beating me!" she cried, "and it is better done. See! I've left some and you haven't. Your row is as clean as a barn floor before a dance, and your stroke is deep and firm."

They worked to the ends of the two rows and were about to start back when an iron bell on a post at the kitchen door rang. They saw Zilla with her hand on its rope, staring at them fixedly.

"That is for us," Mary explained. "Dinner is ready, and Aunt Zilla has a fit when anybody's late. We all try to obey that bell. It was put there long before the war. It was used—you see it is a large one—to call up the slaves. My grandfather had a regular code of signals which he used to communicate with his overseer. In that day there were negro uprisings, slave runaways to be stopped, and all sorts of outlandish things that are now out of date. Girls like me, for instance, never worked in the field those days, but it is better this way. I know I am stronger and more healthy than my mother was, and if I had less to worry about I think I should be happier, for my mother was not a happy woman. I am afraid that she and my father were not as well mated as they ought to have been. I think the match was made by the parents on both sides, a sort of marriage of convenience to tie some property together."

When they were nearing the kitchen door Charles was suddenly embarrassed by the thought that he might be expected to dine with the family; he felt that he was unfit to sit at table with them in his uncouth clothing. Mary seemed to read his thoughts, for she said:

"Don't change your clothes. We have no ceremony here in the working period. We have no time for style. Run up to your room and get the dust off your face and hands, and come right down. Don't make Zilla mad, for all you do."

Coming down, presently, Charles felt a little easier, for Mary was already at the table in the same dress she had worn in the field. She was drinking milk and eating hot biscuits and fried spring chicken.

"You see I didn't wait for you," she laughed, "and you must not wait for any one in the future, either. When the bell rings sit down and eat. It is the only way. Father is not coming, you see. He has struck another Rowland, a loyalist in the Revolution. Do you know, father went all the way to Charleston, South Carolina, last summer, to consult an old will. He spent money we needed to pay farm-hands with, but he had a glorious time. He was entertained in an old historic mansion which had belonged to some of the Rowlands, and brought home photographs of it, and of old tombstones and maps of the first settlers. Oh, he'll bore the life out of you if you let him! He has never been sat down on but once. Old Judge Warner, who went through the war with father, was with us overnight not long ago, and after supper father got out his charts, books, coats of arms and began. The judge listened for a while, then suddenly said:

"'Say, Andy, I'm going to be frank with you. I never have been interested in my *own* ancestry. Wouldn't it seem odd to you if I was interested in *yours*?'"

Charles laughed heartily, for the girl had managed to put him quite at his ease. Besides, he was ravenously hungry and Zilla had brought a big platter of fried chicken and a plate heaping with hot biscuits and put them before him. A pot of coffee stood near him, from which he was expected to help himself. A door of the room was open, showing a flower-garden full of blooming rose-bushes. The midday sun beat down on it. Bees were hovering over the flowers. In some apple-trees close to the door birds were flitting about and chirping. A rooster was crowing lustily at the barn; the cawing of a crow came across the fields. To the wanderer all nature seemed to be swelling, bursting with joy. As he looked into the face of the girl across the table something seemed to tell him that a veritable new life had begun for him, and that she, in some way, was responsible for it. He was full of gratitude to her.

Dinner over, they rose from the table together. "What are you going to do now?" she questioned. "I must tell you that we always take at least an hour for dinner, and on very hot days we don't work till later in the afternoon."

"It is too much fun to stay away from it," he laughed. "It is like playing a new game."

She went with him to the door; she stepped down into the yard. "I must show you a few other things," she said. "That is the blacksmith's shop adjoining the smoke-house. The shop used to be a means of making money. We owned an old slave who was considered the best blacksmith in the county. He used to shoe horses and mend carriages and wagons, but now the shop is seldom used except for the sharpening of tools. Then we hire a blacksmith to come out from Carlin. But he gets three dollars a day, and so we only have him about twice a year."

They were at the old shop now, and Mary drew the great sliding-door open. To her surprise, Charles stepped in, examined the big bellows, forge, and anvil with the air of one who knew what he was about.

"Everything is here," he said, "and in good order."

"What do you know about a shop?" Mary asked, with a smile.

"More than I do about farming," he answered. "The show I was with carried its own shop, and now and then I used to work in it as an assistant. If you will let me, the first rainy day that comes I'll sharpen all the tools."

"Oh, can you—will you?" she cried. "That would be splendid. But if it gets out the neighbors will bore you to death with requests for this or that. You couldn't shoe a horse, could you?"

"Oh yes. That is simple enough," he replied, indifferently. "The big draft-horses we used had to be double shod, and I learned how to do it."

At the door of the shop they parted. Charles went back to the cotton-field and resumed his work there. All the afternoon he toiled. Digging the mellow soil and cutting down the succulent weeds and crab-grass was a fascinating pastime rather than a disagreeable task. The sun sank behind the hills. The dusk fell over the land. Presently he looked up and saw Mary at the end of the row which he was finishing.

"This won't do," she chided him. "In a little while it will be too dark. Didn't you hear the bell?"

He had not, and he stared at her, abashed.

"Well, come on," she said, sweetly. "Aunt Zilla is not angry. It is such an odd thing to see a man willing to work that she was laughing over it. I think she likes you already, and it is queer, for she does not take to strangers readily. She is a close observer and she says that you have a sad, lonely look about the eyes. I didn't agree with her, for you seem very cheerful to me. You are not—not homesick, or—or anything of that sort, are you, Mr. Brown?"

"I think not at all," he answered. "How could I be homesick, for I have no home?"

"Then Aunt Zilla may be right," Mary observed, quietly. "You may be sad because you have no home; perhaps that is what she reads in your face. Now that I come to think of it, you do seem to look lonely and isolated. Somehow I can't imagine your being contented here with us. You are so different, somehow, from our young men. I don't know in what way, particularly, but you are different, and so I am actually afraid that you will decide to—to go somewhere else. If you do, Mr. Brown, don't let anything I have said about—about needing your help stop you."

They were on the path approaching the house; he paused suddenly, and they faced each other. "I wish I could remove those ideas from your mind for good and all, Miss Rowland," he said, almost huskily, in his earnestness. "It is the second time you have mentioned the subject and I want you to understand the truth. My life for the last year has been one of restless torment. I gave up traveling with the circus to settle down on a farm. Something told me I would like it, but nothing told me that I would find work with such kind persons as you and your father. The truth is, I am so contented here that I am afraid"—he was laughing now—"that I shall wake up and find myself in that rumbling freight-train again, with canvas to unload, ropes to stretch, and stakes to drive."

"Well, I'll not bring it up again," she promised, with a sigh of relief. "I wouldn't have done it, but Zilla set me thinking on that line. I do want you to feel at home here, and it is not all selfishness, either. I've had trouble—I'm having plenty of it now—and somehow I feel that you have had more than your share somehow, somewhere."

The words were half tentative; she eyed him expectantly, but he made no response. They were at the veranda now, and he turned into the hall and went up to his room. He found that his bag had come, and, quickly putting on the suit of clothes it contained, he hurried down. The suit was a good, well-fitting one, bought with his old taste for such things, and in the lamplight he presented quite a changed appearance. He remarked the all but surprised look in Mary's face when he met her in the dining-room, but she made no comment. She had not changed her dress, and was waiting for him in her place at the head of the table.

"Father has eaten and gone back to his books," she said. "He takes very little nourishment. That is one good thing in ancestry worship, it saves food in his case. He can live on a biscuit and a glass of milk a day if he is on the track of a fresh twig for our tree."

When supper was over they went out to the front veranda. Leaving Charles seated on the end of it, Mary went into the big parlor behind him. He saw the light flash up as she struck a match and applied it to a lamp. A moment later he heard her playing the old piano. Its tone was sweet and her touch good. She was playing old plantation melodies, some of which he had heard before, and a wonderful sense of peace and restfulness crept over him. Presently, as if drawn by the music, Rowland rose from a rustic seat under an oak on the lawn and came to him.

"She learned that from her mother," the old man whispered. "My wife was graduated at a Virginia college for young ladies, and in her day was considered a fine performer. Mary sings, too, but—There, she is beginning now."

He checked himself, for his daughter was singing an old hymn, and Charles thought her voice was wonderfully sweet and sympathetic. But it suddenly quivered, a lump seemed to rise into her throat, and she stopped. There was stillness for a moment, then Charles heard Zilla's voice.

"Don't give way lak dat, missie!" she said. "Raise yo' pretty haid up. Dem boys is gwine ter come thoo dis spree same as de rest of 'um. Don't give up, chile. Ol' Zilla gwine ter go 'stracted if you do. You is too young en' sweet en' lightsome ter give down lak dat."

"It is those boys," Rowland muttered. "She's like her mother was, full of worry when they start to cut up. As for me, you see, I know that wild oats must be sown. I certainly ought to know, for I cut a wide swath in my young day. It must run in our blood. There was a young Sir George Rowland among the first settlers in South Carolina, and, judging from his will, of which I have a copy, he was as dissolute and extravagant as a royal prince. Yes, yes, blood will tell, and history is only repeating itself in my boys."

He turned into the parlor. Charles heard his voice gently admonishing his daughter, joined to that of Aunt Zilla, and presently Mary was heard ascending the stairs to her room. She had a lighted candle in her hand, and Charles caught a glimpse of her when she was half-way up the flight. She looked to him like an old picture of Colonial days; the light elongated her figure and gave to her trim gown the effect of an elaborate train. He was sure that the impression he had of her at that instant would never leave him.

Saying good night to Rowland, Charles went up to his room and undressed. A few minutes before he had been conscious of a sense of infinite peace and content, but already the feeling was gone. In its place was a growing desire to lift the sinister shadow that hung over the young girl. He could hear her soft step in her room across the hall. He had put out his light and now saw from his window that old Rowland was still strolling about the lawn. Presently all was still in Mary's room. He was very tired, but his brain was too active for sleep. The long straight rows of cotton-plants haunted his mind. In thought he was cutting out the weeds with Mary at his side. He heard again her sweet, merry comments and wise suggestions; he saw the wondrous lights and shadows in her beauteous face and the moving grace of her form. He was her servant; she belonged to the social class which he had renounced forever. Owing to the blight upon his name and character, he could never aspire to be more than a laborer on her father's farm, but it didn't matter. Nothing mattered but her happiness, and he told himself that she should have happiness if he died to give it to her.

CHAPTER VI

He waked before the sun was quite up the next morning. The pale light reflected from the eastern sky was creeping in at the windows when he opened his eyes. His mind was not clear, and at first he thought he was in his room at his old home. In a half-dreaming state he fancied Michael was at the door, telling him it was time to rise and catch a train. Next he thought he heard Ruth's voice calling to him, as she was wont to do at times before she was out of bed. Then the vague outlines of the old furniture took clearer shape and he sat up. In a flash his new life had reopened before him. He dressed hurriedly and went down-stairs. The front door was open, and the dewy lawn lay in the yellowing light. The peak of the nearest mountain pierced the fleecy clouds. He was turning around the house to go to the cotton-field when the blind of Mary's room was thrown open and she looked down and smiled.

"Good morning!" she cried. "I wonder if you are headed for that cotton-patch?"

He answered that he was, and she laughed.

"Not before you have your breakfast," she commanded. "That is against the rules. It will be ready soon. Wait for me. I'm coming right down."

He went to the veranda and saw her descending. When she came out into the full light from the shadowy house he remarked the lines of care in her face, and they threw a damper on his spirits.

"How did you rest?" she asked.

"Very well," he returned, "but I am afraid that you did not."

She was silent, her head downcast, and he wondered over the impulse that had emboldened him to make such a personal comment. He was about to beg her pardon, when she raised her face and looked at him confidingly.

"Oh, I know I show it, Mr. Brown," she exclaimed, "but I can't help it. I've been half crazy all night long. I slept only a few minutes at a time, and even in my sleep my fears clung to me. It is my brothers. I have worried over them before, but never like this. From what I heard yesterday the spree they are on is the worst they ever had. They were with their vilest associates, moonshiners and gamblers, over at Carlin, drinking harder than ever before."

Here Zilla came to the front door. Catching her mistress's eye, she cried out, excitedly: "Young miss, I see er hoss en' buggy 'way down de road. It got two mens in it. Looks ter me like de boys. Dey is whippin' de hoss powerful en' ercomin' fast."

Ascending the veranda steps, Mary looked down the main road toward Carlin. "Yes, it is my brothers," she said, frowning. "Why they are hurrying so I can't make out. The horse looks as if it is about to drop."

She said no more, but hastened to the front gate, where she stood, her tense hands on the latch, waiting for the vehicle to arrive. In a moment a panting, foaming bay horse was reined in at the gate and the two young men sprang down from a ramshackle buggy.

"Where is father?" Kenneth, the older, a tall, dark young man, asked, hurriedly.

"He is in the library, I think," his sister answered, "Kensy, what is the matter?"

"Oh, don't ask me!" he cried, impatiently, a wild look in his eyes. "Keep the horse there ready, Martin. But never mind. What's the use? It is all in. We'll have to leave the main road, anyway. We must skip for the mountains."

"Oh, brother, brother Kensy, what is it?" Mary cried, in sheer terror, as she clutched his arm.

Drawing it from her impatiently, even roughly, he cried out to Zilla: "Call father! Hurry! No, I'll find him."

"Oh, Martin, Martin, what is it?" and Mary turned to her younger brother, who was short, rather frail-looking, and had blue eyes and reddish hair.

"Nothing, nothing," he said, his glance following Kenneth into the house. "Don't ask me, sis. It is all right."

"But I know something has gone wrong!" Mary cried. "You and Kensy look it; you can't hide it. What is it?"

He shrugged his shoulders, lifted his brows, and then said, reluctantly: "Well, we got in a little scrape, that's all, and had to make a break to get away. The sheriff and a deputy are after us."

"After you! after you!" Mary gasped. "What have you done?"

Martin hesitated sullenly, his eyes on the grass.

"Tell yo' sister de trufe, boy," Aunt Zilla suddenly broke in. "Be ershamed er yo'se'f, keepin' 'er awake all night wid worry. Tell 'er what's de matter. Don't yer see she's half 'stracted over yo-all's doin's?"

"Oh, well," he responded, "it was a little shooting-scrape. Ken and Tobe Keith had a dispute in Gardener's pool-room about an hour ago. Tobe drew a knife. Some say he didn't, but I saw it; I'm sure I saw it. I grabbed him around the waist, and—well, Ken was a little full and had a gun, and while I and Tobe were wrestling he fired."

"And killed him!" Mary cried. "Oh God, have mercy!"

"No, no, don't be a fool, sis! Please don't! He was just wounded slightly, that's all."

"But why did you run away, then?" Mary's pale lips shook as the words dropped from them.

"Because," he frowned—"because some of the mountain boys advised us to, and Sheriff Frazier lived around the corner and had heard the shots. This horse and buggy was loaned to us by Steve Pinkney. He'll be here after them. Zilla, feed and water the horse, please. We've got to get away in the mountains till—till we find out how Keith is."

Mary started to say something, but choked up. She put her arm about her brother's neck, but he gently took it down.

"Don't make it worse than it is, sis dear," he faltered. "We are in trouble, big trouble, this time, but we hardly knew what we were doing. If the fellow lives, we will—"

"If he lives! My God! *if* he lives!" Mary moaned.

Her father and her older brother were coming out on the veranda now. The old gentleman had a book and manuscript under his handless arm. Charles noted that he was not even pale, though a certain expression of irritation rested on his patrician features.

"Yes, leave the horse," he was saying. "Get into the mountains. As you say, you know a good hiding-place. I'll remember the directions to it, and we'll get food to you somehow or other. It may not be serious. The scoundrel was attacking you with a knife, you think?"

"Martin thought so," Kenneth answered, "but I'm not sure of it now. Steve Pinkney says Martin was mistaken, and that is why he advised us to run. I was drinking. My nerves are all shattered. I got mad when I saw Keith and Martin struggling, and fired before I thought. I'm sorry, but if is too late now. We must get away."

"Yes, and before somebody sees you here," Rowland said. "Are you hungry?"

"Yes, but we can't wait," Kenneth answered. "Come on, Martin."

Mary had run to her older brother. She held out her arms; she was sobbing in her white fluttering throat. He took her into his embrace, drew her bare head to his shoulder, and stroked her hair.

"We are bad boys, sis dear," he said, tenderly. "We have not treated you right; no one knows that better than Martin and I, and we are getting paid for it. I hope Keith won't die. God knows I do! I really haven't anything against him. It was just a dispute over a game of poker. He was mad and so was I. Good-by. We must go. They will not find us where we are going."

"Hurry!" she gasped, as she slid from his arms. "Hurry!"

Side by side the two boys hastened toward the barn. The little group saw them pass through the stable-yard, climb over the fence, and vanish in the thicket which was the border of the vast forest that reached out, dank and trackless, into the mountains toward the west.

With a little sigh of despair, Mary sank down on the lowest step of the veranda. Her father looked at her for a moment with a childlike stare of perplexity, and then said:

"Come, come, don't act that way! It won't do any good."

"Come in de house, missie," Aunt Zilla said, gently, and as soothingly as a mother to an ill child. "Dem boys is gwine ter give de sheriff de slip en' dat man will pull thoo. Come on. Yo' breakfust is gittin' cold. Mr. Brown wants ter git ter his wuk in de cotton."

To his surprise, Charles saw Mary sit more erect. It was as if by a superhuman effort she had shaken herself temporarily free from the overpowering disaster.

"Yes, you must have your breakfast," she said, smiling faintly at Charles. "Come, let's go to the dining-room."

At the table he found himself admiring the self-control of both Mary and her father. Charles noted that Mary ate but little, and that little she seemed to take without relish. Rowland had his manuscript at his side at the table, and once he consulted it, as if his mind had reverted to something he had been interested in before the arrival of his sons.

"I am sorry that I did not have the opportunity to present my boys to you," he remarked once. "I told Kenneth who you were and assured him that you had given us evidence of your friendly spirit. He is glad that you have come to help us out with the work. One might not think so from his present conduct, but he hates to see his sister do manual labor in the field."

CHAPTER VII

Mary, now a different creature from what she was the day before, accompanied Charles to the cotton-field after breakfast. "You have done an enormous amount for half a day," she said. "You must not drive yourself like that. I know why you are doing it, but you must not. It would be wrong for us to permit it. From your accent I take you to be a Northerner, but you are acting like a cavalier of the old South. I appreciate it—I appreciate it, but I can't let you do so much."

"What, that?" he began. "As if that were anything! Why, Miss Rowland—" His emotions swept his power of utterance away from him, and he stood, hoe in hand, helpless under the spell of her storm-swept beauty and appealing womanhood. He wanted to aid her more materially. He wanted to offer his services in behalf of her brothers. He would have given his life—in his eyes it was a futile thing at best—for her cause; and yet he knew himself to be helpless. A woman's intuition is a marvelous thing, and when it permits itself to fathom a man's love it is as sure as the law of gravitation. She understood. Her dawning comprehension beamed faintly in her stricken face. He saw her breast rise tremulously and fall.

"I think I know what you started to say," she faltered. "And it is very, very sweet of you when you have known us such a short time. Isn't it strange that it should be like this? I know I can trust you—something makes me feel sure of it—and you have impressed my father the same way, and even critical Aunt Zilla."

He leaned on his hoe-handle. He now felt more sure of his utterance. "I want to help you," he cried. "I know how terribly you must feel over this matter. You are too young and gentle and frail for this dastardly thing to rest on you. I must do something to beat it off. I—"

"There really is nothing," she half sobbed. "As much as I love my brothers I'd rather see them dead than on trial for murder. Why, Mr. Brown, the sheriff wants to put them in that dirty jail at Carlin! I saw it once. The cells are iron cages in the center of big rooms walled about with brick. Oh, oh, oh!"

He longed to comfort her, but there was nothing that he could say. The keenest pain of his entire life seemed to be wrenching his heart from his body. The still fields, the slanting sunlight on the long rows of cotton-plants, the cloud-draped mountains, grimly mocked him in their placid inactivity when it seemed to him that the very universe ought to be striving in her behalf.

"Oh, it will be only a question of time," she moaned. "They can't hide in the mountains long, and if Tobe Keith dies—oh, oh! if he dies—"

She had suddenly noticed a horseman dismounting at the gate. He was fat, rather gross-looking, of medium height, and middle-aged. His hair and eyes were dark, and he had a heavy brown mustache twisted to points, which was after the manner of the mountaineers.

"It is Albert Frazier, the sheriff's brother," Mary explained.

"The sheriff's brother!" Charles started.

"We needn't be afraid of him," Mary said, somewhat confused. "In fact, I think he has come to try to help me. He—he is a—a friend of mine. He has been paying attention to me for almost a year. He sees me. He is coming here. Wait. Don't go to work yet. I want you to meet him."

"Paying attention to you!" Charles's subconsciousness spoke the words rather than his inert lips. It may have been the sheer blight in his face and eyes that caused the girl to offer a blushing explanation of her words.

"I don't mean that we are engaged—*actually engaged*," she said. "It is only a sort of—of understanding. He says he loves me. He has done us a great many favors. You see he has influence in various ways. But I have never really encouraged him to—to—You know what I mean. But he is very persistent and very hot-tempered, domineering, too. But, oh, what does that matter—what does anything matter? Right now he may be coming to tell us that—that Tobe Keith is dead."

Charles said nothing, for Frazier was near at hand. His keen brown eyes rested on Charles, half inquiringly, half suspiciously. He carried a riding-whip with which he lashed the horse-hairs from his trousers with a quick, irritated stroke.

"Good morning," he said, as he tipped his broad-brimmed felt hat. "Out here giving instructions, eh? I heard you'd hired help."

She made a failure of the smile she tried to force. It was a pale, piteous pretense. "Mr. Frazier—Mr. Brown," she introduced them.

Frazier did not offer his hand, and so Charles did not remove his own from his hoe-handle. He simply nodded. It would have been hard to do more, for instinctively he disliked the man. The feeling must have been returned, for Frazier all but sneered contemptuously.

"I heard of Mr. Brown at the hotel in town," he said. "Circus man, eh. You fellows are always dropping in on us mountain folks. Well, well, we need your help now in the fields. Niggers are no good."

"Have you heard about my brothers?" Mary here broke in.

"Yes. That's what I rode out for, Mary. I knew you'd be crazy. You are funny that way—as if you can keep boys like these two down."

"But how is Keith?" Mary reached forward and caught the lapel of his coat entreatingly. She appeared quite unconscious of what she was doing, and as he answered Frazier took her frail fingers into his burly clasp, and for a moment held them caressingly, a glint of passion in his eyes. Had she been his wife the sight could not have been more painful to Charles. It did not excite his anger; somehow it only heaped fresh despair upon the depression which had almost unmanned him.

"Oh, Keith? Yes, I knew that would be the first question," Frazier said. "And I made special inquiry before I left on that point, for everything depends on it, of course. Well, little girl, nobody can possibly tell yet. Our doctors in town are not expert surgeons, and they can't decide just yet, it seems. The ball is lodged in the stomach somewhere, and they seem to be afraid to probe for it. It was a good-sized piece of cold lead and the fellow may kick the bucket any minute. You see—"

"Stop! She is fainting!" Charles cried.

He sprang forward, but Frazier had put his rough arm about her and began to fan the ghastly face which now rested on his breast.

"By God! so she is!" Frazier said. "Get some water, man. Quick! I can hold her, all right!"

"No, no, don't go!" said Mary, as she opened her eyes, drew herself erect, and stood away from Frazier. "I felt faint, but it is all gone now. Nothing is the matter with me. Go on! Tell me about my brothers."

Frazier glanced at Charles, half smiled, and shrugged his shoulders.

"Oh, you know as much about them as I do, I reckon," he said. "They came this way. I know where they are by this time. I know, but my brother doesn't," and Frazier laughed significantly. "You see it is like this, little girl; my brother happens not to be on to these trips of mine out here to see you. I have my reasons, and good ones at that, for not letting him know. There is a part of my father's estate that is to be divided when either me or John marries, and if he thought that I was thinking of such a thing it might upset him a little. At any rate, he is in the dark about us, so when he started out this morning after your brothers I made it my business to throw him clean off the track. I told him that they had gone exactly the opposite way and that I was sure they would take a train for the West at Tifton, and show him a clean pair of heels."

"Then—then he won't look for them here in the mountains?" Mary panted.

"Not for a while, anyway," Frazier returned. "And that is what I came to tell you, little woman. I'm no fool and I am going to do everything in my reach to keep the boys out of John's clutch till we can tell how Keith gets on. John and I have worked together in tracking men down, and he doesn't dream that I am against him in this. Thanks to me, he and his deputies are working on a false scent altogether, and I'll keep them at it if I turn the world over. You can depend on me, little girl. I'll keep you posted. The boys will be safe where they are for a while, if you will keep them fed."

"But do you think Keith will live?" Mary demanded, tremulously.

"The Lord only knows," Frazier said. "He is awfully low, it seems to me. I reckon there is no use fooling you as to that. You may get bad news any minute. But even if he dies we'll manage somehow to slip the boys away. I know a feller now in the West. I get letters from him. Fifteen years ago he shot a man in—"

"Don't, don't tell me about it!" Mary pleaded, her agonized eyes turning to Charles, as if for protection that was not available from any other source.

"No, what is the use of all that?" Charles blurted out.

"Don't chip in here!" Frazier thundered. "What do you mean by breaking into my talk? Get back to your work! Are you paid to stand here idle?"

There was nothing he could say, and Charles dropped his head for a moment. Mary was staring at him blankly. So vast was the tragedy hovering over her that she quite failed to sense the tension between the two men.

"Come on, let's go to the house," went on Frazier, continuing to scowl at Charles even while he was putting his arm about the girl. "I have to see your father about some money he wants to borrow at the bank. He wants me to indorse a note for him."

"You know what to do, Mr. Brown," Mary said. "It will take you several days to finish the cotton. After that we'll decide what next to do."

Charles doffed his hat and bowed as she turned away, Frazier's arm still about her waist. He went to the unfinished row of cotton-plants and began to work. His back was turned to the receding pair. How different his outlook was from that of the day before! Then a veritable new existence seemed to have opened out before him, an existence that was a divinely bestowed transition from sordid misery to far-reaching happiness. All the ills of life seemed to have taken wing, leaving him free to grow and expand as the plants he was nurturing; but now there was nothing to face but the grim fact that he was a drudging outcast from conventional civilization. As he toiled on his breast ached under a pain that was superphysical. Had he brought it on himself? he wondered. Was all this the inevitable punishment for the reckless folly of his youth? It might be so, he told himself, and the sacrifice he had made for William and Celeste and Ruth was not sufficient. He had caused his dying mother great mental distress; he had led young men astray; he had been ostracized by his club and college fraternity; he had been sentenced by a judge in a police court; he had disgraced his family. He ceased working and looked toward the house. Mary and Frazier were still in sight. The heavy arm was still about the slender waist. The fellow bore himself with the air of a man confident of the prize he was winning, and yet unconscious of its inestimable value. Charles stood staring till they disappeared in the house, then he resumed his work, but without any part of the interest of the day before. A wonderful thing had happened to him. He had scoffed all his life at the idea of a man's supreme devotion to any particular woman, and yet within only a few hours he had found himself bound hand and foot, mind and soul, to a young girl he had never seen before. What had brought it about? Ah, she was suffering and he was suffering! It was the kinship of his soul to hers. But what could come of it? he asked, gloomily. Nothing, not even if she were to withhold her love from her present suitor, for Charles could never prove himself worthy of her. She belonged to a proud old family, and he was virtually a nameless man. For William's sake he had promised to obliterate himself, and he must keep his promise. He toiled on. The sun was hot and the perspiration oozed from him and dampened his clothing. He worked with the despair of a shackled convict bent on forgetting all that lay beyond his prison walls.

CHAPTER VIII

The next day was a wet one. Charles heard the rain beating on his window when he waked. Dressing hurriedly, for his watch showed that he was late, he went down-stairs. No one was in sight. Going to the dining-room, he saw Zilla putting his coffee at his plate.

"I heard yer comin'," she said, agreeably. "My white folks ain't up yit. Marse Andy al'ays sleeps late on er wet day, en young miss just got back from town en is in 'er room, tryin' ter res'. She saddled de hoss 'erse'f 'bout midnight en rode off. She said she couldn't sleep nohow widout knowin' how Tobe Keith was gittin' on. I tried ter stop 'er, en so did 'er pa, but she would go."

"And did she get favorable news?" Charles asked.

"He's des de same as he was," Zilla replied, with a sigh. "He's powerful critical. She waited dar all night at de hotel wid Miz' Quinby. One minute she'd hear one thing, and den ergin sumpin' else. Po' chile talk erbout war-times en slave days? Dat po' chile has mo' ter bear dan 'er ma en pa ever went th'oo when dey was all fightin' fer de ole state."

The rain was still falling heavily when he left the table, and as he stood in the front doorway and realized that it was too wet for hoeing, he suddenly thought of the blacksmith shop and the work he had planned to do in sharpening the tools. Glad of something to busy himself with, he went to the shop, kindled a fire in the antiquated forge, and began to work. There was something vaguely soothing in the splash and patter of the rain on the low, blackened roof of split oaken boards, the sucking of the air into the bellows, the creaking of the bellows chains, the ringing of the anvil, and the spray of metallic sparks in the half darkness of the room.

It was near noon. The rain had ceased, though the clouds were still heavy and lowering. He was hammering on a red plowshare when Mary suddenly appeared in the doorway. Her back was to the outer daylight, her face dimly lighted by the slow blaze of the forge. She advanced into the shop, paused and scanned the heap of sharpened tools on the ground near the tub of blackened water which was used for cooling the metal.

"What a wonder you are!" she cried, with an attempt at a lightness he knew she did not feel. "You have already done ten dollars' worth of work this morning. You see I know, for I pay the bills."

"It is nothing," he answered. "I wanted to be busy."

"I heard the ringing of the anvil when I waked, and knew what it meant. Yes, you are wonderful, and I am afraid"—she tried to smile—"that you are too valuable for us. I was thinking about you on my way to town last night. You won't stay here. You can't stand this sort of thing—I mean the awful mess you find us in. I wouldn't blame you for leaving us. Why, I'll be frank with you, Mr. Brown—it is only fair to you as a stranger in this locality. There are plantations only a few miles away where you would find more people employed, where they have some sort of amusement, and where the people you'd work for would not be upset and depressed as we are. I did want to save our crops, now that they are planted, but, facing this other thing, the crops count for nothing—nothing at all. If God would show me a way to save my brothers I'd give my very soul in payment. You don't know—no one could know how I feel. I am stretched on a cross, Mr. Brown. I am praying with every breath I draw, but I am stifling under the dread of what may happen. At this very minute Tobe Keith may—may—" she groaned, leaned against the bellows and stood shuddering, cowed and wild-eyed, under the horror her mind had pictured.

"Don't, don't, please don't!" he cried. "Don't give up. Don't lose hope. There is always hope. I lost it once in—in a great trouble, but I lived through it somehow. You will, too. Some wise man has said that God does not lay any burden on any one that is too heavy to bear. Think of that—believe that; it comforted me once. It is comforting me now in the belief that you will escape from this terrible thing."

"Oh, do you think so—*do* you?" and she wrung her hands, lowered her head again, and uttered a little wail that ended in a sob.

He all but reached out his hands toward her in a strange, bold impulse to take her into his arms, but checked himself and stood aghast as he contemplated the catastrophe which might have followed such an unwarranted act. Had he subconsciously leaped back to the free period before his downfall, or, as a regenerated man, had he for an instant felt himself to be on her level? Ah no, it was the kinship again—the kinship of suffering souls. "I'm sure of it," he repeated. "If I thought otherwise I'd see no good in life at all. Men deserve punishment for the wrong they do, but gentle girls like you must not suffer for the mistakes of men. It will pass over—your cloud will blow away."

"Oh, oh!" and she put her hands to her dry eyes while her shoulders shook. "I hope—you make me hope a little, somehow—that what you say may be true. You comfort me more than everybody else put together. It is your way, your voice, your look. You are a good, kind man, Mr. Brown. How strange that you came just when you did! I'll try to be braver. I'll try to stop thinking that every approaching person on the road is coming to tell me the worst."

"That is right," he said.

"And would you pray—would you continue to pray?" she asked, with the timid simplicity of a child groping in the dark.

Their eyes met steadily. "I don't know how to advise you as to that," he said, after a pause full of thought. "I must confess that I am not religious. I used to pray, as a child, but I don't now."

"Well, I shall keep it up," she said, quietly. "There are moments when it seems to help. I prayed to be allowed to sleep this morning, and I did. You see, I need the strength. If I go to pieces all may be lost, for my father can do nothing."

She turned back to the house. The rain had ceased, though the clouds were still thick and lowering. The forge blazed again; the anvil rang as he pounded the yielding steel into shape. He had forgotten himself and his past; the new existence was buoying him up again. Nothing mattered but the woes which had come to Mary Rowland and the necessity of his shouldering them—fighting them.

When the bell rang for lunch he went into the house. He found Mary in the dining-room, packing some food into a basket.

"It is for the boys," she explained. "I am glad it is clearing up, for I must take it to them."

"You?" he cried, in surprise.

"Yes," she made answer, simply. "Father and I are the only ones who know where the boys are. Father is in town now to wait for news and to attend to some business with Mr. Frazier at the bank. Father would not want me to go, but some one must."

"Might I not go in your place?" he asked, and he actually held his breath while he waited for her reply.

"You don't know the way," she said. "It is hard even for me to find."

He looked at the heavy basket. "But you can't carry that by yourself. May I not carry it for you?"

She glanced at him gratefully. "Would you really care to go?" she inquired. "It is a long walk, and difficult even in dry weather."

"Please!" he said. "You ought not to go alone."

"Thank you; but first get your dinner. I don't want any. I have only just eaten my breakfast."

When they started out, half an hour later, the clouds had lifted somewhat, though they were still full of rain. They went through the barn-yard, climbed over the rail fence, and entered the near-by thicket, which stretched on into the sloping woodland of the mountains. The wet weeds and grass were already dampening her shoes, and, noting it, he paused suddenly.

"You really ought not to expose yourself this way," he protested. "Your feet will be soaked in a very short time."

"It doesn't matter," she said. "Nothing matters, Mr. Brown, but the fate that hangs over my brothers. I think I could wade in water up to my knees for days at a time and not be conscious of discomfort. It isn't one's body that feels the greatest pain, it is the mind, the soul, the memory. The pain comes from the futility of hoping. Life is a tragedy, isn't it?"

"Yes and no," he answered, smiling into her expectant, upturned face, the beauty of which had deepened under her gloom. "I have thought so at times, but there were always rifts in my clouds. There will be in yours."

"How sweet and noble of you!" she said, tremulously, in her emotion. Suddenly he saw that she was studying his face closely, feature by feature. Then she continued, as one rendering a verdict: "Yes, you have suffered. I see the traces of it. It lurks in the tone of your voice; it shows itself in your sympathy for me."

Without revealing his new-found passion for her, which surged within him like a raging torrent, there was nothing he could say. Presently they came to a brook several yards in width and he could see no means of crossing it. She was disturbed for a moment, but to her surprise he stepped into the shallow water, took the basket to the other side and, wet to his knees, came wading back to her.

"You must let me carry you across," he said, smiling.

"No, I'm too heavy." She shook her head.

"I could carry one of you under each arm," he jested. "Come!" He held out his hands. She hesitated. A touch of pink colored her cheeks, and then she came into his arms.

"There," he directed, as he lifted her up, "put your arm around my neck and lean toward me. Don't be afraid. That's right. I must be steady, you know, for there are round stones under my feet, and if I slipped we'd both go down."

Reaching the other side, he put her down and took up the basket. His heart was beating like a trip-hammer. The flush was still on Mary's face.

"You carried me as if I were a baby," she said. "How very strong you are! I could feel the muscles of your arms like knotted ropes. What an odd mixture you are!"

"In what way?" he asked, as they moved on side by side.

"I hardly know," she answered. "Well, for one thing, you seem out of place as a common workman in the fields. You have the manner, the way of—" She broke off, and the flush in her cheeks deepened.

"I've been several things," he admitted, with a sigh. "I ought to know something of life, for I've had many experiences."

"I was in your room this morning," she said. "It is a desolate place for a man of your temperament. I must fix it up. The attic is full of old things—curtains, pictures, and even books. You must be lonely at times. I noticed a photograph on your bureau in a frame. It was that of a child, a beautiful little girl. She was so refined-looking, and so daintily dressed. She resembled you, about the eyes and brow."

Charles stared fixedly. He looked confused. "Yes, I think we do look alike," he finally replied. Probably she expected him to say more, but how was it possible to explain?

"I think I understand," she said, almost in an undertone, as she strode on ahead of him. "I now know why you look homesick at times. You must miss her."

He saw that she did not fathom the truth about the child, but he was not prepared for an adequate explanation and so he remained silent. However, the girl was making deductions.

"It must be," she thought, as she forged her way through the damp bushes still ahead of him. "It is his child. His wife must be living and they are separated, or he would speak of her. Poor fellow!"

CHAPTER IX

For four miles they walked over very uneven, rocky ground. Deeper and deeper they went into the mountains. There were hills to climb in places where there was no sign of path or road; there were yawning gulches to cross; dank, stream-filled cañons filled with dead and leaning trees to pass through. He felt that she was leading him aright, for her step was firm and her progress rapid and sure. Now and then she would look at the western sky where the presence of the sun was indicated by a somewhat brighter spot than the rest of the dun expanse.

"We really must hurry," she kept saying, "for we'll be overtaken by night on our return if we don't get to them pretty soon."

"Have you a landmark to guide you?" he asked.

"Yes, there to the left. Do you see that mountain peak? Well, their hiding-place—it is a little cave they know about—is in the thick jungle at the foot of it, on this side. We can't go all the way in. It would be impossible. I shall get nearer and whistle for them to come out. They know my whistle. They taught me how to do it when I was little. It is like this," and she clasped her hands together tightly, leaving an orifice between the thumbs into which she blew her breath sharply. A keen whistle was produced. "There is no mistaking it," she continued. "They would know it anywhere. Every pair of hands makes a different sound."

Half an hour later they were on the edge of the dense jungle of which she had spoken. A veritable riot of dank undergrowth was massed beneath giant trees and around green, moss-grown boulders. The greater part of it was a miasmatic swamp, the boggy soil of which could not be walked upon with safety even in dry weather. Mary paused on a spot where the ground was firm and folded her hands. "Be still and listen," she said. "If they are there, they will answer. They will know that I'd not whistle if it were not safe."

The flutelike note rose on the still air; it was echoed from a near-by cliff and died down. No sound followed. Mary looked perplexed, worried. She whistled again. This time a distant whistle caught up the echo. It was a coarser tone than hers but produced in the same way.

"That's Kensy!" she cried, in relief. "Listen! Hear the twigs breaking? He is coming—maybe both. She whistled again, now more softly, and in her excitement tremulously. The sound of bending bushes and the cracking of dry branches was growing nearer.

"Hello, brother!" Mary suddenly cried out. "Here we are. Come on."

"Hello, sis! Who is with you—father?"

"No, Mr. Brown."

The sound of his movements ceased. "Who?" he asked, dubiously.

"Mr. Brown, you know. He is working for us. Come on. It is all right, Kensy."

"Oh!" Kenneth was heard ejaculating. "All right. Coast clear, sis?"

"Yes, yes, Kensy. We've got some food."

"Food, thank God! We are starving, sis. We haven't had a bite to eat since the night before we left home." With this he appeared from a clump of weeping willows, and stood before them. She introduced him to Charles. Kenneth simply nodded. He was coatless, without a hat, and besmeared with the dark mud of the morass from head to foot.

"I fell down back there," he said. "My foot slipped while I was on a log. I was wet, anyway. We were away from the cave, trying to kill some birds to eat, and got caught in the rain. Afraid to make a fire, anyway. No matches."

"I have some in a dry box," Charles said. "Won't you take them?"

"Never mind. I put plenty of them in the basket," Mary said. "Where is Martin?"

"In the cave. He had his clothes off, trying to dry them, and so I came out alone. He is all right, but acting like a baby. Oh God! what have you got, sis. He had the basket in his muddy hands and was removing the napkin which covered the contents. There he comes now. He couldn't wait."

The other boy now appeared, barefooted, his trousers rolled up to his knees. On being introduced he shook hands timidly. He ignored the basket of food. His glaring, dark-ringed eyes rested on his sister's face. He panted as he bent toward her. "How is Keith?" he asked.

"Yes, how is he?" Kenneth echoed, glancing up from the contents of the basket.

Charles thought it was significant that Mary hesitated for an instant before replying. "He is just the same as he was—no better, no worse," she answered.

"No better? My God!" Martin seemed to shrink together like a touched sensitive-plant. "Then—then he may die?"

Kenneth had his hands full of baked chicken, but he lowered them and, leaving the food in the basket, he stood up. "Is it as bad as that, sis?" he faltered, his lips betraying a tendency to shake.

"I hate to say so," Mary faltered, "but I must not deceive you and make you reckless. This is the only safe place now." She told them of Albert Frazier's aid in misleading his brother.

"He is a good one," Kenneth said, more at ease. "He is sharper any day than his blockhead of a brother. If he stays on our side we'll be all right, even—even if—"

"Don't say it, Ken!" Martin's young mouth was twisted awry. "I can't bear it. I can't—I simply can't!"

Kenneth uttered a forced laugh of defiance. "He is like that all the time," he said. "He didn't sleep a wink last night. He cried. He prayed to God and to mother's spirit: 'Save Tobe Keith—save Tobe Keith! Don't let 'im die!'"

"It is because I held him," Martin feebly explained. "You see, I had him so he couldn't move, and—and when Ken shot I felt his body sort of crumble up and hang limp in my arms. If he dies it will be my fault, for—for he could have dodged the shot but for me. If he dies, sis, it will be my fault and it will mean the rope and the scaffold."

Kenneth had bent to the basket again, but he refrained from taking up the food. He faced his sister. "We'll have to stay hid," he said, grimly. "Don't offend Albert Frazier, for all you do. He won't let his brother find us. Even if he found us, I'll bet Albert could keep him from making an arrest. He owes Albert money, I've heard. They always work into each other's hands. Albert had some trouble himself once that the sheriff squashed."

Charles was now looking at Mary. There was an expression about her face, and all but swaying body, that was akin to that of her fainting-spell in the field the preceding day. She had locked her hands together and he saw a flare of agony in her tortured eyes. There was a fallen tree near her and she sank down on its trunk and lowered her head. Finally she accomplished what he knew she was trying so hard to do; she mastered her weakness.

"Martin, sit here by me," she said, pleadingly, and the younger boy obeyed, the far-reaching terror still in his bland blue eyes. She stroked back his matted hair and picked the fragments of leaves and grass from it. "My sweet boy!" she faltered, "I don't know what to say to comfort you and quiet your fears about—Tobe's condition. I'm glad mother is not alive, Martin. She could not have borne this. You are so young—just a boy—and you are sensitive and imaginative. It looks worse to you than it really is. I feel down deep in me that Tobe will get well. We are sure to get good news before long. Now eat something."

"I was hungry this morning, but it is gone," Martin said. "The sight of the stuff almost sickens me."

Mary put both her arms around his neck and kissed him. "You are making yourself sick," she said. "Eat, won't you, for my sake?"

His brother was eating now, and Martin went to his side and took a piece of chicken and a biscuit. Mary watched them for a moment with wide-open glittering eyes—the sort of stare that sometimes seems to float on a rising tide of tears invisible. Then her head sank again.

"Look here," Kenneth said, suddenly, as he glanced toward the western sky. "You and Mr. Brown have a long walk before you to get back before night. You are doing no good here now. Hadn't you better start?"

Mary stood up. "Yes, we must be going. Are you comfortable in the cave?"

"Yes," Kenneth returned. "It is good enough. We have a big bed of dry leaves and grass, and if Martin would only sleep we'd be all right."

"I try, but I can't," the blue-eyed boy said, in an uncertain, half-abashed tone. "There was a night-owl near us last night, and it was hooting, and, my God! sis, the thing seemed to talk. I never had anything against Tobe Keith in my life. In fact, he and I used to fish and swim together when we'd run away from school, and to think that I actually—Turn around, and I'll show exactly how I clamped his arms and how he was bent down when Ken fired."

"No, not now," Charles protested. "Your sister is very nervous. She almost fainted just now."

"No, don't go into it," Kenneth mumbled, his mouth full. "I haven't anything against Tobe, either. We were both drinking, but they tell me the law doesn't excuse a fellow on that account. I didn't know what I was doing, but I couldn't prove it to a jury. I reckon they would call it deliberate. You see, Tobe and I had had words the day before over another matter, and I remember I made some threats about what I'd do to him. Oh, if he dies they will have a case against us. I know that well enough, and we must stay under cover till we can get West."

"I thought Tobe had a knife," Martin said, piteously. "I was sure I saw him draw it, and I held him to keep him from stabbing Ken. You know Tobe did rip a fellow open once in a fight. They say I was mistaken and that it was just a spoon he had been eating oysters with, and that he dropped it as soon as I grabbed him. Sis, will you let us know how he is as often as you can?"

"Yes, yes," the girl promised, "and if you don't hear it will be a sign of good news. Remember that, and, brother, do try to sleep to-night. You look sick."

She glanced at the sky again. She kissed them both and walked away. They had gone only a few paces when Charles suddenly turned back and joined them.

"Your sister may not be able to come every time," he said. "But I know the way now, for I took note of the landmarks, and I'll come by myself."

"That will be bully of you," Kenneth said. "By the way, we must have a signal, so that I'll know who it is. Suppose you whistle twice slowly and three times fast, and I'll answer and come out."

Mary was looking at Charles from sadly inquiring eyes when he caught her up a moment later. "What did you say to them?" she asked.

He told her and she forced a wan smile, while a warm glow of gratitude rose in her eyes.

"How sweet and kind of you!" she said. "You have proved yourself to be a friend, and we have known you such a short time."

"I'd give my life to help you out of this," he suddenly said, surprised at his boldness of speech and the raging storm of sympathy which had fairly forced the words from him.

"Your life?" She was close at his side, for he was holding the dripping bough of a mountain cedar aside for her to pass. "That is a strong expression. Your life? That is all one has, you know."

"My life is worthless to me and to every one else," he said, frankly, and as he uttered the words he was viewing his career in a flash-light of memory from its beginning to the present. "Yes, Miss Rowland, it is no good— absolutely no good. That's why I feel as I do for your brothers, and—I mean it—I'd give my life to-day to lift you out of this trouble and see you as I did that day in the store when you hired me."

"*Hired* you? Don't use that word," she suddenly cried out, and she put her hand on his arm in a gentle stroke of protest. "Mr. Brown, it seems to me—I don't know how to explain it, but it seems to me that I've known you for ages and ages. I can see that you are sad at times, and I know that you have suffered somehow, somewhere. That picture of the pretty child in your room—she is linked with your trouble, is she not?"

"Indirectly," he admitted, not seeing her drift. "Yes, it was partly on her account—for her own future—that I left home."

"I see, I see; and her mother?" Mary's voice had sunken almost to inaudibility; the cracking of the twigs under their feet all but drowned its sound. "Did you leave her with the child?"

"Oh yes! They are inseparable," he answered. He felt that he was admitting too much, and he turned the subject to that of the lessening sunlight on a cliff to their left. He thought the dense clouds massing behind them indicated a high wind and a heavy downpour of rain.

But his companion was not thinking of the state of the weather. "You will go back to them some day, of course," she persisted.

Charles shuddered; she was probing a subject that he felt honor bound not to touch upon. She repeated her words, steadily fixing his eyes with her own.

"No," he repeated, firmly, "I shall never go back, Miss Rowland—never in the world. My future home is here, anywhere, but never there again."

"And you do not like to speak of your family? Is that it?" Mary went on, softly, sympathetically.

"I can't—I haven't the moral right to speak of them now. That is all I can say. I'm dead to my past, Miss Rowland. I am blotting it out. Serving you in any capacity helps kill memories that ought to be dead. There are memories that reproach and torture one. I have my share of them."

CHAPTER X

For perhaps a mile they trudged along in silence. Presently Mary stopped and turned on him.

"A drop of rain fell in my face," she said, looking up at the sky.

His eyes followed hers. Along the brow of a mountain to the west clouds as black and thick as the smoke of pitch were massing. The tops of the trees in the near distance were swaying violently and the breeze had become cooler and was full of swift and contending currents. Little whirlwinds lifted the leaves at their feet and sent them sky-ward in shafts and spiral columns. More drops of rain fell. The brighter spot in the west was becoming cloud-veiled, and it was growing dark on all sides.

"We are sure to get caught," Mary said, in alarm. "It is an awful storm, both wind and rain. They are terrible here in the mountains when they rise suddenly like that. See, it is coming fast. What shall we do?"

He could offer no helpful suggestion. There was no sort of shelter in sight. Still they hurried on breathlessly, Mary leading the way. At times, in her haste, she plunged as aimlessly into tangled undergrowth as a pursued animal, and had to be extricated by his calm, firm hands.

"Running like this won't do any good," he advised her, gravely. "I'm afraid of one thing, very much afraid, and that is that we may lose our way. You see, up to now we had the light in the west to guide us, but it is all gone now. Those shifting clouds are very misleading."

"Oh, I'm sure we are right as to the direction," Mary said, "but I am afraid of the storm. See the lightning over there, and hear the thunder. The storm is getting nearer, and it is dangerous among trees like these at such times. They are shattered and torn up by the roots very often."

It was raining sharply now, and the darkness had thickened so much that it was impossible to discern the landmarks which Charles had made note of as they passed the spot before.

"Ah, we are right!" the girl suddenly cried. "I know that flat-faced boulder there, but it is miles and miles from home. I know the way now, but we can't possibly make it in time to escape the storm."

In a veritable sheet the rain beat down now. The thunder roared and the lightning flashed about them. The black clouds hurtled along the mountainside and drooped down from the threatening sky. The water was running in streams from Mary's bonnet. Charles jerked off his coat and was putting it about her when she protested.

"No, don't!" she cried. "You'll need it." She tried to resist, but, as if she had been an unruly child, he drew the garment about her forcibly and buttoned it at the neck.

"You must," he said, simply; "you must!"

"Must!" she repeated, sharply. "How dare you speak to me like that?"

"Pardon me, Miss Rowland," he said. "I don't want to offend you, but you must keep it on. You are not well. I have noticed your tendency to faintness. Your trouble, loss of sleep, and worry have weakened you. Your feet are wet, and—"

"Thank you; I was wrong," she answered, as the wind bore his words away and the rain dashed into her face.

For a little while they forged their way through the wet bushes, wild vines, and mountain heather. Suddenly she paused again.

"We are in for it," she sighed. "There used to be an old hut of logs near the flat boulder. It is somewhere here. If we could find it we would be sheltered for a while."

"A hut?" he echoed. "Then we must find it if possible. The storm is just beginning. To be exposed to it might cost you your life."

"I think it is over that way," she replied, and they turned sharply in the direction she indicated. It was now so dark that they could scarcely see where they were walking. Streams newly made from the accumulating water on the heights above flooded their feet to the depths of their shoes, and the rain fell upon them as if by the pailful. Once Mary slipped and fell, and he lifted her as tenderly as if she had been a sick child.

"Too bad! too bad!" she heard him saying, and then: "Excuse me, but I must hold you." With that he put his arm around her waist. She shrank back for a moment, but she made no protest, and side to side, like a pair of lovers, they struggled along. Sometimes she stumbled, sometimes he, but the footing of one or the other always held.

"The hut must be here somewhere," Mary said. There was a vivid flash of lightning, and in it Mary saw a giant oak which she remembered. "We are right," she exulted, aloud. "It is just beyond that oak."

But other difficulties were to be met. A torrent of water coming down from the mountain ran between them and the goal. Again he lifted her in his arms, this time without protest on her part, and bore her across. The rain, broken into a mist by the wind, filled their mouths, nostrils, and eyes. They could scarcely breathe, or see. Once he took a clean handkerchief from his pocket, unfolded it, and without apology wiped her face.

"You treat me as if I was a baby," she said, but the act had not displeased her. It was significant that he called her "Miss Rowland" the next moment, and that he wore the same air of humility as when she had "hired" him in the village store.

Another flash of lightning revealed the dark, low roof of the hut, and with his arm around her waist they hastened to it. Its door was closed, but not locked, and he easily pushed it open. Drawing her inside, he stood facing her. Neither spoke; both were panting from the loss of breath.

"This will never do," he said. "You will take cold in those wet things. I must make a fire."

"A fire?" she said. "How could you?"

"I have matches in a water-proof box," he explained. "But I'll have to be careful in opening it. My hands are dripping wet."

"Shake them out on the floor," Mary suggested, "and you can then pick them out separately."

"Good! I shouldn't have thought of it," he laughed. He took the box from the pocket of his coat and carefully emptied the matches on the floor a little away from where they were standing. "Now," he said, picking one up. "Here goes."

It failed, owing to the water dripping from his hands. He tried again. This time he was successful and he raised the burning match above his head. The tiny flame lit up the room. Bare walls of logs from which the dry bark was falling, a floor of planks, a roof of split-oak boards, a chimney of logs plastered over with clay, and a broad stone hearth were all they saw, save a heap of fire-wood and small pieces of pitch-pine in one corner.

"Fine!" he cried. "That wood will burn like tinder. It looks to be very old." A gust of damp wind from the door blew the light out. Again they were in the dark. "Wait," he advised. "I'll gather up some of that dry bark, and then we'll set it on fire."

"Yes; it will burn easily," she agreed.

He noted that she spoke as if she were shivering with cold, and he made haste to get the bark. With his hands full, he groped to the chimney and bent down over the ashes in the fireplace. She picked up a match and succeeded in striking it. She held it against the heap of bark. The bark ignited. He hastened for more, and then, as the flame was now sufficient, he added small pieces of wood, and then larger sticks. Soon a fine fire was crackling and blazing in the crude stone fireplace.

"You must get dry," he said, taking his coat from her shoulders. "Everything depends on it."

She laughed almost merrily, as they stood side by side in the rising steam from their drying clothing.

"You must sit down, and put out your feet to the fire," he declared. "I'll make a seat for you." He brought some logs from the corner and made two heaps of them about five feet apart, and then raised one of the loose floor boards, and laid it across, thus forming a sort of bench. She smiled gratefully; sat down and put out her feet to the flames.

"You must take off your shoes and stockings and dry them," he said, with the firm confidence of a family doctor.

"Must!" She repeated the word to herself, and bit her lip; she made no motion to obey his wishes.

"Surely you are not offended at what I said," he went on, after a little silence. "It is a serious thing, you know. Dry feet at such a time as this are more important than a dry body."

"Oh, I don't mind!" she answered, and she bent down and began to fumble the strings of her shoes; but the water had drawn the knot tight and her fingers were benumbed with cold.

"You must permit me, Miss Rowland," Charles said, calmly. He sank on his knees before her and, without waiting for her consent, he skilfully loosened the knotted string and drew her shoe off. "Now the other, please."

She thrust it out, but rather reluctantly. "You have such a strange way about you!" she said, coldly. "That is, I mean—sometimes."

The string he was now working on seemed to be more tightly tied, and she heard him mutter something impatiently: "I don't want to cut it." (Surely he had not heard her last remark, she thought.)

But he evidently had heard, for when he had removed the other shoe he said, "So you think I have a strange way about me at times, do you?"

He had seated himself on the bench beside her. Her head, neck, and shoulders in the red glow of the fire formed an exquisite picture. She had removed her hat, and her damp hair shone like a mass of bronze cobwebs. She was so dainty, so frail, so appealing! Not only had her young soul been torn to shreds, but the very elements had pounced upon her defenseless body. In her he saw the richest embodiment of a long line of patrician ancestors. How strange the whole situation! There she was storm-bound with a man whom the law held as no better than a felon, a nameless wanderer with no possibility of a respectable future ahead of him. She was silent, and he repeated what he had said.

"I don't mean anything wrong," she replied, smiling on him sweetly. "Now I suppose you will order me to take off my stockings. I don't have to, for they are drying as they are. See!"

She had put her small feet out to the fire. Her whole form was veiled in the rising vapor. It seemed to him to be a mist of enchantment out of which her eyes shone and her voice came like inexplicable music. An exquisite fancy held him in its grasp. His life and hers were but of a night's duration. They were besieged in an impenetrable forest by wild beasts, the prey of elemental forces. For the moment she was his, all his own. Frazier, her family, conventions, his own misfortune, would ultimately part them, but now in his ecstatic vision she was his, and the world might end with the dawn, for aught he cared. But one thing he suddenly began to fear, and that was that thoughts of her brothers' trouble might again depress her. So he bent all his energies toward her entertainment. He told her of a trip to Europe he had made just after leaving college, filling his account with amusing anecdotes. Her eyes were bent on him with a stare of profound interest.

"How wonderful," she exclaimed, "to meet one who has been there so recently! It has always been like a dream of heaven to me. My mother went when she was a girl, and she used to tell us about it when we were children. There were some far-off cousins of hers living in London. The head of the house had a title. I don't remember what it was—my father knows. Strange to say, he is proud of it, as if it would help us now. I suppose—I suppose"— her voice shook and mellowed as it fell deeper into her throat—"that those people over there would not care to keep up with us, now that we are so poor and my brothers are—like they are. I have an idea that old English families are very particular when it comes to the violation of the law."

"Don't think of your brothers' trouble," he pleaded. "Let us try to have cheerful, hopeful thoughts."

"I am trying," she responded, but even while she was speaking her face and tone showed the futility of her effort. "Poor Martin!" she went on. "Do you know, somehow, I feel more for him than for Kensy. Kensy is rougher, harder, less sensitive, less imaginative. Martin has always been my baby of the two. He was sick once several years ago, and I waited on him, nursed him, and petted him nearly to death. This is terrible on him. He may be awake now in that cold, damp cave, and with those ghastly thoughts to keep him company. Oh, life is a tragedy, Mr. Brown! As a child, I thought it was an endless dream of beauty and joy, and I have waked to this—to this!"

He tried again to cheer her with his stories, but her sweet face held shadows which he could not banish. Now and then she would smile faintly, but he saw that she was forcing herself to do so.

Something he said about his school-days evoked a sudden question for which he was not prepared.

"You speak of your home, but you have not yet told me where it was," she said.

He looked down at the pool of water which had dripped from his clothing, and hesitated. His pause brought a quick remark from her.

"Pardon me, I have no right to ask," she sighed.

"But you *have* the right," he floundered, conscious of the flush on his face and the agitation in his manner. "It is only that—that I have put it behind me forever. It is mine no longer, you see."

"Never mind. I'm sorry I touched upon it." She sighed again and looked through the open door out into the raging wind and rain. "I'm always prying into your personal affairs, as when I spoke of the photograph of the pretty little girl in your room."

"Oh, I'm glad you noticed the picture of Ruth," he said, still embarrassed, "for I love her very dearly."

"You miss her, I know you do," Mary said, softly. "The picture looks as if you had carried it in your pocket for a long time."

"I used to do that," he confessed, "but I found that it kept the past too close to me. Now I see it only just before going to bed."

Suddenly Mary leaned toward him; a portion of her wonderful hair fell against her cheek; her eyes gleamed as if with coming tears. "Mr. Brown," she said, "you are so good and kind and noble that I am going to pray for one thing in particular to happen to you. God may have wise reasons for withholding it from you just at present, but I am going to pray that He will some day give you back your child."

"*My* child!" He groped for her meaning. "She is not my own child. She is only my niece."

"Oh, then you are not married!"

"No, and I never have been. In fact, I never can be. My conduct in the past has made that impossible. Other men may marry and have children, but I am not like them."

"How strangely you talk—how very strangely!" Mary said, her eyes still tensely strained toward his. "You talk as if—as if there were certain dishonorable things against you. Why"—here she actually laughed in derision—"if you were to lay your hand on an open Bible and say that you were dishonorable, or ever had been, I'd not believe it! It isn't in you; it never was. My intuition tells me so, and I know I am right."

"I am what I am," he said, sighing. "I won't go into it all; it would do no good. I have no right to a decent place in any society. I want you to know me for what I am, Miss Rowland. God knows I'll not make false pretenses while I am under your father's roof. I am here to work for you both. What I was when you picked me up in my filth and squalor I still am and shall continue to be."

Mary stood up and turned her back to the fire, to dry her clothing. He rose as she did and stood beside her. He looked at his watch. It was near midnight. He showed the dial to her in the firelight. She nodded thoughtfully, but was silent. The rain was steadily beating on the roof, a newly made brook was gurgling and swashing past the door. The wind had died down. Drops of water fell through the low chimney into the hot coals, but not in sufficient quantity to depress the fire. He put on some more wood. His vision of the short-lived possession of her companionship still swirled about him like ineffable, soul-feeding light. He could have touched her with his hands; he almost felt that she would not have been deeply offended; the yearning to do so rose from depths that could not be fathomed. She was looking at him steadily from beneath her long lashes, the lashes which gave to her features the evasive expression he could not describe.

"How strange you are!" she said, softly, sincerely. "I don't know why it is, Mr. Brown, but when I'm here with you like this my troubles seem to stand aside. I almost hope. I do—I really do."

"I was wondering if your father will worry, knowing that we are out in the storm," he said.

"No, he won't, but it would have driven my mother crazy with anxiety. Even if she knew we were sheltered here she would worry. She belonged to the old school. The fact"—Mary laughed softly—"that we have no chaperon would be a terrible misfortune. But don't think I care about such things. This is a new age and I'm simply a hang-over from an older one. Even if the rain were to let up we couldn't make our way back in the dark. There is nothing to do but wait till daylight."

"Your clothing is quite dry," he said, touching her sleeve, "and so is my coat. Would you like to recline here by the fire and take a nap? I can put the coat down. It would be a hard couch, but—"

"I'm not sleepy—not a bit!" she assured him; "but you must be, and tired, too, after all you've been through. Suppose you lie down by the fire, and I'll keep watch over you."

He smiled and flushed as he declined, and then his face became grave.

"You touched upon something just now," he faltered, "that perhaps I ought to think about. Since your mother would not have quite approved of your being here like this with a stranger, there may be others in the neighborhood who might gossip about it. If you would not be afraid to remain alone, I could go on home and send some conveyance. I can find the way, and as for the rain, it's nothing. I have often worked all day and part of the night up to my knees in water."

"How silly of me to have said what I did!" she exclaimed, and caught his arm. He felt the warmth of her pulsing fingers through the thin sleeve of his shirt as she turned him toward her. "Why do you hold that against me? I wasn't thinking how it sounded. Why did you speak of it?"

"Because I'd rather die than be the cause of the slightest whisper against you," he said, reverently. "I know how narrow-minded small communities are, Miss Rowland, and I know better than any one else how little I have to recommend me to strangers. I am worse than nothing in the eyes of the world, and it is beyond my power now ever to change their view."

A pained look crossed Mary's face. She sat down again and put her feet out toward the fire. She folded her arms. "I wish," she said, compressing her lips, "that you would stop abusing yourself. The rest of the world may condemn you, as you say they do, but I shall not. I have known a good many gentlemen in my life, but I've never met one in whom I had more confidence. I could swear by you. You may think that strange, but I could. I feel the truth streaming from your whole personality, your voice, your eyes, your very silence at times. I don't know how it was, but in some way you have not been fairly treated. You have not! You have not! I thought it might be perhaps an unfortunate marriage, but since it is not that it is something else. You seem to me to be the loneliest man in all the world, with a great aching heart; but notwithstanding that you are thinking and acting only for me. Do you think I can overlook that sort of thing? Mr. Brown, you are helping me, and if I am not able to help you some day I shall never be content."

He shrugged his broad shoulders. "Don't think of me at all," he sighed. "I am responsible for my position in life, but I am not unhappy—I really am not. There is such a thing, Miss Rowland, as throwing off an old shackled life for a new, freer one; and the new one will be normal, if the old one is crushed out completely. It is simply a psychological fact. The most wonderful thing in the world is autosuggestion. If one holds before himself constantly the thought that things are beautiful they will be so. If he thinks otherwise, he thereby damns himself. When it became necessary for me to adopt my—my present way of living, I determined always to look upon it as a sort of rare adventure, and it has been one full of something like hope. Since I came to work for you and found you in trouble I have thought of nothing but the prospect of seeing you happy again."

The girl was strangely moved. She had lowered her head, and he looked down now only on the mass of wonderful, firelit hair that hid her face from view.

"Sit down, please," she suddenly said, huskily, and he obeyed. She was silent. The rain still beat heavily on the boards overhead; the mountain streams still gurgled and sang. The wind had died down. The darkness was heavy and thick.

Presently Mary seemed to find her voice. She raised her head and smiled sweetly as she remarked: "How strange we two are! Life is beating, pounding, crushing us—you in one way and me in another; and yet here we are like two ants huddled together on a floating chip, drifting we know not where. I cling to you for support, and I wish it were so that you could cling to me. The only difference is—well, you know why I'm on the chip, but I may only surmise why you are on it. I'll bet I know, though; I'll bet I know," was her afterthought.

"You know what?" he asked, startled slightly, and he sat wondering what she would say as she locked her hands and seemed to hesitate.

"Well, I'll bet there is one true explanation. The thing you are—are involved in—the thing that caused you to leave home, has to do with the welfare of others."

"Why do you think that?" he asked, half fearfully.

"Because you are that rare type of man," she returned.

"I have nothing in the way of self-defense to offer," he answered. "My early life was a mistake. I may be atoning for it a little. I sometimes hope so.

You are right in one guess—some others are the better and happier for my absence. It is so that I can never return; that is settled for all time. The new life is all that I have, but I assure you it isn't bad. It is heaven compared to the one I renounced."

So the night passed. The rain ceased toward dawn, but there was little light till the sun was up. Then they fared forth over the wet, rain-washed ground for home. The sun was breaking through a cloud when they reached the old house.

Rowland was on the back porch when they appeared before him, wet to the waist from contact with the dripping weeds and bushes through which they had made their way. He seemed not much surprised.

"I thought you'd find shelter somewhere," he said, casually. "I sat up most of the night on my book. I was trying to tie the main branch of the Westleighs to our line through the Barbadoes record, and I noticed how hard it rained."

"How is Tobe Keith?" the girl broke in to ask.

"He is just the same—no better and no worse," Rowland answered. "That is a late report, too. I got it from Tom Gibbs, who passed along just now and stopped to let me know."

"Oh, I'm glad, I'm glad he is not worse!" Mary's face beamed faintly. "I was afraid we'd get bad news. Poor Martin! He may think the worst has happened." She turned to Charles. "Will you get your breakfast now, or wait till you change your clothing?"

"I don't mind the dampness," he smiled. "Is it ready?"

It was on the table and he went in alone, while Mary ran up to her room. Returning half an hour later, she found that he was gone.

"He was in de kitchen des now, young miss," explained Zilla, "en' he seed de basket er stuff I had fixed raidy fer de boys t' eat, en' picked it up en' said he was gwine tek it ter um."

"What?" Mary asked. "You don't mean that he has gone back?"

"Yassum. Mr. Brown say Martin is worried, en' he wants ter tell 'im dat Tobe Keith ain't no wuss dan he was yistiddy. I tol' Mr. Brown ter wait till you come down, but he said dar wasn't no time to lose. He said Martin looked sorter puny-like en' needed 'couragement. Yo' pa seed 'im start out, en' didn't say nothin' erginst it."

It was as if Mary had something further to say, but she restrained herself. She went back to her room, ascending the stairs rapidly. Her window looked out toward the hiding-place of her brothers, and crossing a little glade beyond the barn she saw Charles, the basket on his arm. He was striding vigorously toward the forest. In a moment he was out of sight and Mary turned from the window. By her bureau she stood motionless, full of thought. Presently she heard Zilla calling to her, and, answering, she went slowly down the stairs.

CHAPTER XI

About noon Charles returned. Mary, at the window of the kitchen, saw him emerge from the wood back of the barn and come toward the house. There was a vague droop of weariness on him of which he seemed unaware. She met him in the front hall; his eyes fell under her stare and he flushed.

"Why did you go?" she asked, reproachfully.

He gave one of his characteristic shrugs and began to fumble in his coat pocket for a note which he finally handed her.

"It is from Martin," he said. "They managed to keep dry last night, I understand. They were glad to get the basket. The water spoiled most of the other things and they were hungry."

She read the note.

It ran: "Dear Sis,—How sweet and good of you to send Mr. Brown back so quickly! I couldn't have stood the suspense any longer. I was afraid Tobe was dead—I thought it all night during that awful rain. I couldn't sleep, but maybe I can now. Don't let Mr. Brown leave us. He sat and talked to us this morning for an hour, and I've never heard from human lips the sort of things he said. He helped me a lot; he was so kind and gentle and kept putting himself up as a man who had made mistakes and suffered. Oh, he is wonderful, wonderful! Even Ken listened close and seemed affected. He is our friend. He shows that. He wants to help us, and he will if he can. He used to drink, but gave it up; he says it is easy. He has made me decide to act differently in the future—that is, if Tobe lives."

Mary read the rest of the note, folded the paper, and thrust it into the bosom of her dress. Charles stood at the foot of the stairs, his hat in his hand, his boots covered with mud.

"I didn't want you to tire yourself out like that," she said, gratefully, "but I'm glad you went. From this note I see how much good you have done my poor brothers. Now listen to me—I will have my way about this. Go up to your room, take off those damp things and go to bed. I am going to be your nurse for to-day, anyway. I'll bring you your lunch and you may take it in bed, and then go to sleep."

He laughed lightly and shrugged his shoulders. "Really, you must not make a baby of a great hulk like me, Miss Rowland. I've been through things ten times as bad as that little walk. I simply couldn't eat in bed. I'll be down in a few minutes."

She was about to protest, but he left her and ascended the stairs.

Coming down a few minutes afterward, he saw a saddled horse at the gate and heard voices in the parlor.

His spirits sank, for he recognized the horse as the one Albert Frazier had ridden when he had first seen him. He caught a few words the visitor was saying in his gruff, unpolished way.

"You are too high-strung and nervous, little girl. All is well so far. Leave my brother to me. I'm pulling the wool over his eyes, all right. I've made 'im think the boys are on their way to Texas, and if Tobe lives—"

Unwilling to listen, Charles passed on into the sitting-room. Glancing through the open doorway into the dining-room, he saw that the cloth was not yet spread on the table for luncheon, and he sat down to wait. The voices still came from the parlor, but he did not catch any part of what was being said. Zilla entered the dining-room and spread the cloth on the table. Presently Frazier was heard leaving. His heavy boots clattered on the steps, and the gate-latch clicked as he went out. Then Mary came in. She did not know that he was there and he surprised an unreadable, almost hunted expression on her face.

"Oh!" she exclaimed, on seeing him, "so dinner is not ready? Mr. Frazier could not stop. He is working hard to keep the sheriff off my brothers' track. He says when he left town Tobe Keith was just the same. The doctors at Carlin are afraid to probe for the—the ball. They have held a consultation, and agreed that the great specialist, Doctor Elliot of Atlanta, might operate and save him. They refuse to undertake it themselves."

"Then this Doctor Elliot ought to come and see him," Charles said.

"But Doctor Elliot is so busy that he never leaves Atlanta, except in instances where enormous fees are paid. The Carlin doctors say that Tobe ought to be taken to him. They say it would be safe to move him that distance."

"Then he must be moved," said Charles.

"Yes, he must go," Mary agreed. "The only thing is that it will cost considerable. You see, Tobe and his mother (she is a widow) are awfully poor. Yes, the money must be gotten up, and I must get it."

"You?" Charles cried. "Why should you?"

"Because no one else will do it. Even my father has the silly idea that we ought not to have anything to do with it, because it would look as if we admitted the boys' guilt. That is rubbish. A man's life—three lives—are at stake. Yes, I must raise four hundred dollars. They say it will cost that much, including transportation, nurses, and the like. I may be able to borrow it from some one, but we are hard run. Father is over his head in debt. I know where I can get the money—in fact, it has been offered to me already—but I don't like to take it. I have my reasons for—for not *wanting* to take it."

"It was offered you this morning—not many minutes ago," Charles said, fiercely and impulsively.

She looked up in mild surprise at his tone and the rebellious glare in his eyes, and then said, slowly and wonderingly:

"Why do you think *that*?"

"I don't know, but I am sure of it," he blurted from the depths of his restrained passion. "Something tells me that this Mr. Frazier wants to furnish it, and also that you shrink from being in his debt."

Mary avoided his desperate gaze. "You are a great reader of minds," she faltered. "Many men would make me angry by saying what you are saying, but I can't be offended with you. It is strange, but nothing you could do or say would annoy me. Well, you are right. As I told you once, Mr. Frazier and I are not actually engaged. Somehow, I want to be free in that way a little longer. I'm so young, you know, that marriage does not appeal to me yet. Mr. Frazier has helped my father raise money in several instances, but I have never felt that those transactions bound me in any way; but I know, and he feels, that this particular offer of his—" Her voice sank and trailed away into inaudibility.

"That if you accepted this offer it would be binding?" Charles threw into the gap.

It seemed to him that she flushed slightly. She was very erect, very stately. Somehow he thought of her as a captured young queen suffering under the indignities of her enemies. She made no answer, and, leaning toward her, he repeated his words even more earnestly and in greater agitation.

"Yes, as I look at it, the acceptance would bind me," she finally gave out. "I could not take the money otherwise, for I simply have no way of paying. He put it that way himself; that he was as much interested in my brothers as I, because, in a sense, they would be *his* brothers."

Charles was pale; he was trembling; he knew that his voice was unsteady, for his whole being was surcharged with a passion which his reason could not justify, and which his sheer helplessness only intensified.

"You must not accept his money; you must not bind yourself," he cried.

"Why?" she asked, with the half-eager look even a desperate woman may wear when facing the evidence of a man's growing passion for her.

"Because you don't love him," was the reply which further fed her curiosity as to his trend of thought. "You couldn't love such a man. He is incapable of appreciating you. For two such persons to marry would be a crime against the holiest laws of the universe."

"I can't quite agree with you," she replied, as she slowly shook her proud head. "You see, Mr. Brown, there are things more important than even marriage. It is important that I save my brothers, for their own sakes. I don't count. If I should have to accept this money, it may save Tobe Keith and my dear boys." She laughed half-bitterly. "What would I care after that? Do you think I would begrudge the price? Never, and I'd be as true a wife as ever was bought in a slave-mart in the Orient. Always—always after that I'd know positively that I'd accomplished some actual good in life."

"Never! never!" he cried. "It would be wrong unpardonably wrong!"

"How can you say that—you, of all men?" she suddenly demanded. "Didn't you intimate last night that by giving up your home and becoming a wanderer you had helped make others happy?"

"That was different," he flashed out. "I was a worthless drunkard, a disgrace to my home, relatives, and friends. I was compelled to leave, anyway. I could not have held my head up another day. But it is different with you. You have been nothing but a help and a blessing to your family and friends. You deserve all that life can possibly give to any one, and you must get your just dues."

She smiled and slowly shook her head. "You are a poor witness for your argument," she said. "When the time came you forgot yourself, and that really is the ideal course. You have intimated that the decision, whatever it was, has not made you unhappy, and I think it will be the same with me. Thousands of women have been contented after marriage with men they did not love very deeply. Women have even married for sordid reasons alone, and led normal lives afterward. Why should I not take the risk with such a motive as mine would be? No, if Albert Frazier is the means of saving Tobe Keith's life and restoring my brothers to me, I shall withhold nothing from him that I can give. Already he is working night and day to prevent their arrest. I couldn't bear to see them behind the bars of a jail. Kensy could stand it, but not my poor, sensitive, fanciful Martin. Let's not talk about it any more."

Tears were in her eyes, and her lips were twitching under a flood of emotion about to burst from its confines. Here the bell was rung for luncheon.

"You go on in," Mary said, huskily. "I am not a bit hungry. You will excuse me, won't you?" She turned toward the stairs to go up to her room, and, like a man walking in a dream, he went to his place at the table. What a mockery the act of eating seemed when his soul was in such turmoil! On his walk home he had felt very hungry, but his appetite had left him. He ate perfunctorily, so much so that Aunt Zilla showed concern.

"What ails yer, sir?" she asked. "Yer ain't gwine ter mek yo'se'f sick, is yer? Dat strain, two trips in one, thoo all dat mud en' slush, was onreasonable, 'long wid no sleep."

He smiled up at her. His contact on a level with the lowest of mankind had broadened his sympathies for humble people, and he felt drawn to her, for her tone was unmistakably kind.

"No, I'm all right, Aunt Zilla," he answered.

She went to the kitchen for some hot waffles, and when she put them before him she said: "I'm gwine tell you some'n', Mr. Brown. I'm gwine ter tell you, 'kase you is er stranger in dis place en' orter know. I know nice white folks when I sees 'um, en' I know dey ain't nothin' wrong 'bout you. I'm gwine tell you ter look out fer dis yer Frazier man. He won't do. He ain't de right stripe, en' ef we-all wasn't po' now he wouldn't be let in at de front do' er dis yer house. Bofe him en' his brother come fum low stock. Deir daddy was a overseer dat couldn't write his name. You kin tell what dis one is by de way he set at de table en' handle his knife en' fork en' spout wid his loud mouf when Marse Andy is talkin'. Yes, I'm gwine tell you what I heard 'im say ter Marse Andy when dey was in de settin'-room des now. Marse Andy tol' 'im what you went to de mountains fer, en' he fairly ripped en' snorted. He was mad 'kase dey-all let you know de boys' hidin'-place. He said you couldn't be trusted; dat you had some secret reason fer helpin' out wid de boys. He said de sheriff was on de lookout fer some housebreakers dat was wid de circus, en' done lef' it ter 'scape fum de law. De low rapscallion said he was bounden shore dat you was one of 'em. He said he was des lyin' low, right now, but dat befo' long when dey got de papers ter serve on you, dey was gwine arrest you."

Charles laughed softly. "Well, I am not a house-breaker, Aunt Zilla," he said. "I am not boasting of what I am. I make no claims of any sort, but I am not one of the men the Fraziers are looking for."

"Marse Andy tol' 'im dat," the woman went on, "but it des made 'im all de madder, en' he went on tryin' ter 'suade Marse Andy ter send you off. Marster has ter take er lot off'n 'im 'kase he owes 'im some money, I hear 'um say. Dey was talkin' about you when young miss come in en' hear 'um."

"Oh, she heard!" Charles exclaimed. "I'm sorry she did."

"Huh! young miss don't believe it!" Zilla cried. "She tol' 'im so ter his face, en' was purty sharp erbout it, too. She woulder say mo' on de same line ef she wasn't afeard he'd turn erginst de boys. I seed she was good mad en' tryin' powerful hard ter hold in. She come in de kitchen while 'er pa en' Mr. Frazier was talkin' en' tol' me, she did, dat I mus' not listen ter anything he say erginst you. She say you is had trouble en' is all erlone in de world widout kin en' er home, but dat you was er honorable gen'man. Shucks! I already knowed dat. I knows white folks of de right stripe es soon as I see how dey handle black folks."

Charles thanked her warmly and left the table. The soil was too wet for working in the field, and he was about to sit down on the veranda when Mary suddenly came from the parlor and faced him.

She was smiling sweetly. "Do you know what you are going to do?" she demanded, playfully and yet firmly. "You are going right up to your room and take off those damp clothes. Then you are going to cover up in bed and take a good nap."

"Am I?" he retorted, and yet he was deeply touched. He was reminded of the days in his boyhood when his mother kept watch over his well-being, and of a later period when Celeste had nursed him after his unpardonable debauches. He had been a homeless wanderer for a long time, and here in this out-of-the-way place he was being treated kindly, almost lovably. He told himself that he was unworthy of it, and yet it was sweet, so comforting that he hoped he would never lose it. He had made friends of the two boys, of the old, preoccupied gentleman, of the black serving-woman, and, above all, he had the friendship and gratitude of the marvelous young creature before him.

"Yes," she persisted, "you must go; and don't wait, either. While you were walking your wet things were not so bad, but you are inactive now, and may take cold."

With a smile he obeyed her. In his room, as he undressed, he caught sight of the picture of Ruth on his bureau, and for a moment his eyes lingered on it. It was the only visible link between him and a life that was never to be his again, but he didn't care. How wonderful the new life was! How good to feel that he was helping that particular family to bear its troubles! What did his own amount to? Nothing at all. They had become non-existent.

He was about to lie down when he heard the sound of a horse's hoofs in the yard below, and, going to a window, he looked out. Mary was mounting the horse Zilla had led from the stables to the block at the gate. The girl had donned a black riding-skirt and she wore an attractive little cap; she took her place in the saddle very gracefully. In a moment she was galloping away toward the village. He surmised what it meant. She was going to get news of the wounded man's condition.

Charles knew there was no sleep for him. How could he sleep when his mind was in its present turmoil? It was impossible. He gave up the effort, and, dressing, went down-stairs.

CHAPTER XII

It was well for Charles's state of mind that he was unaware of what had happened at his home at the time of his disappearance and shortly afterward.

Two weeks from the day of the exposure of the affair at the bank, a personage of great importance in the estimation of the Brownes arrived from Europe. It was an uncle of William and Charles, an elderly man of considerable wealth, a childless widower, who, having long since retired from business, lived on a private income and traveled extensively, that he might pass the remainder of his days with less monotony than the quiet life of Boston afforded; he was a lonely old man who cared little for club life and had no tastes in art, music, or literature.

James Browne reached the home of his nephew one Sunday morning just as the little family were leaving the table. They were expecting him, but not quite so soon, for they had thought that he would stop as usual for a few days in New York, where he had landed.

He was tall and slender, with a pink complexion and rather long snow-white hair and beard. It was plain that he was angry, and it was evident in a moment that he had been so since he sailed from Southampton a week before. He shook hands with William perfunctorily and kissed Celeste and Ruth as if it were a mere matter of form which the relationship demanded. He was about to speak, when Celeste interrupted him by rising and leading the child to the door, where she was turned over to a maid.

"We think it best for her not to hear anything about her uncle," Celeste said. "She simply thinks he has gone away for a while. She was devoted to him."

"She may as well know," the old man retorted, gruffly. "She will hear it quickly enough. I heard it even in London. You see, my name was mentioned along with all the rest of you. The papers, even over there, had accounts of it. It was thought the scoundrel had sailed for England under an assumed name. My bankers asked for particulars. They are more blunt about such things over there than we are. Well, well! has he been caught yet?"

"No, not yet," William answered, and both Celeste and his uncle stared at him. His face was very rigid and had the bloodless look of a man who was in a low nervous condition.

"Where do they think he is?" the old man demanded.

"No one knows," William managed to say, "He has not been heard of since he left."

The elder Browne sniffed in disgust and stroked his beard with his carefully manicured fingers. William noticed that their nails glistened in the light from the window. He noticed the loose English cut of his uncle's tweed suit, and the quaint watch-fob which had been picked up somewhere abroad.

"Do you think he will be caught?" the old man went on.

"I don't know. I can't say," was William's slow reply. "The police have not—not consulted me as to that. The bank officials don't mention it, either. They are very considerate. In fact, they are very kind and anxious to have me feel—feel that they do not hold me responsible for what happened."

"I suppose so," the elder Browne said, promptly. "I read that you had made the loss good. Have you?"

"Half of it is paid already, and they know where the rest is coming from in a few days. They are well secured and satisfied."

"I was going to speak of that debt later," the old man said. "We are all one family, and a disgrace like this against our name and blood ought to be shouldered equally, as far as cost is concerned. William, I'm going to pay half of that shortage. I'll give my check for it to-morrow. I'll see Bradford in the morning. Do you know, I don't want the scamp brought back here. I think when the loss is paid the chase will let up. What is your idea?"

William was astounded by the unexpected offer, so much so that he hardly noted the questions which followed it.

"I'm afraid," William answered, "that the police will not be influenced by it. A reward has been offered and the detective force of the city is trying to win it. The offer has gone to other cities as well."

"Well, I don't want him brought back and tried and sent up," the old man went on, frowning and jerking his beard. "The papers would be full of it again, day after day, and everybody would be pitying us. I don't want any one's pity. I've tried to live decently myself, and at my time of life I don't deserve all this publicity for no fault of mine. I must say that I liked the young scamp, even at his worst. You see, I never thought of his being anything but a drunkard, and a rather good-natured one at that. He was always doing kind things. I've heard of some. Michael once told me of quite a sum Charlie advanced for him when he needed it. Where is Michael?"

"He has gone to New York," Celeste explained. "His mother lives there, and is not very well again. We are expecting him home soon. Yes, Charlie was kind to him, and Michael is heartbroken by what has happened."

"Have you discovered what the boy was investing in?" the old man asked. "How did he lose such a large amount, or did he really take it with him, as some think?"

William had become pale. He lowered his eyes. He had the look of a man on trial for his life. The ordeal was more severe than any he had passed through since his brother left. His friends and associates had seldom broached the topic, but the present questioner saw no reasons for reserve. Seeing that her husband was overlooking his uncle's last question, Celeste answered it.

"I don't think he had a large amount of money when he left," she said, in crisp, firm tones, and William felt her eyes sweep steadily toward him as she spoke. "That seems to be out of the question, and I am sure that William agrees with me."

"I—I've never said anything about that," William stammered, without looking at either his wife or his uncle. "I only know that Bradford, the directors, and the—the police department have made no report on that line."

"Any one could keep such transactions hidden, could they not?" Celeste asked. "By acting through secret agents outside of Boston, for instance."

"Yes, oh yes!" the old man answered. "Many men who are important heads of great concerns and who handle the public's funds often speculate that way, on the quiet. Banks would lose their depositors if such dealings were known. Agents can easily be found who will hold their tongues. So you think the boy may have some associate, Lessie?"

"I didn't say that, exactly," Celeste retorted, coldly. "I only thought that William might know if such an agent could have been employed."

No reply was forthcoming from the pale man of whom she was speaking, and suddenly the new-comer turned upon him. "What is the matter here, anyway?" he almost fiercely demanded.

"Matter?" William asked, with a start. "Where? What do you mean?"

"Why, we don't seem to be getting anywhere," the old man answered, petulantly. "Both of you somehow seem changed. You don't seem to know much about the affair. I expected, when I saw you, to learn something more than has been published, but you both talk in riddles and in a shifting, roundabout way."

To his astonishment, Celeste got up and left the room, closing the door behind her.

The two men stared at each other. "You must excuse her," William finally said. "She is all upset over it. She has shut herself in and doesn't go out at all now. She has refused to receive several callers. She goes about with Ruth a little, but that is all."

"Ah, I see—the shame of it, I presume!" the old man said. "Well, I can sympathize with her. She thought a lot of Charlie. Perhaps she can't find it in her heart to blame him seriously. Women are that way, you know. She used to overlook his wild conduct, I remember. Well, well! Perhaps we might as well not talk about it before her. She seems different to me— looks as if she were soured on everything and everybody. Now when I said just now that I was going to pay half the loss, instead of looking pleased I thought she half resented it."

"You must not blame her," William said, with drawn lips. "She has a lot to bear. She feels the—the disgrace of it on Ruth's account."

"We all feel the disgrace of it," the old man answered, "but women are more sensitive, imaginative, and high-strung than men."

"Celeste may have gone to see about your room," William said, just as the church-bells began ringing. He caught their tones and hoped that they would somehow interrupt a conversation which he felt he could no longer sustain. The old man was on his feet now, having risen at the departure of Celeste, and he began to stride back and forth across the room. He folded his hands and wrung them together. He muttered some words which William failed to catch, as he paused at a window, and then he came back.

"If it is hard for me, I presume it is even harder for you to bear," he said, aloud. "On the way over, as I sat in the sun in my steamer chair, with nothing else to think about, I often pictured you there at the bank with those associates. My reason tells me that they are sympathetic with you and must feel a certain regret for allowing you to pay back such a large amount; still, if I may be allowed to say so, you must feel awkward. You must meet big depositors who—well, who think perhaps that you ought to have had better judgment than not to have kept track of the boy's plunging. To have retained a dissipated young scamp like that in your employment was imprudent in itself, to say nothing of all the rest."

"They may blame me," William said, reluctantly. "I don't know how they feel, or how they talk together in private. I only know they still seem to have confidence in me and in my business judgment. God knows I am doing the best I can to run things straight, and I keep showing them the figures. They laugh at me for being so particular, and assure me that it is unnecessary, but I intend to keep it up."

"This is a hidebound, Puritan community," the old man responded, with a slow frown, "and I feel that you are against conditions at the bank that you don't yet fully realize. Bradford and the others are sly, long-headed business men, and they are not going to tell you all they think."

William stared, his mouth falling open, a heavy hand splaying over the cap of his knee. "I don't understand," he faltered. "What could they be keeping from me?"

"Well"—and the old man seemed to be probing his vocabulary for adroit words—"it may be like this. In a community of this kind there is perhaps a certain class of well-meaning people who have the—the old-fashioned idea that dishonesty runs in the blood of certain families. I remember that when I was younger I imbibed that idea from some source or other. It is silly, of course, but it may exist, and if there is any place that it would be apt to thrive it would be among a lot of nervous bank depositors and stockholders. Now that is one thing I have come to fight by my influence *and with my money.*"

William's groping, even bewildered, stare showed that he did not understand what his uncle was driving at, and in a few halting words he managed to say so.

"Why, it is like this, my boy," the old man explained. "I know Bradford well, and several of your directors, and when I plank down my half of the missing money to-morrow I am going to take such a firm, fatherly stand behind you that—well, two of us fighting for the family honor will be a stronger force than one, that's all. I stand well here in Boston, I know that, and I am going to back you."

"I haven't really felt that I was in need of—" William was breaking in, but his uncle did not suffer him to finish.

"Well, you do need it," he said, sharply. "I can see it in your looks. You have lost weight. You look nervous. You have an agitated manner. You speak in jerks. This thing is killing you. Your mind may break under the strain. Yes, I'm going to hang about the bank. I'll transfer my chief deposit— and it happens to be a big one just now—from New York to your bank. I'll buy all the floating stock I can pick up. I'll be in the market for it at all times. Now—now what do you think of that?"

"It will help wonderfully," William declared, with faintly rising fervor which in a moment seemed to pass away, for Celeste was entering the room. She came in softly and resumed the chair she had left a few minutes before.

"Suppose you tell her what I am going to do," the old man said to his nephew. "It may brace her up, you know."

A helpless, bewildered expression filled the face of the younger man. He hesitated, licked his dry lips, and then wiped them with a handkerchief which he had kept tightly balled in his hand. "You can do it better than I," he managed to get out. "It is most kind, and—and thoughtful of you."

"It is nothing but an effort to defend the family honor," the old man began, and he repeated what he had just said to his nephew, and with some elaboration of details. "What do you think of that?" he ended, with a straight look into the face of the quiet listener.

"It is kind of you," she answered, coldly. "It will be a great help to my husband at the bank. By the way, between you two do you expect to do anything at all toward helping Charlie?"

"Help him! How can we?" the old man asked, with a startled glance at his nephew. "Do you mean, my dear, if we intend to help him escape pursuit?"

"If he has to escape, yes. What can he do alone, and out in the world as he is without friends or money?"

"Money? I guess he has plenty of that, from all accounts," and her uncle suppressed a mirthless smile. "Don't you think so, my dear?"

"I have an idea that he was almost penniless," Celeste answered, her eyes on the floor, her thin white hands clasped firmly in her lap.

"Have you any positive evidence of that?" the old man inquired.

But to his surprise, Celeste made no answer beyond saying:

"I have a strong feeling that he needs both friends and money."

"But," her uncle fired up impatiently, "how can we help him? Even if we could find him, and didn't let the authorities know, we would be aiding, abetting, and even concealing a lawbreaker. Oh no, my dear, the thing for us to do is to make it thoroughly known that we have cut him off, that we are ashamed of the relationship, and that we are honest, if he isn't."

Celeste shrugged her shoulders; an evanescent sneer curled her lip, but that was all. Presently she said: "Your room is ready. You must be tired and dusty. I'm sorry Michael is not here to wait on you, as he used to do."

As she spoke she rose, and, with stilted courtesy, so did the two men. The older man started up to his room, leaving Celeste and her husband face to face.

"That is a wonderful plan your uncle has," she said, coldly. "I presume it will work well in your behalf. Yes, they will be influenced at the bank by your uncle's money and backing. If they have ever blamed you for employing Charlie they won't any more."

"I am glad for Ruth's sake—and for yours," William added. "My affairs are in better shape now, anyway, and if I were to die—I assure you I don't feel very strong—you and the child would be fairly well provided for, along with the heavy life insurance I carry."

"I am not afraid that you will die soon," Celeste said, in a low, firm voice. "I have the feeling that you will be permitted to live long enough to straighten out everything in your life that should be attended to."

He took her arm, leading her toward the door. "I want you to know one thing—I want you to think of it constantly," he said, tremulously. "I mean it when I say that I'd rather die than bring trouble down on you and our little girl. In a situation like this there are some things that are worse than death. And you must remember that men sometimes take risks for the sake of those they love that they would not take for themselves."

The face of the little woman darkened rebelliously. She frowned and drew her arm from his fawning grasp. She started to speak, but choked up, and, lowering her head, she went up the stairs hurriedly as if to hide her rising emotion. Alone in her room, she stood listening to the ringing of the church-bells. She went to a window and looked out.

CHAPTER XIII

When Mason parted from Charles at Carlin he went straight to New York without stopping. It had been his intention to remain in the city only a few days, but, chancing to find his old room at Mrs. Reilly's unoccupied, he took it; he would wait for letters from home before deciding what to do in the future. Having sufficient funds to pay his way for a while, he felt rather independent.

One morning he happened to be passing through Washington Square when he came face to face with a man whose features were strangely familiar, and yet Mason could not tell where he had seen him before. It was evident, too, that the stranger had recognized him; indeed, there seemed to be a flash of surprised delight in the man's eyes. He passed on, and Mason, looking back, saw that the man was looking back also, though he quickly turned his head and walked on, now more slowly.

Seating himself on a park bench and opening a newspaper, Mason, by looking over its top, kept the man in view. Where had he seen him? he asked himself. Was it among the professional followers of the circus; perhaps he was some one he had chatted with at a restaurant? These questions were unanswered till a little thing happened. It was the surprising act of the stranger in pausing behind the great arch at the entrance of the park and peering stealthily at him. In a flash it came to Mason that it was the plain-clothes detective whom he had first seen at Madison Square a year before, who had followed him and Charles to their rooms, and from whom they had so narrowly escaped by flight at night.

"This is a pretty mess!" Mason muttered. "Now he will perhaps nab me as a witness and I'll be put through some sort of a third degree to force me to tell where Brown is and what I know about him. I'll make a move and see what he will do, anyway."

With this thought, and lowering his paper, Mason rose, sauntered carelessly along the walk to another bench, and sat down. Looking toward the arch, he saw the stranger coming in his direction. Opening the paper, Mason pretended to be reading, though he could still see the approaching man. He reached him, but, to his surprise, passed on. However, he came to a halt near by, and, with his hands in the pockets of his short coat, he stood staring hesitatingly at Mason. "He may be waiting for a policeman to help him take me in," was Mason's dejected mental comment. "I think I am in for trouble this time sure. I don't see any bluecoat about. I wonder if I'd better make a run for it?"

He decided that such a course was impossible; the detective would blow a whistle and some one in the crowd would stop him; besides, the man looked as if he might be swift of foot. "We thwarted him before, and he will run no chances this time," Mason decided, gloomily, and he began drawing mental pictures of himself seated in the midst of a group of uniformed officers bent on locating the man in whose company he had been seen. The big price on the head of his friend was, no doubt, still offered, and that was inducement for extra work. Mason decided that he would lie with as straight a face as possible, though he was afraid that he might become tangled in his statements; the detectives might uncover discrepancies which could be turned against himself. There was no doubt that he was in a "pickle," as he put it, and he was both angry and alarmed. Charles had never alluded during their long friendship to the published charges against him, but somehow Mason had come to believe that his friend was not guilty.

The stranger, with what looked like an absolutely timid expression of face and mien, was coming toward him. There was nothing to do but to brazen it out, and Mason braced himself for the most difficult ordeal of his life. The man stopped in front of him, bent forward, and said:

"I beg your pardon, sir, but it seems to me that your face is somewhat familiar, and I was wondering if we have ever met before. I am a stranger in the city, sir, but I have an idea that I saw you a year ago here in New York."

"It may be," Mason answered, conscious that he must make as few admissions as possible and yet not appear to be keeping back anything. Suddenly his line of procedure became clear to him. He would simply say to this man, and his associates, that he had not seen Charles for more than a year. How could they prove otherwise, for if they had known Charles to be with the circus they would have taken him? That point was clear and Mason now felt more confident. He found that he could calmly return the stranger's bland stare. In fact, he began to study the fellow. He fancied he knew the exact spot under the man's lapel where his metal badge was concealed.

"It was in the crowd at Madison Square where I saw you," the stranger went on, as if eager to remind Mason of the fact. "You were listening to the speakers."

"Yes, I remember going there," Mason said, taking out a box of cigarettes. "Do you happen to have a match about you?"

The man fished one from a vest pocket with fingers which seemed to quiver slightly, and there was no doubt as to the look of suspended excitement in his mild eyes. Mason decided that he would not offer him a cigarette. "I think I recall seeing you there," he remarked. "In fact, as you passed me just now your face seemed familiar. You say you are a stranger in the city?"

"Yes, I only come here once in a while."

Silence fell. A lame Italian was playing a wheezy hand-organ at the end of the walk, and a group of ill-clad children were dancing near by. Charles wondered what his companion would do if he suddenly got up and left. Would he then declare himself in his official capacity or dog his steps as formerly? Mason somehow wanted the thing settled for good and all. How could he sleep or have any peace of mind with an uncertainty like that hanging over him?

"I think I may venture to be plain with you, sir," the stranger broke the silence to say. "The day I saw you you were in the company of a—a young man that I desire very much to meet."

"Oh, let me see," and Mason deliberately flicked the ash from his cigarette. "Who was I with that day? I ran with several chaps about that time."

The stranger described Charles accurately, and all but held his breath as he waited.

"Oh, *that* fellow!" Mason exclaimed, carelessly. "He was a stranger to me. I met him by accident at the house I roomed at. So you want to meet him?"

"Yes, very much. He is an old friend of mine."

"I see," Mason answered. "Well, I'm sorry I can't help you find him. He and I parted about that time and I have not seen him since. I'm rather sorry, too, for I found him a rather agreeable chap."

"So you don't know where he is?" The stranger's face fell, and a shadow of absolute gloom seemed to come into his earnest eyes. "When I saw you just now, sir, I hoped that you might put me on the track of him."

"He dies hard," Mason mused, now more at his ease. "No, I can't help you," he said, aloud. "If I remember rightly he said something about working his way to England on a cattle-ship."

"England? My God! then I'll not find him at all!" the stranger sighed.

"It would be a difficult job," Mason went on, with real pleasure in the tale he was concocting. Then suddenly he was emboldened to pursue different tactics. "Say," he said, "I think you are the man I saw hanging about our house the night after I noticed you in Madison Square. Am I right?"

Something like a sigh escaped the lips of the stranger. Surely, if he was a detective, he was either a poor one or a most accomplished actor. Mason suddenly decided that he was dealing with the latter when his companion answered:

"Yes, I followed you both to that house, sir. I wanted a word with my friend. I tried to catch his eye in the crowd at Madison Square, but failed."

"But if you wanted to speak to him, or see him, why didn't you do it while he was with me?" Mason demanded, with no little pride now in his skill at cross-examination, and a growing sense of his own security.

"There were reasons why I should not," was the slow answer. "I wanted to see him alone, sir. I watched the house that night till—" The stranger paused as if he had said more than he intended.

"Till I came out and made you run away?" Mason smiled. "I didn't intend to spoil your game, whatever it was."

"I came back and watched the house after that," the man went on, dejectedly. "I saw you both come out with your things. I followed you up-town and across to the river. I saw you at the boat-house. I didn't know you intended to cross over till your boat had started; then it was too late. You see, sir, I am pretty sure that you do know more about my friend than you are willing to tell. I've got to know more about him, and I'm going to stick to you till you help me locate him. You see, I don't believe the story about the cattle-ship. Men don't go to New Jersey in a small boat at night to ship for England. Now, do they, sir, really?"

"But you see, it was after we got across that he thought of England," Mason added, carelessly. "Come on, my friend, spit it out. What is it that you have up your sleeve, anyway?"

"I am sorry, sir," the stranger answered, regretfully, "but I cannot take you fully into my confidence. You see, if it were my affair alone it would be different, but, as it is, I cannot say more."

"Sly dog," Mason thought. "I've seen a few detectives at their game, but I never knew that any of them ever played the part of absolute idiocy to gain a point." "Well," he added, aloud, "we may as well change the subject. Have you ever noticed how gracefully these street kids dance? Watch that slim girl waltzing with the tiny tot. Why, she—"

"Excuse me, sir," the stranger broke in, "but I am not satisfied about what you have told me. I don't want to doubt your word, sir, but this is a very grave matter. I have been looking for you for a year, hoping that if I met you I'd learn something about my young friend. You yourself make me doubt the story of the cattle-ship. It is the way you tell it, I suppose. I think, sir, that we are playing at cross-purposes. I'm sure, sir, that my young friend must have placed confidence in you. He showed that, it seems to me, sir, by leaving the city with you as he did that night. Nobody but two close friends would act as you did. You see, I kept you in sight all the way to the boat-house. I crossed over myself the next morning, and looked all about over there, but saw nothing of you." Mason stood up. He was no longer afraid of the man, and yet he was irritated by his persistence. He looked at his watch. "I must be going," he said. "I have an appointment down-town."

The stranger was on his feet also. "Don't leave me like this, sir," he implored. "I have reasons to believe that our young friend would be glad to see me if he could safely do so. Somehow I feel that he is here in the city and that you know where he is."

"You are barking up the wrong tree," Mason said, crisply. "I know nothing more than I have told you."

"But I have caught you in a contradiction—about the cattle-ship for England, you see," and the man actually grasped Mason's lapel and clung to it desperately. "I don't want to go back to Boston without some favorable news. He has one true friend there who would do anything to get news of him—a good kind lady and a relation of his. I haven't much money, sir. I am only a poor servant with a sick mother to support out of my earnings, but if you will give me some helpful information I am willing to pay you."

"Pay me? Come off. What do you take me for?" Mason drew back and detached his lapel from the man's clutch. "Do you think I don't know your game? Well, I do, and let that end it. Good day."

Turning suddenly, Mason strode off toward Broadway. "That will settle him, I guess," he muttered, "unless he calls a cop to take me in. That was mushy sob-talk he was giving me. I guess he thought it would go down, but it didn't. Good Lord! a man that can act like that ought to be playing Hamlet. He is after that ten thousand dollars and he is willing to work for it. Good gracious! he no doubt knows where I hang out. Perhaps he dogged my steps here to-day and that startled look of recognition was all part of his game. He and several others may now have Mrs. Reilly's house under watch. Gee! that mountain town is the place for poor Brown, after all!" He had reached the edge of the square when, happening to glance back, he saw the stranger following him. "My Lord! what is he up to now?" Mason said, under his breath. The man was signaling to him with his handkerchief.

"Wait, sir!" he called out. "I must see you a moment."

Mason turned back into the walk he had just left, and advanced to meet the man. "I'll have it out with him and be done with it," he decided. "I can't stand this. I'd as soon be in jail myself. If he wants to take me to the police I'll go. I'll stick to the cattle-ship yarn, and let them disprove it."

CHAPTER XIV

One evening, several days after Charles's trip with Mary to the hiding-place of the two boys, he and Rowland sat on the front veranda. It was dusk and supper was almost ready.

"We may have to wait a little while," the old gentleman explained, in his languid way. "Mary is looking for company, I understand, and he may be slow getting here. He is sometimes, for he is a little careless about such things—more careless, I know, than I used to be in my courting-days."

With a sudden depression of spirits Charles surmised that the expected visitor was Albert Frazier, and he made no comment. Presently Mary came down the stairs. She had changed her dress, rearranged her hair, and looked very pretty as she stood in the doorway and glanced down the road toward Carlin.

"You and Mr. Brown need not wait, father," she said. "You know how slow Albert is. I'm sure Mr. Brown is both hungry and tired. He has finished the cotton and started on the corn. Albert and I can eat later. I want to get news from Tobe Keith. Albert promised to go by his house before starting out."

"I am not at all hungry," Charles declared, as Mary disappeared in the parlor.

"Well, I am," Rowland said, "and I shall not wait longer for Frazier, or any one else. I have some notes to make after supper, and this delay is upsetting me. Come, let's go in and leave the two sweethearts to eat and coo together. They won't eat much, I reckon. By the way, in my genealogical research I find that there are many family names of French origin in our mountains. This Frazier—'Frazyea' would be the French pronunciation— may have had fine old Huguenot ancestors away back in the early settlement of South Carolina. He has his good points. He is not exactly the stamp of man I would have wanted my daughter to marry in the old days, you know, but things are frightfully changed. The financial shoe is on the other foot, you see, and it is money that founds families."

Their supper was soon ended, and on their return to the veranda they found Mary still watching the road. "I see him, I think," she announced, wearily. "It looks like a man with a broad-brimmed hat on. Yes, that is Albert."

The rider drew in at the gate and dismounted, leading his horse into the yard and up to the steps. "You must excuse me, little girl," he said. "I couldn't make it earlier and get the news you wanted. The doctor was making an examination and was delayed. Tobe fainted several times. He is weak, the doctor says tell you, but there is still hope." Here catching sight of Charles, he continued, gruffly: "Say, fellow, put up my horse. And, say, give him a pail of water from the well and some shelled corn and a bundle of fodder."

Starting in surprise, Charles was about to thunder out a furious reply; to save himself from such a display of temper in the presence of a lady he simply turned back into the sitting-room.

"Did he hear me?" he heard Frazier asking his host, in a rising tone of anger.

"He was not hired for that sort of work, Albert," the old man said, pacifically. "He has been in the field ever since sunup. Zilla takes care of our own stock. Come, I'll go with you and show you the stall and the feed."

Frazier swore aloud and muttered something about "tramp farm-hands" which Charles could not catch; then he and Rowland led the horse to the stable. Charles was standing in the center of the room when Mary came in. She walked straight up to him and laid her hand on his arm.

"Don't let that bother you; please don't!" she urged, excitedly. "I don't want you to have trouble with him. He is a dangerous sort of man. If he takes a dislike to you he will do his best to injure you, and he has it in his power to do all sorts of things, along with his brother as an officer of the law."

"I understand. I have already heard a few things he has said about me," Charles replied, still furious, and yet trying to calm himself. "I know the kind of man he is exactly. But you are in trouble, and I shall not worry you in the matter. If he insults me again I'll try to overlook it—I *will* overlook it."

"Thank you," Mary said, gently and sweetly, in a voice which quivered with curbed emotion, "but he mustn't do it again. I must talk to him. He has no right to come here giving orders like that to people who have been as kind and unselfish as you have been. Oh, I don't know what I am to do, Mr. Brown! When he was telling about how weak Tobe Keith was my very soul seemed to die in my body."

The room was dimly lighted by an oil-lamp on a table in the center of the room. She stood facing him, her wondrous eyes filling with tears of anxiety, her lips twitching, her brows knitted, her hands clasped over her snowy apron.

"I don't know what to say to comfort you," said Charles. His voice shook and he tried to steady it. "I am ashamed of myself for sinking so low as to be angry with that man at such a time as this. You are stretched on the rack, Miss Rowland, and you are being tortured. I wish I could take your place—as God is my judge, I do! I can't bear the sight of it. It is unfair, hellish, satanic! It must not go on like this."

"I want you to—to think well of me," Mary said, haltingly, "and I believe you will. You must not think me shallow if I appear to be light-hearted to-night with Mr. Frazier. You see, everything depends on him now. He knows where the boys are, and if I were to anger him or rouse his suspicions in any way he would turn against us. I am sorry he is like that, but he is. I see now that I made a mistake in allowing him to pay such constant attention to me, but I am only a weak girl and couldn't help it. You see, at first he offered to take me to places, parties, picnics, and I wanted to go, as any girl would in my place, and that is the way it began. Then he became dictatorial and jealous, and so it went on till—well, you see how it now is. My father is indebted to him and so am I now."

"Surely you haven't obligated yourself—" stammered Charles.

"Not in so many words," Mary broke in, "but it amounts to the same thing. He wants me to let him furnish the money to pay Tobe Keith's expenses to Atlanta, and I see no other way than to accept his offer. If it goes that far, I shall consent to be his wife. If he saves my brothers from the scaffold I'll be his slave for life. Love? I don't expect love. What he feels for me is not love, and what I would be giving would not be, either. Love is a dreamlike thing, more of the soul than the body."

"I know what love is now," Charles thought. "I never knew before, but I do now."

The steps of the two men were heard coming from the barn, and Mary went hastily out of the lamplight and into the gloom of the hall.

"Our supper is ready, Albert," Charles heard her say. "Come on before it is cold."

Passing through the dining-room, Charles managed to reach the yard by means of a side door without having to meet Frazier. He found himself standing among some fig-trees and grape-vines in the dewy grass, surrounded by what had been beds of flowers in the day when the place had been well kept. An unshaded window of the dining-room was before him, and through it Charles saw Frazier and Mary approaching the table. The man's arm was actually about the girl's waist, his coarse lips were close to her pale cheek. He was smiling broadly, and laughing as if over some jest of his own making. Charles would have withdrawn his eyes, but he was held as if spellbound by the tragedy which was being enacted, with him as the sole spectator. Charles noted that Frazier sank heavily into a chair without first seeing that Mary was seated. He saw him take a cigar damp with saliva from the corner of his great mouth and place it on a plate at his side. He saw him reach out and take Mary's hand and fondle it patronizingly as he continued to talk. Even in the dim lamplight Charles read in the girl's face the growing desire to resent the fellow's coarse familiarity.

Charles uttered a groan and turned away. Off toward the barn he wandered, finding himself presently at the blacksmith's shop. The wide sliding-door was open, and for no reason of which he was conscious he went into the dark room and sat on the anvil. Money was now the thing he wanted above all else in the world. If only he could anonymously send to the suffering girl the funds needed for Keith's treatment, how glorious it would be! So small a thing and yet it might free the girl from a union that would be a lifelong outrage against her sensitive spirit. Only four hundred dollars! He remembered having spent more than that in a single night at a card-table—more than that on a drunken trip to Atlantic City in the company of reckless associates. Obtaining the money, however, was out of the question. He might get it from William, but he had pledged his honor never to enter his brother's life again; besides, the time was too short. The window of the dining-room gleamed in a sheen of light through the boughs of the trees about the house. He fancied he saw the pair again, and the thought maddened him. Marry that man! Could she possibly work herself up to the ordeal? Yes, for she was simply ready to sacrifice herself, and Charles knew from experience what self-sacrifice was like. He groaned as he left the shop and went toward the barn. The dense wood beyond it, lying under the mystic light of the rising moon, lured him into its bosom, and he decided that he would walk there, for no reason than that he hoped in that way to throw off the gnawing agony which lay upon him.

He had climbed over the fence and was about to plunge into the thicket when he heard a low, guarded whistle. He recognized it as the one Kenneth had used in response to his own as he approached the secret hiding-place. In a low whistle he answered and stood still.

"It's him!" He now recognized Kenneth's voice. "I knew him as he got over the fence. Come on, stupid! It's all right!"

"Yes, it is all right. I'm alone," Charles said softly.

"Come here to us, then," Kenneth proposed. "The bushes are thicker."

Charles obeyed, and soon stood facing the two bedraggled boys.

"What does this mean?" he asked, aghast over the risk they were running.

"It means that we've made up our minds to hide closer to home," Kenneth half-sheepishly explained. "Nobody's looking for us here in the mountains; you said so yourself. Sister said Albert Frazier was keeping the sheriff off the track. We don't like it out there, and—"

"How is Tobe Keith?" Martin's tremulous voice broke in. "What is the use of so much chatter about smaller things? How is he?"

"The doctors say there has been no vital change," Charles informed the quaking boy.

"No change? My God! when *will* there be a change?" Martin groaned. He was covering his pale face with his hands, when Kenneth roughly swept them down.

"Don't be a baby, silly!" he snarled. "Blubbering won't undo the matter. If he dies, he dies, and we can't help it." Kenneth forced a wry smile which on his soiled, bloodless face was more like a grimace in the white moonlight. "Martin behaves like that all the time, morning, noon, and night. That is one reason I decided to come nearer home. He needs sister to cheer him up and pet him. I don't know how. Then our cave is damp and chilly. I'm afraid he will get sick. He don't eat enough. I get away with most of the grub. Here is my plan, Brown. You are a good chap, and a friend, too. We may as well sleep in the hay in the loft of the barn. We'd have nothing to fear in the night, and through the day, with all of the family to keep a lookout up and down the road, we could get away even if the sheriff did come."

Charles informed him of Albert Frazier's presence in the house and that he might remain over night. At this the two boys exchanged dubious glances.

"Well," Kenneth opined, slowly, "I am sure he can be trusted in the main. As long as he and sister understand each other he will be on our side. He has stood behind the old man often in raising money; though, take it from me, Brown, Albert is not made of money. He owes a lot here and there and has to be dunned frequently even for small amounts. In her last note sister said that he would raise the money to send Keith to Atlanta. He can get it, I guess, by some hook or crook."

"Sister mustn't let him furnish the money," Martin faltered, his voice raising in uncertainty and ending in firmness.

"Mustn't? What do you mean, silly?" and Kenneth turned on him impatiently.

"Because she doesn't want to accept it from him, that's why," Martin stated, almost angrily. "She doesn't want to bind herself to him like that. I know how she feels about that fellow. She was just amusing herself with him and was ready to break off when this awful thing came up. If she takes the money and binds herself we'll be responsible, for if we hadn't been drunk that night at Carlin—"

"Oh, dry up! dry up! you sniffling chump!" Kenneth retorted. "We are in a hole, and we have got to get out the best we can."

"She mustn't take the money from him," reiterated the younger boy, turning his twisting face aside. "If she takes it she will marry him, and she is no wife for that dirty, low-bred scoundrel. You and I know all about the girls he has ruined. Didn't Jeff Raymond come all the way from Camden County to shoot him like a dog for the way he treated his niece, and then the sheriff stepped in and smoothed it over? Pouf! do you think I want my sweet, beautiful sister to marry a man like that to save my neck? I'll tell you what I'll do, Mr. Brown, if she starts to do that for my sake I'll drown myself. She is an angel. She has had enough trouble from me and Ken. We have treated her worse than a nigger slave ever was treated."

"For the Lord's sake, let up!" thundered Kenneth. "This is no camp-meeting. If sis wants to take the money, let her do it. Now, Brown, I'm willing to trust Albert Frazier to some extent, but he need not know just yet that we are bunking in the barn. Let him keep on thinking we are at the other place. Tell the others about it, though. We've had enough to eat to-night, but please have Aunt Zilla get us up a warm breakfast in the morning. It will tickle the old soul and she will spread herself. You see, I'm in a better mood than Martin is. I don't cross a bridge till I get to it, but he has attended Keith's funeral a hundred times in a single night, and as for the other"— Kenneth uttered a short, hoarse laugh and made a motion as if tying a rope around his neck—"he has been through *that* quite as often. That boy is full of imagination. Mother used to say he would write poems or paint pictures. He has 'painted towns red' with me often enough, the Lord knows. Some say I am ruining him. I don't know. I don't care. If a fellow is weak enough to be twisted by another—well, he deserves to be twisted, that's all."

"I don't blame anybody but *myself*," Martin whispered from a full, almost gurgling throat. "I know I never let sister twist me, and I ought to have done so. A man is a low cur that will bring his sister down to this sort of thing, and that's what I am. But she shall not marry Frazier if I can help it. The trouble is, I can't help it!" he ended, with a groan. "By my own conduct I have sealed her fate and mine. If our gentle mother were—"

Kenneth abruptly turned his back on his brother. "Come on," he said to Charles, with a frown of displeasure, "let's go to the barn and put the baby to bed in the hay. Then you may go tell sister, if you will be so kind."

CHAPTER XV

When they had disappeared in the barn, Charles, for precautionary reasons, skirted the stable lot, plunged into the thicket at the side of the house, and entered the yard at the front gate. The parlor was lighted, and he knew that Mary was there, entertaining her visitor. He tried to walk noiselessly, but his tread made a low grinding sound on the gravel, and the broken steps creaked as he ascended them. To his consternation he heard Mary coming. She stood in the front doorway, staring in agitation.

"Oh!" she cried out, in relief, when her glance fell on him. "I thought — thought that you might be a messenger from town. Mrs. Quinby said she would send word if a dangerous change came."

"I must see you about your brothers —" he was beginning, when they heard Frazier's heavy tread in their direction.

In a flash of comprehension she acted. Stepping close to him, she whispered, softly, "After he goes up to bed — meet me under the apple-trees out there!"

She stepped back to the doorway just as Frazier was emerging from the parlor. "Yes, I thought it was a messenger from town," she said, aloud. "Good night, Mr. Brown."

"Good night," Charles answered, and he passed on to the stairway and went up to his room. He heard the voices of Mary and Frazier on the veranda. They were walking to and fro, for he could hear their steps side by side.

Charles did not undress. He did not light his lamp, but sat waiting. There was a certain undefinable comfort in the knowledge that he was serving Mary, that she had made the appointment to meet him later. At all events, her uncouth suitor did not have her full confidence. But how slowly the time dragged along, how irritating the thought that the girl was tortured by suspense over his interrupted disclosure!

It was eleven o'clock when he heard Mary saying good night and Frazier went clattering up the stairs. He carried a lighted candle in his hand, and Charles, peering from his darkened coign of vantage through the half-opened door, beheld the sensual visage in a circle of light. How he detested it! Frazier turned into the guest-room at the head of the stairs, the windows of which overlooked the lawn in front of the house. The door was closed after him. Charles heard the key turned and the bolt rattle into its socket. Frazier was evidently a cautious man even in the house of friends, and it was known that he had enemies who would not hesitate to take advantage of him. He always carried a revolver. He was permitted to do so by the law as an occasional deputy under his brother.

Frazier continued his noise. He made a clatter as he doffed his heavy boots. A rickety old chair creaked under him as he sat in it. Charles heard even his dull tread as he thumped about in his bare feet, removing his outer clothing. A window-sash was thrown up with a jarring bang. Then the groaning of the mahogany bedstead announced that he had retired for the night.

Charles went to a window and looked out. He could see the apple-trees Mary had indicated, and he was glad that they were not in view of the windows of Frazier's room. He waited, wondering if the visitor were a quick and sound sleeper. He took off his shoes that he might as noiselessly as possible descend the stairs. He decided that he must go at once; it would be discourteous to let Mary reach the rendezvous first. So, with his shoes in his hand, he started down. In the great, empty hall the creaking of the worn, well-seasoned steps seemed to ring out sharply as exploding gun-caps. After each sound he paused, waited, and listened to see if Frazier had been aroused. All was still, and he moved on. Reaching the outer door, he found that Mary had left it unlocked. He was soon outside and under the trees at the side of the house. He could see the window of Mary's room. It was dark. She had not retired, of that he was sure; like himself, she must be waiting somewhere in the dark. The moon was higher now, and its pale, star-aided light fell over the fields and mountains and the long, winding road to the village.

Presently he saw Mary coming. She wore slippers and was very swift of foot. As lightly as a wind-blown wisp of smoke she flitted across the grass toward him.

"Are you here, Mr. Brown?" she asked, her voice trilling like the suppressed warbling of a bird.

"Yes, Miss Rowland," he answered, softly, and he advanced toward her.

"Thank God!" she ejaculated, fervently. "I was afraid you would not be able to get down past Albert's room. What is it you have to say? Oh, I'm crazy—crazy to hear!"

He told her, watching her face closely. She started, narrowed her eyes in perplexity, and then, unconsciously, put both of her hands on his arm and held it as she might have that of a long-tried and trusted friend.

"Oh, what do you think? What do you think?" she all but moaned. "Will it be safe?"

She had lifted her sweet face close to his. Her touch on his arm was a thing never to be forgotten. It seemed to rivet his very soul to hers.

He weighed his decision deliberately. "I cannot really see that they are in much more danger," he finally got out. "It is a fact, as Kenneth says, that, with us to keep watch on the road, we could warn them of any approach that had a suspicious look. After all, perhaps the very last place the officers would think of searching would be one so close at home. At any rate, the boys want to be near you—Martin especially."

"My poor baby!" Mary suddenly broke down and began to weep.

"Don't, don't! Please don't!" Charles put his arm around her; he drew her to him. He wiped her eyes with his own handkerchief; his toil-hardened fingers touched the velvety skin of her cheeks. She did not resent his action.

"He is just a baby!" she sobbed; "he is as gentle and timid at times as a little girl. I must see him to-night."

"To-night!" Charles exclaimed, in surprise.

"Yes," and she drew herself from his embrace as if unconscious of having yielded to it, though her tear-wet face was still raised to his, the tremulous, grief-twisted lips never before so maddeningly exquisite. "Yes, I must see him to-night. I'll go alone. I can whistle and they will know who it is. Kensy may be asleep—he no doubt is—but Martin will be awake, poor boy!"

"May I not go with you to—" he began, hesitatingly.

"No, I'd better go alone. You see, if I happened to be discovered I could make some excuse, but it would be different if we were seen together. Don't wait for me. Please go back to your room. You are tired. We are making you do both night and day work, but, oh, I am so grateful! Good night."

"Good night," he echoed, as she flitted away from him like a vanishing sprite produced by the moon and starlight.

At the steps he took off his shoes again. No experienced house-breaker could have turned the bolt of the great door more softly than he did, and yet an accident happened. The large brass key, which was loose in the worn keyhole, fell to the floor just as he was opening the door. In the empty hall it sounded to him as loud as a clap of thunder. He stood still, holding the door ajar for a moment, and then softly closed it. Cautiously he crept up the steps, and was half-way to the floor above when a harsh command from Frazier's door rang out, followed by the sharp click of the hammer of a revolver.

"Halt!" cried Frazier. "Stand where you are, and hold up your hands. If you value your life, don't move."

Charles stood still, but did not raise his hands. "I'm going up to my room," he said, calmly. He now saw Frazier in his white underclothing, leaning over the balustrade, the revolver aimed at him.

"To your room, with your shoes in your hand?" was the incredulous retort. The revolver was lowered reluctantly and Frazier swore in his throat. "Is that the way you come and go in the house of decent people?" he went on, insultingly.

Beside himself with rage, Charles silently pursued his way up the stairs. Frazier seemed surprised at receiving no answer, and, with the weapon swinging at his side, he muttered something under his breath and retreated to his room door.

"I'll look into this," he called out. "I'm sure Mr. Rowland doesn't know this sort of a thing is going on under his roof."

In a flash of far-reaching insight Charles saw the disastrous consequences of a nocturnal row with the bully. Mary was then outside the house, and if Frazier were to catch her returning no sort of explanation except the truth would satisfy him. What was to be done? In an instant Charles took the only available course, crushing his pride to accomplish it.

"I am sorry I disturbed you, Mr. Frazier," he said to the white figure in the doorway. "I took off my shoes to make as little noise as possible. I am sorry, too, that I have forgotten something and must go back after it. I'll try not to disturb you when I return."

With a low growl, Frazier vanished in his room. Charles heard him drop the revolver on a table and the creaking of the bed as he sank on it. Down the stairs Charles went. Slipping on his shoes outside, he crept around the house toward the barn, over-joyed by the discovery that Mary was not yet in sight. At the barn-yard fence he paused. He could hear low voices from the dark loft; now it was Mary speaking, now Martin, now Kenneth. Charles crept to the main door and softly whistled. Immediately there was silence within the building. Then a whistle sounded. It was Mary's, he was sure, and he heard her descending the narrow steps from the loft.

Frightened she must have been, for when she reached him she was all aquiver and her voice hung dead in her throat.

"Don't worry," he said, promptly, to allay her fears. "All is safe, but I had to warn you."

Kenneth and Martin were now at her side, and he explained the situation to them all. "I was afraid you might come in at the front door and be seen by him," Charles said. "You see, he may not go to sleep easily, and—"

"I was going in that way," Mary broke in. "He would have caught me, and I would have had to tell the truth. He mustn't know the boys are here. The truth is, I am a little bit more afraid of him than I was. He—he holds everything over me that he finds out. He talks about our marrying more than he did. I can get in by the back stairs, and I'll go up very soon. Don't wait, Mr. Brown. He is sure to lie awake till you return. Lock the door after you. Don't remove your shoes this time. Show him that you don't care what he thinks."

Charles found the way clear for him on his return, and as he passed Frazier's room he noticed that the door was closed; he heard no sounds within.

"*Show him that you don't care what he thinks!*" Mary's last words were ringing in his ears. Somehow they were the sweetest words he had ever heard. They warmed, thrilled, encouraged him. He took them to sleep with him. They followed him through strange turbulent dreams that night. They were back of his first waking thoughts the next morning. "*Show him that you don't care what he thinks!*" He could have sung the words to the accompaniment of the rising sunlight as it bathed the fields in yellow. With them she had thanked him for the service he had rendered, and the service had been her protection against that particular individual. Marry him? Could she marry a man she feared? And yet she had said she would under certain conditions, and the conditions were on the way to fulfilment. Great God! how could it be? His short-lived hope was gone; the music of her magic words had ceased. He heard the clatter of Frazier's boots in his bed-chamber. As he passed down the steps, he heard the burly guest emptying soiled water from his wash-bowl out of a window upon the shrubbery below. How he hated the man!

CHAPTER XVI

A few days later Mary left on horseback immediately after breakfast. From Rowland, Charles learned that she was going to see certain persons who owned near-by farms, with the hope of borrowing money for the removal of the wounded man to Atlanta and for his treatment there by the famous surgeon, Doctor Elliot.

Charles was at work, hoeing corn, when from the thicket bordering the field Kenneth and Martin stealthily emerged and joined him, having crept around from the barn.

"It is all right," Kenneth said, with an assuring smile. "Nobody is in sight on the road for a mile either way. We can dodge back any minute at the slightest sound. It's hell, Brown, to stay there like a pig being fattened for the killing. This is monotonous, I tell you. I can't stand it very long. That man must get to Atlanta. Mary is off this morning to borrow cash for it. Our credit is gone. Nobody will indorse for the old man but Albert Frazier, and I think his name is none too good here lately."

"He will get the money for sister, see if he doesn't," Martin spoke up, plaintively. "She is trying to keep him from it, though; that's why she went off this morning. She doesn't care for him—she doesn't—she doesn't! She knows what he is. She couldn't love a man like that. I hate him. He claims to be helping us, and he is, I reckon, but he has an object in view, and I'd die rather than have him gain it."

"No, I don't want her to marry him, either." Kenneth's voice had a touch of genuine manliness in it which Charles noticed for the first time. Moreover, his face was very grave. He shrugged his shoulders and flushed slightly as he went on. "I've been watching you, Brown. Having nothing else to do all day long, I've watched you at your work and seen you come and go from the field to the house and back. I envy you. To tell you the God's truth, I'm sick and tired of the way I've been living. They say I am responsible for Martin being in this mess, too. I reckon I am, and I know I am the cause of sister's worry and the disgrace of all this on the family.

They say an honest confession is good for the soul, and I say to you that if this damned thing passes over I'm going to take a different course. I see the pleasure you get out of working, and I am going to work. The other thing is not what it is cracked up to be."

Kenneth's voice had grown husky, and he cleared his throat and coughed; the light of shame still shone in his eyes.

"He means it," Martin said, throwing his arm about his brother and leaning on him affectionately. "Last night when he found me awake he came over to my corner and sat down and talked. He said he'd got so he couldn't sleep sound, either. It was wonderful the way he talked, Mr. Brown. I didn't know Ken was like that. He talked about mother and about sister's brave fight against so many odds—and, may I tell him, Ken? You know what I mean."

"I don't care what you say," Kenneth answered. He was seated on the ground, his eyes resting on the gray roof of the house which could be seen above the trees, outlined against the blue sky and drifting white clouds. "I'm not ashamed of anything I said."

"Why, he said," Martin went on, "that he admired you more than any man he had ever run across. He said what you told him about how you used to drink and gamble—when you could have kept it to yourself—and how you had quit it all and put it behind you because it was the sensible thing to do—Ken said that was the strongest argument he had ever heard, and that he liked you because you seemed to want him to do the same thing."

"I did appreciate that talk, Brown," Kenneth admitted. "You put it to me in a different light from any one else. You spoke like a man that had burnt himself at a fire, and was warning others to stay away from it. I don't care where you come from or what you were when you landed here, you are a gentleman. You have made me feel ashamed of myself, and I am man enough to say so. I've been bluffing in this thing. I have felt it as much as Martin, but wouldn't let on. I've not been asleep all the time when he thought I was. God only knows how I've lain awake and what I've been through in my mind."

Suddenly Kenneth rose; his face was full and dark with suppressed emotion, and he stalked away toward the barn.

"He is not like he used to be," Martin remarked, softly, his eyes on his brother. "All this has had a big effect on him. It is strange, but I often try to comfort him now. He is worried about Albert Frazier."

"About him?" Charles exclaimed, under his breath.

"Yes. He doesn't like to feel that we are in his power so completely. He is afraid sister will marry him, and she will, Mr. Brown, if she fails to get that money elsewhere. I don't think she really wants to marry him. She pretends to like him, but that is all put on to fool me and Ken. He is working for us. Every day he tells the sheriff something to throw him off our track. He actually forged a letter that he showed to his brother which he claimed was from a friend in Texas saying that me and Ken had been seen at Forth Worth, on our way West. When sister told Ken that it made him mad. A week ago he would have chuckled over it, but now he hates it because it sort o' binds sister to Frazier. A man that will fool his own brother like that is not the right sort for a sweet girl like my sister to live with all her life. Father wouldn't care much, but Ken and I would. We have been running with a tough crowd, but we know that we've got good blood in our veins."

Presently Martin left, went to keep his brother company, and Charles resumed his plodding work in the young corn. He gave himself up to gloomy meditation. What a strange thing his life had been! How queer it was that nothing prior to his arrival there in the mountains now claimed his interest. William, Celeste, Ruth, old Boston friends, college chums, business associates—all had retired from his consciousness, almost as if they had never existed. The fortunes of this particular family wholly absorbed him. He could have embraced Martin while the boy was talking, because of his resemblance in voice and features to Mary. He respected Kenneth for his fresh resolutions, and pitied him as he had once pitied himself. His hoe tinkled like a bell, at times, on the small round stones buried in the mellow soil. The mountain breeze fanned his hot brow. Accidentally he cut down a young plant of corn, and all but shuddered as he wondered if it, too, could feel, think, and suffer. He saw a busy cluster of red ants, and left them undisturbed. They were sinking a shaft, he knew not how deep, in the earth. One by one they brought to the surface tiny bits of clay or sand, rolled them down a little embankment, and hurried away for other burdens. That they thought, planned, and calculated he could not doubt. He himself was a monster too great in size for their comprehension. Had he stepped upon them their universe would have gone out of existence. He wondered if they loved one another, if their social system would have permitted one of their number to go into voluntary exile and in that exile to find a joy never before comprehended.

CHAPTER XVII

Mary rode to house after house on her way to Carlin, but met with no success in the matter of borrowing money. It was near noon when she entered the straggling suburbs of the village. At a ramshackle livery-stable she dismounted and left her horse in the care of a negro attendant whose father had once been owned by her family. She called him "Pete"; he addressed her as "Young Miss," and was most obsequious in his attentions and profuse in promises to care for her horse.

Opposite the hotel stood a tiny frame building having only one room. It was a lawyer's office, as was indicated by the sanded tin sign holding the gilt letters of the occupant's name—"Chester A. Lawton, At'y at Law."

He was a young man under thirty, who had met Mary several times at the hotel when she was visiting Mrs. Quinby. He was seated at a bare table, reading a law-book, when she appeared at the open door. He had left off his coat, the weather being warm, and on seeing her he hastily got into it, flushing to the roots of his thick dark hair.

"You caught me off my guard, Miss Mary," he apologized, awkwardly. "I know I oughtn't to sit here without my coat in plain view of the street, but the old lawyers do it, and—"

"It is right for you to do so," Mary broke in, quite self-possessed. "I only wanted to see you a moment. I wanted to ask you what is customary in regard to fees for getting legal advice."

Lawton pulled at his dark mustache, even more embarrassed. "I—I—really am rather new at the work, Miss Mary; in fact, I'm just getting started," he answered, haltingly. "I suppose that such things depend on the—the nature of the case, and the research work, reading, you know, and—oh, well, a lawyer sometimes has expenses. He has to travel in some cases. Yes, fees all depend on that sort of thing."

He was politely proffering a straight-backed chair, and as she sat down she forced a smile. "To be frank," she went on, "I don't know whether I really ought to employ a lawyer or not, and I was wondering how much it would cost to find out the probable expense."

"Oh, I see!" laughed Lawton, as he sat down opposite her, leaned on the table, and pushed his open book aside. "Well, I'll tell you, Miss Mary. I don't know what the older chaps do, but I make it a rule not to charge a cent for talking over a case with a person. That is right and proper. If you have any legal matter in mind, all you've got to do is to state it to me—that is, if you have honored me by thinking my advice might be worth while—and if I see anything in your case I'll then advise you to proceed, or not, as I deem best."

Lawton seemed rather pleased at the untrammeled smoothness of his subdued oratory, and waited for her to speak.

Mary was silent for a moment, and then she said, "You see, I don't know whether I really ought to seek legal advice yet, at any rate, and—" She broke off suddenly.

"Miss Mary," said Lawton, trying to help her out, "may I ask if you are referring to—to the little trouble your brothers are in?"

She nodded, swallowed a lump of emotion in her throat, and looked him straight in the eyes. "Father wouldn't attend to it, and I got to worrying about it—about whether advice ought to be had or not. We are terribly hard up for ready money and have got into debt already."

"Well, I'll be frank with you, Miss Mary, and I'm going to tell you something that may be to your interest. Now if you had gone to—we'll say to Webster and Bright, across the street, they, no doubt, would expect you to pay and pay big whether you needed a lawyer or not. Old law firms have strict rules on that line, I understand. Everything is 'grist that comes to their mill,' as the saying is, for they will tell anybody that they are not paying office rent for fun. But it is different with a young chap that is just getting on his feet in the profession. Now, knowing you as I do, and having had several agreeable talks with you, I'd hate like rips to charge for any advice I can give unless—unless it was of great benefit to you; and the truth is, I am not at all sure that you need a lawyer."

"Oh, you mean—But I don't understand!" Mary exclaimed, not knowing whether his words boded well or ill for her.

"Why, it is like this, Miss Mary. There are tricks in my trade, as in all others, and as matters stand in the case of your brothers—well, if Tobe Keith should happen to pull through, the charges against them would be so insignificant that the courts would be likely to dismiss them entirely. That, no doubt, is a slipshod method, but it is peculiar to us here in the South. You see, your father stands high—nobody higher, in fact; he fought for the Confederacy, has always been a perfect gentleman, and has no end of influential kinsfolk. Why, the district attorney himself is a sort of distant cousin, isn't he? Seems to me that I have heard him telling your father one day that if he ever printed that family history he'd subscribe for several copies, because his name was to be in it, somehow—on his mother's side, I think. Then the Governor is akin, too, isn't he? I thought so" (seeing Mary nod) "and the Kingsleys and Warrens. Oh, take it from me, Miss Mary, if Tobe Keith does get on his feet your brothers will not even be arrested. So I'll not take any fee from you—yet awhile, anyway; and I'm going to say, too, that I'd keep the boys out West. It is a good thing they went to Texas. I suppose they are out there, dodging about. I heard Sheriff Frazier say so the other day (his brother Al had picked up the news somehow or other), but he hadn't decided to institute a search till there was a change in Tobe's condition."

"Have you heard from him to-day?" Mary asked, and she all but held her breath as she steadily eyed the lawyer.

"No change at all, I understand," Lawton answered. "The doctors still say he must be taken to Atlanta to get the ball out."

"Yes, that must be done," Mary sighed, and her face became graver. "I am trying to raise the money—four hundred dollars. Mr. Lawton, can you tell me how to do it? I have no security."

"I'm sorry, Miss Mary"—Lawton's color heightened and he screwed his eyes up in embarrassment—"that I can't help you out on that line. Everybody I know is in debt or short of funds. The bank is awfully strict, and high on interest, too. Your father and Albert Frazier drew up some sort of a paper at this table the other day. I think Frazier went his security, put his name on a note at the bank. I heard them talking about how difficult it was to get money. I think Albert has about run through the little pile his old daddy left him. He is a high-flyer for these times—free and easy with his money as long as it lasts."

"So you can't tell me any one to go to?" Mary rose and began to adjust the veil on her hat.

"No, I can't, Miss Mary. There ought to be a public fund for such cases of need as Tobe's. Yes, you must take some steps in his behalf. It would look well from any point of view. Tobe didn't know what he was doing, and neither did your brothers. If Tobe gets over it, it may be a good lesson to all three."

Mary was at the door now; he followed and stood bowing her out, while she thanked him for his helpful advice.

She was crossing the street when Albert Frazier, seated in a buggy, with his brother, drove by. She thought he might get out and speak to her, but he simply tipped his hat and transferred his gaze to the back of the trotting bay horse. She noted that the sheriff, whom she had never met, had not noticed her nor his brother's salutation.

She went into the post-office to get some stamps, and when she came out Albert Frazier was waiting for her on the sidewalk.

"I would have got out when I passed you just now," he said, beaming on her admiringly, "but I was with John, you see; and—well, to be plain, he doesn't know about me and you, and right now especially I don't want him to get on to it."

"I understand," she said, coldly, looking away from him. "Aren't you afraid he will see us now?"

"No. He has gone on home. His wife isn't well. Say, little girl, you are not mad, are you?"

"Oh no," she answered, forcing a smile.

"Well," he bridled, "it is for your own good and the boys'. I'm having a tough job keeping John from suspecting the truth. If I hadn't got up that bogus letter from Texas he might have had his men searching the mountains, or watching you and that hobo circus man take food out to them in their cave. I'm doing all I can for you and I think you ought not to get on your high horse as you do sometimes."

"Forgive me," she said, tremulously, the muscles of her lips twitching. "I know what you are doing, and I appreciate it from the bottom of my heart."

Her grateful words put him in a better mood. They were about to cross the street again; a wagon loaded with cotton-bales was passing. He was hardly justified in doing so, for she needed no assistance, but he took hold of her arm, and she felt his throbbing fingers pressing it. She drew away from him. "Don't!" she said, impulsively.

"There you go again," he cried, but not angrily, for her natural restraint had been one of her chief attractions. Other girls had given in more easily and had been forgotten by him, but Mary was different. There was, moreover, always that consciousness on his part of her social superiority. He wanted her for a wife, and, situated as she now was, he had never felt so sure of her.

"When are you going to let me give you that money?" it now occurred to him to ask. "Tobe must be removed, you know."

A look of deep pain struggled in the features she was trying to keep passive. "I haven't quite given up the hope of getting it elsewhere," she finally said. "If I quite fail, I'll come to you. I've said so, and I'll keep my word."

At this moment a farmer came up to Frazier and said that he wanted to speak to him a moment. Excusing himself and bowing, Frazier left her.

CHAPTER XVIII

As she walked on Mary was glad that Frazier had been called away before he had asked her whither she was going, for she did not want him to know that she had decided to call at Tobe Keith's home and inquire personally about his condition. It struck her as being incongruous that she was already keeping things from the man she might eventually marry. And at this moment various thoughts of Charles fairly besieged her brain. Somehow she could not imagine herself keeping any vital thing from him. How strange, and he such a new friend! She found herself blushing, she knew not why. What was it about the man that appealed to her so strongly? Was it the mystery that constantly enveloped him, and out of which had come such a stream of generous acts, or was it the constant heart-hungry and lonely look of the man who certainly was out of his natural sphere as a common laborer?

Her way took her through the poorest section of the little town. Small houses, some having only two and three rooms each, bordered the rugged, unpaved little streets. Part of the section was known as the "Negro Settlement," and there stood a little steepled church, with green blinds, the walls of which, in default of paint, had received frequent coatings of whitewash at the hands of the swarthy devotees. She had no trouble in finding her way, for she already had a general idea of where the mother of the wounded man lived, and only had to ask as to the particular house.

"Can you tell me where Mr. Keith lives?" she inquired of a little negro boy amusing himself in a swing.

"You mean the man that was kilt?" the child asked, blandly, as he halted himself by thrusting his bare feet down on the ground.

"The man that was—hurt," Mary corrected, shuddering over the way the boy had put his reply.

"De las' house at the end er de street, on dis yer side. You cayn't miss it. Miz' Keith got grape-vines in 'er front yard, en' er goat en' chickens en' ducks."

She found it without trouble. The house had four small rooms and a crude lean-to shed which served as a kitchen. A slender, thin woman of the lowest class of whites, about fifty years of age, scantily attired in a plain print skirt and a waist of white cotton material, her iron-gray hair plastered down on the sides of her face from a straight part in the middle of her head and drawn to a small doughnut-shaped knot behind, sat in the doorway smoking a clay pipe with a reed stem. As Mary arrived at the little gate, which was kept closed by a rope fastened to a stake and from which hung a brick for a weight, she looked up, drew her coarsely shod feet under her, and took the pipe from her mouth. She must have recognized the visitor, for she contracted her thin brows and allowed a sullen, resentful expression to spread over her wrinkled face and tighten the muscles of her lips.

"May I come in, Mrs. Keith?" Mary asked, holding the gate partly open and dubiously waiting for a response.

The pipe was clutched more firmly and the woman stared straight at her. "You may come in if you want to," was the caustic answer. "We don't keep no bitin' dog. I didn't 'low the likes of you would want to come, after what's happened, but if you do I can't hinder you an' Tobe hain't able to prevent it, nuther."

"Who is it, mother?" came a faint voice from within the house.

"Never mind, sonny, who it is," the old woman called back. "I'll tell you after awhile. Remember what the doctor said, that you must not get excited an' lift your fever."

There was silence in the room behind the grim sentinel at the door, and Mary lowered her voice almost to a whisper.

"Perhaps I'd better go away, Mrs. Keith," she faltered. "I thought I might see you alone. That's why I came. I don't want to disturb your son—I wouldn't, for all the world. Mrs. Keith, I am unhappy over this, too."

"Huh! I don't see nothin' fer *you* to be upset over!" sneered the old woman. "Your brothers lit out fer new fields an' pastures with money to pay expenses with, like all highfalutin folks manage to git, while us pore scrub stock o' whites has to suffer, like Tobe is thar on his back, unable to move, an' with barely enough t' eat except what neighbors send in."

No seat was offered the visitor; the speaker grimly kept her chair, her stiff knees parted for the reception between them of her two gnarled rebellious hands and the clay pipe.

"I came to ask—I had to come," Mary faltered, her sweet face whitened by the rising terrors within her. "I came to see if any arrangements are being made to—to—I understand the doctors advise your son's removal to Atlanta, and—"

"They advise anything to shuffle the blame off their *own* shoulders," blurted out the stubborn woman. "They see they ain't able to do nothing, an' they want my boy to die some'r's else, to save the county the expense of—of—" and she choked down a sob, a dry, alien thing in her scrawny neck. "I don't believe he'll ever be sent, so I don't. Sis Latimer, my cousin, a preacher's wife, has traipsed over two counties, tryin' to raise the four hundred dollars, and now says it can't be done. That was the last straw to Tobe. He lay thar, after she left, an' I heard 'im cryin' under the sheet, to keep me from hearin' him. He says he hain't got nothin' ag'in' your two brothers now. He says they was all to blame, an' if they hadn't been drunk an' gamblin' it wouldn't 'a' happened. Tobe's a odd boy—he forgives in a minute; but I hain't that way. I know how your brothers felt. They looked on my boy like dirt under their feet because you folks used to own niggers and live so high in your fine house with underlings to run an' fetch for you at every call. Kenneth Rowland would have thought a second time before pullin' down on a feller in his own set. Oh, I heard the filthy name he called Tobe, an' I didn't blame my boy for hittin' him, as they say he did, smack on the jaw. A blow with the bare hand, after a word like that is passed, doesn't justify the use of a gun while another feller is pinnin' a man's arms down at his side so he can't budge an inch. I'll tell you what you may not know, an' that is that if my boy does die them two whelps will be hunted down and strung up by the neck till they are dead, dead, dead! Thar never was a plainer case o' murder—cold-blooded murder. They say—folks say your brothers are livin' like lords in the West on money sent to 'em by rich kin to escape disgrace. The sheriff said so hisse'f, an' he ort to know. He's jest waitin' to see what comes o' Tobe. Your turn an' your stiff-backed, haughty old daddy's is comin', my fine young lady."

The faint voice was heard protesting from the interior of the house, and Mrs. Keith rose and stalked to the bed on which the wounded man lay. He said something in a low, guarded tone and Mary heard his mother answer:

"I wouldn't do that if I was you, honey. Let 'er go on. I can't stan' the sight of 'er, after what has happened. She looks so uppity, in 'er fine clothes an' white skin not touched by the sun, while me an' you—"

The man's voice broke in, plaintively rumbling, as if from a great distance. He must have been insisting on some point to be gained, for he continued talking, now and then coughing and spitting audibly.

"Well, well," Mrs. Keith exclaimed, "I'll tell 'er. I think it is foolish, but I'll tell 'er. Do you want me to comb your head a little an' spruce you up some?"

He evidently did, for Mary was kept waiting ten minutes longer. Then the sullen virago appeared in the doorway. "Tobe wants you to come in and see 'im," she reluctantly announced.

Despite the feeling that she was unwelcomed by the woman, Mary saw no alternative but to go in. She regretted it the instant her eyes fell on the wasted form on the unkempt bed and beheld the eager orbs peering at her from deep, dark sockets beneath shaggy brows. The room seemed to swing around her, the crude board floor to rise and fall like the waves of a rocking sea, the bed to float like a raft holding a starving derelict. Grasping the back of a chair for support, Mary leaned on it for a moment, and then, slightly recovering, she sat down, wondering if she could possibly bear the impending ordeal.

"I'm glad you thought enough o' me to come, Miss Mary," Tobe began, in the instinctive tone of respect that his class had for hers, "an' I want to say something to you." He hesitated and lifted his eyes to his mother, who was standing at the foot of his bed. "Ma," he said, "will you please go out a little while—just a little while?"

"Me! Why, I'd like to know?" she fiercely demanded. "Surely you hain't got no secrets from me?"

"I hain't got no secrets, but I want to talk free an' easy like to Miss Mary, an' somehow when you stan' lookin' like that an' thinkin' what I know you are thinkin'—well, I just can't talk, that's all."

"Humph! I say! Well, this is a pretty come-off!" Mrs. Keith fairly quivered with suppressed rage. "Can't talk before me, eh? An' me your mother at that. Well, well, I won't hender you, though you know the doctor told me to keep you perfectly quiet, an' here you are—Well, well, I'll go; if you feel that-away I'll go! A mother's feelings is never paid attention to nohow."

Mary tried to protest, but could think of nothing to say under the circumstances; besides, the angry woman was already whirling away. Mary heard her treading the creaking boards of the adjoining room.

"Please move your chair up a little mite closer," Tobe requested. "I've got just so much wind, an' no more, an' I can talk easier when you are close to me."

She obeyed, feeling like an inanimate thing pushed forward by some designing force. His thin hand lay within her reach. It was a repulsive object, and yet the same force directed her to take it; she did so, and with the act all her fears, all her timidity, left her. She pressed it gently; she leaned forward and stroked it almost caressingly with her other hand. Tears welled up in her eyes; they broke their bounds and fell upon her hands and his. He stared in slow astonishment, his lower lip quivered; he closed his great, somnolent eyes as if to give himself up to the dreamlike ecstasy of the moment. She saw his breast shaking, his throat moving as if he were swallowing rising sobs. Silence fell, broken only by the creaking boards in the next room, the clucking of a busy hen in the yard, the chirping of little chickens, the thwacking of an ax at a wood-pile not far away. Tobe turned his face from her. She saw him stealthily wiping his eyes on a soiled handkerchief.

"I'm gittin' to be a fool, a babyish fool," he said, presently. "Lyin' here like this is calculated to make a feller that-away, an' you bein' so kind an' gentle, too, is—is sorter surprisin'. A sick man can hear a lot o' ridiculous things when he is down like this. You see, I'm surrounded mostly by women, an' they chatter a lot. Anyways, you hain't nothin' like most of 'em say you are—too proud an' stuck up even to inquire about a feller in my fix. Yes, I'm glad you come, so I am. I hain't heard anything lately but revenge! revenge! revenge! The idle women that huddle about me through the day talk hate from morning to night. They got Ma at it; she hain't that-away as a general thing. I wanted to see you. I've seen you at a distance an' always wanted to get a closer look. They all say you are pretty, an' so you are. By all odds, I should count you the prettiest young lady in this part o' the country. I know I hain't never seed one that could hold a candle to you. I want to talk to you about Ken an' Martin. Miss Mary, them boys hain't bad at heart. La! I used to love 'em both, an' they liked me, too! It was just rot-gut liquor. Mart didn't mean no harm by holdin' me when that scrimmage begun, an' Ken may have *thought* he saw a knife in my hand that I was about to stab into Martin. I understand that's what he claimed before they made off to the West, an' it all may be so, for a drunk feller will think all sorts o' things. I wanted to see you because, if I *do* peg out—an' it looks like I'm goin' to—I want you to write this to the boys. I want you to tell 'em, Miss Mary, that you saw me an' that Tobe Keith said he didn't bear no ill-will an' died without hard feelin's. Tell 'em, too, that I said I hoped they would show the law a clean pair o' heels, for it looks like they will have trouble if they are fetched back here. Oh, I'm sorry for 'em! I saw, while I was lyin' thar, how sorry them boys looked when they saw what had happened. It sobered 'em in a minute, an' they would have stayed to help me if their friends hadn't got scared an' told 'em to run, that the sheriff was comin', an' the like."

"You mustn't say you are going to die, Tobe," Mary faltered, huskily, still gently stroking his hand. Beads of perspiration were on his sallow brow, and with her handkerchief she wiped them away. "The doctors say that if you go to Atlanta, to Doctor Elliot's sanatorium, he can—"

"I've given that up." He smiled faintly. "The money ain't in sight an' never will be. Besides, they only want to experiment on me. I know my condition better than they do. Surgical skill may be all right in many such cases, but mine has stood too long. I hain't afeard to die, Miss Mary, but I am sorry my going will be so serious for Ken an' Martin. Do you know, I was to blame chiefly. I was the one that furnished the whisky for that racket. I got it from a moonshiner I know. That is between you an' me, Miss Mary, for I broke the law when I went to his secret still an' got it without reportin' him."

CHAPTER XIX

Mary remained twenty minutes longer, and when she was going out at the gate she met Doctor Harrison, who had just alighted from his buggy and was hitching his horse to a portable strap and iron weight near the fence. He doffed his straw hat and smiled from his genial, bearded, middle-aged face and twinkling blue eyes.

"So you've turned nurse, have you?" he jested. "Well, I'm glad you came, for more reasons than one."

"You think it was right, then?" she answered.

"Decidedly, Miss Mary. At such a time as this we should not listen to gossip, but simply act humanely."

"I hardly knew what to do, for some persons thought that it would look as if I—I admitted that my brothers were—"

"I know," the doctor broke in, "but, nevertheless, I'm glad you put that aside. If I were on a jury—" He hesitated, as if he realized that he was on ground forbidden by due courtesy to her feelings. "Well," he started anew, "it can't possibly do any harm, and I am sure you will feel all the better for it."

"What are the chances for his recovery?" Mary asked, with bated breath, as she met his mild gaze with her steady eyes.

He looked toward the cottage door, placed his whip in the holder on the dashboard of the buggy, and then slowly swept his eyes back to her face.

"I am sorry to say—to *have* to say—that he is not doing so well. He seems a little weaker. However, when he gets to Atlanta—I hope I am not betraying secrets, but I met Albert Frazier just now and he told me that you had about concluded arrangements to supply the money. He did not say that he was telling me in confidence, but he may have meant it that way. People often say things to doctors, you know, that they would not make public, and if it *is* a private matter—"

"It is not, Doctor. I know—at least, I think I know—where I can get the money, and I shall not care who knows that it is from me. Tell me, please, do you think it best to send Tobe to Atlanta?"

"It is the only thing to do," was the decided answer. "You see, here in this small place we haven't the facilities, the surgical skill, the equipment for such a critical operation, and the truth is we all of us here balk at it. A doctor like Elliot can afford to take the risk, you see. If he should fail, you know there would be no criticism, while if one of us here were to do so we'd be thought—well, almost criminally wrong."

Mary's face was brooded over now by a shadow. She shuddered; her eyes held a tortured look. "So you think he ought to go at once?" she said.

"The sooner the better, Miss Mary," was the prompt answer. She gave him her hand, and he wondered over the change in her mood as he lifted his hat.

"I'll let you know very soon, Doctor," were her parting words. "Please don't mention it, for the present, anyway. I think I know where I can get the money that is needed."

Mary walked on, now toward the square. Her step was slow, her eyes were on the ground.

"Oh God! how can I? And yet I must!" she groaned. "He means to make me take the money; that is plain. He understands what it would mean, and so do I; but, oh, I don't want to marry him. I'd rather die—I would, I would, I would. And yet if I died—if I died—"

She had to pass through the square to get her horse, and she dreaded the possible encounter again with Albert Frazier. She felt relieved, on entering the square, to notice that he was not in sight. The plate-glass window of the bank, with its gilt-lettered sign, caught her eye. Why not try there to borrow the money, as a last resort? Perhaps the banker would consider lending her the money on her own name. She had heard of loans being made to women who had no security. Yes, she would try. It would be a last effort, but she must make it.

Entering the little building, she went to the opening in the wire netting and asked the cashier if Mr. Lingle were in. She was answered in the affirmative and directed to a half-closed door bearing the words, "The President's Office."

She opened the door without knocking, and saw the back and shaggy head of a man of sixty, without his coat, his collar and necktie loose, his sleeves rolled up, busy writing. Hearing her, he turned, suppressed a frown of impatience, stood up and bowed. His face was round, beardless, and reddish in tint.

"Oh, Miss Mary, how are you?" he asked, awkwardly extending a fat, perspiring hand. "Want to see me, eh, personally? Well, I'm at your service, though these are busy days for us. What can I do for you?"

Her voice seemed to have deserted her. She was conscious of the fear that no words at all would come from her, and yet immediately she heard herself speaking in a calm, steady tone. She was smiling, too, as if she knew that what she was saying had a touch of absurdity in it.

"I've come to bore you," she said. "I need some money, not on my father's account now, Mr. Lingle, for I know about his debt to you, but for myself, this time. I have no security beyond my word and promise to pay. It is a very serious matter, Mr. Lingle. You know about Tobe Keith's condition and that he must be sent to Atlanta. No one else will pay for it, and—"

"So you are going to mix yourself up in that mess, are you?" asked Lingle, frowning till his shaggy iron-gray brows met and all but overlapped. "If you were my daughter—Oh, what's the use? I'm not your teacher, but if you were in my charge I'd make you stay out of this. I know, I reckon, what's the matter. You feel responsible because your brothers were held accountable; that's like a woman. But all that is neither here nor there. I can't let you have any money at all. I'm going to be plain. Maybe it will open your eyes a little to the facts. My dear girl, I hold a mortgage on all the crops in the ground at your place, on the very tools, cattle, hogs, and horses. Your father—I hate to say it—but your father is as helpless in business matters as a new-born baby. He belongs to the old order. He is up to his neck in debt to every friend he has. I can't let him have any more money, and I can't let you have any. I wouldn't let you have it for what you want it even if you had good collateral to pin to your note. I couldn't conscientiously do it, for it would be throwing it away. That drunken roustabout hasn't one chance in a thousand to live, anyway, and the country would be better off without his brand. As for your brothers—well, you'd better keep them in the West. Men of your father's stamp don't have quite the influence they used to have. Our courts are being criticized for their lax methods so much that our judges and juries are becoming more careful in administering justice. If Tobe Keith dies—well, your brothers had better stay away, that's all."

"So there's no use asking you to—"

"No, Miss Mary, this bank can't mix up in such matters as that. Folks from up-to-date towns are making fun of us, too. One drummer was telling it around in Atlanta the other day that any stranger could cash a check here by simply inviting us to take a drink or handing us a cheap cigar. We are making new rules and sticking to them." With that the president of the bank turned toward his desk and reached out for a sheet of paper on which he had been writing.

"I thank you, Mr. Lingle," she faltered. "I am sure that you know best."

He held his paper in his left hand while he gave her his right, and made a sort of scraping movement with his foot as he executed a bow.

As she went back into the main room she was conscious of the fear that Albert Frazier might have discovered her presence at the bank and be waiting for her outside. Why, she asked herself, was the thought actually so terrifying? He might propose that he should have her horse sent out and that he be allowed to drive her home. In that case it would all be over. She would have to give the promise he had so long sought and she had so long withheld. A thrill of relief went through her on finding that he was not in sight anywhere about the busy square. She walked rapidly now toward the livery-stable, still with the fear of pursuit on her that was like the haunting dread of a nightmare. She was soon in the saddle and galloping homeward. At the point where the village street gave into the main country road she checked her speed. What, after all, was she running from? If the thing was inevitable, what was the use in putting it off? Was not the delay injurious to the end she was seeking? Might not even another day count fatally against Tobe Keith's recovery? Yes, the answer was yes, and nothing else. If it had to be done, why wait longer? She actually tried to turn the head of her horse toward the village, but the animal had scented home and the food to be had there, and refused, allowing the taut rein to bend his neck but not to guide his limbs. She finally came to regard it as an omen to be obeyed and allowed him to gallop on toward the farm.

As she neared her home the sun's rays were dying out of the landscape and the dusk was gathering. Coming to meet her from the house she saw Charles, and she wondered what had happened, for he never left the field before sundown; moreover, it struck her that he was walking rapidly, as if to reach her before she got to the house. He could not be coming to take the saddle from her horse, for Kenneth or Martin at the stable could do that. She summoned a smile as she greeted him at the barn-yard gate and he reached up to catch the bridle-rein. To her surprise he failed to return it. She had never seen a graver expression on his face as he held up his strong arms to help her down.

"What is the matter?" she asked, now alarmed.

"Don't get frightened," he said. "After all, it may amount to nothing, but still, I had to reach you and put you on your guard. I was afraid you might call out or whistle to your brothers, and that wouldn't do. After you left, they were so quiet, and remained out of sight so persistently, that, as the time passed, I became concerned about them. Usually, you know, they steal out and go into the woods for recreation or join me at my work. To-day they did not appear, so I went to the barn about two hours ago. Fortunately I did not whistle, but went directly up to them in the loft. They explained it. It seems that Kenneth had observed a strange man moving stealthily in and out of the woods, sometimes watching me, sometimes the house, and sometimes the barn."

"Oh!" and Mary went white from head to foot. "It is one of the sheriff's men. Don't you think so?"

"I don't know. Kenneth says he got a good look at him and that he is sure he is a stranger here. To be plain, Kenneth thinks that the sheriff has sent for a detective and that the detective may suspect the thing we are trying to hide—that the boys are not in the West, but here at home."

Mary said nothing. The deepening pallor of her face rendered it grim and firm, but it was none the less beautiful in its unwonted lines. He took off the saddle, opened the gate, and turned the horse into the lot.

"When the boys hear the horse in the stall," he said, "they will know you are back. Will it be necessary for you to go in to them? I mean—you see, if the fellow is still watching; in that case he might draw deductions from your being there. While if you go on to the house now—"

"I understand, and you are right," Mary said, with tight lips. "No, I'll go to the house. It is awful—awful—awful!"

He closed the gate and walked by her side till they reached the path leading down to the field. Here he turned to leave her.

"Where are you going?" The tone and words carried an almost desperate appeal to him not to leave her. In her wonderful eyes something seemed to burn not unlike the celestial resignation of the ancient saints before approaching torture. But, withal, she seemed to want to lean on him for moral or physical support.

"I think I'll go back to work," he answered. "It is still not quite time for supper. Besides, from the field I can keep a better watch on the woods while I appear to see nothing."

"Well, well, you are right," she said, sighing, "but please don't be late, and tell me if you see anything."

As she was nearing the house she saw her father returning home by a small private road which led to some of the farms north of his property.

"Where have you been?" she asked, as he joined her at the front gate, gallantly opened it, and stood aside for her to enter before him.

"I went over to see Tankersley," was his answer. "I heard he had some money he might lend, and—well, I thought maybe I'd get it and send it to Tobe Keith. But as soon as the old miser heard what I wanted it for he laughed and sneered in my face. He was very impudent. His standard is money, and nothing higher. Of course, I couldn't afford to get angry with a man so low bred, and I came away."

"I didn't know you had thought of raising money for Tobe," Mary said, wistfully. "In fact, I thought you would oppose my trying to get it."

"I admit I did think we ought not to go that far at first," Rowland said, as they reached the steps of the veranda, "but after you left this morning I was talking to Mr. Brown. He is a most remarkable man in many ways. He is quite a philosopher and has a wonderful vocabulary when he gets to talking. He swept everything away except the fact of Tobe's life being at stake, and the terrible consequences his death would have on the—the future state of mind and ultimate character of the boys. I confess he set me thinking. He had the courage to scold me pretty sharply, too, about—well, about my inactivity just at this time. He said I ought to lay everything aside and think more of you and my sons. He is right. I don't know who he is or what sort of ancestors he had, but he is a man of moral convictions, and I respect him. He is a gentleman at bottom. He has met reverses and taken up this mode of life through necessity. I told him I would try to get the money from old Tankersley, and he seemed glad when I went away for that purpose."

They were on the veranda now. Mary could think only of the strange man who had been seen about the premises, and she was trying to make up her mind as to whether it would be expedient to mention it to her father when she saw him looking down the road toward the village.

"That is Albert's horse," he said. "Yes, he is headed this way. That means that he will stay all night again. I think I could get that money from him, but I don't want to ask for more right now. He has done as much as I could expect already. No, I'll not ask him for it. Besides, of all the discourtesy known, to borrow money from a guest seems to me to be the worst. He seems worried over what you intend to do in his case," and Rowland was smiling pointedly. "He says you won't say one thing or another positively. He seemed to be hinting the other day that he'd like for me to take a hand in it, but I'll never do that. You must be your own judge. He is away beneath you in the matter of birth, but—"

"Father," Mary suddenly broke in, "you have not let him know that the boys are in the barn, have you?"

"No, I never let on about that," Rowland said, wearily, his eyes on the approaching horse and buggy. "I promised you I wouldn't, and, while I saw no reason—"

"He mustn't know; he mustn't know!" Mary broke in again. "I can't tell you now why, but he mustn't know that. He must not put up his horse, either, unless the boys are warned. It is getting dark and they may not see him coming. But keep him here, chat with him, and I'll slip to the barn by the back way and warn the boys."

"Well, I'll do that," Rowland promised, "but hurry on back. I can't entertain him. He comes to see you, not me. He is daft about you—actually crazy. He'd give his right arm to have you agree to—"

But Mary had vanished into the hall and with lowered head was scudding through the shrubbery to the barn. The buggy was stopping at the gate, and Rowland went down the walk with a stately step to meet the incongruous suitor for the hand of his daughter.

CHAPTER XX

In his corn-field, Charles took up his hoe and set to work. Now and then his eyes furtively swept the thicket on the hillside where Kenneth had seen the lurking stranger. Something seemed to tell Charles that the man was still in the neighborhood and was only waiting for the darkness to veil his further operations. He heard the sound of Frazier's horse on the road and saw Mary slip from a rear door of the house and steal rapidly down to the barn, but he did not understand what it meant. It became plain a moment later when Mary was seen hurrying back and the sound of hoofs and wheels at the gate had ceased. That it was Frazier making another call he did not doubt, and a sense of helpless discontent descended upon him, seeming to gather weight and substance from the very thickening darkness, and disconsolate voice from the dismal croaking of the frogs in the near-by marshes. Fireflies were flitting over the corn and about the shrubbery bordering the walk to the house. Charles now gazed more frequently and keenly toward the thicket. It was growing so dark that he felt that his pretense at working could not be kept up longer without exciting undue suspicion in the mind of the possible observer. He had decided to stop, when something among the branches of the young trees on the hillside caught his eye. To his astonishment he saw the vague outlines of a masculine figure emerge, stand out from the trees, and then slowly advance toward him. That he had been under the eye of this person the greater part of the day and was still being watched he did not doubt. That the man knew he was there and was coming toward him for a purpose he was sure. What could it mean other than that the man, if he was a detective, had decided to reveal his purpose and seek an interview from a man so recently hired that he ought to be a disinterested witness? That must be it, and Charles steeled himself for an ordeal he dreaded in many ways. With his hoe on his shoulder he made his way between two rows of corn toward the path leading up to the house. The man was still approaching. He was not a hundred feet away when, as Charles was turning toward the house, the stranger suddenly and softly coughed.

"Ahem!" the man cleared his throat, coughed again, and waved his hand. Charles turned quite around and stood hesitating.

"Wait! Please don't go yet, sir," a strangely familiar voice exclaimed, in a low, urgent tone. "I must see you."

"Great God! Mike, is it you?" Charles lowered his hoe and stood peering through the gloom.

"Yes, sir, it is me, Mr. Charles," was the faltering reply. "I hope you won't be angry, but I felt that I must see you. I waited till night, thinking it would please you for me to do so."

"My God! Mike!" was all Charles could say, as he reached out his hand and dropped his hoe.

"Yes, sir. I hope you will forgive me. I haven't the right to do all this, considering your wishes, sir, but I couldn't keep from it, sir. I saw you about a year ago in Madison Square in New York. You were with a friend, sir, and I dared not address you then, so I followed you and him."

"My Lord! You were that fellow!" Charles laughed out of sheer relief in finding that his greater fears were ungrounded.

"Yes, sir, and I stood watch over the house, hoping to see you alone, but you both got away that night, and—"

"Thank God! Mike—I'm glad—rejoiced to see you!" and Charles affectionately wrung the hand that was in his. "How are the people at home?"

"All well, sir—your brother, the missus and the little girl. She is always asking about you—can't seem to understand like—like—well, like the others."

"I see," and a sudden chill passed over Charles at the thought now in his mind. "But, Mike, how did you happen to locate me? Surely they don't know at home that I am down here."

"Oh no, sir! That was just my discovery, sir."

"Your discovery?"

"Yes. You see, I've been making rather frequent trips to New York to see my mother, and when I was there I was always on the lookout for you. You see, I didn't then know but what you and your friend might return from New Jersey and be hiding somewhere in New York. So a short time ago, sir, happening to be in Washington Square, who should I see but a man who looked so much like your friend that I determined to get a closer view. It turned out to be Mr. Mason, sir; but we were playing at cross-purposes, Mr. Charles, for he thought I was a plain-clothes detective. He had spotted me that time a year ago in Madison Square and, sir, your friend—he will do to trust—he shut up like a clam. He lied like a good fellow, sir. I don't know what he didn't tell me with as straight a face as a parson at a funeral. We had it up and down, sir, for quite a while, and him thinking every minute that I would show my badge, whistle for help, and take him in as a witness against you. Presently, however, he seemed to get tired of the tack we were on and made a bluff, sir. He got up and just as good as told me to mind my own business. He walked off, madlike, in a huff, as if he had had enough of me. But I couldn't let him depart so, Mr. Charles. I went after him again, and then he came back and we had it out. To make a long story short, I finally convinced him that I was your friend, sir. In fact, he said that you had honored me by mentioning me to him. It was the money, however, I think, that clinched the matter."

"Money? Mason didn't accept money from you, did he?" Charles asked, in bewilderment.

"Oh no, sir! He is the soul of honor, Mr. Charles! I mean the money I owe you and which I told him I had then in the bank to pay you. He said you were—I think he said 'strapped,' sir, down here in the neighborhood of Carlin, and he was sure you needed the cash, as you were so hard up that you were going to work on a farm. And this is the way I find you, sir, dressed like a common laborer. Thank God, I've got the money, Mr. Charles. Here it is in a roll. It is burning a hole in my pocket, sir. You ought not to have left Boston without it."

Charles's heart bounded at the sight of the money Michael was now extending toward him. He took it. He fondled it. His eyes beamed through the dusk. "Oh, Mike," he cried. "You can never imagine how much I am in need of this. I wouldn't take it from you, but I really must, for it is going to help a sweet, beautiful girl out of serious trouble. I'll tell you about her later. She is the daughter of the gentleman for whom I am working."

"Was she the young lady who came on a horse and whom you assisted at the barn, sir?"

"Yes. Did you see her, Mike?"

"Yes, sir, and a good look I had, too, sir, for I was hidden behind some thick bushes only twenty yards from where you and she stood with the horse. Oh, she is indeed beautiful, sir, and must have a fine character. Pardon me, sir, but I think I understand. You could not keep from—from—no natural man full of young blood could keep from—admiring her. Ah, sir, I congratulate you. I see now that maybe you need not be so—so lonely and unhappy in your new life."

"There is nothing between us, and never can be, Mike," Charles sighed. "You know of the cloud hanging over me. That will forever prevent my marrying. This is a fine old aristocratic family, Mike. But, Mike, this money may save her from a marriage that is repulsive to her. It will have to be used secretly. I mustn't be known in it."

"You don't mean, sir, that you are giving the—the money away as soon as you get it? Ah, that is like you, Mr. Charles! You are never thinking of yourself—always of others, as you did in my case and many others. But I had hoped—when Mr. Mason told me of your condition down here—I had hoped that the money would come in handy to—"

"It is worth my life to me," Charles interrupted, grasping the hand of his companion and pressing it fervently. "I would have given my right arm to have gotten it anywhere for her use."

"Then it really *is* love, sir," Michael opined, simply. "And considering what I've seen of the lady, I can imagine how you feel under the fear, sir, of her going to some one else who is unworthy of her. Yes, I'll have to be satisfied."

At this point the bell at the kitchen door clanged. "It is for me, Mike," Charles explained. "I'm late for supper and must go now. But I must see you to-night. Are you stopping at Carlin?"

"Yes, sir, at that remarkable inn. It was there, from that talkative clerk, sir, that I learned of a circus man being employed on this place."

"Well, go back now, Mike, and I'll be in to see you to-night. It may be as late as eleven o'clock, but I'll not fail. Wait up for me. There are many things to be inquired about, but first that other business must be attended to."

"About the young lady, sir?"

"Yes."

"I'll be there, Mr. Charles, and I'll be guarded in my conduct, you may be sure. I'll get directions from you later. Come straight to my room, sir."

"One other question, Mike, before you go." Charles lowered the hoe which he had put on his shoulder and leaned on it.

"Did the—the thing I did at the bank harm my brother financially? Is he still employed there? You see, I was afraid that, on my account—"

"Oh, that is all over with, sir. Your brother, if anything, stands higher than ever. You see, that was due to your uncle James."

"To Uncle James!"

"Yes, sir. You know he came home from Europe very soon after you left. He took a high hand at the bank—bought up all the floating stock and only recently was made the president. I have hoped, sir, that, that being the case, the charges against you would be dismissed. You see, I know, Mr. Charles, and they must know, that you were unconscious of what you were doing. I myself have seen you, sir, when you were in a condition that—"

"Well, never mind that," and Charles seemed to shrink within himself, shouldered his hoe, and turned. "We'll talk it all over at the hotel to-night."

On reaching the house he found that the family and the guest had already supped. He went into the dining-room and sat in his accustomed place. He heard voices from the veranda, and knew that Mary, her father, and Frazier were seated there. Aunt Zilla brought his supper, and he apologized for his delay.

"Dat's all right, Mr. Brown." She smiled significantly. "Young Miss done tol' me dat you was doin' er favor fer 'er. You could stay till daybreak, fer all I care—she is in so much trouble. My Gawd! ef you des could 'a' looked at 'er while she was settin' eatin' 'side dat low rapscallion ter-night, you'd 'a' pitied 'er like I done do. I could 'a' poured de scaldin' coffee down his thick bull neck fum behind when I fetched it in. Why, you kin tell fum de looks of 'im dat his money is all he got! Huh! I say!"

She vanished through the door of her sanctum, letting it shut with a bang that shook the wooden partition.

Presently Charles was conscious of the entry into the room of some one whose step was soundless. It was Mary. She fairly crept into the circle of lamplight from the unlighted hall and sitting-room. Sinking into the chair next to his, she whispered:

"I slipped away. I had to. I couldn't wait to know. Did you find out what—who—"

She was at a loss for words, and he smiled reassuringly. "It was all a mistake. The man Kenneth saw was looking for me. He is an old friend from up North, and a trusty one. He acted oddly, but—but he is rather eccentric, and he was somewhat afraid that I might not want to see him."

"Oh! then it wasn't a detective?"

"No, only an old friend of mine whom I have not seen for some time. I'm sorry it caused you such a fright."

"That doesn't matter." Mary rose, her eyes on the door leading to the veranda. She stood as if listening. The alternate mumbling of two masculine voices came in on the sultry air. She sighed, looked down at Charles, and he saw that the light of relief which had illumined her face had already died down.

"That is out of the way," she whispered, as if to herself in part, "but something almost as bad has come."

"You mean—?" He stood up to keep her company, and saw her sweep her eyes furtively toward the door again.

She nodded as if he had finished a remark that she fully understood. "Albert says that the doctors held another consultation just before he left Carlin this afternoon. They decided that Tobe must be removed to-morrow night at the latest. He came to tell me and to drive me to town with him in the morning."

"And you are going to—allow *him* to furnish the money?"

She nodded again, her face averted. "I've tried everywhere, and so has father. This is no time for sentiment. I shall do my duty."

There was a sound of steps approaching through the hall. There was no mistaking that careless, blustering stride. With a startled, almost frightened expression, Mary whirled toward the kitchen and disappeared just as Frazier entered the sitting-room. An instant later and Frazier would have seen the two together.

"I was looking for Miss Mary," he said, and he glowered on Charles, who had resumed his chair and taken up his knife and fork. Charles thought with lightning swiftness. He did not want to give the man the slightest information, so with a steady, contemptuous stare he simply made no answer.

His manner and silence fairly stunned Frazier, who, in default of anything else to do, simply glared at him for a moment and then turned back toward the veranda. Charles was glad he had taken the course he did, the next moment, for he heard Mary's voice on the veranda speaking to her father. She had slipped out at the kitchen door and had hastily made her way over the grass back to the front. Charles finished his supper and, having nothing just then to do, he started up to his room. He intended to go to the village as soon as he could leave the house unnoticed, and that meant waiting till the family and the guest had retired. As he was ascending the stairs he heard the angry voice of Frazier raised above a normal tone.

"He simply glared at me when I spoke, sneered and didn't open his lips. Now I tell you that if it hadn't been here in your house, Mr. Rowland, I'd have given him a licking that he would remember all his life—a common, roustabout circus tramp acting in such a high and mighty way with me!"

Charles heard Rowland's faint voice in response, but failed to catch his words. It was ten o'clock before he heard the others go to their rooms, and he waited half an hour afterward before stealing down the stairs and starting on his walk to the village.

CHAPTER XXI

The following morning Charles went to his work after breakfasting alone. Aunt Zilla said the others were not yet up. From his corn-field he saw Frazier lead his horse up to the gate and hitch it to his buggy, which had been left there. Presently Mary came out, and was assisted into the vehicle. Frazier attentively tucked the lap-robe about her feet, waved a parting hand to Rowland at the gate, and they drove away. The buggy seat was a narrow one and the couple had to sit close together. Frazier, in a very loutish way, had dropped his right foot over the edge of the buggy, and it was swinging to and fro close to the wheels, like a pendulum.

"I want to warn you and your father both against that fellow," he was saying to the thought-immersed girl, who, pale and rigid, sat by his side. "I am sure there is something crooked about him. He has all the earmarks of a suspicious character. I have helped my brother in several detective cases and I never saw a man I suspected more. It is not all groundless, either, little girl. You see, the last time I was here to stay all night I heard him coming in away after midnight, slipping up the stairs with his shoes in his hand, and this morning between two and three he did the same thing. The first time I stopped him with my gun in my hand, but this morning I let him pass. I intend to give him plenty of rope and watch him. Some suspicious characters were connected with the circus he left, and my frank opinion is that this Brown dropped off here, and is working on your place merely as a blind to cover up some shady game."

"You say you heard him come in this morning between two and three?" Mary said, wonderingly. "Are you not mistaken?"

"No. The truth is I thought I heard him go out about eleven, but was not sure, so I left my door slightly ajar. I am a light sleeper when I want to be, and I heard him at the front door and watched him creep up the stairs without his shoes again. A fellow like that may stare at me and not answer a decent question, but it won't pay him. He doesn't know who he is fooling with."

Mary said nothing. She was wondering what could have taken Charles out at that hour. Finally she thought of the old friend he had mentioned and decided his going out must have been connected with him. But—again she found herself perplexed—why had the "old friend" acted so strangely the preceding day? Why had he hidden in the thicket for so many hours before approaching Charles, and why had he waited for the darkness to fall before accomplishing his purpose? It was queer, very queer, but not for a moment did she doubt that all was as it should be. She found herself actually too miserable to attempt a defense of Charles against Frazier's insinuations. After all, what could be of importance beyond the object of her mission to the village that morning? Frazier had said that he would go to the bank as soon as they reached Carlin and get the necessary money. Whether the life of the wounded man might be saved was very doubtful at best, but one thing seemed settled beyond recall, and that was her marriage to the man by her side. Could it be possible? she kept asking herself, to the thudding accompaniment of the horse's hoofs; yes, yes, it was now inevitable. She was glad, vaguely glad, that Frazier forebore mentioning the subject during the drive. He evidently felt that after the price had been paid she would be ready to complete the bargain. She was beginning to feel herself a slave, but she was a haughty, uncringing one, and well knew the value of what she was giving.

They were entering the village. He told her it was nine o'clock and the bank would be open for business. He could, by going only a short distance out of his way, drop her at Keith's house. How would she like to stop and tell Tobe the good news while he went on to the bank for the money?

It was just what she desired, for she shrank from being seen at the bank on such business. The president, at least, would understand and make mental, if not open, comments. So at the gate of the cottage Frazier left her, promising to come back very soon.

No one was in sight about the place, though the front door was open, and as she entered the gate she heard the grinding tread of thick-shod feet on the boards of the floor within.

The buggy was disappearing down the street as she timidly reached the door. She stood there a moment, and then summoned up the courage to rap on the lintel.

"Go see who it is, Ma," she heard Tobe say. "Maybe they are here already."

Then Mrs. Keith appeared. Her facial expression was more cheerful than it was the day before, her form more erect and confident. She was even courteous in her unlettered way.

"Come in, come in," she said, smiling. "Tobe, it is Miss Mary. He is daft about you, Miss Mary; he hasn't talked about a thing since you left but the sweet way you acted and spoke yesterday. He has a lot to tell you, but I reckon you have heard by this time. News spreads like fire in dry broomsedge in a little place like this."

"I have heard nothing new," Mary answered, wonderingly.

"You say you haven't? Well, everybody else has, here in town, I'll bet a horse. Tobe, she hain't heard. You tell her. He can do it to the queen's taste." Mrs. Keith laughed in a chuckling way.

"You can't fool me with that prim look of yours, Miss Mary," the wounded man said, smiling wanly from his pillow, as Mary bent over him. "You know all about it. I'm not such a fool as to think that two big things would just happen together like you being here yesterday and that other piling in so quick afterwards."

"What do you mean by 'that other'?" Mary asked, in groping surprise.

"Listen, Ma, listen at her!" Tobe laughed. "You know women better 'n I do. Ain't she just making out?"

"She looks to me like she's really puzzled," Mrs. Keith answered. "The truth is, Miss Mary, the money for the Atlanta trip was sent last night, an' we don't know who it come from; but Tobe declares you are at the bottom of it."

"I believe it, and nothing won't shake me from it," Tobe insisted, still smiling confidently.

"You say—you say that you got the money!" Mary fairly gasped in surprise.

"Not only that, but a cool hundred over the amount," Tobe went on. "You'd as well get off your high perch, Miss Mary Rowland. You see, I've got evidence."

"Evidence! I don't understand." Mary was truly bewildered.

"Yes. I had no sooner mentioned it to Mrs. Bartlett this morning than she told about how you was riding from place to place to borrow the money. I can put two and two together easy enough. You simply got the money and are trying to keep from being known in it, that's all."

"I give you my word, Tobe, I know nothing about it," Mary answered, her head hanging in embarrassment. "I confess I *did* try to get the money, and—and I intended to try again to-day. Of course, I'm glad it has come."

"I believe she is in earnest, Tobe," Mrs. Keith said, her gaunt hands clutching the foot of the bedstead. "Well, it is awfully strange, Miss Mary. It happened like this. I was up with Tobe to give him his fever mixture about two o'clock this morning, when down the street, alongside Mrs. Bartlett's picket fence, I saw two men coming. It looked like one was trying to persuade the other to do something that he didn't exactly want to tackle, an' my first thought was that they were niggers trying to rob some hen-roost. But while I was watching, sorter scrouched down on the door-sill, so as not to be seen, the two men come on to our gate and halted. Then in the starlight, that was pretty bright, I saw they was white men. I was still, an' so was they for a minute; then I heard one of them say, sorter peevish-like: 'Go on. Knock at the door, an' when somebody comes out hand it to 'em and say what I told you to say. That ain't hard to remember. Nobody won't hurt you.'"

Tobe laughed merrily from his bed. "'Fraid he'd get shot, I reckon. Think o' that, Miss Mary—afraid he'd have somebody pull down on him when he was out to do a kind deed like that!"

Mrs. Keith's smile blended into her son's mood, and she went on:

"The feller that was doing the ordering opened the gate an' sorter shoved the other one in and stayed back behind hisse'f. On come the other one then, and found me settin' on the door-sill. It seemed to scare the very wits out of 'im, for at the sudden sight of me rising from my seat he made a gruntin' sound, and would have bolted outright if I hadn't halted 'im. I asked him what he wanted. For a minute he was tongue-tied and then he hauled out something that I took for a gun at first, but which was a big fat roll o' Uncle Sam's currency wrapped in tissue-paper.

"'It's a present from a friend an' well-wisher of the young man that was hurt. He hopes he will use it and get well.' That was all he said or would say. He had a sort o' Irish twist to his tongue, I should say, and he had on a nice suit of dark-gray clothes. He was a plumb stranger in this place, it seemed to me. I know I never laid eyes on him before. Well, sir, he just bolted, an' him an' the other feller made off towards the square at a lively gait. I didn't then know what was in the roll, for I had only the feel of my fingers to guide me, but you bet I hustled in and turned up the lamp. You can't imagine my astonishment. I was so crazy that I could not count the stuff. Tobe was asleep, and thar I stood at that center-table with all that boodle. Tobe woke up and saw me, and I told him as well as I could what had happened, and me an' him counted the stuff bill by bill—some tens, some twenties, and as high up as fifties. Five hundred dollars! I locked the front door. I wanted to bolt down the winders, hot as the night was. I thought about getting out Tobe's revolver. As I say, I was plumb off my nut. I knowed I ought not to 'a' done it, but I stayed awake and let Tobe chatter till daybreak. He was in for sending to the doctor an' letting him know at once, but we didn't till about seven o'clock. And Doctor Harrison heated the wires hot between here and

Atlanta. It is all ready fixed down there, and our tickets bought. We are to take the one-o'clock through express. The doctor is going along, too, an' a nurse, just for the trip. The doctor engaged the drawing-room in a sleeping-car, whar he says thar hain't a bit of jolting, and plenty o' space for Tobe to stretch out comfortable. Four buck niggers from the cotton-warehouse is coming to tote Tobe on a cot to the train, and a whole drug-store o' mixtures is going along. The doctor is powerful pleased, and said we was taking it just in the nick o' time. In fact, he said we mustn't be too hopeful, as all depended on what Doctor Elliot would be able to do down thar. He said we was too excited, for one thing, an' that we must calm ourselves down—that a trip like this would be hard enough on Tobe, anyway. I promised I'd keep Tobe quiet, but how can I? Every minute somebody drops in to find out if the tale going about is so, and we go over it again."

"I am afraid that I am exciting him now," said Mary, as she rose. "I must be going. I came in this morning, Tobe, to—to find out how you are," she said, haltingly, "and I am delighted to hear the good news."

"I know you are—I know that," Tobe answered, extending his pale hand. "I'm glad you come, Miss Mary. Coming like you have has wiped out all hard feeling between me and your brothers. If I get well I'll do my level best to keep the thing out of court, and if I die I'll leave word that I was as much to blame as the boys."

CHAPTER XXII

The sensation which came over the gentle girl as she went out into the cool morning air was indescribable. She felt almost as if the balmy sunlight were some joy-giving fluid to be drunk like wine. Her step was buoyant. She told herself that a veritable miracle had happened. She could not explain it, but it had happened. Her unspoken prayer constantly framed in heart-sinking desire had been answered. She didn't want aid to come from Albert Frazier, and it had not.

This thought reminded her that she must try to see him before he had put himself to the trouble of getting the money at the bank. So she hastened toward the square.

She was soon entering the bank, and in the little vestibule she saw Frazier in earnest conversation with an employee of the bank. Frazier's heavy brow was clouded over as with displeasure. He failed to note her presence at first, and she heard him say, angrily:

"I don't see any necessity of waiting for him. It is a mere matter of form, anyway. I'm in a hurry right now."

The embarrassed clerk was about to reply when Frazier noticed Mary and turned to meet her, his hat in hand.

"I've been delayed by these idiots," he said, fuming. "I've always had my check honored without delay, but simply because I overchecked a little yesterday they want me to wait and see the president. Bosh! I'll show them a thing or two! We need another bank here, anyway, and I'll get one started. These fellows have a monopoly and are getting entirely too particular. I suppose you got tired waiting for me, and—"

"No, it wasn't that," Mary corrected him. "The Keiths have already got the money."

"Got the money!" he repeated. He took her arm, and in almost benumbed astonishment led her out to his buggy in front. She explained as well as she could, and noted the slow look of sullen chagrin steal over his face. "And you say they don't know who sent it? That sounds fishy to me. Who ever heard of such a thing?"

Mary was unable to make an adequate reply. His face was clouded over and growing darker every minute.

"Well," he asked, "what are you going to do this morning?"

"I want to call on Mrs. Quinby at the hotel," she answered. "I promised to come the next time I was in town. You mustn't bother about me. I shall take dinner with her."

As she spoke Mary turned toward the hotel, and Frazier walked along with her, taking care to be on the outside of the pavement, as was the custom. The look of disappointed anger was leaving his face and a shrewd expression was taking its place.

"I'll be around to take you home after dinner, then," he remarked, his glance failing to meet her upturned eyes. "The truth is, I must see my brother and have a roundabout chat with him in regard to the boys."

"In regard to them?" Mary said, in a startled undertone.

"Yes. It is like this," he went on, his shrewd expression deepening. "Things are not quite in as good shape as they were, little girl. I didn't intend to tell you yet, but I reckon I may as well. It seems that the grand jury has been criticizing my brother in a roundabout way for not making a more thorough effort to—to locate the boys, and I'm a little bit afraid that he may telegraph to Texas and make inquiry of the man whose name was signed to the letter I showed him. I'll have to watch him closely and try to prevent that, you know."

"Oh!" Mary muttered, in alarm. "Then he might—"

"Yes, if he got on to that trick he would be furious and maybe see through the whole thing—find out about my interest in you and all the rest. He saw me with you the other day, and I had to pretend that I was pumping you on the sly to help him locate your brothers. It went down, for he is none too bright, but there is no telling when he may suspicion the truth and then, you see, he might take a notion to search the mountains. That would be bad, wouldn't it? But I'm going to work hard to-day to throw him off. If he should happen to see us together I'll tell him—you see, he knows I've had financial deals with your father—I'll tell him that you came to pay me some interest or something like that. As a last resort I may—I don't say it would come to that—but as a last resort I may just come out flat with the truth and tell him, you know, that you are—well, what you are to me, and throw our case on his mercy. I don't know how he would act about it, I'm sure, but he might, you know, give the boys a chance to—to—"

He seemed unable to proceed further in his crude diplomacy, and Mary, blinded by terror to his designs, suppressed a deep sigh, and with tight lips remained silent. They were now at the entrance of the hotel.

"I'll find out all I can," he said, as he was leaving her, "and will let you know when I come for you this afternoon. By the way, I'll drive around to the rear door, and we can go out by the back street without passing through the square. We have to be very careful. It is a wonder folks haven't got on to my trips out your way, but they haven't so far, it seems, and they must not just now. It might upset things awfully."

Mary went into the office of the hotel. Sam Lee was behind the counter, and came to her quickly.

"How d' do, Miss Mary?" he cried, flushing to the roots of his smoothly matted hair, which lay over his eyebrows like the bang of a mountain school-girl. "Mrs. Quinby is out the back way, buying a load of frying-chickens from a farmer. She will be in in a minute. Will you wait here, or will you go up to the parlor?"

Mary decided to go to the parlor, dreading the entrance of some acquaintance and not being in the mood for greetings or conversation. Sam accompanied her, gallantly opening the parlor door and going in to raise the blinds of the shaded windows.

"Oh, by the way, Miss Mary," he said, as he was about to leave, "how did you come out with that circus man I told you about that wanted to do farm work?"

"Very well," the girl replied.

"And he is satisfactory?"

"Yes, quite," Mary answered.

"I was wondering how he would suit," Lee pursued, thoughtfully, "for he seemed a sort of a misfit to me. You see, I meet all sorts of characters from everywhere, almost, and I'd never have put him down as a good farm-hand."

"He does very well," Mary said, evasively. "We are entirely satisfied."

"Well, he is odd in many ways," Lee continued, observantly. "He never comes in town in the daytime, but always at night, and late at that. He was here last night about midnight. There was a queer chap here that refused to register. I say refused, but I can't say he did that, either, for he simply paid for a whole day in advance at the transient rate and was assigned a room. We always require a guest to register, but he was so busy asking questions about the people and the town that I overlooked it. Well, if that looks odd, it seems a little more so that your man should come in last night, wake me up after twelve, and want to see the fellow. The funny part of it was that when I asked him who he wanted to see he didn't know, or pretended that he didn't, anyway. He set in to describe him—said he had on a dark-gray sack-suit and wore a green necktie, and the like. It was No. 37 that he was after, all right, and I showed him up to the room. They must have had an appointment, for Thirty-seven was up, reading a paper, when I knocked. Then I remembered that he had questioned me about the circus and the men that dropped out here. I remembered then that I told him about getting Brown a job on your farm. It was all odd, but I run across so many strange things here in this joint that I have quit keeping track of 'em. However—now I hope you will take this as coming from a friend, Miss Mary?—I believe, if I was you, and in as much trouble as you are already, why, I'd be on my guard with that fellow Brown. I heard the sheriff talking one day to his brother about the outlaws that was with that circus, and I must say, while I am not a detective of the first water, I think for a common hired hand your Mr. Brown is a mystery. I noticed that the two did not shake hands, and that looked as though they had met that day before. They just waited till I left, and then the man in the gray suit closed the door. They must have stayed there an hour or more, and then—now comes the strange part—they come down, passed through the office, and went out on the square. They may have been gone an hour when the fellow came back alone and slipped up to his room."

"A dark-gray suit!" Mary said to herself, recalling Mrs. Keith's description of the mysterious visitor at her house, "and a friend of Mr. Brown!" Her heart was beating rapidly now. She was afraid that the clerk would note the excitement which was fast mastering her, and she abruptly changed the subject. Going to the window, she looked out, and then said:

"I see Mrs. Quinby is coming in. Please tell her that I am up here, but ask her not to hurry on my account."

"I will—I'll do that, Miss Mary," said Lee, backing from the room, a mystified look in his observant eyes. "Yes, I'll tell her, and she will be right up."

CHAPTER XXIII

It was growing dusk when Frazier brought Mary back to the farm. He did not stop, having some important business to attend to that evening, and drove back to the village. Mary was very unhappy. From a window in the parlor of the hotel she had seen Tobe Keith taken to the train, and the silent awe of the bystanders, the grave looks of the doctors, the nurse, and Mrs. Keith in her best dress induced a feeling of vast depression. She had heard people on the pavement below saying that Keith would never be cured—that no man in his condition could stand the operation that was proposed. She thought, too, that Mrs. Quinby had failed to give her much encouragement. Indeed, it was almost as if her good friend were trying to prepare her for the worst.

Finding no one in sight about the house, Mary went straight to the barn to acquaint her brothers with all that had taken place. She tried to shake off the morbid feeling which clung to her so persistently, not realizing that it was due to the fact of her still being, in a sense, in the power of Albert Frazier. It was true that he had not paid for Keith's expenses, but he had managed to make her feel her absolute dependence on him for the safety of her brothers. She shuddered, and fairly cringed, under the thought that she had not repulsed him when he had put his arm around her in a secluded spot on the road home and kissed her on the cheek. The spot stung now as if it were a wound which her rising flush was irritating.

She had seen her brothers in their loft, and was entering the house, when she met Charles descending from his room.

"You are late," he smiled. "We have had supper already."

"So have I," she answered. "I took it early with Mrs. Quinby at the hotel. We drove rapidly, as Mr. Frazier had to hurry back to town."

She sat down on the veranda, and he stood, with an unusual air of embarrassment, quite near to her.

"Sit down, please," she said. "I know you are tired from your work."

He obeyed willingly enough, but it seemed to her that there was a certain undefinable restraint about him. They sat silent for several minutes.

She was watching his face attentively. At any other time she might have been amused. Did he not realize that his failure to inquire about Tobe Keith was an indirect confession of the part he had played the night before?

"Well, they took Tobe to Atlanta to-day," she suddenly announced, still eying him closely.

"Oh, did they?" he exclaimed.

She said nothing for another moment. "I suppose you think that Albert furnished the money?" she continued. She smiled now at his look of confusion, and as he made no reply she went on: "Well, he didn't. When I got to Mrs. Keith's this morning I learned that some one else had given her the necessary money. No one knows from whom it came."

"That's strange," Charles said, feebly.

"Yes, it was very strange. It seems that the man who brought it was an absolute stranger. He turned it over to Mrs. Keith, but refused to say who sent it. The whole town is talking about it."

"Very strange indeed," Charles said, still awkwardly. "I hope the poor fellow will stand his journey well."

"Yes, sending money like that was very strange," Mary persisted. "Most persons do their charity differently. They blow a horn, sound a trumpet, or get it into the papers; but this is genuine charity. However, it will leak out. You can't keep things like that hidden long."

"What do the doctors think—do they think that his chances are good for recovery?"

Again Mary ignored his remark, smiling faintly through the dusk as she watched his obvious floundering. "No, a deed like that is too rare and fine for the author of it to keep hidden. Oh, if you could have been there with me this morning and seen that poor mother's face and her son's as they told about how the money came, you would have felt like crying for joy. I did. I couldn't help it. I broke down. I think I know now what heaven is like. It is like I felt at that moment. They were like two happy children, and I was happy, too, and grateful." Here Mary actually sobbed. "I was grateful to some unknown person who had saved me from—from the most humiliating thing that ever threatened me. I was willing to give my life rather than accept that aid from Albert Frazier, and it had come in that mysterious way like a gift from God at the very last moment. You must help me—help me find out who did it, Mr. Brown. Will you?"

He stared like a man in a bewildered dream. "Yes, yes," he stammered, "I will, but why bother about it now, anyway?"

"'Bother about it'! How can you use such words? You see, you are not in my place. You can't realize how I feel. I want to see him. I want to look into his face, as — as I am looking into yours now, and tell him just how I feel and what he has done for me. I want to repay him. I want to tell him that there is nothing — nothing under high heaven I would not do for him. I want him to tell me what to do in all this darkness that has gathered about me and is stifling hope and life out of me, young as I am. I want to be his faithful friend till the end of time. I want to serve him — to be his slave — anything."

Charles rose to his feet awkwardly. "I—I see how you feel, Miss Rowland," he said. "But I am afraid I am keeping you from your duties. By the way, your father has gone over to Dodd's. He came by the field and asked me to tell you that he would not be back till about bedtime."

Mary got up also. She reached out and took his arm and walked with him to the other end of the veranda. He felt her hand trembling. She pressed his arm against her side. "You shall not go yet!" she cried, passionately. "I have been beating about the bush. I know that you did that thing. I've known it all day. No one else knows, but I do — and it has made me so happy. I could not have taken it from any one else, but I want to take it from you. I want to take it, because I know you wanted to give it. I know how you feel about me, and I want you to know how I feel about you."

Had the heavens split above him, dropping flames of celestial fire, he could not have felt more ecstatic. She had suddenly paused and lifted her wondrous face to his. Her beautiful lips hung quivering like drooping flowers. He was a man of remarkable restraint, but sometimes acted under impulse. He took her face between his hands, he bent to kiss her unresisting lips; then suddenly he checked himself. A picture of his whole past flashed before him. He was a man with a price on his head and liable to exposure at any moment. What right had he to the heart of such a girl as this — to win it under her father's kindly roof through the agency of a just act to a suffering man. He dropped his hands. With his face full of deepening agony he simply looked at her fixedly and remained mute.

"What is the matter?" she asked. "You are troubled about something; I see it. I've known it a long time."

"Miss Rowland—" he began.

"*Miss Rowland!*" she cried, impatiently. "Charlie—don't you see I call you Charlie! I have called you that a hundred times to myself since finding out what you did. I used it when I prayed to you — actually prayed to you this afternoon to forgive me for allowing that man to kiss me on the way home."

"To kiss you!" She saw him start and stand quivering under her earnest upward stare. She saw him lower his head as a slave being scourged with thongs of steel—a slave who was determined to show no signs of suffering. "He kissed you! Then—then—my God! you are engaged to him! After all, you are engaged to him!"

"No, not quite that!" she cried, in almost piteous appeal, "but I was afraid, from the way he talked—Oh, Charlie, you can't understand! It is true that I did not have to take his money to-day, but I am still at his mercy."

"Still at his mercy!" Charles groaned, his eyes ablaze with blended lights of fury and despair.

Falteringly she explained Frazier's veiled threats. As she ended she put her hands on his shoulders and again she lifted her face to his. Again he was swept by the flames of desire; again he held himself in check; again the shackles of his hopeless condition bit into the flesh of his memory, sinking to the very bones of his consciousness. What could he do? He might tell her of the blight on his life which had isolated him from all others, but what good would that do? And had he not promised William that the truth should never be known? No, his fate was sealed. He had won her, but he must lose her. No honorable man could ask such a woman to share such a precarious fate. She would be less unfortunate even as the wife of a man like Frazier. Charles was a social outcast who had crept into the shelter of unsuspecting hospitality. One loophole, and one only, flashed before his eyes on the screen of temptation, and that was to go back to Boston and demand his moral rights. But that would mean that he was failing to make good those sacred obligations. That would mean the degradation of William, and the terrible blight upon his family whom till now he had saved from humiliation and pain. No, that course would rouse condemnation even in the heart of the girl before him. Was there anything she would not do or suffer to save her brothers? Could such a selfless creature approve of a man less selfless? Her wondrous face, the all but visible halo about it, was his answer.

"What is the matter, Charlie?" she asked. "Have you lost respect for me for allowing him to kiss me? I could have died when he did it—I hated myself so, for I was thinking of what you would think if you knew. But I was afraid—afraid of him. If he were to become angry and turn against me, he would give my brothers up at once. He would lead in the search for them, and if he knew or suspected—"

"Suspected what?" he interrupted, as she paused and stood shuddering, her eyes filling with shadows.

"If he suspected that I—if he suspected how I feel to you—he would try to kill you. Already he is your enemy, already he suspects you of—"

"Suspects me of what?"

"—of being a fugitive from the law who left the circus to avoid being arrested. It is absurd, ridiculous! Only such a man as he is would dream of such a thing. If ten thousand persons testified under oath that such was the case I'd not believe them."

"You'd not believe them?" he echoed, and he hugged to himself his inherent right to her faith in him as an honest man, for dishonest he had never been.

"No, I'd not believe them. It seems to me now that I believe only in you. In all humanity I know of no one I trust so much—my father, my brothers, even my sweet dead—" She hesitated, then finished, fervently: "Yes, even my mother. She would forgive me if she were here and understood."

Again the infinite yearning to take her to his breast swept over him. He put his arm about her; he was drawing her to him, when, with a groan of tortured resolution, he released her. His face was white in the dusk as he stood grimly silent.

"I can't understand you, Charlie," she whispered, tenderly, and yet in a groping, bewildered tone. "Somehow I know—I'm *sure* that you—love me."

"Oh, I *do!*" he said, quickly, "but I have no right to do so. I can't explain. It would do no good, anyway. I am bound by honor not to reveal certain things, even to you."

"I see, I see; now I begin to understand *a little*," she said, wistfully. "And I won't press you to tell me, either. It may be that you are bound to others, as I am bound. Though I have the sweet comfort of talking to you about it. I couldn't bear it all but for you, but I shall be braver, less complaining, from now on."

She lowered her head; she stood back from him. An overwhelming sense of losing her pressed down on him like a pall. He wondered if in her mute attitude lay any touch of womanly resentment against him for the stand he had taken. He held out his hands to her, but she simply sighed and slowly shook her head.

"What is it?" he asked, tremblingly.

"It must be as you say," she answered. "I wonder why God brought us together like this. It is strange—strange—strange!"

He could not answer. His arms sank to his sides. She turned and left him.

CHAPTER XXIV

Like a sheer mechanical thing, actuated by some external force, he went down the steps and on to the lawn. Standing near the front gate, he saw Rowland coming down the road, and stepped aside to avoid meeting him. He was in no mood for mere passing platitudes such as the old man often dealt with. Charles crept around the house on the dewy grass, and found himself in the vicinity of the barn. Suddenly, despite his own depression, he felt a surge of pity pass over him at the thought of the plight of the two boys. They were her brothers, and on that account he loved them. He wondered if they were asleep already. Presently, while he stood looking at the dark, sloping roof of the barn, he saw a figure steal out from the kitchen door and move across the sward toward the barn. It was Mary. She passed close to him, but made no sign of having seen him. Again his fears of having offended her womanhood besieged him. She had said that she understood him, but she could not know how vast and grave his obligations were. Was there any way by which he could make them known and still be true to his vow? He could see none, and to suffer under her displeasure might only be another burden to bear. He walked back to the front of the house. He saw Rowland ascending the stairs with a candle in his hand on his way to his room. Twenty minutes passed and then he saw Mary returning. How it was that he had the boldness to advance toward her he could not have explained, for, despite her open admissions in regard to himself, he still felt that he was only what he appeared to the outer world to be—a hired man of no social standing.

"I was hoping that I'd see you again to-night," she began, in an even tone. "I've just been to see my poor boys. Martin has a cold and I am giving him some medicine for it. I wanted to make a confession to you before I went to sleep to-night. I took the liberty of telling them something which you may not want them to know."

"About you and Frazier?" he ventured.

"No, no!" she answered, with a near approach to the sweet tone which she had used on the veranda. "Have you held that thought all by yourself here on the lawn? Was it that which made you stand like a post as I passed just now? No, I did not mention his name. They don't like him. They don't want me to—to—I sha'n't use the word. I think that is why you are so gloomy to-night—I mean because I said I was still at his mercy. This is what I told the boys. I could not help it. I could not keep it back. They won't tell, anyway. They promised, and do you know they would not displease you for anything; they admire you intensely. I told them who it was that sent Tobe Keith that money. I was partly guessing, but I told them that you sent it, too, by the friend who came here to see you and caused them such a fright."

Charles could find no words with which to answer; he heard her laugh softly as she stepped close to him and put her hand to his lapel and held it as she might have done were she pinning a flower upon it.

"Your good deeds tie your tongue," she said, "but you can't lie. You would lie out of this if you could. You tried to hide that act of goodness by what really was a sly trick, but I saw through it. I saw through it because I wanted it to be that way."

He caught her hand and held it, telling himself that it was a brief offense surely when he had made up his mind to give her up forever. But, oh, how it throbbed and pleaded in his clasp! Each little finger seemed to have a soul of its own. He dared not look into her eyes. Their drooping lashes seemed breakable bars between him and a life of eternal bliss.

"Are you angry because I told them?" she asked.

"Not if it pleased you," he said, passionately. "That is all I live for—to please you."

"Do you mean it? Do you mean it, Charlie?" and she pressed his fingers—his calloused fingers—in her soft ones. She raised her face to his. "Oh, I know you do, but I am dying to hear you say so."

He nodded. He took a deep, quivering breath and slowly exhaled it; she felt him trembling; his face was grim and pale.

"I have no right," he said, "to talk to you this way—to allow you to— to talk to me in a way that would be impossible if you knew my whole history." He was speaking now as a man might just before the black cap was placed over his face. "I ought not to have come here to your father's house without—without telling him and you the full truth. I am a fugitive from the law. I can say that much without breaking my word to others. At any moment I may be caught and imprisoned. In that case your family would be mentioned as harboring me, and I had no right to let you unsuspectingly run that risk."

"You—you a fugitive from the law?" Mary cried. "You!"

He released her hand and mutely nodded. He kept his eyes now on the ground.

With a motion as swift as the flight of a hummingbird she caught his hand. She held it against her breast and forced his eyes to rise to hers. "I won't believe it! I won't! I won't! I won't! God will not let that be true, Charlie. You've come into my tormented life like a sweet dream of everything that is good and noble. You can't make me believe it. You have reasons for deceiving me. What they are I don't know, but what you say is not true. It would kill me to believe it. When Albert Frazier mentioned it I knew that it was too absurd to think about."

"Well, he was wrong about *that*," said Charles, seeing her drift. "There were certain men in the circus who left about the time I did, and there were warrants out for their arrest. I was not one of them. I left for fear that certain questions regarding my identity might be put to me that I could not answer, and for the additional reason that I was sick of the life I was leading. The — the offense with which I am charged dates further back. I did not think that I'd ever have to tell you these things, but I find that I must. I am not a safe man for you to know — certainly not a man worthy of — of the things you have said to-night. This living here and helping you a little has been like heaven to me, but it can't go on. I am a misfit in life. I am an outcast for all time. You may be holding a sort of ideal of me — women in their deep purity will do those things sometimes — but I must undeceive you. You must see me as I really am. I was a drunkard, a gambler — disgraced in the town I lived in, expelled from the clubs I belonged to, found guilty in court; I came away to hide myself from the eyes of all who knew me. The new life has changed me to some extent. I see things differently. I think I have a keener moral sense. Adversity seems to have awakened it in me, but Fate is punishing me severely, for the consequences of my past, it will always — always stand between me and the things I now want."

Mary still clung to his hand. Through his desperate recital she had looked steadfastly into his eyes. "I don't care what you have been," she said, under her breath. "It is what you are now that counts with me. The greatest men and the best in history have made mistakes when they were young. It is for you to judge whether — whether we can ever be anything more to each other than we are now. I don't think it amounts to much which it is, if only we love each other. That is the main thing. I don't know how you feel, but I can never love any other man — never!"

He lowered his head, but she saw that his eyes were ablaze.

"I think"—he was speaking now very earnestly, very despondently—"that I shall leave you as soon as my summer's work is over—that is, if you are out of your trouble by then. I could not go while you are so unhappy. I couldn't stand that."

"Oh, you mustn't go!" she sobbed, pressing the back of his hand to her wet eyes. "Why need you go?"

"Because the longer I stay the worse it will be for both of us, and I am afraid that my presence here will be discovered. I am using my own name. I never threw it off. I must not be taken here. There are a thousand reasons why I should avoid a chance of that. You are the main one."

"Yes, that would kill me," she asserted. Almost unconsciously she kissed his hand, she fondled it as a mother might that of a dying child. "I couldn't live after that." Suddenly, and after a pause, she fixed her eyes on his face again. "I want you to do something for me," she faltered.

"What is it?" he asked.

"I don't want you to tell father or my brothers what you have told me to-night."

"Why?" he wondered.

"Because they would misunderstand it all. They don't know you as I do, and I could not bear to have them misjudge you. You may have broken the law, but you said you were once in the habit of drinking too much. I am sure that if you did wrong you really were not conscious of what you were doing. No man with your nobility of character could do wrong knowingly. It is not in you and never was. Don't tell my father and brothers. Will you?"

"If you don't want me to do so, I shall not," he promised. "I only wished you to understand my situation and be on your guard. It may be that a man's adoration of a woman may stir her sympathy and even cause her to imagine that she reciprocates his feeling, and you must have known how I felt about—"

"Yes," she interrupted, "I know. That night in the cabin—oh, that night! I've kissed its memory a thousand times. That night I saw love born in your eyes and I knew that for you no other girl existed. Is it any wonder that I loved you when I saw how humbly and unselfishly you were striving to save me from pain? Imagine that I reciprocate, indeed! There is no imagination about my feeling for you, Charlie. This morning, when I discovered who it was that had sent that money to Tobe Keith, and knew that you were trying to keep me from discovering that you did it, I was so happy that I could not speak. In my mind I saw you stealing out of the house at night, meeting your friend at the hotel, and his slipping up to that cottage door while you remained hidden from view. Is it any wonder that I gloated in triumph over the fact that it was you who did the act of mercy rather than Albert Frazier? Is it any wonder that when he kissed me—It was just on the cheek, my darling, just here and it was as cold as ice. Kiss me, Charlie, kiss me—kiss me." Her face was raised to his, her lips were poised expectantly.

A storm of doubt swept over him, and then he clasped her in his arms and pressed his lips to hers.

CHAPTER XXV

It was just after sundown, two days later. Charles was at work in a patch of cabbages near the outer fence of the farm, not far from the barn. Presently, happening to look toward the thicket, he saw a man in a gray suit of clothes and a straw hat cautiously emerging. Their eyes met. The man waved a handkerchief and then stood still, partly hidden by the bushes among which he stood. Charles glanced toward the house and, seeing no one, he put down his hoe and walked toward the man. They met in the edge of the thicket and clasped hands.

"You are back already—or did you really go to Atlanta?" he questioned, eagerly.

"Yes, sir. I would have written, Mr. Charles, but—well, I thought it might not be best. You didn't say that I might. Yes, sir. I attended to everything the best I could. I was at the train when they got there with the poor fellow, and saw them take him from the Pullman at the station and put him into an ambulance from the sanatorium."

"How did he look? How did he seem to stand the trip?" Charles asked, anxiously.

"I couldn't tell, sir. I couldn't see his face. The police kept the crowd back, but the old woman—his mother—looked worried, and I thought the doctor from here did also, and the nurse that came along. I think they gave him a stimulant. I know I saw a bottle and a glass in the doctor's hand. They drove slowly, and so I had no trouble keeping up with them afoot. I saw them drive into the grounds of Doctor Elliot's sanatorium, and I felt relieved. I would have telegraphed you, but did not know how to reach you here in the country."

"Well, that was two days ago," Charles said. "Have you heard anything more?"

"They operated last night, sir. I was there early this morning. I went into the grounds, hoping to get information, but a guard stopped me at the door and refused to tell me anything. I was trying to persuade him, sir—I know how to deal with such persons, as a rule—but this fellow, although I showed him some money, refused to talk at all. I was greatly worried till

Mrs. Keith chanced along and saw me. She recognized me, sir, and she ran out and grabbed my hand. She wanted me to go into the public sitting-room, but I refused. Oh, she was crowding me with questions; they came so fast, sir, that she wouldn't let me get a word in! However, she was so—I may say so gay, sir, that I began to think she had good news. Finally, Mr. Charles, she told me that the operation was done, and most successfully. In fact, sir, she says Doctor Elliot says her son's recovery is almost assured, though it was a narrow escape."

"That is good news, Mike—wonderful news!" Charles exclaimed. "It will make some people very happy."

"The young lady especially, I presume, sir?"

"Yes, her most of all, Mike."

"Well, I think she need not worry any more about the poor fellow. I am sure, from all I hear down there, that he will soon be on his feet. That old lady, Mrs. Keith, fairly hung on to me, Mr. Charles. I can hold my own with the average man in a shady deal of this sort, but not a woman out of her head with gratitude and curiosity combined. Why, sir, I thought once that she'd have me arrested to force me to tell her who sent the money. It was only by lying straight out that I got away from her clutches. I told her, I did, sir, that I'd go down-town and ask permission to let the cat out of the bag and return. That was the only thing that saved me. I'd have been there yet but for that little trick."

"So she doesn't know that, anyway?" Charles said.

"No, sir, she hasn't the slightest idea. She tried to make me say that I did it, but of course I couldn't allow that, sir. So I simply stuck to it that I'd been sent by some one else—a friend, a well-wisher and—you know what you said to tell her."

"And what are your present plans?" Charles asked.

"I must return home, sir. I want to stop in New York and see my mother, and then go back to Boston. I have been away as long as I can manage it now, sir."

"You have been of great service to me, Mike," Charles said. It was growing darker now. The twilight was thickening, the yellow glow in the western sky above the mountain-tops was fading away. They strolled down a path toward the house. "Yes, Mike," Charles continued, "no man on earth could have done me such a valuable service. If you hadn't come that poor fellow would have died and half a dozen persons would have been stricken down with grief and overwhelmed with disgrace."

"And the young lady—the beautiful young lady, sir—you say she would have suffered most of all?"

"Yes, most of all, Mike. But you mustn't go away with the thought that—that there is anything of a serious nature between me and her, for there isn't. No one else here knows the truth, but I have told her—given her to understand—that something is hanging over me which will forever keep us apart. She belongs to an old and honorable family, Mike, and I am what you see me now in these old clothes; I am a servant and can never be anything else. So you are going back? Well, I want you, if you can, to see Mason in New York and thank him for sending you to me; and as for the people at home—"

"I was going to ask what I might do in regard to them, Mr. Charles," Michael said, suddenly, as Charles paused. "Your brother and your uncle, who lives with us now, will not ask questions, but the missis—she will. She is sure to, the first opportunity."

"You think—" Again Charles lost his way to satisfactory expression.

"Yes, sir. You see, she has always questioned me on my return from New York, to find out if I have heard anything. She will want to know this time, too, sir, and I confess that it will be hard to fool her. She looks one so straight in the face, you know, sir, and the truth is she loves you as if you were her own brother, sir. Nothing wins a woman's heart like being tender to her child, and she knows how you loved the little lady, sir. Pardon me, Mr. Charles, for making a suggestion. The missis can be trusted where you are concerned. She'd die rather than betray your interests. Would you mind if I frankly told her that I have seen you and that you are well and safe? I think, sir, that it would only be fair to her, after all the worry she has had about you. It would make her very happy, Mr. Charles. You see, as it is, she does not even know if you are dead or alive, and—and—But it is not for me to advise, sir."

Charles hesitated. Then he said: "I think you may tell her, Mike. I couldn't risk writing back, but I can trust you with that news of me. Give her my love, please, and tell her to kiss Ruth for me, and—and, well, tell her anything you like. She won't betray me. After all, I'm glad to be able in this way to relieve her mind."

So closely were they occupied with their parting words that they failed to see a figure approaching from the direction of the house. It was Mary, and she was close to them when they heard her step and, turning, saw her.

"Oh," she exclaimed, on seeing the stranger, "I thought it was one of my—" She checked herself abruptly.

For a moment Charles stood as if dazed, and then recovered himself. "This is my friend, Michael Gilbreth," he said. "He is the one who aided us so substantially the other night."

"Oh, and I have wanted so much to meet you—to thank you," said Mary. She held out both her hands to the astonished servant, and he awkwardly took them.

"I'm pleased, I'm sure, miss, to meet you, but—but," he stammered, "you must not thank me. Mr. Charles is back of all that. You see, miss, it wasn't expense out of *my* pocket—"

"I know—I understand, but you kindly delivered it," Mary said. "And that was a great service. It may result in saving a human life and avert much misery and misfortune."

"But, you see, I owed the money to Mr. Charles," Michael went on, simply. "He advanced it to me a long time ago when I was in need myself. He is always doing the like, miss, and it is strange, for the minute I pay him back out it goes to somebody else; but—"

"Mike has just brought good news from Atlanta," Charles, hot with embarrassment, broke in.

"Oh, have you?" Mary cried.

Michael hesitated, looking at Charles, who answered for him: "Yes. The operation was highly successful. Keith's recovery is now practically assured."

"Oh, that *is* good news!" Mary cried, her eyes flashing with joy, and she prevailed upon Michael to tell her all the details. When he had concluded she looked toward the barn. "I must hurry and tell my—tell my brothers." She was starting away when she turned back. "You must stay with us, Mr. Gilbreth. We have plenty of room. Any friend of Mr. Brown's is welcome at our house."

Michael threw an awkward glance at Charles and then said: "I thank you, miss, but I must hurry away. My time is up."

"Then I'll say good-by." Mary held out her hands. "I shall never forget your kindness, and I wish you a long, happy life."

The two men lapsed into silence as she flitted away in the gloom.

Presently Michael, with a deep sigh, said: "Now I understand, Mr. Charles—I understand how you are placed. Why, sir, she is the most exquisite young lady I ever saw! She's not only beautiful, but, sir, she is the real thing in womanhood, and her voice—I have never heard one like it. It is like music, sir, full of sweetness and gentleness and human sympathy. Oh, I can't blame you for wanting to stay here and cut out all the rest. Labor such as you are doing now with such companionship—"

"You mustn't misunderstand, Mike," said Charles, and his voice sank low in his throat. "She can never be more to me than a friend. You know why well enough. I am trying to be of use to her, that's all."

"But your *heart*, Mr. Charles," Mike said. "You'd not be a natural man if you could keep from loving a lady like her, sir. In fact, I see it in you. You never were struck that way at home, sir. Among all the fair ones you knew up there, none of them—"

"We mustn't talk of that, Mike," Charles broke in, huskily. "I don't allow myself to think of the impossible. How are you going to Carlin?"

"Afoot, sir. I like it. I can easily make my train to-night. Well, sir, you will have to be going in and I'll say good-by, Mr. Charles."

"Good-by, Mike. Your coming has been a great help to me."

Tears suddenly filled the servant's eyes, and, turning swiftly, he walked back toward the thicket and disappeared.

As he neared the house Charles saw Mary coming from the barn. Her head was cast down and she was moving slowly. They met near the kitchen door.

"I've just left them," she said, in a voice full of joyful emotion. "Oh, I can't describe all that took place. They have both been in abject despair night and day since Tobe was taken away, and when I told them the news they—I can't describe it. The joy seemed to bewilder them, stupefy them. Kenneth sat still on the horse-trough—I couldn't see his face in the dark, but I heard him catch his breath, and when he tried to speak he choked up. And Martin—he came to me and put his head on my breast and cried like the child he really is at times. Oh, Charlie, life is wonderful! I am in heaven to-night, and my reason tells me that I never could have reached it in any other way than through what I've suffered and your help. Yes, you—you did it. But for your money all would have been lost."

"You forget that you yourself would have paid it if I had not," Charles argued, "or rather, it would have been paid by—"

"No, there's where you are wrong," Mary protested. "My father tells me that the bank would not have cashed Albert's check that day. He has met with great losses in some enterprises, and is on the verge of bankruptcy. No, if it hadn't been for you all would have been lost. When your friend said just now that you were always doing kind deeds he said only what I already knew to be the truth. You are the most unselfish man I ever knew. Is it any wonder that I—" She did not finish, but suddenly turned and left him.

CHAPTER XXVI

Two days later Rowland came back from the village. He brought the news that Keith was well on the road to recovery, and that he had had a talk with the district attorney, who had intimated discreetly that it was unlikely that grave charges would be made against his sons, owing to the disposition of the Keiths to drop the matter. The boys might be charged with disorderly conduct and fined, but an arrest would not be made and the case might not reach the court at all, owing to the sympathy of the judge, who felt that Kenneth and Martin had already been punished enough.

The next morning after this Charles found both the boys at the breakfast-table when he came down. To his surprise, they announced that they were going to help him in the field, that they were willing now to run the risk of being seen by passers-by, though they were going to keep out of sight as much as possible. So, accordingly, they both secured hoes and set to work in the cotton-field.

All that morning they worked with energy, which, no doubt, was due to their long confinement and the exhilarating sense of freedom. Mary came down herself at noon and brought them all a delightful lunch which she had prepared with her own hands. It was a warm day, with plenty of sunshine, and they all sat in the shade of some oaks which stood on the edge of the field. When the lunch was over Mary got ready to go home and the boys hastened for their hoes, to resume work.

"You are wonderful!" and Mary smiled up at Charles, who was helping her put the things back into her basket.

"Because I eat so much?" he jested.

"Because you are having the most remarkable effect on my brothers. Even Kenneth has changed. He says he wants to be like you. He sees what your industry is producing for us. We have never had such promising crops before. Then—then your talks have done them good. I mean your talks on moral lines."

"'Moral lines,'" he repeated, sadly. "Take it from me that I am a most unworthy adviser. I do not want to sail under false colors. Your brothers are fortunate in having had their lesson without fatal and lasting consequences.

As I have told you—as I have tried to have you understand—I shall always be what I am—a man without a home, without a family, without a country, for I cannot legally cast a vote. What your brothers are escaping from—long imprisonment—I am in danger of every hour. So far I have escaped, but I may not be able to keep it up. Do you know—and I must say it now, so that you will understand thoroughly—do you know, while I dread being taken back home in shackles, I dread another thing far more, and that is being arrested here. Your friends would laugh at you for being hoodwinked by a criminal tramp in whom you have such absurd confidence as to give him food and shelter."

Mary's eyes were full of unshed tears. She hastily crammed the table-cloth into the basket. "Why are you talking to me like this to-day, when I was so happy?" she gulped.

"Because you insist on saying things about my—my worthiness, when I am so overwhelmingly unworthy," he answered, grimly, standing over her, his fine brow wrinkled with inner pain and bared to the sun. "Besides, as I say, you must be prepared for it if I suddenly leave without a hint of my intentions. If I could live a thousand years and be trained in the highest modes of expression I could never tell you how much peace and happiness I have found here. This," and he waved his hand over the growing crops— "this has been like the fields and meadows of Paradise into which I walked suddenly like a man who was born blind receiving sight. You say you believe in the existence of God. Sometimes I do, but I wonder really how He could have allowed me to grow unsuspectingly from infancy into dissolute manhood, and then send me here? Why did He direct my repentant steps to this spot—to this soul-soothing spot which I have enjoyed only to lose?"

"Oh, because of all you have been to us!" the gentle girl softly sobbed, as she stood by his side. She would have taken his hand but for the nearness of her brothers. "You say you have done wrong in your past. I don't believe it; but I shall not dispute with you over it. I only know that God could not make a man so helpful, so useful as He has you without eventually rewarding him. As Kenneth and Martin are escaping, so shall you escape. Your troubles will not last. As for your going away, you shall not. I say it. You shall not, I could not live without you. I know that as well as I know that you are standing there. I'd follow you to the end of the world. If you went to prison I'd go, too."

"You can't mean that." He bent toward the ground and uttered a low moan, and yet his face was ablaze with triumphant light.

"I do mean it," she reiterated, "and if you think your running away would save me from silly, weak-minded embarrassment, you must know that it would kill me. Yes, Charlie, I tell you now that if you leave me and I fail to see you again I'll end my life."

She had stepped close to him and he suddenly drew back.

"Your brothers are looking this way," he warned her.

"I don't care," she blurted out, desperately. "They may know. They adore you as I do. I'll tell them how I feel. They are human. They will understand."

"They would not want you"—Charles sighed—"want you to care for a man who may any day be thrust into jail. Brought up as you have been brought up, with your family back of you, they could not want you to care for a man whose life is the deplorable wreck mine is. Our parting is inevitable. I've tried to see it otherwise for a long time, but in vain. I am responsible for the blight that is on me, and I must bear it to the end. Maybe I can tell you more, honorably tell you more, some day, but I cannot do so now. But, after all, even that mild justification would do no good. I shall never forget you, but it is your duty to forget me. Women do forget such things, but I shall hold you in my mind and soul forever."

Kenneth was approaching to ask some question of Charles, and in order to hide her distraught face from her brother's view Mary lifted the basket and moved away.

That night the family, including the two boys, sat on the veranda after supper. Rowland deported himself as if nothing very remarkable had happened in the escape of his sons, but they themselves acted like persons completely changed in character. Kenneth had lost his vaunting air of self-assertion and overconfidence, and was very quiet. Martin was effervescing with the sense of his release from the dangers he feared and half lay, half sat with his head in his sister's lap. Mary's hands were gently stroking back his hair, and now and then she bent and whispered something mother-like and tender in his ear.

Dreading another reference from the family to the part he had played in their rescue, Charles got up and went to his room. He was tired, but not conscious of it, and not at all sleepy, for his brain was in a whirl with thoughts of what had happened, together with grim cogitations on the course he was trying to lay out for his future guidance.

His reason told him that two courses only lay before him. The more logical seemed to be his abrupt disappearance from the spot which had become so dear to him. The other alternative was to return to Boston and appeal to William to release him from his agreement. This temptation was by far the greater, and for a moment, in his fancy, it mastered him. That girl—that wonderful girl down-stairs with her brother's head in her lap—might then become his wife. "Wife! wife! wife!"—the very word thrilled him through and through. He was seated on the edge of his bed, his hardened hands clasped between his knees. His muscles were taut, his face was wet with perspiration; it trickled in cold drops down his neck onto his strong chest. Then another vision was spread before his mental sight. He pictured William as he had last seen him at his desk in the bank at night. He saw himself standing there telling the brother, whom he really loved, that he had come back to undo the thing that he himself had proposed. He saw the dumb appeal in the cowering man's eyes.

"But you were free," William seemed to say, "and this means death to me. Charlie, it means death!"

"I know, but I now love a noble woman," he heard himself pleading, "and for her sake I must live, and now I have learned what life really means. William, my brother, I have failed in what I undertook to do. I am not an angel. I'm only a man of flesh, blood, and bone—a primitive man who knows no law but that of his heart's desire."

He fancied that he saw William's head sink to his desk, the death stamp of agony on his face. He could hear him say: "You are right. I am the one to suffer, not you. Leave me alone this time. I have the same means here in my drawer. I won't fail now. Go home, say nothing, but be there to comfort them when the news is brought."

He saw himself turn away, pass out at the big door and into the lighted streets. It was the old walk home across the Common. Familiar objects were here and there. Celeste met him at the door. He led her into the parlor and turned on the light. They faced each other. She, too, had the shadow of death upon her face.

"I know why you've come," he heard her say, resignedly. "I've been expecting it. No man could be unselfish enough to accomplish what you undertook." The light of her affection for him had died out of her eyes. She quivered now in fear and dread.

"I had to do it," he imagined himself saying, in the tone of an executioner hardened to grim duty.

"I understand. We are ready—Ruth and I are ready."

"May I see the child? If she is asleep I won't wake her. But may I have just one look? I have her picture, but that is all of her that was left to me."

She seemed to lead him up the stairs. How like a dream it all was! Celeste moved through the space his thought created as silently as a creeping ray of moonlight. She opened the door of the child's room. The gas burnt low. There was the snowy bed. He dared not look at it quite yet. Around the room crept the eyes of his thought, seeking respite from his growing remorse. There hung dainty dresses. There in the open closet were other things—little boots, slippers, shoes with skates attached, toys, dolls—and there on the bed—how he loved the child! How he pitied her as she lay asleep with that pink glow of life's alluring dawn upon her, unconscious of the blade he had unsheathed.

"Yes, she must be told now," Celeste seemed to say, in vague, ethereal tones. "She is young to shoulder it, but justice must be done even by a child like her. She must not rob you of a single right or privilege."

The child waked. Startled joy blazed in her opening eyes. She uttered a scream of delight and held out her arms. He took her to his breast and clasped her tightly, her fragrant cheek against his own, her warm body filling his chilled soul with fresh life.

"I can't do it," he heard himself deciding, and forthwith, the pulsing thing on his breast became the cold drops of sweat which his agony had forced from him. "No, I can't do it," he repeated. "I'll wander again. I've given my word, and I'll keep it."

CHAPTER XXVII

The voices on the veranda seemed louder now. He thought he heard Mary uttering a startled command of some sort; and then there were steps on the stairway and Kenneth and Martin softly knocked on his door. He opened it.

"Some one is driving up the road," Kenneth explained. "Sister thought it might be Albert Frazier coming to call on her. Anyway, she said, as he doesn't know that we are at home, we'd better keep out of sight. He may want to stay all night, and in that case we'll have to go to the barn again."

The three men went to a window and cautiously looked out. A horse and buggy were stopping at the gate. Frazier was alighting, while Rowland went down the walk to meet him in accordance with his hospitable habit.

"I can't stop long," Frazier was heard saying. "Leave the horse there. He'll stand, all right. I only want to see your daughter a few minutes."

"Thank God!" Kenneth exclaimed, in relief. "Then we can get to bed, Martin. Oh, how I hate that man!"

The boys left Charles alone. He heard them creeping down the hall to their room at the end of the house. Later he heard their father pass on his way to his room. Charles sat down on his bed again. A different mood was now on him. Hot fury raged through him as he thought of what might be taking place below. That man might be urging the gentle girl to marry him. He might still be holding threats over her, and Mary might accept him. He heard their low voices. Frazier's dominated. Its coarse monotone rumbled through the hall. He seemed to be explaining something. Charles closed his ears, for the sound was maddening.

"It is rather late to call," Frazier was saying, "but I had to see you, and this was the only time. I've thought it all over about me and you, little girl. I don't know, but maybe I'm not as tough a proposition as I appear to be. The truth is, I'm all in. I've lost every cent of money I had. I plunged too reckless. I lived too high. It was come-easy-go-easy with me. I've been a bad man, but you were always what I wanted. I reckon it is because you are so good at heart, but I knew that you'd never love me. I knew that, and so I resorted to that other game. I am sorry, for it was a sneaking thing to do. But, as I say,

I'm all in financially. I could not maybe for many years give you what you deserve, and so I've decided to tell you about it and move away from here. I have a chance of getting something to do in Seattle. My mother's brother has an opening for me there and I am going at once. You never cared for me, did you, little girl? Now be honest."

"I don't think I ever loved you," Mary responded. "It was because you were so—so kind to me and father and the boys—that—"

"Oh, I know. That was part of my dirty work," Frazier sighed. "I was looking a long way ahead. Your father is as simple as a child, and I was using him, tempting him to let me indorse for him. However, he owes me nothing now. I am a bankrupt and the bank that advanced the money to him with my security will look to him for it. Your crops are good this year, and he will be able to make a substantial payment on account when they are marketed. That man you picked up is a wonder. My brother thinks there is something crooked about him and is looking him up. The fellow acts strangely, but he is doing your place no harm, and perhaps you ought to keep him. There is some mystery about him, but I've seen others like him who turned out all right in the end. I think he has secret associates. In fact, I have an idea that some friend of his advanced the money for Tobe Keith's operation. I started to make investigations on that line, but my crash came, and all that is off."

"Do you think Tobe's chance is good to recover?" Mary asked, falteringly.

"That is one thing I came to tell you," Frazier answered. "The latest news is even more favorable. I heard this afternoon from Doctor Harrison that he is doing splendidly."

"Oh, I'm so glad!" Mary cried. "You can't imagine how much it means to me!"

"I think I can, little girl, for you are a mother to the boys, young as you are. I came to say something else, too. I wanted to wipe my slate off as clean as possible before I go, and so I set to work on my brother. He now knows all about how I felt to you, and, as he is a good fellow, he promised to help all he could. He is sure now that the boys will never be seriously punished and has promised me not to arrest them."

"Does he know that they did not go West, after all?" Mary asked, anxiously.

"Yes, he does now. The boys were seen working in the field by a mischievous neighbor, who reported it, but no harm will come of it now. You can depend on my brother. He will not molest them. They've had their lesson. They never were a bad sort, but only a little wild. They have good blood in them and will come out all right in the end. My brother really hates to have me leave, and he will stand behind any friend of mine. I'm a rotten egg, little girl. Wanting to tie to you was my best point, and that was a doubtful one, for I was unworthy of you, and knew it all along—all along. I reckon a man ought to be as clean as the woman he marries, and I was wrong, too, in trying to get you by the methods I was using."

The horse at the gate was pawing the ground impatiently. Frazier looked over the landscape musingly. The moon was just appearing above a mountain-top. The old house which had blazed with the festive light and rung with the merriment of buried generations stood swathed in darkness, its roof-edge drawing a line against the dun sky. Ghosts of the past, earth-anchored by sweet memories, perchance, came and went through the old doorway and strolled about the moonlit grounds.

"It is time I was going," Frazier announced. "I don't know what has come over me of late, little girl, but I know that I am different from what I used to be. If I hadn't been I'd never have said what I've said to-night. I hope you will be happy. You'd never have been so with me—never! Good-by!"

"Good-by!" she echoed. She was crying. Why? She couldn't have answered. She went with him to the gate. She held his arm in a gentle grasp of pitying gratitude. They shook hands over the gate. He took up the reins, got into the buggy with his old ponderous movement, raised his hat, and the impatient horse bore him away.

She turned and glanced up at the window of Charles's room. He was standing there, looking at her, but she could not see him through the murky panes.

"Now go to bed, darling," a voice from the past whispered in her subconscious ear, "Mother is watching over you."

CHAPTER XXVIII

The next day, in the afternoon, Charles and the boys were in the blacksmith's shop repairing a plow that was to be used immediately. Kenneth was at the bellows, and Charles at the anvil, his sleeves rolled high on his brawny arms. Martin stood in the doorway. Presently he whistled softly, and ran to Charles just as he was about to strike the red-hot plowshare which he was holding on the anvil.

"Don't make any noise!" he said. "I see a buggy and horse stopping at the gate. It looks like the sheriff's rig, and I think he is in it."

Charles dropped his tools, and he and his companions crept to a crack in the wall and peered through it.

"That's who it is," Kenneth informed Charles, in a startled voice. "I wonder if—if Tobe has become worse, or—or—"

"I couldn't stand that," Martin cried out. "Oh, don't think it!"

Charles said nothing, and there was no response from Kenneth, who was grimly peering through the crack. They saw Rowland, bareheaded, walking leisurely from the veranda to the gate. They saw him shaking hands over the buggy-wheels with the sheriff. They could not, at that distance, read his face. Of what was taking place the three watchers could form no idea. Presently they saw Mary come down the walk, pass through the gate, and shake hands with the sheriff.

"Sister means to find out if anything has gone wrong, so she can warn us," Kenneth said. "Brown, this looks pretty tough on us. We were thinking everything was all right, but this looks bad."

Still Charles said nothing. His face, only half illumined by the light through the crack, which struck across his fixed eyes, was grim and perplexed.

They saw Mary at her father's side, but the hood of her sunbonnet hid her face from view. The three stood talking for several minutes; then Mary was seen leaving and turning in their direction.

"She's coming to tell us," Kenneth said. "Now, we'll know. Keep still. Maybe she is afraid we'll be seen or heard at work."

Mary appeared in the doorway. She removed her bonnet and smiled reassuringly. "Frightened out of your skins, I'll bet," she jested. "I came to tell you. He is not looking for you. He said so plainly, for he saw how worried I was. In fact, he said that Tobe was still improving, and hinted—he didn't say so in so many words—but he hinted that he knew you both were about the place, and that he was not going to molest you now that Tobe is out of danger."

Charles was staring at her fixedly; the animation that should have been in his face was absent. "Then he wanted to see your father about something else?" he said.

"Yes, some business, or—" Mary broke off, and with a sudden shadow across her face she stood staring at him. "I don't know what he wanted to see father about. It seemed to me that it was of a private nature, and so—so that's why I came away."

"Gee! what does it amount to, since he's letting us go?" said Martin. He stepped to his sister's side and stood with his arm around her waist. For once she seemed unaware of the boy's presence. She was recalling something Albert Frazier had said about the sheriff's opinion of Charles. Could the present visit pertain to him?

"Thank the Lord, he's off!" Kenneth exclaimed. "Bully boy, that chap!"

The brothers went to the doorway, looked all around, and then hastened away to meet their father, who was slowly coming toward the shop. They joined him.

"Where is your sister?" he asked. They told him, and he went on, as if only partially conscious of their eager questions.

"Oh, that's all right!" he said, impatiently. "He is not going to bother you. Oh, Mary, where are you?"

"Here, father," she answered, as she came out, accompanied by Charles. "Did you want me?" It seemed to her that he now glanced at Charles with a look of vague displeasure on his face.

"Yes, I want to see you. Come to the house with me, please."

Mary was sure now that something pertaining to Charles had happened, for her father was treating him in a manner that surely indicated it; the old man had taken no notice of him, and that was most unusual.

Leaving the others in the shop, Rowland led his daughter toward the house. "I wanted to see you about a little matter that may be rather serious," he began. "The sheriff didn't come to see me about the boys at all, but about Mr. Brown."

"About him!" Mary said, faintly. "What about him?"

"He put a lot of questions to me in regard to Mr. Brown," Rowland said, "but I couldn't answer a single one of them. He seemed surprised— astonished, in fact, for he said he didn't see how any sensible man could take in a stranger like Brown unless he had proper credentials. I couldn't even tell him where Mr. Brown came from, who he was, or anything. I tried to explain that Mr. Brown had been so gentlemanly and useful that we hadn't thought such a course necessary, but the sheriff only laughed at me for being so easily hoodwinked."

"Hoodwinked!" Mary protested. "He hasn't hoodwinked us, father. I'm sure he is all we have given him credit for being."

"Well, it seems that the sheriff thinks there is something very suspicious about him. Warrants are out for a number of men who left the circus when Mr. Brown did. The sheriff says that Mr. Brown has been leaving our house at night, and has been seen in town on several occasions. Quite recently he met a stranger at the hotel, a queer fellow with a Northern accent who had refused to register. They were out together the night the gift was made to Mrs. Keith that everybody is talking about, and the man that turned the money over to her answered the description of the stranger that Mr. Brown was with."

"But surely the sheriff is not fool enough to think that giving money away like that was a sign that Mr. Brown was—was a suspicious character!" protested Mary.

"The sheriff thinks that very thing is ground for suspicion," Rowland went on. "He says it may be that Tobe Keith knows more than he has ever let out. It seems that he was seen drinking with some of the circus men. The sheriff thinks that the money was paid over by persons who were afraid Tobe would make some sort of death-bed statement that would implicate Mr. Brown and others. The sheriff found out through one of his men that the same man who met Mr. Brown at the hotel was seen at the hospital in Atlanta where Keith is, and then again here with Mr. Brown. I don't want to be unfair or suspicious of innocent persons, but—now I must be plainer, daughter. I've been afraid that you and Mr. Brown—But I'm sure you know what I mean without my going into it."

"I know what you mean, father," Mary faltered.

"I don't want to offend you, my dear," Rowland went on, "but it seems to be my duty to bring it up. He is an educated man and has the manners of a refined gentleman. In fact, when I used to contrast him with Albert Frazier it seemed to me that a young girl like you could not fail to be impressed with him. He is a good talker and has seen something of the world, evidently. I must say I like him. I like him so much that I almost feel that it is my duty to be more open with him than I can be, for I promised the sheriff that I'd say nothing to him of this. He wants to have him watched for a week or so. In any case, he thinks that under some pretext or other he may arrest him and force him to give an account of himself."

"An account of himself!" Mary repeated the words to herself. Then, touching her father's arm appealingly, she said, aloud: "Do you think you ought—Surely, father, you will not let this change your manner toward Mr. Brown?"

"Why do you ask that?" he demanded.

"Because just now in the shop you treated him coldly. I'm sure he must have noticed it. He is an unhappy, lonely, sensitive man, who—I think—has had some great trouble."

"I didn't mean to treat him differently," Rowland said with regret. "Perhaps I was absorbed in what I had to tell you. But the truth is I must be careful, more careful with you than I have been. I see now that I was wrong to allow you to—to see quite so much of a stranger as you have of this one. You remember you and he were out one entire night—"

"Oh, don't bring that up!" Mary cried. "You know as well as I do how that came about."

"Oh yes, but, nevertheless, you and he were together, and, as I said, he is an attractive man. Right now you are defending him. Think of that, daughter, you are defending a man we know absolutely nothing about, and who I must frankly say has not treated our hospitality with due respect in not producing proper credentials. The profession he was in before he came to us was a queer one for an educated gentleman. You must admit that. Your future and your happiness is in my hands, and a young lady with the ancestry you have had ought to look—"

"Don't mention my ancestry, father," Mary broke in. "It interests you, but it does not interest me. Life, as it is, is too grim and earnest to spend any part of it in digging up the dry bones of dead lords and ladies."

"Blood will tell," Rowland frowned in sudden displeasure. "We are poor and have our troubles, but we know who we are. Yes, I must be more careful with you, my dear. And if Mr. Brown cannot show who and what he is he doesn't deserve my friendship nor your faith in him. Women are sentimental. Whatever they want to be right they think is right. The sheriff has set me to thinking. He just as good as told me that I was crazy to harbor this young man under the circumstances. I won't say anything to Mr. Brown, but I hope you will be careful. You must not let it be said—if the sheriff *does* arrest him—that you were ever anything more to the young man than—"

"I know nothing wrong about Mr. Brown," Mary broke out, now flushed with anger, "and I know much that is good—much that I cannot tell you. I do not intend to let a coarse man like that sheriff influence my opinion in the slightest. He doesn't know Mr. Brown and I do."

"Still, you must be careful," Rowland urged.

"I don't know what you mean," Mary said, stubbornly. "I don't know as I want to know. I shall have to treat Mr. Brown as my conscience tells me to treat him. I know what he has done and is doing for us, and that is enough for me."

"I know, but you must be careful," her father repeated. "Even the boys must be put on their guard."

"On their guard, indeed!" the girl sniffed. "If you haven't eyes to see that Mr. Brown is making men of them, I have. If you thought as much about your children as you do about your forefathers you would have noticed the wonderful change in their characters that Mr. Brown has brought about by his talks and his example."

"I take your rebuke, my dear, because in a way it is deserved. I have been too much absorbed of late in my history, but the book is about done now, and I shall have more time for other matters. If Mr. Brown has helped the boys I shall be grateful for it; still, good deeds sometimes are done by persons who, to say the least, are unsafe. That reminds me. A letter I once wrote to a branch of the Rowland family happened to reach a man by the name who was serving a long term in prison, and the fact is that he gave me more substantial help in what I wanted than many others who had their freedom and whose respectability was not questioned."

"Why not state in your book"—Mary half smiled—"that the best information you could get about the Rowlands was from a prison?"

"I call that flippant, daughter," Rowland answered, "but it doesn't matter. A sense of humor is a family heritage which has come down from the women of your mother's line, who were noted for their brilliant repartee. I have recorded scores of bright sayings in my book. Your great-great-great-grandmother once said to Washington—"

"I remember it," Mary said, crisply. "The same thing was told of a number of other Colonial dames. Bright remarks must have been scarce in that day of scalps and tomahawks."

Rowland was thinking of something else, and did not smile. They were at the house now, and with one of his unconscious bows he left her to go to his room.

CHAPTER XXIX

One night, two days later, Rowland had retired early, and the boys, having worked hard all day, soon followed him. Charles was seated on a rustic bench on the lawn. He had noted the change in Rowland's manner toward him and had promptly coupled it with the sheriff's visit. That something of a serious nature was impending he did not doubt. Several times he had caught Mary's glance, and each time he had felt that she was trying to convey some hint that she wanted to speak to him, but that no suitable opportunity had presented itself. Something told him now that she would join him where he sat; he knew that she had not yet retired, for now and then she passed the window of the lighted sitting-room. The anticipation of meeting her was not that of unalloyed joy, for he felt more and more that he had no moral right to the trust she was so blindly placing in him. She had bared her soul to him; he was unable to do the same to her. Loving her as he did more than life itself, yet he was sure he had no right to foster love in her breast. The burning tobacco died in his pipe as he held it in his tense hand between his knees and again thought out the sinister situation. For the sake of his love's life and hers he might wreck the hope and happiness of a whole family to whom he had pledged fidelity; but if he did that even Mary herself would spurn him. Yes, for had she not been ready to sacrifice herself on a bare chance to save her brothers? No, she loved him for what she thought he was, not for what he would be if he failed in his righteous undertaking. He might tell her how he was bound, but that would sound like self-glorification and would do no good, since her only chance for happiness lay in forgetting him.

He felt rather than saw her as she approached soundlessly on the dewy grass. He stood up. The seat was short, and the wild thought flashed through his brain that he had no more right to sit close beside her than the humblest subject beside his queen; so he stood bowing, and with his hand mutely indicated the seat. She took it, and then, as he remained standing, she suddenly reached out, caught his hand, and drew him down beside her.

"What is the matter?" she asked, insincerely, for she knew the cause of his restraint.

"Nothing," he answered.

"Oh, I know there is; but never mind," she continued, still holding his hand. "I had to see you to-night, Charlie. I could not have waited longer."

"Is it about Albert Frazier?" he asked.

"No, you know it is not. Besides, he has gone away for good and all. He released me from my—my understanding with him. We are not even going to write to each other."

The heart of the listener bounded, but it sank a moment later, for, pressing his hand, as if to console him, Mary went on:

"I wanted to see you about yourself, Charlie—yourself."

"I can guess," he said, grimly. "It has to do with the sheriff's visit the other day. I felt that something was wrong from the way your father acted. He tries to treat me the same, but can't."

Mary lowered her head. She toyed with his big fingers as a nervous child might have done. "I think Albert started his brother's suspicions against you soon after you came to us," she said, gently.

"Suspicions?" Charles was speaking merely to fill awkward pauses.

"Yes, it is outrageous, but he has you mixed up with the men who left the circus when you did. I suppose his idea is to get information from you if he can—force it from you by unfair means. A man like him will balk at nothing to gain his point."

"I can give him no information," Charles answered, in a low, forced tone. "I knew such men were with the circus, and that they had left about the time I did, but I did not even know them personally."

"I know that," Mary said, her hand now like a lifeless thing in his clasp, "but you do not want to be arrested and—and questioned, do you?"

He started, stared steadily, and then released her hand. "No," he answered, after a pause, "I don't want to go through that. I am sorry to have to admit it to you, but it is a fact. I am—am really not prepared for—for that. In fact, that is why I left the circus just when I did. The report was out that the entire company was to be grilled, and I had reasons for—for—But I think you know what I mean. I've tried hard to make you understand that I am unworthy of—"

"Stop!" Mary cried, sharply. "This is no time to go through all that. I know you are worthy, and that settles it. But I have not told you all. Charlie, you are being watched day and night."

"Watched?" he exclaimed.

"Yes, the sheriff told father so, and I myself have seen the men. One in the day and another at night. At this very moment we may be under the eye of one of them."

"What is the sheriff's object?" Charles asked, in a tone of dead despair. "I mean in having me shadowed this way?"

"I think he has an idea that the friend of yours who was here the other day is in some way connected with the men he is after, and that he may return to see you."

"Thank Heaven, Mike is gone, and is out of it!" Charles said, half to her and as much to himself. "It would have been terrible if that poor chap had been drawn into it. Well, well, you see what I have brought down on you for so kindly giving me work and shelter and treating me as an equal when I am simply an outlaw trying to escape imprisonment."

"Hush! hush!" Mary cried, fiercely. "I shall not listen to you."

He had made a movement as if to rise, but again she caught his hand and detained him.

"I know what you are at heart, and that is all I want to know of your affairs. You have said you were bound by honor not to tell everything, and I would not want you to break your word even to enlighten me."

His face was set and pale, his lips twisted awry. Again he drew his hand away. "Have you any idea when they will arrest me?" he asked, hollowly.

"Not for a week or so, anyway," Mary responded. "The sheriff said that you would not be allowed to leave here. Do you want to get away, Charlie?"

"It would do no good to try," he sighed, and yet bravely, for he was not thinking of himself at all. "It would be an open admission that I was avoiding the law." He sighed again and stood up. "Pardon me," he said, "but I mustn't let you compromise yourself like this. You say I am watched, and it would be unfair to you—to your father—to your brothers—for your name to be associated in the slightest with mine."

"Oh, what can I do?" Mary was standing by him now, her hand upon his arm. "I thought I was unhappy over my brothers, but, now that they are out of trouble, I am in agony over you. Oh, Charlie, don't you see—don't you understand—"

Her voice broke in a sob. He was swayed by a storm of emotion. He was about to take her in his arms, when the thought of being seen by a hidden observer checked him.

"You must go in now," he said. "See how the dew is settling on your hair."

She nodded mutely, and side by side they went to the house. The sitting-room on the left of the hall was lighted, the parlor on the right was dark.

"Come into the parlor," she said, in a low, firm tone. "No one could see us there, and—and—oh, Charlie! I can't part with you like this! I can't bear it. I'd lie awake all night."

In the silence of the big room they stood facing each other. Their hands met like drowning persons afloat in a dark, calm sea. He could see her eyes in the gloom. They seemed like portals of escape from a living hell. Her quick breath fanned his face; the warmth of her being drove the deathlike chill from his body. He took her face into his hands, and bent and kissed her lips. She put her head on his breast, her arms about his neck, and held him tightly.

"They shall not part us," she whispered against his cheek. "Never, never, never!"

CHAPTER XXX

The Boston family were at breakfast. William was in his place next to his wife, and his uncle, who now lived in the house, sat opposite him. The two men were talking of stocks, bonds, securities, and insurance rates. Celeste was taking no part in the conversation. In her morning dress she looked as frail and dainty as ever.

Presently the maid who was waiting at the table bent over her shoulder and, smiling, whispered something to her.

"Oh, is he!" Celeste exclaimed. "Tell him to wait. I want to see him after breakfast."

"Who is it, dear?" William asked.

"It is Michael," she returned. "He has got back from New York. I want to find out how his mother is. He has been away longer than usual. I am afraid she may be worse."

Raising his coffee-cup to his lips, William dismissed the subject and continued his chat with his uncle.

"We certainly have made the bank pay," the older man said. "As you know, it was not in the best condition when I took hold of it. I had no idea running a bank was so interesting. I have handled my end well and you have yours. I have heartily enjoyed my work, but sometimes I am in doubt about you."

"About me?" William's eyes met the upward glance of his wife, and both looked at the old man inquiringly.

"Yes. You always seem nervous, overworked, and worried. I've tried to make it out. Are you sure you are entirely well? You are getting gray, my boy, and your signature often has a shaky look. You don't smoke too much, do you?"

"I think not," said William, and his eyes fell under the calm, penetrating stare of his wife. "But I *am* nervous, and seem to be getting more so. I am thinking of a vacation."

"That is right, take it," his uncle said. "I can run the old boat awhile by myself."

Celeste remained at the table after they had left the room. She listened attentively and heard them closing the door as they went out into the street. No sooner were they away than she rang for the maid.

"Please tell Michael that I want to see him," she said to the girl. "He is still there, is he not?"

"Yes, madam."

In a moment Michael appeared, his hat in hand.

"When did you get back?" Celeste asked, after she had greeted him and he stood at the end of the table, the dust of travel on his gray suit and in the hollows of his earnest blue eyes.

"At four o'clock this morning, madam; I'm pretty well done up."

"How did you leave your mother?" asked Celeste, and her eyes swept him from head to foot. It was plain to the servant that her questions were merely perfunctory.

"Very well, thank you, madam. It is very kind of you to ask."

"I am glad to hear it, Michael." Celeste faced him more directly now. "I was afraid she was worse, for you know you were gone longer than usual."

"A few days longer, madam," Michael said. "I had no idea of being detained, but I actually ran across a trace of Mr. Charles, and, knowing your anxiety, I—"

"You have found him—you have seen him!" Celeste interrupted. "I know it from the way you look, Michael."

"Yes, madam, I found him. After some trouble and quite a journey I located him and managed to meet and talk with him."

"Sit down, Michael, sit down; you are tired."

He drew a chair back from the table and sat in it, his travel-stained hat on his knee.

"Now tell me about him. Is he well?"

"A perfect picture of health, madam," Michael beamed. "He is living on an old plantation down in the mountains of Georgia, working like a common laborer, but he seemed satisfied."

"Like a common laborer!" Celeste repeated, sadly. "Go on, tell me everything, Michael."

At some length the old servant recounted his experiences from the moment of his meeting with Mason in New York till he had joined Charles in the South.

"And the girl you speak of—the planter's daughter. You say she is—"

"The most beautiful and refined young lady I ever met, madam. I cannot tell you how well she impressed me. You could see by a look at her that she was of fine stock. She was very nice to me. I saw her father, too, but I did not meet him—a fine figure of a gentleman. A little run down in appearance, madam, but a courtly gentleman at bottom. The house was a fine old place. You could not blame a young man like Mr. Charles for wanting to settle there, after all the roving he had had to get away from—You understand what I mean, madam?"

Celeste nodded breathlessly. "You must tell me, Michael," she urged, "if, in your opinion, Charles is in love with the young lady."

Michael hesitated; he fumbled the rim of his hat; he blinked under her steady stare.

"Answer me, Michael," Celeste insisted. "Surely he would not object to my knowing it if he is. You see, I am anxious to hear that he has found such happiness."

"I may as well tell you that he made no secret of it, madam, but I regret to say that it has not brought him full contentment."

"Then she cares for some one else," Celeste said, regretfully.

"On the contrary, madam, I am sure that the feeling is mutual. I could see it in the way she looked at him, and in the way she treated me merely because I was a friend of his, as he told her in my presence."

"But I don't understand," Celeste pursued. "If they love each other—" She went no further, knitting her brows perplexedly.

"It is this way, madam. Oh, Mr. Charles spoke plainly enough that night at the little hotel when he came to see me! You see, madam, he is conscientious—Mr. Charles is remarkably so, and he will not, he says, think of asking such a young lady to be his wife when he is—well, under a cloud."

"Oh! Oh! That is it!"

"Oh yes, madam, and in that respect he is to be pitied. Even if he were willing to keep his—his little mistake from the young lady herself, he could not show her family proper credentials as to who he is. You see, he is at present a common farm-hand. The young lady seems to understand him, I should say, but her people and the community don't. You would be sorry for him if you could see him and hear him talk in his brave, manly, and patient way."

At this point Michael told of the timely aid which had been given to Keith, the motive behind it, and the successful outcome of the operation. As he told it, it was a dramatic story which held Celeste spellbound.

"And he gave even *that* money away!" Celeste cried. "I know he loves her, Michael, but, as you say, he is only a farm-hand and the other thing hangs over him. I know him well enough to understand that he'd never think of marriage in his condition. Oh, he must be unhappy, Michael! As you say, she may be the one woman in all the world for him, and yet he has to give her up. Poor, dear Charlie!"

"Yes, he is unfortunate, madam. He no longer drinks. All that is over. He is a man among men, madam. His simple life and regular habits have improved him wonderfully. He is a young giant of a man. His skin is clear, and his eye bright, but he is sad—yes, he is sad and thoughtful, especially when he speaks of home and the little girl. He cautioned me not to mention him to her. He wants her to think of him as dead, because the young soon forget those who die."

Celeste rose suddenly. "I'll see you again," she said, clearing her husky throat. "I must go now. I thank you, Michael. No one else could have done what you have done." At the door she suddenly wheeled on him. "Michael, wait, please!" she said. Her lips were twitching, her brows were contracted as if in deep, disturbed thought. She rested her thin white hands on the back of a chair and grasped it as for support. "Michael," she continued, "did it ever occur to you that Charles may have been drawn into that trouble by others and may not have been *wholly* to blame?"

"I can't say that I thought that, madam," said Michael, swinging awkwardly from one foot to the other and blinking. "I did always think, and believe, too, that he wasn't at himself when it happened. I told him I thought that once, and he did not deny it. That is why I've been so sorry for him, for a man ought not to be punished all his life for a thing that was done when he was—well, like Mr. Charles used to get."

"I see; I see what you think," and Celeste nodded as if in affirmation of some thought of her own. "And you say you think the two are in love with each other?"

"Oh yes, madam, and that is the sad part of it."

"And that but for Charles's secret trouble they would be married?"

"Yes, madam. I have no doubt of it."

"Thank you, Michael. You may have done him a great service by—by going to see him when you did. I mean," she added, starting as from some inner fear, "that reaching him just when you did with that money—"

"Oh yes, madam, Mr. Charles spoke of that a dozen times. You see, as I have tried to explain, it lifted a load from the young lady."

"I understand that," Celeste said, musingly. "And she is very pretty and sweet and gentle, you say?"

"She is everything a lady ought to be, madam, and, oh, I must say my heart ached for her, too, for I could see how she felt about him. She is full of spirit. She is the kind that would fight for a man to the last ditch and drop of blood. But, oh, madam, it seemed so sad! There he was in a farmer's clothes, his hands as hard as stone, and she—why, madam, he treated her like she was a princess of royal rank, and all the time with that old, sad look he used to have when he was scolding himself to me after one of his little sprees around town. Almost the last thing he said to me, madam, was that when he had helped her all he could he intended to slip away, for her own good, and take up his life somewhere else among strangers. It was then, madam, I assure you, that I almost lost my religion. I've been taught, madam, from my mother's knee—and she is a saint, if one ever lived—I say I've been taught that our Saviour died to help men who repent, and there was Mr. Charles bowed down like that without a hand held out to him. He gave up all he loved here—you, the little girl—his 'Sunbeam,' as he called her down there—and his brother, and now, when he has found some one that he loves, he must give her up also and start to roving again. I shed tears. I couldn't help it, and it moved him. I could see that. We were in my room at the hotel. His face turned dark as he sat there on my bed trying to be calm. He stood up and shook himself and smiled. 'Mike,' he said, 'nothing counts that we do for ourselves. It is only by forgetting ourselves and helping others that we accomplish anything worth while.'"

"Thank you, Michael, I'll see you again soon," Celeste said, moving toward the door.

CHAPTER XXXI

"'Nothing counts that we do for ourselves,'" Celeste repeated, as she was ascending the stairs to her daughter's room. At the door she paused and listened for a moment, then, softly turning the bolt, she entered the room. The blinds were down to exclude the sunlight which was growing warm. On the great white bed Ruth lay asleep. One plump bare arm, shapely wrist, and hand lay against the mass of golden hair. Celeste stood at the foot of the bed, and with a mother's parched thirst drank from the picture before her eyes. How beautiful the child was! How exquisite the patrician brow, the neck, the contour of nose, mouth, and chin! How temperamentally sensitive, imaginative, and high-strung! How proud of her father, of his social and financial standing and his old name of Puritan respectability! How affectionate she was with her mother, how adored by the servants and by her absent uncle!

"She is all I have now!" thought Celeste, as she choked down a sob, "Can I do it—am I able to do it?"

She sat in a rocking-chair near the bed, her gaze still on the child's face. A sudden breeze fanned the shades of the windows inward. She locked her hands in her lap, her thin, blue-veined, irresolute hands in a lap of stone. "'Nothing counts that we do for ourselves,'" she quoted, uncompromisingly. "If I refuse I'll not be acting for myself, but for her—my baby—my darling baby! Charlie loved her enough to undertake her rescue, and I must help him carry it through. Yes, I can do that conscientiously. It would kill her to learn that her father was a convict. She couldn't grow up under it. It would blight her whole existence. At school she would hear it. In society it would be whispered behind her back and thrown in her face. Oh, it can't be! God would not allow it to be. He would not allow the sins of a father to fall on shoulders so frail and helpless. Some coarse children would think nothing of it; it would kill my baby. She would brood over it—oh, I know my child! She would hold it in her mind night and day. From what she now is she would become an embittered cynic, soured against life and her Creator. She would never marry. She would not want to bring children into a world so full of pain. And yet, and yet—" Celeste rose and went to a window and stood looking out, peering through the small panes as a hopeless prisoner might.

"And yet—justice must be done." Her white lips framed the words which shrank from utterance. "Charlie has *his* rights, and so has the girl he loves. He undertook our rescue without knowing the cost. He was full of repentance at the time over his trivial mistakes, but now he must see it differently. Shall we drive him to roving again? Would God give my child a happy life at such a cost? Would He blight the lives of two of His children for one—and those two wholly innocent? No, justice must be done. It must! It must! It must! But I can't be her executioner. Why, I'm her mother! She is all I have in the world!"

Celeste crept back to the bed and bent over the sleeping child. Her hand went out as if to caress the white brow, but her fingers lifted only a fragrant lock of hair, and this she bent and kissed as soundlessly as the sunlight's vibration on the rug-strewn floor.

The next day was Sunday. Leaving her husband and his uncle smoking over their papers in the dining-room, her child in the care of a maid, Celeste slipped away unnoticed. She did not often attend church, but she was going to-day. Why, she could not have explained. It was as if a building with a spire and chimes, altar and surpliced clergyman, white-robed choristers and bowed suppliants, would help her make the decision that a long, sleepless night had withheld. She felt faint as she entered the family pew and bowed her head, for she had taken little nourishment since her travail began. Somehow her own death seemed a near thing, but she did not care. There were other things so much worse than mere death.

She failed to comprehend any part of the sermon which the gray-haired minister was delivering in that far-off, detached tone. She noticed some rings on his stout fingers and wondered how such mere trinkets could be worn by an ordained helper of the despairing and the God-forsaken. As soon as the service was over she hastened homeward. She told herself that she would act at once and face her husband with a demand that either he or she should perform the bounden duty. But as she entered the door and heard the voices of the two men in the dining-room, and smelled the smoke of their cigars, her courage oozed from her. She could not tell them both. Her talk must be for William alone; it would be for him to inform his uncle, and he would do it. William, once shown the right road, would take it. She knew him well enough for that. His wavering for the past year had been like hers, but when he knew all and was faced with the call of justice, as she was facing it, he would obey.

At the foot of the stairs in the hall she paused. Should she go back to the two men, or—It was the rippling laugh of her child up-stairs, who was being amused by a maid, the joyous clapping of a small pair of hands, that drew Celeste up the carpeted steps and into the child's presence.

"Oh, mother, see what she has put on me!" Ruth cried, gleefully, as she sprang into the middle of the room robed in a filmy pink gown which had been made for her use in a class in interpretative dancing, and held out the skirt, forming wings like those of a fairy floating over beds of roses. A circle of artificial flowers rested on the golden tresses. Ruth's eyes were sparkling with delight as she bowed low in one of the postures she had been taught, and then glided gracefully into her mother's arms.

"Oh, we've had so much fun! Haven't we, Annette?"

"Madame will pardon me," the French maid said. "I know it is Sunday, but she was so full of joy when she waked that—"

"It doesn't matter," Celeste said. "You may go. I'll dress her for dinner myself."

And as she did it, that morning of all mornings to be remembered, Celeste was the most pitiable of all pitiable creatures. Her coming sacrifice was not like that of Abraham in his offering of Isaac to his God, for, while he was a child of God, Abraham was not a mother.

"Justice must be done!" she kept saying. "The happiness of two against the misery of one—two against *two*, in reality; but I don't count, I mustn't count. Charlie said to Michael that nothing counts that we do for ourselves, and this protesting ache within me is self, for my baby is myself. Sweet, sweet little daughter! Mother has the blade ready and must thrust it deep into your joyous heart. Oh, if my cup would only pass, and my will might be done instead of God's!" She held her child on her knees as she took off the pink symbol of dawn and robed her anew. She was laying her child on an altar before God and no sacrificial ram was in sight.

CHAPTER XXXII

All the rest of the day Celeste was with Ruth. She walked with her in the Public Gardens. She stayed away from home, fearing that some one might call, and she felt unequal to the mocking convention. Surely this was no time for smirking formalities. When, as the sun was going down, she and the child returned home she found no one there except the servants. She felt relieved, for she was not prepared yet to meet her husband's eye, for surely he would know that something unusual had happened to her. She was glad that he did not return till just before the supper was served. She took Ruth down-stairs and into the dining-room as soon as the meal was announced. William and his uncle had met again in the parlor and were talking there in low tones. She and Ruth were in their places at the table when they came in.

"Yes, we certainly put it over on them," the old man said, with a chuckling laugh. "I felt sure the market was firm and sent my wire at once."

"I was confident, too," William answered, "but I never knew you to take a risk, and it may have been due to that fact that I was so undisturbed."

"Well, I think I can say as much for you, William," the old man answered. "Since I have been with you at the bank you have been the most conservative business man I ever knew. I have sometimes thought you were too careful, but caution can never be a fault."

They took seats. The business talk continued. The bank was to become the greatest in the state—every indication was in its favor. Celeste failed to hear Ruth's pretty prattle at her side. As she looked at the two men her determination, which had been held so firmly all day, grew weak and vacillating. How could she carry out her plan before them? She sank more deeply into the mire of misery than ever. The whole world seemed black and mad under the contending forces of right and wrong. How frail was the spirit flag she was striving to hold aloft in all that clash and rush of evil!

No, the right thing could not be done—by her, at any rate. Charles would have to remain the self-elected lifelong victim that he was. After all, he would be saving her; he would be saving Ruth; he would be saving his brother whom he had always loved. *Saving* his brother! But was he? Could it be done so vicariously? And as this question pounded upon her brain she looked for the first time with scaleless eyes at her husband. Why had she not noticed it before? William was the mere withering husk of the man he had once been. His deep-sunken, shadowy eyes told his story; his parchment-like skin, his furtive, haunted look, repeated it; his constantly enforced attention to what was being said by others, his Judas-like manner, the quivering of his mentally handcuffed hands, confirmed it again and again. Why, William was dying—dying from the sheer poison of his putrefying soul. Only his great, staring eyes seemed alive, and they lived only in their dumb quest of mercy. Poor William! No one could save him but himself. Charles's nobility, Charles's sacrifice, would not do it. He must do it himself. Ah yes, that was the key, and it had dropped down from heaven! The thing was settled now. She would see him before the dawn of another day. She would suffer. Ruth would suffer, but William would be saved. Ah, that was the point too long overlooked! His only child would be paying the price, but in the far-off future Ruth herself, with the spiritual wisdom of age, might thank the memory of her mother for the opportunity given her.

The family retired before ten o'clock that night. Celeste sat by her daughter's bed, and with a soft, soothing song lulled her child to sleep. Gradually she felt the tiny fingers losing their grasp upon her own. Shortly afterward Celeste heard William ascending the stairs to his room adjoining hers. She heard him close his door. He always closed his door. At night or in the day he closed his door. Even at the bank he closed the door of his private office, perhaps in order that he might release the drawn cords to those perpetual curtains of his secret self.

There was another door between her room and his. Even that was shut. If she wished to see him before he retired she must hasten. She went into her own room, but did not turn on the electric light. She stood in the center of the room, shivering from head to foot as from cold. Presently she knocked on his door. Then there was a moment of tense silence. The sound must have startled her husband; and when at last he did fumblingly turn the bolt and open the door he stood there in the dark, facing her wonderingly, speechlessly.

"I—I didn't know who it was—at first!" he stammered. "I thought— thought—"

"Excuse me," she said, stroking the death-damp sweat from her brow and sliding past him into his room, "but I wanted to see you. I wanted to talk to you. It is something important, it seems to me. I couldn't do it before uncle, and you were with him all day. May we have a—a light?"

"Need we?" fell from his lips impulsively, then: "Yes, dear, of course. I quite forgot. I—I sometimes undress in the—the dark in the summer-time."

He groped for the button on the wall. "Yes, I was right," he thought. "She has had something on her mind all day and last night, and she says it is important. My God! important! Only one thing is important—can it have come up again?"

His fingers touched the button. He pushed it in and the white glare filled the room like a photographer's flash-light, revealing their set visages to each other. William certainly looked old now, for a storm of terror was laying waste his whole suppressed being. She turned from him in sheer pity of his swaying frailty. She sat down in a chair, and, like the ill man that he was, he sank into another. He had unfastened his scarf and collar and the ends of both hung in disorder on his breast.

"You say it is something important?" he muttered, and with his hand he made a pretext of shading his eyes.

"Yes, William, it is important, as I see it," she answered, her stare on the floor, her bloodless hands in her lap, tightly clasped. "It is about—about a subject we have not mentioned between us lately."

"I think I understand," he breathed low. "Then you have heard from him, or at least you know where he went."

"Yes, and through Michael," she added. "Michael owed him some money and so he searched for him till finally—"

"Oh!" burst eagerly from her listener. "Then it was not the detectives—not the police. You see—you see, I thought—"

"No, he is safe in that respect, for a while, at any rate," Celeste said. "Michael found him in a retired place down in the mountains of Georgia, and—"

"Why, I—I thought he had gone abroad!" and there was no mistaking the sudden uneasiness in William's tone. "But you say he is still here in this country? Are you sure about that?"

"Yes, Michael has seen and talked with him. William, Charlie is very unhappy. Don't think that he is complaining, for he is not, but a new life has opened out before him and he is still young. William, justice must be done to him."

The hand-shade fell lower over William's eyes, but she could still see their fixed pupils just beneath the flesh-line of his palm.

"Justice!" he gasped. "Surely you are not going to—to hint at that suspicion of yours again. Haven't I shown you—told you that it would make you miserable for life?"

"It is not merely a suspicion now, William," she said, grimly. "I know it to be a fact that Charlie is wholly innocent, and that you—But, oh, you know what I mean!"

Like a murderer faced by skilled accusers confident of his guilt, William could formulate no denial. His sheer silence condemned him, that and the furtive flight of his eyes from object to object in the room. They reached everything except her set face. He and she were silent for a moment; then William spoke:

"So he talked to Michael. Probably he said a lot of things to him, and Michael has come back full of—of—"

"He said nothing of that sort to Michael," Celeste corrected, quickly. "Charlie is still true to his agreement with you. He lets Michael think that he did it when under the influence of drink. Michael hasn't the slightest idea that another is to blame."

"I see, and in spite of all this, and even Charlie's confession over his own signature, which I showed you, you still hold the idea that—"

"Yes, I know that the poor boy was innocent, and that he did it all—the written confession, the going away, the shouldering of the disgrace here, and the nameless life among strangers as a common laborer—he did all that for your sake and mine and Ruth's. Don't—don't deny it any more, William—*don't lie to me*! I won't stand for it! I won't! I won't! I *can't*!"

He gave in. He could have crawled like a worm before her in his weltering despair.

"You know it is true, don't you, William?" There were pity, gentleness, and even abiding love in her tone.

He was conquered. He covered his ashen face with his gaunt hands, and, with his elbows on his knees, he sat leaning forward, dumb and undone. Then she told him his brother's story. It fell from her lips like the sweet consolation of a consecrated nun to a dying penitent, and yet it rang full and firm with Heaven's demand for justice. With a wand of flaming truth she pointed the way—the only way. He sobbed. William for the first time sobbed in her presence. His lips hung loose and quivered like those of a whimpering child.

"Have you realized the cost?" he asked, presently. "Do you know what it will mean to you and to Ruth? As God is my judge, Lessie, I am not thinking of myself. In fact, I was thinking only of you when I did it!" Here he made a confession of how he had prepared to kill himself that she might escape the long-drawn publicity of his trial, and how his brother had thwarted the effort.

"Yes, I realize the cost," Celeste answered, "but Ruth and I must pay it. It seems to me now that a greater thing in God's sight than paying our own debts is paying the debts of others. Charlie is trying to pay our debts, but he shall not. William, he shall not. You are dying under the strain that is on you. It is God's way of blighting His fruitless trees."

"You are right," he faltered. "A felon's cell, a convict's chains, would furnish relief compared with the tortures I have been enduring. But you and the baby—oh, Lessie, that is unbearable! That thought has haunted me for over a year."

"I know, but don't think of it now," she said. "Act at once. See uncle to-night before he retires. He is still in the library. He said he had something to read."

"I'll tell him at the bank in the morning," William said. "It is the proper place for it. Yes, yes, I'll tell him. You look as if you doubt it, but I'll keep my word. If you stop to think of it, you will see that there is nothing else to do."

"Wait!" Celeste rose and went out into the hallway. She leaned over the balustrade and peered downward; then she came back. "I see the light in the library," she said. "He is there now. Go. It must be settled to-night. I am holding myself to it with all the strength of my soul. I am afraid I will weaken. Another night and I might. Charlie's rights and Ruth's are in a balance, and they are seesawing up and down. Hurry! Hurry! Go this minute!"

He rose and staggered from the room. Celeste sat down and leaned forward. She listened, all her soul in her ears. She remembered that the old stairs had a harsh habit of creaking when one went down or up them. They were uttering no sound now. Why? she wondered. Softly she got up and crept out into the hall. There in the darkness stood William on the first step, a hand on the railing. His face was turned toward the foot of the stairs. The narrow strip of carpet stretched down toward the dim light below. He was staring at the light as if turned to stone by its gruesome import. She crept to him, touched him on the arm. He turned his death-mask of a face to her, and moved his flabby lips soundlessly.

"Go on," she said.

"You forget one thing, Lessie." His voice came now in a rasping whisper. "You forget that this thing was Charlie's own suggestion. He proposed it. He would expect me to live up to it, as well as he himself. You mentioned Ruth. She was in his mind at the time, as well as you and me. Then there was another thing. He had—he said so himself—he had disgraced himself here. He had acted in a way that made him want to disappear, never to be heard of again. This would bring all that up again. I have no doubt that he would want the matter to rest just as it is."

"Yes, he would, and for that very reason it shall not," Celeste flashed out. "He loves a good girl, and she loves him. If you are silent to-night they will be parted forever. The thing is killing you; it will kill me, too. Are you trying to force me to be your accomplice?"

His head rocked negatively like a stone poised on a pivot, but still he did not move forward. Gently she caught his hand, the one still on the railing, and as she did so his fingers automatically clutched the wood as if he were afraid of falling down the stairs.

"I'll go," he said. "You see, I was wondering just how to put it to uncle. He will be humiliated in a peculiar way. I hardly know how to say it, but he has all along felt the—the stigma of Charlie's—of what he thinks Charlie did—felt it so keenly that he has overdone his—his praise of me. You understand—of *me*. He has boasted of my—my moral stamina and ability on all occasions, in that way, you see, to make up for Charlie's—or what he thinks was Charlie's bad conduct. It will upset him terribly. It will fill him with chagrin, for—for I and the bank and its success have become his very life. I dread the effect on him. He is old, you know, and not so very strong. What would we do if it were to result disastrously—I mean to him, you understand? If Charlie hadn't done this thing of his own accord—"

"Stop, William," Celeste said, with a resolute sigh. "I see how hard it is for you to do. Let me do it. I'll know what to say perhaps better than you. Besides, if you consent to my going to him it will be the same as if you did it. In fact, I'll tell him you sent me."

"No, I'll have to put it through," said William, suddenly. He barred the way by thrusting his disengaged hand against the wall, the other still holding on to the balustrade. "Go to your room. I'll attend to it."

He moved forward now, and, standing still, she saw him slowly descend the stairs and vanish at the library door. Then she went back to her own room. But she did not disrobe nor turn on the light. She remained sitting in a chair at a window through which the rays of a street lamp fell. She would wait for William's return. She loved him; she was sorry for him; she wanted to cry, but could not.

CHAPTER XXXIII

William found his uncle at a writing-table, sheets of paper and a note-book before him, a fountain-pen in his hand. He looked up and smiled a pleasant greeting. "Thought you had turned in," he chuckled, softly. "I told Lessie I had a book to read, but it wasn't that, really. I've been here figuring on my holdings. I love to do it. It makes the things I've fought and won stand out, you see, before my eyes, as you might say. It furnishes me with a fresh surprise every time I do it. It always seems bigger, solider, you see. Sit down, my boy; take a cigar—there are several pretty good ones. No, you won't? I see, it will keep you awake, eh? Well, I must say I admire it in you. The best business men are careful, and you are one of them. I owe you a lot, my boy," he went on, as William sat down and clasped his cold knee-caps with his shaking hands. "Do you know what you did for me? I see; you are too modest to confess it. Well, you actually did this: I had practically given up the financial game. I was trifling my time and income away in Europe when this great family trouble clutched me and pulled me back into harness. And what has been the result? Why, I've not only enjoyed the game of defending our blood, but every venture I have made has shoveled gold into my bin."

William nodded. He could not find his voice. He was glad that his uncle's enthusiastic face was bent over his writing.

"And don't think I am not realizing that I'm no longer young, either," the steady voice went on. "I'm not a silly fool. I sha'n't claim more than ten years more of life, at the furthest, and what do you think I expect to do with my effects? You saw the little item in *The Transcript* the other day, stating that I might make a big donation to several charitable institutions? I know you must have seen it. Well, nothing could be farther from my intentions. I am going to leave all I have to a young fellow that I think had a pretty hard time of it. Of course, you don't know who I mean, Billy. I didn't think I'd ever want to provide for any particular person, but when I got back from Europe and saw you haggard and unstrung, putting up practically all you had in the world to pull our name from the mire—well, it changed me on the spot. You see, it was a quality I didn't think a man could have, and I'd found it in you."

"Wait! Stop, please!" William gulped. "I—I—"

"Too modest, eh?" the old man laughed. "Now you keep quiet. I am holding the floor, and the chairman says you are out of order. Huh! if you are too modest to want this for yourself, think of your wife and child. I've grown to love them as if they were child and grandchild of my own. I want to see them happy, and when I make them so you will be, too, Billy, in spite of the rascally thing that has been done to you. You shall be president of the bank; you shall run the whole thing, and I'll sit back and take life easy to the end. Do you know that old men enjoy life more than the young? Well, it is true. Aside from the bad conduct of your brother—the lasting sting of it—there is nothing in my life to regret. I am actually happy in the realization that I am doing so much for the happiness of you and yours—and mine. Yes, they are mine, too."

There was a pause, but William was unable to fill it. He reached out and took one of the cigars from the table; he struck a match and lighted it, but it burnt for an instant only. The old man was looking at him steadily. "You are not well to-night, are you, Billy?" he asked, in a sudden swirl of affectionate concern.

"No, not very," William heard himself saying. "I—I—"

"Well, perhaps you'd better turn in," his uncle suggested. "This is your day of rest, you know. Later I'll give you the details of what I am going to do for you."

"Uncle," said William, desperately, standing up and leaning forward like a storm-blown human reed, "I am unworthy, absolutely unworthy of—"

"Bosh! Go to bed!" the old man cried, in an ecstasy of delight. "I'm to be the judge of worthiness in this case. It is a scarce commodity these days, and when I see a man actually trying to stave off his just rewards—why, he is a miracle, that's all—a miracle of unselfishness! Stupid, think of that bonny child of yours! Don't you want to see her take her proper place in the social world? What have you lived and toiled for? I'll bet Lessie won't treat this thing as you do. I'll bet she will kiss her old uncle, and—"

William lost the remainder of the remark. A sudden sense of respite brooded over him like a protecting cloud. Had he the right now to step between his wife and child and such a princely inheritance? In the face of it would Lessie herself not feel impelled to take a different stand? What normal mother would not? To disillusion the old idealist now would ruin the chances of a good woman and a helpless child. Yes, at any rate, he told himself, he must see Celeste and lay the matter in its new form before her.

"Well, I'll go up," he said, as casually as was in his depleted power. "I'll see you at breakfast. I—I am rather tired."

"Yes. Good night, my boy. Sleep will do you good."

Somehow William had the odd sense of being bodiless as he ascended the stairs. As he approached his wife's room he saw the handle of her door move, and then he knew that she was standing waiting for him just inside the room. They faced each other in the deflected flare of the street lamp. She reached out and took his hands and clung to them.

"I've been listening. I expected a scene, a commotion, but I heard nothing of the sort," she whispered. "It must have simply stunned him. The blow was too deep even to stir his fury."

William pressed her hands convulsively, appealingly. He put an arm around her, a shaking, half-palsied arm.

"Lessie," he panted, raspingly. "I found out down there—Wait, wait! Give me time." He cleared his throat. "I found out—It was like this, darling. You know how rapidly he talks at times? Well, he wouldn't give me a chance to break in; and finally he told me something that made me—forced me to feel that if you had been there—I mean—"

"What? Go on! Go on!" Celeste breathed quickly.

"He was in a jolly mood. He spoke more freely than ever before. He let out the fact that he is worth several millions and that he intends to leave it all to us—*I mean to you and Ruth*. He has no idea of donating anything to charity, but all to you two. So you see—you see, it put me where I simply had to—to lay it before you. It strikes me as a reasonable idea that with all that money at your disposal you could—why, Lessie, you could make Charlie rich, and surely you cannot stand between our child and all that good fortune. Don't you see, dear? The truth would so infuriate uncle that he would—would drop us all—you, me, Ruth, Charlie—everybody! Old men are like that; they can't seem to recuperate after such a blow. I didn't tell him. I confess I didn't even mention it, for it was my duty to—to show you how matters stand. I'd not be a natural husband and father if—if I had acted otherwise. We have got in this awful mess. How are we going to get out? Remember, dear, I was trying to earn money for you and the baby when it happened, so how can I bear to—to think of going to jail and leaving you penniless? He would be mad enough to send me to jail, dear; he is just that vindictive, and he would not take care of you two, either. You don't seem to realize that it would make him the laughing-stock of the public, and he so sensitive and hot-tempered. You see, I have forced him to be my active accomplice in covering it all up, and he would have to remain silent or turn me over to the authorities. Oh, it is awful—awful! He puts such a high and unjust value on me that when he finds he has been fooled he will—why, he won't know how to control himself! It would be like him to leave the house to-night—this very night—and go to a hotel, where he would chatter even to the bell-boys. Think of Ruth—if not of me; have pity on that sweet, inoffensive child."

"Oh, but Charlie! Charlie!" Celeste found voice to say.

"But don't you remember that Charlie himself proposed going away? Why, he was down and out—sick of Boston and everything in it. He said he never wanted to come back or to be heard of again. That was to save me—just *me*—from—from trouble. Is it likely that he would be willing to have me—to have any of us take a step like this now? How do you know that—that he'd like to—to have his old life raked up again? He is evidently playing a part of some sort. Have we the right, without consulting him, to have all this put in the papers and flashed from end to end of the country?"

Celeste stood like a statue, cold and motionless, in his half-embrace. The dim light disclosed her marble cheek to his sight. Her wide-open eyes caught the flare from the street lamp and gave it back in gleams of indecision.

"You say he spoke of Ruth's inheritance?" she gasped.

"More of her than you or me," said William, grasping at the straw. "He fairly dotes on her. But don't think he would stand by her if—if we anger him by this exposure. He would hate us all, Ruth along with us. In a burst of fury he would cut us all out. Oh, I know him, Lessie," went on William, imbibing hope from the dead stare turned on him. "I have been right at his elbow for over a year. He has given me his innermost thoughts."

"I know," Celeste whispered. "I've noticed it, and knew why it was. He looked upon you as a paragon of nobility because you—because he thought you were sacrificing so much to atone for Charlie's conduct. He told me once that it had given him a new faith in men—that he had not thought such a thing possible. But that was wrong—cursed of God. It was hypocrisy as black as the lowest vats of hell. And I helped you in it. I feared all along that my intuition was telling me the truth, but because I didn't know where Charlie was, because I thought he might be dead, I kept silent. But, husband, it is different now—oh—oh! so different! God has sent us this trial. Charlie's life and happiness are at stake. If we are untrue he will bear the burden meant for us. God knows he has suffered enough for his boyish escapades—that has been proved by his throwing off his old habits and becoming a clean, decent, and ambitious man. He loves and is loved, and yet he is regarded as little more than a tramp by the people around him. William, I am weak, wavering, and all but dying under this. What am I to do?"

He put both his hands on her shoulders, turned her face directly to his, and went on, reassuringly: "Go to bed, darling. Let it be as it is. Remember I gave promise to Charlie not to follow him up. He was to be free forever. Go to bed, dear. This is a tempest in a teapot. You are all wrought up and nervous. You'd never forgive yourself for stepping in between our child and her rightful inheritance. Think of that. How would you like to be treated that way just to satisfy some one else's finical qualms as to right and wrong?"

She allowed him to push her toward her bed, and for no obvious reason other than physical weakness she sat upon it, her staring eyes still fixed upon his insistent face. He thought his case was won. He bent and kissed her on the cheek. He tried to raise her chin that his lips might put the seal of frailty upon hers, but she resisted him firmly, inexorably. This gave him pause. All the terrors of his moribund being gathered, screaming and threatening, from the nooks and crannies into which they had but temporarily fled.

"Don't you—can't you see it as—as I do?" he pleaded, still trying to lift her chin, and realizing his defeat even in that small failure.

"No!" That was all she said, but it was more than enough.

He stood away from her. Indescribable contingencies now waxing into grim certainties hurtled about him—exposure, a felon's cell, the visible hatred of the man who had so completely trusted him.

"No!" Celeste repeated, firmly. "There can be only one course to take, and that is the right one—right if it kills us all. You can't tell him. I must do it. He is still down there."

"Is this final?"

"Yes, final," she said, and stood up. He made a movement as if to stop her; it ended by his dropping his limp arms to his sides. His lips moved, but produced no sound. She left the room first, and he followed. Together they leaned over the balustrade and peered at the light below. Then she drew herself erect and started down the stairs. He watched her till she was half-way down, then turned into his room.

She reached the library door. She saw the old man still bent over his calculations, a glow of satisfaction on his pink face. She heard him chuckle. No doubt he was thinking of Ruth's good fortune. She was about to enter when a grim thought suddenly clutched her as if in a vise. How strangely William had acted as they were parting up-stairs! Once before he had started to end his life. Would he be so desperate now? Why not? The crisis was even greater. She turned quickly, and, holding her breath, she darted back up the stairs and tiptoed into William's room. He was standing at his bureau.

She heard a hard substance strike against one of the smaller drawers as he turned to face her. Darting to him, she grasped his arm and slid her fingers down to the revolver he was clutching.

"Oh, you wouldn't do that—would you, dear?" she panted, as she wrung the weapon from his grasp.

His silence was his answer. He stepped back from her. He had steeled himself for the supreme shock of death. How could he summon mere words at this ultimate moment?

"I see, I see!" she moaned, and she was sure now that she loved him in his weakness as a mother might love her child that was blind, crippled, and in unending pain. She put the weapon into the bosom of her dress, and, with her hands outstretched, she cried: "I didn't tell him, darling. I hurried back to you when I thought—thought—thought of *this*. Something else must be done. Charlie wouldn't be willing to murder you. It was to prevent this that he went away."

Her hands were around his neck. He was still under the chill spell of the ordeal he had faced. She drew his head down and kissed him again and again on the lips, as if to restore life's breath to him.

"Yes, something else—but not *this*" she ran on. "We'll see—we'll see, sweetheart. If Charlie were here he'd stop you—he would—he would, and so must I. I see, you couldn't face it all, could you, dear? I ought to have thought of that sooner. Some one has said that God never puts more on us than we can bear, and that is why He turned me back to you when He did. Now, now, we can go to sleep, can't we, darling boy?"

"Oh, it was wonderful—glorious—ecstatic!" he muttered as if to himself, his blank stare fixed on the space beyond her. "I was afraid—afraid—afraid as I put my hand in the drawer and felt it like the icy foot of a corpse; but when I had hold of it—"

"What are you saying, darling?" Celeste asked, fearfully.

"I'll never invest in stocks again. Down, down, down, and the money not my own. I'll be caught. I can't hide it. The examiners will come and look me in the eye, and—"

"Oh, what is it, dear?" Celeste moaned, and, catching his arm, she shook him.

"When I had hold of it," he wandered on, vacantly, "something said—out of the very darkness down where he and my wife were settling my fate—something said: 'Don't be afraid—it is nothing. It will be only a pinprick and you'll be free.' And I was free. I saw—I saw—I heard—I heard—I *felt*—yes, that is it, I *felt* as a man feels when he is said to be dead and no living soul knows of the great change but himself."

"Oh, William darling, you are ill—you are—"

"Good boy, Charlie! Bully boy, my brother! You were true as steel—you knew it had gone down, down, down to the bottom of hell itself and so you ran away. But I was left with it, brother mine. I was in a vat filled with black, smirking imps. Every day I fought with them, every night. But I'm glad now. Are you dead, too? Is that light, or is it— Who ever heard of light and music being the same thing? It is even more than that, eh, Charlie? It is language—the cosmic speech of the universe, and we are in a sea of eternal bliss."

Celeste, wordless now, took his face between her trembling hands and tried to turn it toward her own, but it was immovable. He was chuckling, laughing, his eyes still fixed on space. Dropping her hands, Celeste ran to the head of the stairs, and, like a hysterical woman giving an alarm of fire, she called out:

"Oh, uncle—come quickly! Quick! Quick!"

"What is it? What is it?" he exclaimed, as he darted from the library and plunged up the stairs.

"Quick! Quick!" she cried back, and vanished from his view. He found her standing over her husband, who was now seated on his bed. Hearing his step, William uttered a low, chuckling laugh, and, staring at him, said:

"Here you are again, Charlie. I missed you. That cloud—that dazzling white cloud—seemed to come between us. I ran back to see Ruth and Lessie. Ruth was asleep, and when children are asleep they ride on the clouds— so a spirit told me. But Lessie was awake, standing over, over it—you know what I mean, over the body that held me so long. Oh, I wish she would hide it! Uncle was there, too, Charlie boy. Never could make the old doubter understand this, eh, Charlie? At first it was strange to us, too, eh? Wonderful, wonderful! I hear my old leathery tongue trying to describe it now. How funny!"

"William, what is the matter?" the old man asked, bending over him.

William looked at him closely; he put his hand on his shoulder and went on, chuckling: "Oh, I see it is you, uncle. I want to tell you. You needn't be afraid of dying, as I was all my life. I held it right over my heart and pulled the trigger. There was a flash, a little, tiny tickling sting, and then Charlie and I—I'll never invest in stocks again. It seemed very easy to pile up all that for Lessie and the baby. Down, down, down—Every morning at breakfast I faced them with those figures on my brain like the slimy tracks of coffin snails. Down, down to doom! to doom—that's it, to my doom!"

The old man stood erect. He moved to a window. His niece followed him like a praying shadow. Their eyes met.

"I am the cause of it," she said. "I tried to force him to confess to you that he was to blame, and not Charlie. He tried to use this," taking the revolver from her bosom, "while I went down to tell you."

"He, and not Charlie!" the old man exclaimed, with a fixed stare.

"Say what you like, *do* what you like," she said, harshly, fiercely, recklessly, her white lip curled in a sneer. "He said you would put him in jail. I wonder if you will—I wonder. I would give my life for him. We don't want your money—understand that. What living man has not sinned? and *he* did it for love. Don't you dare to accuse—abuse him. He is down now and dying, perhaps."

With his eyes on the bent form on the bed, the old man seemed not to hear her. "Oh, my God, this is awful—awful!" he said, under his breath. "Well, there is but one thing to do."

Turning, he suddenly left the room. There was a telephone in the hallway, just outside the door, and he went to it. He took up the directory and then turned on the electric light. His hands shook as he fumbled the pages. The book fell to the floor. He picked it up. His old face seemed withered like crinkled parchment.

"I can't find it!" he groaned. "My God! have mercy! It is awful—awful!"

Celeste was at his side. Like an infuriated tigress defending her young, she glared into his face, and all but snarled: "Do it, do it, if you dare—and we'll hate you, despise you, curse your name! I'll teach Ruth to spit on your grave."

"Lessie, Lessie, my child—my poor child! Do you object to my—"

"Object? Would you send him to jail when his reason is wrecked through fear of you—when he is dying?"

"Why, Lessie, Lessie, darling child, did you think *that*? Why, I am telephoning for the doctor, that is all. I love William and pity him as much as you do. We must save him, child, we must save him!"

CHAPTER XXXIV

About a week later Tobe Keith was brought back to Carlin from Atlanta. He was able to walk through the streets from the station to his home. The news reached Kenneth and Martin as they were working in the cotton-fields. The bearer of the tidings said that the sheriff himself had asked that they be informed. Charles was at work close by, and, tossing his straw hat into the air, Kenneth ran toward him, followed by Martin, who was all aglow with joy.

"I thought it would be so," Charles said, when he was informed of the good news.

With his hat swinging at his side, Kenneth held out his hand to him. "I want to thank you," he said, in a manly tone. "You did it, Brown."

And Martin chimed in, a hand outstretched also: "Yes, you did it. If it hadn't been for you he would have stayed here and died. Sister says so."

Flushing red, Charles was unable to deny the part he had played, though still unable fully to explain it. At this instant they saw Mary coming down the path.

"She's heard, too," Martin chuckled. "It lifts a load off her mind—an awful load of worry. She was always afraid there would be an unfavorable turn down there. And they say Tobe is friendly to us."

The two boys went on to meet their sister, but Charles, feeling that he had no valid reason for following them, resumed his work with his hoe in the cotton. Several minutes passed. His back was turned to the trio on the path and he was constantly working away from them. Presently he heard the soft swishing of a starched skirt against the cotton-plants and Mary was at his side. Looking up, he was surprised to find her countenance overcast with a look of depression.

"They've gone over to Dodd's to tell father," she said. "They are very, very happy."

"But you—?" and he leaned on his hoe. "You don't seem—Has anything gone wrong? Was it—a false report, after all?"

"Oh no, it is true enough." She took a deep, lingering breath and released it in a sigh. "But the man that brought the news about Tobe told me something else—something that everybody in the neighborhood seems to know. Charlie, the sheriff has sent those men back to watch you again. They were seen hiding in the woods on the hillside. They are watching us even now. I thought that was all off, but they say the sheriff has had fresh instructions from the East. The men he is after are hiding somewhere in this part of the state, and he seems to think they are here in the mountains and that Tobe Keith and you know something about them."

Charles looked toward the hillside indicated, and then drew his lingering eyes back to hers. He was slightly pale; his lips were drawn tight in chagrin. He made a failure of a smile of indifference.

"I thought that was over," he said. "I thought the sheriff had turned his attention elsewhere. But it can't be helped. You ought not to have taken me in. I ought not to have stopped here at all."

"Don't talk that way!" Mary commanded, with desperate warmth. "What are we going to do about it? I want the truth. I know you are bound by honor, as you say, but as far as you are able I want you to tell me what to expect. If he arrests you—well, what then?"

Charles dropped his eyes to the soil his hoe had turned up and the weeds he had cut. His fine face was stamped with the misery that permeated his being like an absorbent fluid. "If he arrests me he will want me to do the impossible," he said. "He will want me to show who and what I am. I've tried to tell you that I have no past that I can bring up even—even to stand well in your sight. I shall say nothing to him. I don't think the law would let him torture me bodily, but my silence will be ground enough to confirm his suspicions. A man who has been the daily associate of a bunch of circus crooks, and who refuses to show his record to an officer of the law, will stand a poor show."

"I wonder—couldn't you escape? But, oh, I don't want you to leave! I couldn't bear that."

"I thought of escape when they were hanging round before," he answered, with a pale, frank smile, "but gave it up. Such men would be hard to get away from, now that they are on guard, and, besides, to try it would be a confession that I am guilty of what they charge. No, I'll have to let them have their way about it. The men they are after are a dangerous lot and ought to be apprehended."

"Listen to me, Charlie," and Mary, in her earnestness, put her hand on his arm. "I know *something*—a little something—of all this, and you need not deny it. You are trying to protect some one else in some way. I know it; I feel it; I've been sure of it for some time."

"I am sorry, but I can tell you—even you—nothing," he replied, and the words came out with a low groan. "I'm glad you think so well of me. It is the only good thing that has come my way in a long time, but you mustn't care for me deeply, very deeply, for that would mar your future. You know what I think of you, but I have no right to mention it. Your father is right in warning you, as I know he has done; he shows it in the strange, half-fearful way he now speaks to me."

She averted her face; her eyes were moist; her exquisite lips were quivering like those of a weeping child. "I must go," she murmured. "I am sure they are watching us."

"Yes, don't stay." He took up his hoe and began to work as she turned to go.

She hesitated and stood still. "The sheriff talks freely to father," she said. "In fact, I think father went over to Dodd's to meet him. I am sorry to have to tell you this, but you might hear it and not understand. Father liked you all along till—" She broke off, at a loss for words sufficiently delicate to express her meaning.

"Till the good old man found that I was a menace under his roof," Charles put in, bitterly. "That's what I am, Miss Row—"

"Stop!" she suddenly cried out. "Have you lost consideration for my feelings? Am I to count for nothing in this matter? What if you can't reveal everything to me? I don't care. To me you are the soul of honor; to me you are the noblest, most abused man on earth. Charlie, I'll stand by you; I'll go with you if they put you in jail. They can't punish you without punishing me. I've told my father so. My brothers know how I feel. That is why father—as I started to say—is so worried. He doesn't know what to do. He has his pride; he loves me, wants to protect me, and does not know which way to turn."

"And there is nothing I can do, as I see it," Charles groaned, leaning on his hoe, his great, famished eyes on hers. "If it would help, I'd gladly kill myself, but my death would prove nothing but my cowardice and confirm them in their suspicions."

She stepped back to him. She laid her slender, tapering hand on his arm and looked into his face steadily. "Yes, you are too brave for that," she faltered, giving her proud head a little shake of emphasis. "I've never been afraid of that. You, like myself, were born to suffer, it seems, but we will stand up under it, won't we? Let them all do their worst; it won't kill us, for we love each other, don't we, Charlie?"

He lowered his uncovered head; his grim, ashen face was wrung as from deathly pain.

"We love each other, don't we, Charlie?" she repeated, entreatingly.

A shudder shook him from head to foot. "How can I be glad to hear you say that," he asked, "when I know that it is your ruin and that I brought it on you? I have no right to tell you how I feel—how I've felt ever since I kissed you that night in the parlor and you lay so willingly in my arms and hung about my accursed neck. What can I do—what in the name of God, my tormentor? Shall I throw my sacred promise to the winds and laugh in the face of—of—?"

"No!" she cried out. "No, for I'd be doing it. I'd be your evil temptress. Be yourself, Charlie—be what you were before I met you. I think I know— you are selling yourself for some one else as I was willing to do when my brothers were in danger. Don't let me tempt you—don't let anything tempt you. God brought me out of my darkness—by your aid He brought me out. He only knows what my awful struggle was when I was ready to go to that repulsive man as his wife with your image locked in my breast—with my desire for you wrapped around my soul. God helped me; surely He will help you. What are earthly troubles for if they are not to be conquered, trampled under foot, as we mount to the heights to which we are destined? *You shall not tell me anything.* I know your soul, and that is enough."

She turned quickly and moved away. He saw the heads of her brothers as they wended their way toward Dodd's through the tall waving corn. How steadily, how erectly she walked toward the old mansion of her forebears! He noted the tiny marks of her shoes in the soil at his feet. He could have kissed them; he could have fallen on his knees before them in reverent, worshipful humility.

Charles worked on till the cool, creeping shadows of the mountains told him that the sun was down. Then he shouldered his hoe and listlessly trudged homeward. He heard Kenneth and Martin singing as they returned through the corn. It was a negro plantation melody, somehow maddening now in its trustful suggestion of joy. He saw the boys come out into the path. They were arm in arm, full of happiness, full of the ebullient consciousness of their release. He smiled grimly. He told himself that their nightmare had passed, while his was an abiding reality. He must be the exception that proved the rule of life's cosmic harmony. Some things could be borne with a smile. A man might die for his friend, and jest as the black cap muffled his lips; a man might sing as he was being vivisected for a good cause; but this—this fate belonged to no imaginable category of tortures. He had won the heart of an angel and was forced to wear the garb of an outcast in the kingdom which was her rightful abode.

CHAPTER XXXV

Charles left his hoe in the barn and started toward the front of the house. Was he mistaken, or did he see a group of three men near the steps? Yes, and Rowland was one of them. As he passed through the gate he noted the big revolvers belted around the waists of the strangers. They were strong, well-built, sturdy men of the mountains in broad-brimmed felt hats. They evidently saw him, eyed him steadily as he came up the walk, and stood aside silently as he fearlessly ascended the steps. He thought they were going to arrest him, had no sense of objection to it, and was surprised when they neither spoke nor moved. As for Rowland, he simply nodded coldly and Charles went on up to his room.

He went to a window. It was open and he heard the mumbled voices of the men below, but could not see them. He stood listening.

"Oh, it is all right, Colonel," one of the men said. "You've done all you can do. The sheriff thinks the thing looks shaky, and he wants to be on the safe side. There is a big reward out for those chaps and he thinks the fellow that was so free with his money in Tobe Keith's case, and your man that was with him at the time, are two of them."

"I've heard all that from the sheriff himself," Rowland answered. "You may think it strange of us, but we are all willing to trust Mr. Brown. He has done good work here, and has been more than a friend."

"But you say yourself, Colonel, that you don't know a thing about him," came the answer. "You don't know where he comes from, what his connections are, or anything."

"That's all true," Rowland admitted, wearily. "I've never believed in prying into the private affairs of people. He is doing for us more than he agreed to do, and I am sure he is an educated gentleman who may have met with misfortune of some sort. I've never thought he was a happy man, and I've been sorry for him. I wish I could befriend him; and if you will give me a chance—"

Charles listened no longer. He had made up his mind as to what he would do. Turning, he went deliberately down-stairs and out to the group. They looked at him in surprise as he approached, and appeared to be somewhat abashed.

"Gentlemen," Charles began, calmly, "pardon me for interrupting your conversation, but I have reason to believe that you are here on my account. Am I right?"

"Well, yes," one of the men said, awkwardly, as he shifted from one of his heavily booted feet to the other. "You see, we are deputies under the sheriff's orders."

"I thought so," Charles answered, "and I've come to ask a favor of you. The fact that you are watching me under this gentleman's roof is very mortifying to me, for I respect his kindness and his hospitality, and I want to ask if there is any reason why you may not arrest me and take me elsewhere?"

The question astounded them. The two men exchanged swift glances of inquiry. "Why—why, we have had no such orders, you see," the deputy stammered. "We are only doing as we were directed."

"But a man has a right to decent treatment before he is proved guilty of a charge," Charles went on, "and this constant shadowing of this house because I am here is not fair to me or the family. I am a laborer on this place—that and nothing more—and I demand that you either withdraw from these premises or take me with you for safekeeping."

Charles heard a gasp behind him, and saw Mary standing in the doorway, pale as death and trembling.

"What are you saying?" she cried, and she came forward and caught the arm of her lover. "You are not going! You are not!"

"Daughter! Daughter!" Rowland protested, in a sinking voice, "be careful—be careful! Daughter, be careful!"

"He is not going!" she repeated. "It is a shame, an outrage! Father, if he goes, I go. Understand that for once and all."

An awkward pause ensued. Charles stood like a man of granite, his head up, his eyes fixed on the deputies; across his face the whip of pain had left its mark.

"We have no orders," said the man who had spoken before, "except to hang around here and see if that friend of yours comes back, or any other suspicious stranger. We can't take you till we have orders, and we can't let up on our guard, either. There are four of us—two for night, and two for day work."

Rowland looked at his daughter wistfully. There was a suggestion of slow rising emotion in his wrinkled face as he spoke.

"Tell Sheriff Frazier for me, boys, that I will furnish a bond for any amount in Mr. Brown's behalf, and that I hope he will do what Mr. Brown wishes in regard to lifting this—this surveillance."

"Mr. Rowland," Charles cried out, urgently, "you mustn't do that. I don't deserve it at your hands. I'm a stranger without a dollar to my name."

"He does deserve it, father. You are right," said Mary, as she swept to her father's side and locked her arm in his. "He is the best and truest friend we ever had, and you will never regret this."

The old white head rocked up and down deliberately. "Yes, tell the sheriff what I said, and do it at once if possible."

"One of us will see him right away," was the deputy's answer, as both of them clattered down the steps and strode toward the gate.

Charles started forward as if to utter a further protest, but Mary sprang to his side.

"Hush!" she cried. "Father wants to do this. Let him! It is a poor enough return for what you have done for us."

Turning suddenly, as if to hide her emotion, she went into the house. Rowland and Charles stood facing each other in the gathering dusk. From the direction of the kitchen came the singing voices of Kenneth and Martin, who were unconscious of the tragedy being enacted so close at hand. There was a light rising into the old face of the planter which Charles had never seen there before. Rowland laid his hand on his shoulder and let it lie there gently, almost tenderly.

"You have won the heart of my daughter," he began. "She is the image of her mother, and the man who has such a love has all the world can give that is worth having. I congratulate you, sir. For her sake I must make your cause my own. You have helped me free my sons; you must help me save my daughter. She could not survive your downfall—I know that because I knew her mother. Tell me, as a man facing a man, are these charges true?"

"They are not. I swear they are not."

"Thank God! That is all I want to know!" Rowland held out his hand and, taking that of Charles, he pressed it tightly. He was about to withdraw in his stately way when Charles drew him back.

"Wait," he faltered. "As I've said, these charges are wholly unfounded, but under the circumstances it is my duty to you to tell you what your daughter has failed to mention, and that is that there are things in my life which I have pledged my honor never to reveal—things concerning others more than myself—"

"Then don't mention them," Rowland said, firmly. "Do your duty as you see it and God will take care of you. I have suspected that you may be keeping back something, but that is your right. Now let's go in to supper. But wait a moment. I want to speak of something psychological. Do you know that a man of my age can be turned from almost a lifelong purpose in an instant? You have seen me working on that ponderous genealogy of mine. Well, the other day when my boys were in so much danger my daughter and I were alone in my room. She looked very sad, and all at once it seemed to me that she was an exact reproduction of her mother when we were married. You know in that day when I brought my young wife here we had everything our hearts desired in the way of luxury, comfort, and even what was then considered style. Now it is all gone and we are poor. This change, I reckon, has pained me more than it has my daughter, and I have clung to the past and tried to keep it alive. One of the ways of keeping it alive has been my thinking and writing about the dignity and superiority of my ancestors. I was getting my book ready to hand down to my children and their children, and I would have finished it and published it but for my daughter. On the day I spoke of just now, I happened to tell her that I was thinking of borrowing some money to pay for the printing, when I saw from her face that she wasn't pleased. I asked her what was the matter, and she came and sat on my knee, sir, as she had done as a little child, and as—as her mother had done as a bride. She put her arm around my neck and kissed me, and then she begged my forgiveness for saying what she felt that she ought to say. She pointed out that she and her brothers belonged to a different age from the one I'd passed through. As she saw it, life was too grim and serious for one to foster pride in one's ancestors simply because they, being men and women of gentility, wealth, and influence, had stood higher than others. Mary cried as she begged that I should not spend any money to publish a book which she herself could not take pride in. She said that sorrow, trouble, and adversity had made her see that the common people were nearer God than the opposite class, and that if we expected God to help us out of the great trouble in which my sons were plunged we must humble ourselves. Well, sir, I was changed—in a flash I was a changed man. My young daughter had taught me more in a moment than I had learned in a long lifetime. I laid the manuscript away. If it has any historical value it may be used by some one else in the future, but not by me. It is full of human vanity.

"I felt as if a vast load had been somehow lifted from my old shoulders. I knew she was right and obeyed her. I am telling you this, sir, because you have a right to know the kind of woman whose heart you have won. She is a treasure, sir—a treasure—a treasure!"

Aunt Zilla was ringing the supper-bell. Its tones swept melodiously over the dusk-draped fields. The old man had taken the arm of his companion as he might that of an honored guest in the past, and led him into the house.

"I shall never question your integrity, sir," he said. "Something has told me all along that you are a man among men. My daughter has felt it intuitively, and so have I and my sons. Whatever your personal trouble is, we'll stick to you through it if you will only give us a chance."

Charles found himself unable properly to respond. The family were at the table in the shaded lamplight. The meal passed in quiet dignity, and when it was over the men went out to the front veranda. Kenneth and Martin, who had not been informed of the talk with the deputies, were still in a gay mood and began singing again. Rowland stood on the steps for a moment, and then walked down toward the gate. Finding himself alone, Charles slipped up to his room. He had an overwhelming sense of his need of quiet reflection. He sat down, lighted his pipe, but in his inactive hands it quickly expired. That he would have to face the officers of the law sooner or later he did not doubt. The bond in his favor might mean a few days' delay, but it also meant the certainty of his appearance before the authorities. What would then take place he could not imagine, but of one thing he was sure—a stranger in a strange land who flatly refused to give account of himself when charged with an offense against the law would find himself in a serious position indeed. Then a sudden thought hurtled through his brain and shook him from head to foot, leaving him cold with sheer despair. Why had he not thought of it before? The account of his arrest would be given in the papers, along with the name he had never changed. It would be copied all over the country, and the Charles Browne of Boston, so long sought, would be discovered at last. William would read his doom in the head-lines of his paper at his desk or the breakfast-table. Celeste would know the truth, for William would tell the truth rather than see his brother unjustly punished. The revolver—ah yes! the revolver in the drawer of his brother's desk! It was as clear to his sight now as when he had last seen it. William would use it, without doubt, now, and there would be no delay.

"Where is Mr. Brown?" It was Mary's voice addressed to her brothers below. Charles sprang up and stood listening.

"I think he went up-stairs," Martin said. "He may be tired. He has worked hard to-day."

"Tired!" repeated the grim listener, with a sardonic smile, as if the body counted when the soul of a man was being hounded to such a sinister doom. Mary was still on the veranda. What good could be done by his going to her? How could he act with her as if nothing new had happened when the claws of this unexpected monster were clutching his throat? He crept with the tread of a thief out into the hall and looked down the stairs. He could see Mary standing in the doorway. What was she thinking? How would she view the thing he now feared? He went back into his room and strode to and fro across the uncarpeted floor, his arms locked, his jaws clenched. Presently he heard the sound of hoofs and some one dismounted at the gate and strode up the walk to the steps. Charles went to a window. A restive horse was pawing at the gate. The voice of one of the deputies came up from below:

"I happened to meet the sheriff over at Dodd's, Colonel. He said the bond would be all right, and he has ordered us away. Your man will have to appear in a few days, and you will be informed. He said to tell you that the bond would be drawed up for a thousand dollars and that the fellow would not be arrested yet a while. He said for me to say that you was taking a big risk, as he has fresh reasons for thinking that your man will never be able to show a clean record. He thinks if he had been able to do so he would have put it up before this, considering all that's happened."

Charles started to the stairs, but suddenly checked himself. What was there to say or do? And time to think and try to plan was what he needed. He went back to his room and sat down. He was aflame with the terrible shame of the thing. He heard Mary's subdued voice in conversation with her father and brothers, and the hoof-beats of the deputy's horse as he rode away toward the village. How could he face his friends down there with sealed lips when they were so valiantly and faithfully defending him out of sheer confidence in his veiled integrity? He decided that he would not join them. He sat in his unlighted room till he heard them saying good night to one another, and then he went to bed, but not to sleep. Through the long, warm night he struggled with his problem. Once he half thought he had solved it. He might now manage to escape. It would be leaving Rowland with the bond to pay, but he could perhaps get to William safely, secure the money, and return it. But could it be done? No, for the names of Charles Brown of Georgia and Charles Browne of Boston would be linked together by the detectives, published everywhere, and a renewed search for the bank defaulter would meet with success. No, there was nothing to do now but to wait—if a man of his temperament could wait with a sword like that hanging over him and all he loved.

CHAPTER XXXVI

Charles and the boys were in the field the next morning. The sheer desperate movement of his limbs while at hard work had a tendency to throw off the mental pain that he was still laboring under. It was about ten o'clock, when, happening to glance toward the house, he saw the sheriff drive up in a two-seated trap and sit waiting at the gate. Then, to Charles's surprise, both Mary and her father came out, got into the trap, and were driven away toward the village. Kenneth had noticed it; he came across the cotton-rows and joined him.

"They've gone in to fix up that bond," he explained, in a tone of evident satisfaction. "Father is to sign it to-day in the office of the clerk of the court."

"But your sister?" and Charles wiped the perspiration from his brow and bewildered eyes.

"Oh, I think she went along as a witness to my father's signature, and also to see Tobe Keith and his mother. Brown, she doesn't believe you were connected with those circus men; neither does father. As for me and Martin, you know what we think."

"Thank you," Charles muttered. "It is kind of you all." His eyes were now on the trap and its inmates as they slowly ascended the sloping road half a mile distant. Mary sat with her father on the rear seat. Beyond them rose the rugged mountain, green as to foliage and brown and gray as to earth and stone. Above it all arched the blue sky, with here and there a creeping wisp of snow-white cloud. How incongruous it was! Here he was dodging imprisonment while this gentle family were espousing—blindly espousing his tottering cause. He drew a picture of himself running along the road after the trap, running faster than the horses, overtaking them and panting out a demand that the law should be allowed to take its course. But it was only a futile figment of a weary brain. He had uprooted a stalk of cotton, and he replaced it, raking out the mellow soil with his bare hands, packing it back on the roots, and bracing the plant between two of its neighbors by interlocking their pliant branches.

"Mary! Mary! Mary!" The balmy air, blown from the direction she was taking in his behalf, seemed to sing the name as from vibrant strings stretched from heaven to earth—from shores of matter to boundaries of infinite spirit. Again she was in his arms as she was that night in the darkened old parlor. Her pulsing lips were on his, her clinging arms about his neck. After that spiritual marriage, could heaven or hell tear her from him? Could fate rob him of such a prize? Perhaps, for the prize could not be had at such a price. Mary, who had been a ready sacrifice herself, could not love one less worthy, and she would have to know the truth. He worked on—as a dying man he toiled on through the long, weary day.

CHAPTER XXXVII

On reaching the town, Rowland and the sheriff stopped at the court-house and Mary went to the Keiths'. To her great delight, she saw Tobe out in the little yard, seated under an apple-tree. He got up at once, and with scarcely any limp at all came to meet her.

"Mother is not here," he said, as he shook hands. "It is kind of you to come, Miss Mary."

"I heard you were recovering," Mary returned, "and I was very glad. You know what it meant to me, Tobe?"

"Yes, I do, and that helped me pull through, I think, Miss Mary. Those boys are too young and thoughtless to shoulder a load like that would have been. We were all to blame."

"I hope we will have no trouble with the courts," Mary said. "What do you think about that, Tobe?"

He waved his hands lightly. "Nothing will be done," he answered. "The sheriff and three or four good lawyers told me so. They said it all depended on whether I'd press the charges, and I don't intend to, Miss Mary. I've had my lesson, and the boys have, too. I've cut liquor out and folks say they have, too."

She nodded. "Yes, they have changed remarkably. They are more serious, and they work every day."

Tobe was smiling significantly. For a moment he was silent; then he said: "Miss Mary, me and mother are powerfully bothered about a certain thing. We want to know who furnished the money that came to me that night. As soon as I heard, down in Atlanta, that the stranger that fetched it was a friend of that Mr. Brown on your place, and that Mr. Brown was with him that night and kept back out of sight, why, we was sure that you sent the money, but we heard after we got back that you said you didn't."

"I didn't, Tobe," Mary declared. "I tried to raise it, but failed to get it in time. In fact, I was surprised to hear that you had received it."

"Then you can't tell us anything about that?" Tobe's face fell.

"I think I can, and I think I *ought* to." Mary's color was slightly higher now. "Tobe, you see, since Mr. Brown came to us he has become warmly attached to my brothers, and he was greatly disturbed over the danger they and you were in. I have an idea that the stranger you saw was an old friend of his who came here to pay him some money he owed. I suppose that Mr. Brown did not want to get credit for what he did, and so he got his friend to hand you the money that night."

"Now I understand it better," Tobe smiled. "He must be a fine man, and I don't believe the reports the sheriff and his gang are circulating about him. They say he is in big trouble himself—in fact, that him and his friend belong to the bunch of circus outlaws that are wanted. The sheriff had the cheek to try to tie me up with it, because this money came as it did, but I laughed in his face. I told him he'd have to prove it, and he went off with a hangdog look on him."

"Mr. Brown is not guilty, but he is in trouble over it, Tobe," Mary sighed, as she turned to leave.

Tobe, his hat in his hand, went with her to the gate and opened it, with the unstudied grace of his class. He stood bowing as she walked away toward the square. She was to meet her father at the hotel, and thither she went, vaguely depressed by the talk she had had concerning Charles.

She had reached the front of the hotel when she saw Sam Lee at a canvas-covered wagon belonging to a mountain farmer. The clerk was buying some produce for the hotel table and, seeing her, he left the farmer and came to her.

"I was on the lookout for you," he said, doffing his hat and bowing. "I heard you were around at Keith's. There is some lady friend of yours up in the parlor. She come in on the south-bound about half an hour ago. She is powerful stylish-looking, and wanted to see about some conveyance out to your place, when I told her that you and your pa were in town. She begged me to look you up, and I told her I would. She said she would wait in the parlor. She looks like she may be some of your Virginia kin. I didn't ask her name, for there was no reason for it."

"I can't imagine who it can be," Mary answered. "Well, I'll go up. If you see my father, will you send him up, too, please?"

Mary went into the entrance-hall and up the stairs to the parlor at the end of the first flight. The door was open, and the big room, being somewhat shaded, appeared so dark after her walk in the glaring sunlight that she was at first unable to see distinctly. Presently, however, she became aware of a woman's figure rising from a sofa in a corner and approaching her.

"May I ask if this is Miss Rowland?" a sweet, tremulous voice inquired.

"Yes, I am Miss Rowland," Mary answered. "Are you the lady who wanted to see me?"

"Yes. I asked the clerk about you, and he said he would send you up here. Miss Rowland, I am a stranger, but it is imperative that I see you. There is, I believe, a gentleman working on your place whose name is Charles Browne."

Mary started, stared, and was silent. Her mind fairly whirled in confusion. Charles had hinted at troubles he had left behind him. How could she know that it would be wise for her to speak in any way of him and his affairs to a total stranger? She remained silent. She had drawn herself up to her full height; her head and neck were rigid, her hands clasped tightly before her.

"Oh, I see," the stranger went on. "You don't know me yet, and you are such a faithful friend to him that you don't want to risk the slightest misstep. Well, you are right, and I am wrong. I was in too great a hurry. I see now what I've got to do, Miss Rowland. I've got to convince you that I am his friend, and a faithful one, too."

Mary's perplexed face was still rigid and was growing even pale. Her eyes, more accustomed to the darkened room, were enabled now to get a clearer view of the visitor. She felt strangely drawn by the rather sad and pinched features, the yearning eyes, and the sweet, almost pathetic voice.

"Miss Rowland, I am Charlie's sister-in-law, Mrs. William Browne. I've come here from Boston to tell you and your father something that you ought to know, for, Miss Rowland, I know that Charlie loves you. It came to me through another, but when I saw you come in at that door I knew it to be the truth beyond doubt. You are beautiful, beautiful, and are so true to him that you stand there now, afraid that through me you may harm his interests."

"He has spoken to me of you," Mary said, "and of Ruth." Her hands went out impulsively and clasped those of Celeste. "You must pardon me, Mrs. Browne, if—if I seem slow to—"

"I understand thoroughly," Celeste broke in. "I've come to bring you good, not bad news. My dear, Charlie is the noblest man in all the world—yes, in all the world. Over a year ago his brother, my husband, committed a great offense against the law. On the verge of detection he was about to kill himself and leave me and Ruth under the stigma of it all. Charles sacrificed himself under a sacred agreement with my husband. He left Boston, pursued for a crime he had not committed, and disgraced for life. But the other day Michael, an old servant of ours, came back and told me about you and Charles—that Charles adored you, but was too honorable to think of marriage with you under the circumstances. Michael said Charlie was very unhappy. It made me so, for I wanted him and you to get your rights. I finally told my husband how I felt, and demanded that he do his duty. It drove him out of his mind temporarily. He is now in a sanatorium on the way to recovery. He has confessed everything to his uncle, whose influence at the bank has caused the dismissal of the charges, the financial loss having been made good. Moreover, explanations have been published in the Boston papers which clear Charlie's name in full."

"Oh, I'm so glad! I'm so glad!" Mary now fairly glowed. "You've come just in time to save him from grave trouble." And Mary went on to explain the situation. The two sat side by side on the sofa, holding each other's hands. Rowland found them there half an hour later, and heard the news. He made a most favorable impression on the Boston lady as he stood gravely listening to all she had to say, in the polished manner of the old régime. Then he told them both that he must see the sheriff at once and have the action against Charles suppressed.

In half an hour Rowland came back. Everything had been settled and the bond destroyed. Then he pressed Celeste to return home with him and his daughter, and Mary joined in the invitation. Celeste accepted with delight, for she was eager to see Charles as soon as possible, and Rowland went to order a carriage from the livery-stable. There was, however, a delay in securing a conveyance, and it was near sundown before they had started homeward.

CHAPTER XXXVIII

Charles toiled all that day in the fields. At no time during all his troubles had his depression been greater, due to the humiliating fact of Mary and her father being at work in his behalf. And what good would come of it? he kept asking himself. His appearance at court was inevitable sooner or later, and what could he say in his defense? Nothing and still remain true to the high stand he had taken.

He saw the sun sink below the mountain-top, and felt the coolness of the dusk as it came with its moist suggestion of falling dew. He saw Kenneth and Martin as they left their work some distance away and went singing toward the house. He wondered if Mary and her father had returned. The thought of having to face them in the lamplight at the supper-table was galling to his tortured spirit. He had known them such a short time, and yet was now on their bounty to an unpardonable extent. He bit his lips; he groaned; he cursed his fate. Finally, when it was too dark to work any longer, he started to the house. He was approaching the barn when he saw some one coming toward him. It was Mary, and a fresh sense of his humiliation swept over him like a torrent. What would she have to say? Perhaps the bond, after all, had been deemed insufficient. Perhaps—perhaps—But she was now before him. He dared not look straight at her, and was grateful for the thickening dusk that veiled him from her view.

"We are late getting back," she said, in a voice which, somehow, suggested a tremulous suppression of vast and sweeping emotion.

"I see," he returned. "I thought you'd be back earlier. I'm sorry I allowed your father to do that. I had no idea you were going with him. I ought to have stopped you both. Such a thing has never been heard of! Why, I am nothing but the tramp that I was when I came here! I've not been open with you, and a man who is like that among strangers doesn't deserve—"

"Hush, Charlie!" Mary put her hand on his arm and smiled into his face. "We would do a little thing like that a million times and be glad of the chance. In fact, we have not done enough for you. It is we who ought to be grateful, not you. Charlie, we know all about you now—all about your Boston life—" She broke down and sobbed. She sobbed in sheer joy, but he misunderstood.

"You know, then!" he gasped. "You've found out. They have traced me down. It was the name. If I had changed that I might have had a chance. It got into the papers, I see, and the news of my capture spread to the North. Well, well, you see now who you have been sheltering."

It was Mary's turn to misunderstand. Wiping the glad tears from her eyes, she faced him. She put her hand on his arm again.

"There is a great surprise waiting for you at the house," she said. "Who do you think is there to see you? Who, Charlie, who?"

He stared dumbly, his mouth falling open in limp despair.

"I promised that I wouldn't tell you," Mary went on, "so that you would be surprised suddenly, but you look so—so—You don't seem to understand that all your trouble and mine is over. Charlie, it is Celeste."

"Celeste!" he gasped. "Celeste!"

"Yes, and she has told us everything. Your brother has been ill and has confessed the truth. The blame rests where it should at last, and you are free. Oh, Charlie, you are the noblest, best man in all the world, and when I think of what you have borne and your reason for it I feel like falling at your feet in worship. Oh, tell me—tell me—can you really love me? Since I've heard your story I've been afraid that you—that *such* a man as you—could not really care for a simple country girl like I am. It worried me all the way home. While Celeste was talking it fairly grappled my heart and crushed it. When you and I were both in trouble it somehow seemed possible, but now—" Her voice broke. Quickly Charles stepped forward and took her into his arms. He was quivering in every limb and muscle. Every nerve in his being was strung taut to the music of ecstasy inexpressible.

The clanging of Aunt Zilla's supper-bell awoke them both to the world about them, and arm in arm they went homeward. Celeste was in the parlor, waiting for him, and he went in to her alone. How sad, how changed she looked in the lamplight, how like some consecrated nun contrasted to her former girlish self! As he kissed her and held her thin hands in his calloused grasp he wondered at the lines and shadows in the features which had once been so smooth and free from care. For the first time that day she allowed her emotions to get the better of her. She tried to speak and failed. Suddenly she seemed to him to be a homeless, deserted human waif, and then he comprehended all. The man recuperating in the hospital, though mentally sound, could never be the ideal she had so long striven to make of him. For the second time William had tried to desert her and his child. He was weak; he was a coward; but he was the father of her child, and perhaps ideals were, after all, not to be met in substance. And yet there were strong men in the world, for the man standing before her in the soiled garb of a voluntary outcast possessed the missing requirements. Celeste was happy for him and unhappy for herself. She calmed herself and hurriedly told him the chief things that had taken place in Boston.

"Uncle feels very sorry for his unjust thoughts about you," she said. "All his family pride has centered around you. He is sorry for William, and is not unkind to him, but you are all he talks about now. He is coming down to see you as soon as I get back. I don't know that I have a right to mention it, but I shall, anyway. He has made a will, Charlie, dividing all his fortune between you and Ruth. You are rich now, and are bound to be happy. Mary is a gem of a woman who has proved her worth and fidelity."

She seemed slightly faint. She swayed to and fro, and he caught her arm and steadied her. He had never loved her so much as now. How lonely and bereft she seemed, how frail, how persistently selfless!

"You don't look strong," he said, sympathetically. "You must stay with us for a while, and let us put the color back into your cheeks. The mountain air here is good and bracing."

He felt the brave tremor which a crushed sob gave to her frame. "Thank you, Charlie," she said, "but I must hurry back. I am hungry for Ruth. I have never left her so long before. She is my very life now, Charlie, and—and William needs me."